CRACKED

COMING SOON FROM TITAN BOOKS

Cracked: Rehab Run (November 2016)

BARBRA LESLIE

A DANNY CLEARY NOVEL

CRACKED

TITAN BOOKS

Cracked
Print edition ISBN: 9781783296989
Electronic edition ISBN: 9781783296996

Published by Titan Books
A division of Titan Publishing Group Ltd
144 Southwark Street, London SE1 0UP

First edition: November 2015
2 4 6 8 10 9 7 5 3 1

A CIP catalogue record for this title is available from the British Library.

Printed and bound in the United States.

For my much-missed late mother
Donna Leslie

I hope that wherever you are, the crosswords aren't too hard,
the Chardonnay is on tap, and there's a new episode
of *CSI* every night.

PREFACE

It was November, and I love November. I love the sunny mornings and the slate gray afternoons, and waiting for the first snowfall.

What I hate are perfect July evenings when all the young couples in love stroll around with arms around each other's tanned waists, jeans hanging off their hips in such a way that you know that they just pulled them on after having sex all afternoon. Or maybe they just drove back to the city after being at their parents' summer homes for long lazy weekends, diving off the dock into cold blue water. They wander the streets, meeting other carefree youngsters for drinks on the street-side patios of bars, their voices carrying into the night.

I like that in November, people cover up and walk faster to get where they're going. And I don't have to see young people with the cockiness of a perfect past and a promising future in front of them. Or so they think.

My sister thought that. I thought that once, too. And look at us now.

She's in her grave. And me?

I'm going to find everyone who put her there.

CRACKED

1

A handy tip about addicts:

For every crazy-eyed, brain-fried crackhead you see shambling down the street with flip-flops on in the middle of winter, there are a hundred like me, who stay at home and have their drugs delivered. If you have ready cash and know a dealer (and preferably one who doesn't dabble in his own merchandise), it's not much more difficult than ordering in pizza. But unlike the Domino's guy, dealers drive black SUVs with tinted windows, they never get out of their vehicle, and forget about thirty minutes or it's free.

See, we're not much different to alcoholics. You see boozers on the street drinking two-dollar wine out of paper bags, and you know they're only five steps ahead of your Uncle Eddie, who drinks a quart of Jameson every night and falls asleep on the couch with a lit Marlboro in his hand.

We're like rats: if you see one in an alley, you know there are dozens more, hiding inside somewhere in the dark.

But this isn't about crack.

This is about Ginger.

* * *

It was a typical day for me, or at least a typical end-of-bender day. I'd been up for two days with Gene, my partner in crime. We were watching a stupid comedy on cable, laughing and feeding each other hits. As usual, we were carefully watching the size of the rock sitting on the CD case on the coffee table dwindle, the anxiety building.

For a crack addict, the coming down is so bad that you'd rather keep going until there is no going left.

"Call him," I said, referring to our main dealer, D-Man. "He can get down here and back by rush hour." Gene lit two cigarettes and handed me one. We were a regular forties movie brought to life, we were.

"No, darlin'," Gene said. He always did this, pretended that we should stop. He wasn't the one paying for it. "We can't." It was pure show. As usual, I ignored him.

"If I call him, you have to go outside and get it," I said. For a full-time crack dealer, D-Man wasn't a bad guy, but I didn't particularly like having him up to the apartment. It was not a pleasant experience. He had some kind of paranoid mental illness that he obviously wasn't treating with the right medication, and having him around made me feel like I was in a bad early-90s movie about the dangers of the druggie lifestyle. He was a slightly built but pudgy Slavic guy. He wore Bee Gees or Air Supply t-shirts tucked into combat pants that left very little to the imagination. And I have a good imagination. His real name was Darko, and he had a heavy Eastern European accent. Some days he said he was Croatian, some days Czech, but who was going to argue. The D-Man moniker he had come up with on his own, he said. He was proud of it. He wanted some of his customers, the ones he had never met face to face, to think he was a black dude. The black guys got more respect, he said. I never wanted to tell him that even over the phone, no one was going to mistake his accent, but keeping drug dealers sweet is something junkies tend to aspire to.

D-Man answered on the second ring. At this time of day, late morning, he would have been asleep for about three or four hours, and he always feigned impatience with us when we woke him up. But we all knew that Gene and I were his best customers. He lived way, way uptown, but within an hour, he or one of his scary-ass drivers would be idling at my back door with a little white rock wrapped in Saran.

"Hey, babe," I said, perky and sounding as blonde as I could. My looks were still there, and they still worked for me when I wanted them to. "We watched all our movies. You bringing more down?" This was our stupid code. Hey, don't blame me, blame D-Man. Or Gene. One of them. The cheesy gangster shit was always embarrassing to me – I had absolutely no paranoia, and couldn't imagine that our pissant dealings were important enough to warrant a wiretap. But if I had to play the game to get my rock, then play the game I would do.

"What? You watched all those films already? You people need to get some sleep," D-Man said. I could hear him straining to sit up and lighting a cigarette. He was probably in bed at this hour, and I didn't want to imagine what kind of state his bed was in – even though he didn't smell, per se, I had a vague image of his apartment as something out of a movie about the East Village in the 70s, with cockroaches and a hot plate with tomato sauce burned onto it.

Then again, he was just as likely to have a bourgie middle-class home with wall-to-wall Berber rugs. I'd paid him enough.

"What can I say, we're celebrating," I replied. "You know we like our movie marathons sometimes." Yeah, like twice a week for two or three days at a time.

"What you got for me?" D-Man wanted to know. Ouch. This was always tricky. I had started out paying him huge sums of money, in cash, drawing it out from the bank machine downstairs from my building once or twice a day. Then I graduated to cash advances on credit cards, then to applying for and getting more credit cards. Having been such a nice middle-class girl for so many years meant that I had had a spectacular credit rating, once upon a time. And a lot of credit cards. But when the credit card companies turn on you, they turn nasty. Usually, I only plugged my phone in to call D-Man or one of our other, backup dealers, or when I was expecting a call from them to say they were downstairs. What friends I had left knew to email me, and I would check my email account every few days or so. And Gene and I would head down to our bars every week or so to keep current on the doings in the neighborhood, so we didn't tend to speak to people on the phone much.

I was out of money again. All my cash advances had run out, and while I was expecting a spousal support deposit from my ex, Jack, in a few days, I already owed D-Man upwards of a grand.

"On Friday, D," I said to him. "You know I'm good for it." I always had been, too. As far as he was concerned, I was a cash cow. He didn't have to know that this cow was now bone dry.

"Friday," he said. I could hear him drawing on his cigarette. He liked to pause a lot, as though considering whether to bother. He wanted to keep me on my toes, but we both knew it was a game. He knew Gene and I had options, other people we could go to. But not everyone delivered, and when you've been up hitting the pipe hard for a couple of days, delivery is key. Daylight is the enemy.

"I drew out my maximum this week, sweetie; you know how my bank is set up," I replied. I stubbed my own butt out and motioned for Gene to clean out the pipe so that we'd have some resin to smoke along with our crumbs of crack until D-Man arrived.

The resin is the powdery, ashy remains of the crack that collects on the inside of the pipe. It can be more potent than the actual rock. Ideally, Gene and I liked to time it so that we weren't left jonesing and crashing for an hour or so until D-Man arrived. It was bad news if it was too close to rush hour, because the trip one way could take over an hour in Toronto traffic. "Oh right, your bank, your bank," D-Man said. He was fairly simple for a drug dealer, not as wily as some, and he liked to think that he was our friend, that he was In The Know. "Man, you got to get that sorted out, you know? They can't be holding your money that way. That is your money, Danny."

And yours, too, D-Man. "I know it, D. I know it. So you coming down?"

I could hear him shuffling around. "Gotta make a call. She's on her way."

This was part of D-Man's brilliant code to foil the police. "She" was Bruno, a cabbie friend of D-Man's, a junkie himself who delivered crack all over town in his cab in exchange for free hits. He was a fat old white guy with a nasty dermatological condition that made most of the skin on his hands and face look like it was constantly peeling off. The first time he met me, he shook my hand through the car window and it took every ounce of my nice-girl breeding not to retch in revulsion. After that, every time I met him outside my back door, he kissed me on the cheek and told me he loved me.

Right back at ya, Bruno.

There was nothing effeminate about him, which I guess is why D-Man reasoned that anyone listening would be fooled by the female pronoun. Hey, he may not have been a Harvard grad, but he gave us what we needed.

I hung off the phone and took the pipe from Gene. This was our ritual: he would light it for me while I took a hit. He would set it all up for me, with the foil and the ash and the rock on top like a cherry on the sundae. We were old school with our pipes, MacGyvering them out of empty Tylenol bottles, hollowed-out Bic pens, tin foil, duct tape, and safety pins. He would light it for me, like a gentleman. Even junkies like routine. A year into this habit, I had started to notice Gene was putting less crack in the pipe for me than he was for himself, and it was starting to burn me up. This was my money, and now my debt. Gene couldn't hold down a job – his habit was older than mine, and before crack he had been into regular cocaine – well, so had I, come to think of it – and before that he was just a friendly alcoholic. And a bartender, which is like letting a pedophile babysit your kids: not a good idea. At his last job, he got caught one too many times on the boss's secret CCTV, sitting after hours doing lines off the mahogany bar, helping himself to shots of Jack and playing the trivia machine with money he pilfered from the till.

Despite the fact that we had been joined at the hip for a couple of years, Gene and I were just friends. With the odd benefit. True, we did sleep in the same bed a lot of the time – when we slept, that is. We cuddled and were affectionate with each other, especially in bed. We went to sleep in each other's arms and woke the same way. But we never kissed, and we only had friendly, perfunctory sex about once every few months or so. I couldn't see myself getting over Jack, and Gene was one of those addicts whose sex drive had long since gone down the drain. But affection is good. Friendship is good. And as far as we were concerned, we had all that in each other. We didn't need anybody else. "How long?" Gene asked me.

I shrugged, keeping the smoke in my lungs. It wasn't the best hit, but it would do. Oh boy, it would do, do, do. The longer you hold the smoke in, the better the rush.

"Dunno," I exhaled, dropping my head onto his shoulder. The movie was over, and Gene was flipping stations. "Look. *The Feud* is on." Gene fixed his hit, and for once I refrained from watching how much of the precious leftover resin he put on his.

We sat in silence, watching *Family Feud*. Often we yelled out answers, but just as often we sat in silence. I was more of a talker than Gene while high. Well, I was more of a talker than Gene, period.

We sat like that for an hour, slowly using the last of our stash with Gene cleaning the pipe assiduously, waiting for the phone call. It rang once and we both jumped out of our skins and grabbed for it, but the caller I.D. showed that it was my bank. Fuck you, Bank.

The phone rang again. It was long distance, a 949 area code. My sister Ginger. I glanced at the clock on the DVD player –

noon, so nine a.m. in California. She would have just gotten back from taking the rugrats to school and Fred off to work. She was checking up on me.

"Ginger?" Gene asked.

"I'm not answering it," I said, nodding. Ginger knew about me. She hadn't given up on me either, and I did talk to her once every month or so. I loved her. I envied her. I didn't want to think about her. I let her call go to voicemail, and five minutes later, D-Man called to say that She – Bruno – was outside.

Gene sprang to life, grabbing his jacket and his keys to get back into the building. His boots were already on so as not to waste precious crack time when we got the call.

"Do you have twenty bucks for Bruno?" I asked. That was the price of delivery – even if we didn't have money to pay for the product, we always had to fork over twenty for delivery.

"Shit," Gene answered. He checked his wallet. "I have ten."

I jumped up and checked the pile of coins I kept for laundry money. I had nine dollars in loonies and four quarters. I handed them to Gene. It meant that we only had a half pack of cigarettes between us and no money for more, but who cared.

He smiled. "This is embarrassing," he said.

"Deal with it, dear," I replied. "Go get me my drugs, and make it snappy." Our moods always improved when another eightball was waiting for us outside.

Anticipation. Just like the song says.

"You'll just have to wait for it, bee-yatch," Gene said, all happy tough guy.

"Fuck off and get me my drugs," I replied, happy right back.

Gene left and I got up and went to the bathroom, peed and

brushed my teeth, splashed water on my face. It's important to keep up hygiene whilst consuming large quantities of drugs. You sweat so much while smoking crack that you might as well have just finished a triathlon. I actually kept crack clothes, old worn-out workout clothes, in which I only smoked crack. It was a good thing I'd never been all that vain. Gene was taking a few minutes, which didn't worry me, because usually D-Man called too early, and one of us would be waiting in the cul-de-sac outside the back door of my art deco-era apartment building for ten minutes or more, strung out but coolly pretending to be waiting for our ride somewhere. Just behind me was, literally, the most expensive restaurant in Toronto, a place so upscale that you had to know where it was, located on a back residential street. Limos drove in every few minutes between seven and ten p.m., and Gene and I always thought the valets had made us. However? So far, so good, was our motto.

Inside the apartment, I paced and picked up a couple of glasses, stuck them in a sink full of soapy water, made more ice, got the Murphy's Oil Soap out and had a swipe at the ugly-ass coffee table that my ex had made from scratch. In a previous life, I had been married to a man who had decided to take up woodworking to help quash the demons in his head.

I didn't like to think of my previous life.

But it made me think of Ginger. I picked up the cordless and decided to stay on top of things, the manic hyperactivity of the addict waiting for a fix. I would check my messages!

Five minutes later, Gene came through the door.

"What an idiot," he said, kicking off his boots. "This is twice what we ordered."

I looked at him, my whole body shaking.

"Ginger is dead," I said. "She's dead." I stopped.

My sister. My beautiful sister.

My twin.

2

There were no twins on either side of either my mother's or my father's family, so imagine their surprise, they used to like to tell us, when they were told that Ginger and I were growing together in my mother's womb.

"I thought your father was going to faint, right there in the doctor's office," my mother told us. It was one of our favorite stories, Ginger's and mine. We loved to hear how we began, and to imagine growing nestled together, all safe and warm and protected. There were no stork fantasies in our house; both Mom and Dad were very no-nonsense about the facts of life. "But in those days it was rare enough that the man even came into the doctor's office for these things, so I was proud of him anyway," Mom told us. Dad said that he even drove down to Boston to hear some famous psychologist give a lecture on raising twins.

My parents had five kids including Ginger and me, and they weren't even Catholic. Go figure. My mother, a beauty queen back in the day, didn't know what the hell to do with all of us, and who could blame her. My father owned a couple of dry cleaners in Maine, where I grew up. I guess you could call him successful, but for us, back then, success meant that we had a shit-box summer cabin on a tiny lake and we usually got meat for supper. The steamy chemical smell of a real dry cleaner – as opposed to the storefronts at which we drop our shirts off in the city – always makes me feel eight again. In a good way.

Ginger and I had three brothers. Skipper was almost eighteen years older than Darren, the youngest, and he and his wife Marie lived back in Maine. Laurence, the second oldest, worked in television in New York City. And our little brother Darren, the pet, was a musician, and now lived in Toronto, like me. I had struck out for Canada after high school. Ginger, who had always had her head in a book, had gone off to Bennington, and I had met a Canadian boy who had spent the summer with his grandparents in Downs Mills. When he left for university in Toronto in the fall, I followed him, full of love and craving adventure like I now craved crack. I hadn't been anywhere, and even though I was from Maine, Canada seemed as foreign as Paris.

Of course, the boyfriend didn't last, but Toronto did. And two years later when he finished high school, Darren followed. He was my baby, my pet, and Ginger was engaged to Fred and planning her own life.

Mom had had us, the twins, at forty, and Darren a couple of years later. She called us her change-of-life babies, but until I knew what that meant I couldn't figure how a few more kids could change your life that much. As close as Ginger and I were, Darren was sort of like our honorary third twin. We babied him and dressed him up and for the most part took him with us everywhere we went. The three of us would read together, perched in a tree in the backyard. We shared a stereo, Ginger and I letting Darren take it for two or three days at a time into his room once he passed his twelfth birthday. And when Karen Milton, the love of his sixteen-year-old life, stood him up for junior prom, Ginger and I went to her house, rang the doorbell, and I punched her straight in the face when she answered. Ginger was scared to death, but stood her ground. She might not have been as impulsive as I was, but she never left me to flounder alone. She was always there.

Karen Milton's folks had me arrested. They didn't understand familial loyalty one little bit. I couldn't totally blame them – I did break Karen's nose, and she had supposedly had a burgeoning career as a catalogue model. I found it difficult to believe – I thought she was shaped like a tuber – but I knew better than to say so. My dad was so proud of us for sticking up for our little brother that he bought Ginger and me our first car, an old Buick station wagon with actual wood panel sides. We had the summer of our lives, riding around in that thing, stopping at Dairy Queen and singing out the window at the fireflies, and arguing whose turn it was to drive. We never talked about it, but Ginger could always tell what was bothering me, and I her. If she was in math class and I was in English, sometimes the answer to a quadratic equation would pop into my head, and Ginger would find herself reciting bits of *Macbeth* in her head.

I loved my older brothers well enough, but in some ways they were like foreign creatures to me – blond and athletic and perfect. In fact, I looked like that too, but I always felt darker, as though I should have inky black hair and pale skin. But we all had the quirky, snide sense of humor that made me love my family, when I could bear to talk to them in my angst-ridden teenage years. In my family, the highest form of humor is self-deprecation. Not the "I'm so ugly" kind of thing, but got a long anecdote about having your skirt blow up in front of a class of tenth-graders when you were a student teacher? That story will get told and retold in various guises in my family, with continued appreciation. Bump somebody's car in the parking lot and accidentally leave your dentist's business card instead of your own on the other card's windshield? Hil-arious. In my family, one-upmanship is about how stupid you could be in any given context, not about the money you made or the house you just bought.

Sometimes I thought my being a crackhead was the ultimate manifestation of stupid one-upmanship.

I, Danny, am the black sheep of the family. Literally, now. When my life started taking its sharp sudden downtown after my leaving Jack, when I went from a few glasses of Shiraz once or twice a week to being a full-time crack addict within a year, I dyed my naturally wheat-blonde hair black. Since I had always felt like a goth Sylvia Plath inside the body of a brainless cheerleader, I figured it was time to let the outside match how I felt inside. I'm the only person I know who has blonde roots showing. Dark hair feels much better on me. I don't care how it looks. I don't spend much time in front of the mirror anymore anyway.

When I left Jack – when I felt like I had to leave, to separate myself from the madness that was overtaking him – I wanted to jump into a dark pool and never resurface. And that's what I did. I made almost a career of it, in the beginning. From a young age, I could drink like the Irish girl I was, generations back, and I became a regular at a neighborhood pub, where I learned how to drink like a professional. I found myself enjoying the company of people who lived on the margins; the unemployed actors, wait staff on their days off who couldn't stay away from the place, tweedy retired professors with English accents and broken capillaries, and guys who didn't get work at the union hall that day. I could watch baseball, discuss politics or read a trashy novel with a glass of Shiraz in front of me, and I didn't have to think about a thing. No one judged me. No one asked difficult questions. I was everyone's little sister. The bartender dealt coke, and soon I became one of the people running to the bathroom every forty minutes, becoming more animated every time I came back. Then I met Gene and he introduced me to cocaine's evil cousin.

Crack.

All I can say is, if it didn't feel like a choir of angels all of a sudden bursting into the room and whispering into your ears, I wouldn't do it. Taking a hit off the pipe is like having every good thing in the world rush into your head in one moment, and stay there for a bit, and all the bad things are gone, gone, gone. It's better than a twenty-minute orgasm. Not that I would know.

Crack had me at hello. But it also took my money – I spent over a hundred grand in one year on my habit, without blinking. I had always been a saver; never cared a whit about material things. But crack became my full-time job. I used a lot of creative financing, believe me, and I think most of the collection agencies had me on speed dial. I change my unlisted phone number more than some people I know change their underwear.

Not only did it take away my money, but it also took away

most of my straight friends – what we in the drug world call the normal people, with nine-to-five jobs and mortgages and kids, regardless of sexuality – and most of my family. Not that they didn't try, my family, but my shame meant that I knew they were better off not worrying about what I was getting up to.

But Ginger knew. She knew what I was doing to myself.

Of course she did. She was my twin. I couldn't get away with lying to her about anything important. I couldn't figure out how I hadn't felt her death. I told myself it must have been the crack; it messed with everything in my head, and I couldn't read any signs clearly when I was high – no hunger, anger, love or hate. That's why I did it; that was the beauty of it. Torturing myself that I left Jack when he needed me? Crack, please. Haven't eaten for three days and feeling a bit weak? A couple of stale crackers and another hit will fix me right up without having to go to the grocery store or call for pizza.

And my twin sister had died, without me knowing anything about it. I hadn't felt her death, but I felt her absence.

I used to be a twin. I was Ginger Cleary's twin.

The airport in Toronto was particularly crowded. Word had gotten out that the Rolling Stones were flying in with their walkers to do one of their impromptu concerts at The Horseshoe or some other old-school bar band kind of place. Other than "Sympathy For The Devil," I'm not much of a Stones fan, so I couldn't have cared less if they were standing next to me at the Starbucks getting shots of espresso to shoot into their veins. Now, if Tom Waits was next to me in line, I might have made a sycophantic ass of myself. Or Elvis Costello. Or Kris Kristofferson. God, I'd had it bad for KK when I was a kid. He still did it for me. The whole Rhodes Scholar-troubadour thing. And his version of "Me and Bobby McGee" is probably my favorite recording of all time. But all around me were your basic no-names. Like me.

I scanned the crowd in line at Air Canada, looking for Darren. Darren had paid for my ticket, and he was supposed to meet me here. I didn't have the confirmation number, but he had assured me on the phone that we were booked on the 5:15 flight to LAX, California.

I'd like to say that as soon as I'd gotten Fred's message that Ginger had died, I'd pulled myself together and gotten on the phone with my brothers, trying to arrange a flight. I'd like to be able to say that.

Instead, I'd unplugged my phone, taken a huge hit, and spent the next eight or ten hours with Gene, sitting on my battered green couch. Anyone who tells you that drugs don't help make pain easier to bear is telling only a half truth. When you're high, the pain is a part of you, but bearable. It's when you come down that it gets you, and the pain hits you a millionfold. And therein, as they say, lies the rub.

Gene watched over me, his eyes red from sadness for me and two or three days without sleep, and listened to me talk about Ginger. What a great mother she was. How, being fraternal twins, we looked so different, yet still like sisters. How beautiful Ginger was, how everything that was awkward and uncomfortable about me was somehow effortless and gentle on her. How she had gotten her period a year before I did and when I finally got mine at fifteen and Mom wouldn't let me wear tampons because she thought it would mean I wouldn't be a virgin anymore, Ginger had given me a big box of Tampax and told me to hide them under my bed. She had even, God help her, locked the two of us in the bathroom and showed me the right way to put one in. And made it funny. By the time it was done, we were both laughing so hard that Dad started banging on the door wanting to know what all the commotion was about in there.

The heartbreak when we were eighteen and Ginger decided to go off to Bennington to study French literature.

French literature. That was Ginger. Loved what she loved, and wouldn't be talked out of anything because it might be impractical. When I finally enrolled in college in Toronto, I went from travel and tourism to culinary arts (big mistake – I was asked to leave after I started my second fire in one of the college kitchens), and finally settled into a diploma program in something they called Health and Wellness.

The irony is not lost on me.

Whenever Ginger came to visit me we wouldn't stop talking. We would sit up late into the night while she told me about boys – she and her high-school sweetheart Fred had taken a year's break from each other, and I was a single girl around town – and her classes, and what it was like in Vermont. I would make her laugh, talking about how I felt like I was stuck in one perpetual Phys. Ed. class.

I would just sit on my bed and watch her cleaning her face with Nivea, a ritual that she performed every night of her life. She had never put on so much as a swipe of mascara, not even years later at her own quirky wedding at Cape Cod, when she and Fred had exchanged vows in front of our two families and a half dozen friends. It was a cold day in October, they were both barefoot, and the breakers were so loud that none of us could hear a word that the justice of the peace was saying. Still, it was the most beautiful wedding I have ever attended, and I wasn't the only one crying. And crying is something I was never in the habit of doing. Not then, anyway.

She and Fred were the happiest couple in the world. They had started dating when they both worked at McDonald's at sixteen. I had opted to work in Dad's dry cleaners, but Ginger went for the glamour of the golden arches. Fred and Ginger: it had to be destined, right? Fred was no trip to Hollywood, as my mother, bless her, was fond of saying: he had never grown into the Dumbo ears that protruded from his gigantic head, and the man seemed to have been born without shoulders. But he was funny, smart, kind, a whiz with computers and business later on, as well as being a great fan of early twentieth-century Irish poetry. I always thought Fred was a prize – I think, looking back, that he was my first crush. Even though we were the same age, he treated me with the affection one would reserve for a beloved family dog. And I was always just as loyal as one.

Ginger was what I had always wished I could have been, but have always known deep in my soul that I couldn't. I didn't have her charisma, her loving openness with everyone, even strangers in the grocery store. Her infinite capacity for nurturing.

She was the best of us, and now she was dead.

And in his hysterical voicemail to me, Fred had said it was by her own hand.

* * *

I got to the front of the line at the Air Canada check-in counter, and slapped my passport down on the counter. Thank God it was still valid. I hadn't used it in two years, but before that, with Jack, I had travelled all over the world. I had more stamps in there than all of the Jolie-Pitts combined.

"I'm on the 5:15 to Orange County," I said, not returning the ticket agent's perky smile. "I don't have the confirmation number. My brother has it, but he's not here yet."

The agent slid my passport off the counter and looked at the picture, looked at me.

"You've certainly changed," she said. I'll say. My passport showed a woman with long blonde hair and thirty extra healthy pounds on my 5'10" frame.

"Plastic surgery, Lisa," I said, glancing at her nametag. I met her eyes with a level gaze. She smiled uncertainly, then dropped her eyes. She was clicking away at her terminal. "Aisle seat, please, Lisa, if possible. And please seat my brother, Darren Cleary, next to me." I was trying to sound normal and control the shaking that was starting to take over my limbs. Sometimes after a long enough bender and not enough sleep or food, I could resemble someone with a neurological disorder. I had managed a bit of sleep, so I should be okay without a hit for a while, but I was days past any food other than saltines.

And my twin sister had committed suicide. Ginger was dead. I knew I couldn't think about it now. If I thought about it now, I would sink down to the floor and might not be able to get up again. And this, I had to do. I fantasized about running out the door, into a taxi and back home. Calling D-Man and hitting the pipe until my heart exploded. What did it matter? Ginger was dead. I somehow used every reserve of strength left in me to stay standing. To not flake out on Darren and leave him to deal with Fred and the boys – oh God, the boys – alone. Not to mention Skipper and Laurence and the horrors of funeral planning.

I closed my eyes, and willed myself to be still, and to not vomit.

Lisa the Ticket Agent clicked away further without acknowledging me. She probably had dealt with enough wise-ass freaks today. She was in her forties, tanned to a nice leathery quality, and looked as tired as I felt.

"Sorry if I was rude," I said to her. "I'm going down to California for my sister's funeral. I'm a little…"

I stopped when Lisa the Ticket Agent quickly glanced up at me. Something in her eyes made mine start to water.

"Oh, my dear, I'm so sorry," she said. "I don't know what I'd do if something happened to my sister. She's my best friend." She leaned across the counter and patted my hand. "I'm sorry for your loss, Danielle."

Danielle. The only person who had ever, and I mean ever, called me that was my mother, and she was dead too. Three years ago, she and Dad, driving back from their yearly Florida jaunt, killed by a drunk driver on the I-95.

"Danny," I said, wetness leaking slowly onto my pale cheeks now. "Everybody calls me Danny."

"Well, Danny," she said as brightly as she was able, faced with a scrawny junkie with a bad dye job crying in front of her, "I'll tell you what I'm going to do. Coach is overbooked, so I'm going to bump you and Darren Cleary into first-class. Is that alright?"

I loved Lisa.

I nodded. "Thank you," I said softly. Lisa nodded and whipped my suitcase onto the conveyor belt behind her and handed me my boarding pass. She pointed out the gate and boarding time, half an hour from now. Where was Darren?

"You have a good flight now, Danny," she said. I glanced at her and tried to smile but I think it came out all crooked. I was about to walk away from the counter when a glance at Lisa's face stopped me.

"Danny," she said, in a quieter, different voice than she had used before, "I just had a flash of something. Do you know what I mean?" She was looking intently at me.

"A hot flash?" I asked, confused, and then blushed, because I didn't want to insinuate that she was menopausal. Lisa looked like she cared about her looks. Women who spend that much time in tanning beds don't usually want to be mistaken for anything past thirty-five, even if their skin resembles an alligator handbag.

"Your sister. She didn't die naturally, Danny," she said. She was whispering, and the look on her face made the hair on my forearms stand straight up.

"No, they're saying she committed suicide," I said, locked onto Lisa's face. Somewhere in my brain I couldn't believe I was telling a stranger that my sister had offed herself.

"I don't think she did, Danny," Lisa continued. "I don't think so." She turned away from me for a minute and called out to another agent. "Kimberly, I'm going on break right now, okay?" I stood with my feet glued to the floor, sweating and shivering at once. Lisa looked back at me with her normal face and a hard, shaky tone in her voice.

"You be careful down there, Danny, okay? You be real

careful." And with that, Lisa walked quickly behind the agents to her right and into a room behind counters, snapping the door sharply behind her.

I believe in psychic phenomena about as much as I believe in the Easter Bunny. But I shivered, and I wasn't sure it was just from the lack of sleep, food, and crack leaving my body.

I took my suitcase and walked away.

Now I just had to get through security with a balloon filled with two grams of powdered cocaine and half an eightball of crack stuck as far up my vagina as I could get it. With a length of kitchen string tied around the balloon for easy retrieval in a public bathroom. The coke was to keep me awake and going and get me through times when I had to be on, and in extremis, I could do a fairly decent job of cooking it into something resembling crack. Crack, because, crack.

My lack of paranoia served me well. I smiled and sailed through security and customs in Toronto with a smile on my face and narcotics in my cooch.

Darren was waiting for me at the gate. He pulled me into him and hugged me tightly, not letting go even after I tried to pull away. What started with a sad fraternal embrace ended with us wrestling, me trying to get away from him as he held my head in a vice grip against his chest and sang "Hush little baby, don't say a word, Daddy's going to buy you a mockingbird" loudly, until I was laughing so hard I started to hiccup. A family affliction. Nobody could make me laugh like Darren could. All the other passengers at the gate were watching, some with confusion, most with amusement. At nearly thirty, Darren looked a bit like a younger Brad Pitt. And unfortunately, he knew it.

Handsome, is what I'm trying to say. Even I, his sister, could see it, and I liked to tease him about how long he spent on his hair in the morning, and ask him how the boys in the gay bars were liking him now that he was getting so long in the tooth. Stuff like that. My brother was uber-straight, and a slut to boot.

"You smell like weed," I whispered. This was Darren's only vice. He didn't smoke cigarettes, and wasn't much of a drinker. It was weird that we were related, when you think about it.

"That would be because I just smoked some, Danny Banany," he stage-whispered back.

"Here? In the airport?" Even I wasn't that dumb.

"Duh. In the car, shit-for-brains." We parked on chairs and he put his arm around me, and I leaned into him gratefully.

"Since when do you have a car? Why didn't I get a ride then, ingrate?"

"Wasn't my car, baby. Got a lift from an admirer of the female persuasion." I rolled my eyes at him.

In first class we got the kind of service that I had become distinctly unused to in the past two years of sitting around my smoky apartment, smoking crack. Darren told the flight attendant to "keep the wine flowing" as though he was Dean Martin on the way to Vegas, and the food was better than I had any right to expect. As I shovelled some kind of beef stew into my face, I caught Darren grinning at me.

"The fuck is your problem," I said, and stuck my tongue out, showing him my half-chewed food. He laughed. Sometimes the old jokes are the best jokes.

"Nice to see you eat," he said.

"Happens all the time," I answered, swigging a glass of red wine.

"Bullshit," he answered. "How long since you used?"

I paused. "Twenty-two hours," I answered. I looked at his watch. "And about twenty minutes." Food had made me feel better. Wine had made me feel better. And with crack, if you end a long bender and get some of your basic human needs fulfilled – sleep, food, hydration – you can go a while without using again and feeling too awful. Despite what you see in the media, crack isn't like heroin. Most of us don't need it every day. Unless, that is, we're already on a bender, in which case stopping seems like the impossible dream. And I had already decided to get through the flight clean. I wasn't so far gone enough that I didn't realize that I needed to eat and achieve some semblance of normalcy before I faced Fred and the boys.

"Can't score down there, you know," he said quietly.

We'll see, I thought. "Wasn't planning on it," I said. What I had wouldn't last long, but long enough to score.

Harness the energy that we put into getting our drugs, and you could end world hunger.

Darren raised his eyebrows and said nothing.

"Don't judge me, Darren." I felt my face flush with wine and the beginnings of anger. Addicts and their high horses.

"Wouldn't dream of it, Beanpole," he said, patted my knee, and promptly fell fast asleep. I gazed at him. It was so simple for him. But then again, I thought things had always seemed pretty simple for Ginger. And look how she ended up.

I put my fork down and laid my head on Darren's shoulder. I

wasn't going to tell him what Lisa the Ticket Agent had said. No point in freaking him out.

I was a freak already. I could handle it.

Ginger was alive, and on the plane with us. She kept grabbing at my glass of wine and taking swigs, laughing, holding it out of my reach. It was very important for me to get that glass back. No one else was on the plane, just Ginger, Darren and me. Ginger and Darren were playing hangman, rapt, which confused me, because I'd never seen them doing anything together with such concentration. I looked at Ginger and told her I loved her, even though she was a smart-ass and too perfect to live. Those were the words I used, "too perfect to live." Ginger shook her head at me and took off a white scarf that had appeared around her neck. Her neck was bright red and purple and mottled. I felt sad for her, that it must hurt, like a bad splinter.

"No, Danny, no one is perfect," dream Ginger said sadly. "That's always been your problem."

Then Ginger and I lit up a crack pipe and I inhaled and inhaled and got nothing. I was in a rage of frustration, especially when I saw that she had taken a hit and was holding it in like it was the last breath she would ever take.

Darren was squeezing my hand. "We're landing, drooler," he said. He grabbed a tissue from his jeans pocket and wiped my face. "You're quite a picture."

"Fuck you very much," I said. I rubbed my eyes like a three-year-old, then remembered that I'd actually put eye makeup on this morning. Great.

"You okay?" he said, pushing his chair back to its upright position for landing.

"Crack dream," I said. "Had them before when I've stopped."

"How long do you keep having them?"

"Until you start smoking crack again, I suppose," I answered. Darren sighed.

"Darren," I said slowly. "Ginger didn't kill herself. She didn't." It had been tugging at my faulty brain since I listened to Fred's voicemail message. No way. Not with her boys to look after. Not Ginger.

Fred had said she was found hanging from a shower rod in a motel. Hanging. The image, the thought of it, was seared into my brain and the only way I knew to remove it was to smoke it away.

Darren looked at me, surprised. "Of course she didn't, Beanpole. No fucking way."

We were silent for a bit.

"Why do you think she was at a motel?" Darren told me Ginger's body had been found in some sleazy dive called the Sunny Jim Motor Inn.

He shrugged, staring straight ahead.

"What are we going to do?" I asked. I looked up at him, my little brother, and saw a coldness I had never seen in him before now.

"We're going to talk to the police," he said slowly. "We're going to find out exactly what happened." He tapped a beat on his knee, something only he could hear.

"And if they don't believe us? If they don't help us?"

"Then we'll find out what killed her. *Who* killed her," he answered. He was looking straight ahead.

"And when we find them?"

Darren squeezed my hand again. "What do you think, Danny? What do you want to do?"

I looked him in his cool blue eyes. Mine were reflected in his. "I don't know about you, but I'm going to kill them." I hadn't thought about it, just said it. But as soon as the words were out of my mouth, I knew it was true.

I felt my heart race in my chest like I had just taken a hit. Yes. This was right. This was what had to happen. Wasn't this the natural order of things? I had travelled so far down the rabbit hole that contemplating – actually planning and contemplating killing whoever was responsible for Ginger's death – seemed more than plausible. Why not? Whoever they were, Ginger was worth ten of them, a thousand of them, a million. And if I destroyed myself in the process? Well I was pretty nearly there already. I took a deep breath, and felt an odd peace settle over me, a feeling I hadn't had in recent memory. This could be the end, then. I would do this thing, and I would do it well. And after that, whatever happened to me didn't matter.

Darren leaned past me and looked out the window at sunny California.

"No," he whispered, his eyes trained on the ground. "*We're* going to kill them."

I looked at Darren quickly. My sunny blond brother had a look on his face that I had never seen before. His eyes looked like mine, at that moment. Calm and decided and yet not quite present. He was somewhere else, somewhere where he could do serious damage to anyone who got in his way.

"We've lost too much," I said. "Right?"

"You are right," Darren said, leaning back into his seat and closing his eyes. "Right the fuck on."

But I knew that when push came to shove, I would do this alone. Darren had a life. He had a great, sprawling, messy adventure of a life to look forward to. And as much as he loved Ginger, she was my twin. My other half.

This was my job.

It was only seven-thirty p.m. in California when we landed, and even inside the airport it felt hot. Hot and dry.

"Santa Anas," Darren explained. "There are probably going to be fires again."

"Thank you, Mr. Weather Channel," I said. Probably his only truly geeky habit, an obsession with weather patterns had been with him since he was a kid looking forward to snowstorms and hurricanes in Maine. If I let him go, he would explain the meteorological reasons for such climate patterns, and I would keel over from glassy-eyed boredom. Standing by the luggage carousel waiting for bags to start spitting out, I had a sudden and intense craving, so profound that I wanted to lie down on the spot, curl up into the fetal position, and wait for it to go away. It had been something like twenty-six hours since I last smoked. The longest I'd gone without a hit in ten months. And while I had what I needed tucked safely between my legs, even I wasn't about to try to smoke it in a public washroom in LAX.

"There's my bag," I said, pointing to a lime-green suitcase

coming around on the conveyor. "Bathroom."

I hurried to the ladies' room and thanked the toilet gods that it wasn't crowded. I locked myself into a cubicle and threw up, every ounce of meat and wine violently splashing all over the floor and walls. It wasn't a neat endeavour. It continued until I had nothing left, and I leaned against the wall for support. At home, I would have slumped down to the floor, but by this point there was far too much of a mess for that. I felt sorry for the poor washroom attendant who had to face this. If I could have tipped her, I would have. I felt as empty and hollow and in as much pain as I ever have in my life. I closed my eyes. If it weren't for this, the vomiting that always overtook me for a couple of days after the crack was leaving my system, I might have been able to quit. But anytime I started to feel like this, I would pick up the phone and call D-Man on my speed dial, and within a couple of hours all would be just fine. It wasn't just the vomiting, it was the constant nausea and diarrhea, which lasted even longer. Note to self, I thought: buy water.

I spent a few minutes at the sink trying to clean myself up. I was in a white t-shirt and pale, ripped blue jeans, and both were now brilliantly stained with bright red vomit. Mascara had smeared under my eyes, my skin was gray under the fluorescent lights, and my lips were chapped and bleeding from chewing them, another habit I subconsciously took to when I was without my drug.

Where were the model talent scouts when you needed one?

When I exited the bathroom, Darren was chatting it up with a paunchy guy in a black suit who was wearing a spiffy cap. He was holding a sign.

"Here she is!" Darren said, very hail-fellow-well-met. He was another one in the family who made friends wherever he went. "Look, Danny!" He held up a sign that read "D and D Cleary."

"D and D," I said. "Drunk and Disorderly."

"Dungeons and Dragons," Darren said.

"Dumb and Dumber," I shot back.

"Dark and Demented?" Darren tried.

"Weak," I said. "Bitch, please." The driver was looking at us, an uncertain smile on his face. He was probably in his fifties but he had the red nose and beer gut of the experienced drinker. Ex-cop maybe? Couldn't have a drunk driving record if he worked for a car service though. I might be an addict myself, but I ranked drunk drivers with pedophiles and serial rapists – bad, bad news.

"Danny Cleary," I said, shaking the man's hand. Being around my family always made me want to improve my manners. I was the one with the street skills, not the social ones. Division of responsibility and all that.

Both the driver and Darren were looking at the stains on my clothes, and the ashen, makeup-smeared face. They both looked appalled. I really know how to make a great impression.

"So," I said brightly. "Who sent you, Mr. Driver?"

He snapped his eyes away from my t-shirt. Or was it my breasts? If it was, he'd have to look pretty hard. I still had them, but everything I owned was two sizes too big for me now. "Mr. Lindquist," he answered. "He sent me to come and fetch you up."

Fred had sent him. He must be in rough shape if he didn't come himself. "Well, fetch away," I said. "Take me to your leader." Driver looked uncertainly at me. I motioned for the door. "You

41

know – let's go. Let's blow this pop stand. As it were."

Darren nudged me as we trailed behind the man out of the terminal. "Be nice," he hissed. Then, slightly louder, "Did you puke, or what?"

"No, I just grabbed somebody else's off the floor and rubbed it on myself."

I rooted around in my bag for an Altoid. "Why do you think Fred didn't pick us up himself?" I wanted to know.

Darren shrugged. "His wife just died, Danny. He's got a funeral to plan, two boys who just lost their mother, and a house full of relatives on the way." I nodded. We were quiet for a minute, and when we left the airport, the driver indicated that we should stay put and he'd pull the car around. I could get used to this, I thought.

"I don't know how he's going to live without her," Darren said.

"And the boys," I said. "Oh God, those poor boys."

"Fred told me that the funeral will be closed casket," Darren said. I nodded. I hated open casket funerals. "I have to see her," he continued.

I took a deep breath. Crack, crack, crack, crack. Crack, please.

"Me too," I said.

"We're family, they have to let us," Darren said. "Don't they? By law or whatever?"

"Fuck the law," I said, nodding at nervous-looking No-Name Driver as he opened the back door for me to get into a gaudy stretch Hummer limo. Liberace would have been at home in here. Or Elton John. "We're going to see our sister."

* * *

Rush-hour traffic was still heavy, and Darren and I sprawled in the back of a car that was bigger than my apartment. Smelled better, too.

Darren was examining the crystal decanters thoughtfully provided by the limo company.

"Scotch," he said, smelling one and making a face as he put the stopper back on. "I hate scotch."

"What's that one? Vodka?" I pointed to a decanter filled with clear liquid. Darren smelled it.

"Gin," he said.

"Yuck," I said. "Find me the vodka." It was too surreal. It was sunny, even through the tinted windows, and three hours earlier. My twin sister was dead. I was going to kill someone.

That was the only thought that gave me any peace.

Darren gave me a raised eyebrow, but he smelled another clear decanter, and rooted around in a little fridge until he came up with something to mix it with. As we cruised slowly through the SoCal evening, past the palm trees and strip malls that I hadn't seen in three years, Darren fixed me a vodka and cranberry. It was heavy on the cranberry, light on the vodka. I took a sip and looked meaningfully at Darren.

"You just puked, Danny," he said. "Think you might want to take it a little easy, get some more food in your stomach?"

He was right of course, and I chose not to give him a tart reply. I held on tightly to my heavy crystal glass and looked outside.

We'd left the 405 and were heading to the Pacific Coast Highway.

"Scenic route," I said. Darren nodded.

"I wanted to see the ocean," he said. I looked at him. He was wearing his sunglasses, and I realized he must have had a word with the driver. This was as hard on Darren as it was on me, and I had to remember that in the days to come. I leaned over and grabbed his hand, squeezed it, and said nothing. We sailed through the beach communities Ginger had loved. I took a big swig of my drink and tried to think of nothing.

We drove through Huntington Beach and didn't stop.

"Hey. This isn't the way to Fred and Ginger's," I said.

"They moved, brainiac. A year ago. Remember?"

Vaguely. Something about a new house in Newport? Close to the country club?

"Have you been down?" I asked him.

He hadn't. I watched as we passed some of the bars I remembered down here, places that tried on the outside to look like friendly little crab shacks but there were more Rolexes inside than in all of Geneva.

I was nervous, and I could tell Darren was too. I hadn't seen Fred or my nephews in close to three years, and who knew what state they were going to be in. Matthew and Luke were eleven now, twins like Ginger and me. And like us, not identical – Luke was blonder and had Ginger's glow about him, where Matthew was a bit darker and more pale. More like me, as I recalled, but I hadn't seen them in a long time.

And look at the state I was in. I debated getting the driver to pull over so I could pull a clean t-shirt from my suitcase in the trunk, but even the little bit of vodka I was drinking had put lead into my thighs. I didn't want to move.

The driver took a hard left and we wound our way through streets with houses you couldn't see from the road, with huge private gates and lush bougainvillea along the side of the road. Eventually, we pulled into a driveway with a huge gate in front and with a click on something on his visor, the gates smoothly pulled open.

Darren and I looked at each other. The driver hadn't buzzed the security panel outside the gate, he had his own clicker.

"This is Fred's car," I whispered. "This isn't a limo service."

"He can't hear you," Darren said, indicating the privacy glass separating us from the driver.

"How do you know," I said, as the car swung around a circular driveway, paved with what looked like Italian marble, to a mansion. There was no other word for it. It looked like a small hotel, all pale yellow stone and actual turrets, with a gigantic fountain out front and a fit-looking man in a black polo shirt and black cargo pants hurrying down the steps toward us.

Darren and I looked at each other. "We're on," he said. He looked closer at me. "You have a cranberry moustache." With that, he climbed out of the car. I swiped frantically at my lips with the back of my hand.

"Ms. Cleary," the butler, or bodyguard, whoever he was, said to me, reaching his hand in to help me out. He looked kindly into my eyes, ignoring the vomit-splashed clothes and the juice stain above my lips. He was so good, it was as though he hadn't seen them. "I'm so sorry for your loss. We're all devastated at Mrs. Lindquist's passing. Just devastated."

Mrs. Lindquist? My sister had servants now, and they called her Mrs. Lindquist?

"Thank you," I said, shaking his hand.

"James Rosen," the man said. He had a slight accent I

couldn't quite place. Israeli maybe? "You can call me Rosen. Or James. Whichever you prefer."

"Just don't call you late for dinner?" I blurted and caught Darren rolling his eyes off to my side.

Rosen smiled kindly and nodded, obviously not knowing what the fuck I was talking about. Good thing – neither did I. I have been known to babble a bit when nervous.

Darren and I stood by, watching the driver and Rosen unload our luggage from the trunk of the limo. Neither of us was used to being waited on like this, and all I could think of was, where is Fred? Where are the boys? Why haven't they come outside? Did they see the vomit on my shirt and are hiding behind the curtains? I wondered frantically if Rosen wanted to share a pipe with me. Then the thought made me laugh out loud.

Rosen and the driver – whose name, Darren seemed to know, was Derek – glanced up as I started giggling frantically and uncontrollably. I couldn't breathe. I started hiccupping in a very ladylike fashion, and before I knew it I was bent over at the waist. Then there was a sound coming from somewhere, a horrible keening sound, and when Darren put his hand on my back, I realized it was coming from me.

Ginger was dead. My twin was dead. It couldn't be right. It was as if every sadness I had ever experienced – losing my parents, leaving Jack – was trying to make itself heard.

I am not one to cause scenes, but I sat right down on the ground. I didn't feel like my legs could bear my weight any longer. I was rocking back and forth and I couldn't seem to catch any air.

I didn't look up, but I could see that everyone was standing stock-still around me. Then I could feel Darren's hand on my back and under my arm, pulling me up.

"They were twins, she and Mrs. Lindquist," he said to the two men. "Think one of you could show us to a bathroom?"

As Rosen led the way inside, all was quiet. No sign of Fred or the boys, and the only human I could see was a squat little woman in a maid's uniform Windexing a mirror in the hall as though her life depended on it. I felt like I was watching a movie. This couldn't be real, could it?

"Uh, James?"

"Miss?"

"Where is our brother-in-law? And the boys? Where is everybody?"

Rosen paused and turned around, looked at us. "I thought you knew," he said.

"Knew what," Darren said. I could tell his throat was dry.

"Mr. Lindquist is being held at the Orange County jail. He's been arrested. The police think he killed Mrs. Lindquist."

"He said she… did it herself," I said. Darren hadn't moved.

Rosen shook his head. "That was the initial…" he started, but didn't seem to be able to finish.

I sat down suddenly again on a conveniently placed velvet chair in the hallway and put my head between my legs. I thought maybe I was going to be sick again, I was so lightheaded. I didn't want to puke on Ginger's beautiful floors.

"And the boys, where are the boys," Darren continued, ignoring me.

"Oh dear. No one has talked to you," Rosen said. "It all happened so quickly."

"Where the fuck are my nephews?" Darren said, his fists clenched. His voice was quiet, but his knuckles were white.

Rosen regarded him seriously. "I'm afraid to tell you, sir, that until this matter is sorted, in the absence of family to take them," here, Rosen's voice changed a bit, "last night the police removed the children from the home and have placed them in the care of Social Services."

I sat bolt upright, my vision clearing. No. No way. No fucking way.

"I'm going to change my shirt, and then I'm going to get Fred out of jail," I said to Darren. "You get those kids back home."

Darren nodded, and looked at Rosen like he wanted to hit him. "You take the limo," he said to me, still looking at the poor valet. "And maybe Rosen here can give me a phone number of whoever came and took the kids. How long have they been gone?"

"They were taken yesterday, sir," Rosen replied. "We presumed that someone would have called the family." He took a step forward, put a hand on Darren's arm, which I thought at the time was a very brave act. "I'm so sorry. We would have been happy to keep the boys here. We all love them. They are like our own children. Marta hasn't stopped cleaning since they left. She hasn't slept a wink." Behind him, the maid I had seen earlier peeked around the corner and started talking away in Spanish, tears flowing down her kind face.

Darren went over to her and hugged her, like he had done to me at the airport. The two of them stayed together like that, both of them rocking back and forth and crying. Something hardened in my chest. I felt more sober than I had ever felt. Rosen and I looked at each other.

"Where's my room, James," I said. "I need to change."
I hadn't thought about crack in nearly ten minutes. A record.

3

I was glad it was finally dark as Derek the driver steered the big car skillfully along the much quieter streets. He kept glancing at me in his rear view. The partition was down because I had asked him to lower it – I had planned to ask him questions about Fred and Ginger and the boys. But I found I couldn't yet. Not until I had talked to Fred. I planned to get in to see him, even if I had to blow a corrections officer to do it.

Okay, not really. And despite the clean shirt and a freshly washed face, I doubt any of them would want me to. I wasn't exactly looking like a sex bomb. I had neglected to change my vomit-splattered jeans in my rush to get to the lockup. And as I ran my hands through my hair, I thought I felt something sticky in there too. Lovely. But I doubted Fred would notice, under the circumstances.

Every time I thought about the twins in some kind of group home or in foster placement, or whatever they did with kids whose mothers had died violently and had their father sent to jail for it, I felt like somebody had punched me in the solar plexus. I had to keep taking deep breaths and had to concentrate. Crack had addled my brain, and coming off it made it worse. I just wanted to lie down on the backseat and sleep for ten hours.

Maybe more. Maybe until I woke up in heaven with Ginger.

Except I doubted that Ginger and I were going to wind up in the same place in the afterlife. She was perfect, and me? Not so much.

We pulled in through some wire gates and talked to a security guard. I couldn't hear what they said, but the guard motioned us through.

Derek pulled the car out in front of the building. "I have to stay with the car, Miss Cleary," he said nervously. He sounded like this was the last place he wanted to be. I wondered if he had spent a night or two here himself.

He didn't open my door this time, and I realized that I had already come to expect such treatment. A person could get used to this kind of life. Is this what had happened to Ginger and Fred? Had all this wealth done something bad to them? I couldn't imagine it. They were the nicest people in the world.

I approached a guard who was sitting behind a glass booth.

"I'm here to see Fred Lindquist," I said to him. "He was brought in yesterday. He's my brother-in-law. He was apparently charged with killing my sister." Babble some more, idiot.

The guard just stared at me, then started tapping away at a computer.

"His arraignment is tomorrow morning. No visitors."

Jesus Christ. "Please," I whispered.

"No, ma'am," the officer said. "Only his lawyer and detectives working the case are allowed to see prisoners unless there is a visitation order. Besides," he added, looking down at the papers in front of him, effectively dismissing me, "there are no visitors after six."

The man didn't look like he would respond to flirting, so I didn't try. Instead, I tried tears. It wasn't hard. I seemed to be getting good at this crying thing.

"Please," I said, letting the tears flow down my face unchecked. "I just flew in and found out that the police think she was murdered, and that Fred was charged for it, and I don't know where their kids are, and I don't know what to do."

The guard sighed. "I'm sorry for your troubles. I really am. But without a visitation order, I can't let you in to see him. I can give you a request for visitation, though," he added, pushing a form through the partition to me. I glanced at it.

"Can you tell me the name of his lawyer, then?"

"I'm not supposed to," the guard said warily.

"Please. I'm begging you. I need to talk to him."

The guard sighed again, looked over his shoulder, and tapped away at the computer a few times. He took a piece of scrap paper and wrote a name and phone number down on it. I looked at the guard's bright red hair and acne scars, saw him as another vulnerable human suddenly, and thought that he was the nicest person I had ever met.

"Thank you. Thank you so much," I said. I had seen payphones by the front door, and I headed back to them. Then I paused and turned around and went back to the guard. "You wouldn't have change for the payphone, would you? I'll pay you back."

This time the guard actually smiled. "You're pushing your luck, ma'am," he said, fishing a few quarters from his pocket and pushing them across the counter to me.

"What's your name, officer?" I asked him, scooping up the coins.

"Greg," he answered. "Greg Tobolowski."

"I owe you one, Greg."

"All you owe me is seventy-five cents, ma'am."

I started to walk away. I turned back again. "Greg?"

"Ma'am?"

"Don't call me ma'am. Call me Danny."

Greg smiled and nodded at me, and I went to the payphones with a lighter heart. Over the last couple of years, I had strayed so far from straight society that I always assumed that there was an invisible barrier dividing me from people in positions of authority. Even bank tellers seemed to be the enemy. Once upon a time, though, I had been moneyed myself – not like Fred and Ginger, of course, but I wore a significant cluster of rings on my left hand and paid five hundred dollars a month on my haircuts and highlights. I was never much of a shopper, but I hadn't looked at the price tags on clothes, and had eaten in nice restaurants three or four times a week. Bought nine-dollar bottled water in those restaurants too. On top of the wine, of course.

But that was a lifetime ago, and in the here and now, I was a crack addict standing in a jailhouse in California, trying to get my brother-in-law's lawyer on the phone to find out why they thought he murdered my sister.

I couldn't think about the twins. That was Darren's job. If I thought about them right now, I wouldn't be able to function.

I looked at the scrap of paper in my hand. Chandler York, it read, with a phone number scrawled underneath. I dialed the number and slipped a couple of quarters in the phone, hoping against hope that the man would still be in his office at this time in the evening. With a name like Chandler York, he probably charged a thousand bucks an hour. If I could charge that for anything, I'd be putting in pretty long hours.

I was just about to leave a message on his voicemail when I heard Greg talking to someone. A lean, fifty-something man in a million-dollar suit, with salt-and-pepper hair and a tall, tightly coiled grace. Greg was pointing in my direction, and the man turned to face me. My heart started pounding harder and I broke out into a light sweat along my hairline. When you're a drug addict, you don't want men like that looking at you while you're standing in a jailhouse. It's just instinct. Older white men in authority positions don't usually take a shine to crackheads. They tend to ask awkward questions. Unless, of course, they're paying them for their time in a motel somewhere.

I hoped he didn't notice that I had started to sweat, because at that moment I realized I still had a balloon full of drugs shoved inside me.

The man approached. "Miss Cleary," he said, smiling at me. He wasn't handsome, exactly. His teeth were slightly crooked as though he had grown up without great dental care, but the whole package was somehow elegant. He carried himself as though he had seriously studied martial arts. "I'm Chandler York. I understand you're looking for me."

"Golly," I said. It was probably the first time in my life that I'd said the word, and I hoped it would be the last.

"Let me just say, I'm so sorry for your loss." He grabbed one of my hands with both of his.

"Fred didn't kill her," I blurted out. I extricated my hand from his. They were too cool, his hands, like he'd just come from the morgue. I shivered.

"Of course he didn't," the lawyer said, as though the idea was ridiculous. "I've known Fred for a couple of years now. We met at a fundraiser," he said. "Salt of the earth. Beautiful wife." Then he looked mortified for a moment, realizing that he was talking about Ginger. He started to apologize, but I shook my head. I didn't want to waste time on niceties.

"So why is he here?"

Chandler York sighed, as though the weight of the world rested on his wide shoulders. "Would you like to see him? I might be able to arrange it. But only for a few minutes. And I would have to be present, of course."

"Yes," I said. "Yes. I would be very grateful." Maybe I wouldn't have to blow someone tonight after all. The thought made me almost start to laugh hysterically again. I really needed sleep.

Oh God. I needed crack.

"But where are my nephews? Did you know that Social Services has taken them?"

He nodded. "It's protocol," he said. "Sadly. They should be released into your custody tonight, now that family is here. I argued a last-minute motion yesterday to have the household staff watch them for the night before you and your brother arrived today, but I wasn't successful." I felt an inch calmer. One night, that was all they had been away. Darren would be able to pick them up tonight. That, at least, we could do for Ginger.

The lawyer said a few words to Greg the Guard, and I was asked politely to remove everything from my pockets and to submit my purse at the front desk. We walked down a hallway, I went through a metal detector, and a female guard waved a security wand over me as though it was the four hundredth time she'd done it that day. Which it probably was.

Another hallway, then a guard led Chandler and me into a room and shut the door behind him. We sat in silence for a moment or two before Fred, dressed in an orange jumpsuit, was led in by a different guard, his hands in cuffs, his ankles manacled.

I stood up. "Fred," I said. I started over to hug him, but the guard stopped me.

"No contact with the prisoner, ma'am." I was ma'am all over the place tonight.

He looked like he'd aged twenty years since the last time I'd seen him. His formerly sandy-red hair was now mostly gray, and he looked like he'd dropped twenty pounds. It made his sticky-out ears seem even more pronounced. My heart turned over. What had he gone through? Could this all be from the last days of horror? Or had something been happening before? I sat back down in my chair.

"Hi, Danny," Fred said quietly. He placed his handcuffed hands carefully on the table in front of him.

"Officer," Chandler York said to the guard, "would it be possible to remove my client's restraints for a few minutes?"

"No, sir," the guard answered, eyes straight ahead. "Sorry."

"How've you been, Danny?" Fred said quietly, looking into my eyes. "Keeping out of trouble?"

"Not so's you'd notice," I answered lightly. I wondered quickly, wildly, if I could excuse myself to the ladies' room to fish the balloon out of my vagina and manage a quick line of coke. "Fred. What's going on?" I found myself fighting back slight hyperventilation. I couldn't breathe in here. Why weren't there any windows?

"I got the call the next morning," Fred said, as though we'd been in the middle of a conversation about it already. "She'd been gone all night, but that had... that had happened before."

Ginger? Staying out all night at motels? This could not be right. I shook my head to clear it. I must have missed something.

He cleared his throat. "It was in a shitty little motel. The Sunny Jim. Can you believe that?" He laughed, almost as though he found something funny. "The Sunny Jim, for fuck's sake."

"Fred," I said, but he kept talking.

"We were about to head out for school," he said. "Matt and Luke and me. I was driving them. You know they're in sixth grade?"

I shook my head. To my shame, I didn't really know. If I had thought enough to do the math I could have figured it out, but I had travelled so far down the highway of bad living that I couldn't remember such things anymore. School and grades and car pools were for real people. I was a shadow of one.

Fred nodded. "They're smart. And both pretty good athletes, too. Get that from the Clearys, you know, the athleticism. You remember – I always threw like a girl."

I smiled. I did remember. In high school, I'd pitched for the girls' softball team, and Fred often came to my games with Ginger and joked that they should open up the pros to girls. My siblings and I had always been strong and physically coordinated, and we all tended to be attracted to people who could break their ankles falling off a sidewalk. Other than my Jack. But Jack had no place in my life anymore. He couldn't help me now.

I hoped Fred wouldn't ask how the boys were. I didn't know if he knew that the twins had been taken away last night. I hoped he didn't know. We'd have them back tonight, I kept thinking. Tonight.

Chandler York cleared his throat. "Fred," he said, "we don't have much time here."

Fred looked down at his hands, and I noticed he was going bald, his exposed skull freckled. "She knew about you, Danny. She knew all about what you were doing."

"I know," I whispered. My heart hammered inside my chest. "I mean, I tried not to lie to her. Not to Ginger."

"You never picked up your phone. You never returned her calls."

"Oh, Fred," I said. "I'm so, so sorry. I just… couldn't. You know?"

"She wanted to save you," Fred continued, as though I hadn't spoken. "She said that you were the other half of her, that she had always had the sense that you were put on this earth to do something special. And she couldn't stand what you were doing to yourself. She said she had to understand it. To help you."

I took a deep breath and closed my eyes, willing myself not to cry, and not to speak.

"It's your fault," he said. Matter-of-fact.

My heart stopped. "What?" I asked.

Fred looked square at me. "Ginger's death, Danny. It's your fault. It was because of you." I stayed silent, scared that if I opened my mouth, Fred would clam up and I would never hear the rest of what he had to say.

"She got involved with some bad people, Danny, all because of you. Because of trying to save you. And do you know what they did to her? Do you know yet?" He wasn't whispering anymore. The guard took a step forward, and Fred lowered his voice again.

"They gave her an overdose of something and then they

hung her from the shower rod. They tried to make it look like she killed herself, hanged herself." Fred looked down, and I could see that his face was wet. In slow motion, I looked at Chandler York.

"It did look like suicide immediately, Miss Cleary," the man said gently. "But the post-mortem showed that she was, uh, hanged, after she had already passed. It was an overdose," he said. "It was some bad dose of heroin."

"Heroin?" I couldn't believe it. If Ginger had somehow wanted to replicate my life, my experiences, heroin wouldn't have been on the menu. Smoking crack was bad enough. Shooting heroin was in another league, and I had never injected myself with anything, ever.

Chandler nodded. "But it was the opinion of the forensic pathologist that Mrs. Lindquist was not a habitual user. In fact this might have been the first time. There were no other needle marks on her body."

No, no, no, no. This didn't make sense.

"But why do they think you did it, Fred? You don't do drugs. I don't understand." I was calm. I would stay calm. I would stay calm until I found who did this to my sister, and then I would be able to let my rage out.

"Because I'm her husband. That's what they always think."

Fred had started to cry, great gulping sobs. Snot bubbled out of his nose. Chandler took out a handkerchief and raised his eyebrows to the guard, who nodded, and Chandler cleaned up Fred's face. Gently, like you would a five-year-old. It seemed an oddly incongruous gesture, but sweet. And Fred barely seemed to even notice, just let Chandler wipe his face as he would a child's.

I couldn't figure it all out, how any of this could be true, even remotely. But I would find out.

Calm, calm, I told myself. You can smoke crack later. In a few hours, maybe less, things will be easier to bear.

"Fred," I said. "Who did this to her? Who was it?"

Fred shook his head. "I don't know, Danny. You tell me."

I went cold. "What do you mean?"

"The suicide note. The fake suicide note, that someone made her write. It was addressed to you." Fred got up and walked toward the door, and the guard opened it. He turned back around and gazed at me. "Oh, and, Danny?"

I couldn't look at him.

"Don't come here again. I don't want to see you again." He stood up, and the guard led him out of the room.

Chandler York followed me back to Fred and Ginger's house. His shiny black Porsche – a car I had always seen as a midlife crisis car, a penis on wheels – seemed incongruous for a man of his stature and gravitas. He should have had a stately sedan, a Mercedes 600-series, or a Jaguar. But then again, I was riding around in the back of a stretch limo, so image-appropriate automobiles were not the order of the day. I kept glancing behind me on the drive back to the house, and Chandler was right behind us. I could see that he spent most of the ride talking on a cell phone. Probably explaining to his wife why he wasn't going to make the opera gala, or whatever other tony event would occupy a normal evening for a man like him.

I looked out the window and tried to erase the image of my sister hanging from a shower rod from my mind.

Darren was still gone when we got home. Rosen was there at the door when I got out of the car. I wondered if he ever rested. He didn't look like he needed rest. He looked like a high-end hitman. But in a good way.

"You saw Mr. Lindquist?" he asked. It had started to rain, a light mist, and Rosen held an umbrella over my head as I walked to the front door. So much for Darren's Santa Anas.

"I did," I replied. "James. You don't think that Fred could do this, do you? Do to my sister what…" I couldn't finish.

"Absolutely not," he interrupted. "It is inconceivable."

I nodded and stood outside the front door as Chandler York unfolded himself from his Porsche. I had to hand it to him, he was pretty graceful. Martial arts? Maybe a former Eastern bloc gymnast who'd lost the accent? My mind was whirring away, doing its best not to think of Ginger.

Inside, Marta, who looked like she'd been crying since I left the house, brought us green tea and little lemon cookies in a living room the size of a ballroom. I hadn't seen this room yet. In fact, other than the grand front hallway and the staircase up to my room, I hadn't seen much of anything.

Chandler and I arranged ourselves on sleek Bauhaus-style furniture. He sipped his tea, and so did I.

"Well," he said, breaking what was turning into the awkward silence of awkward silences. "I'm sure that wasn't pleasant for you."

I gave him a look.

"I spoke to the police on the drive over here. Detective Miller."

"Like Barney Miller," I said. God, I had watched too much 70s TV.

"Uh. Right. Except his given name is Harry." He smiled at

me. "I've crossed paths with Miller a few times over the years, seen him at court. Seems decent enough." I nodded. What did that matter now, I thought. Fred was already in jail. Chandler cleared his throat. "Danny. When, after Ginger's … passing… did you talk to Fred?"

"I didn't," I replied. "He left me a message, and the rest I got from my brother."

"And the rest of your family, when do they arrive?"

"I don't know," I replied. I wasn't sure. Darren had been the family conduit in this situation. I loved my brothers, Skipper and Laurence. I loved them, but I hadn't returned an email or a phone call from either of them in many months. I assumed they knew I was still alive, because they never stopped trying. I shifted in my seat, about to excuse myself to go and finally remove the drugs. Having a latex balloon shoved up your lady parts isn't the most comfortable way to spend a long day. Between an international flight and a visit to a jail, I was happy I hadn't had to undergo a body cavity search today.

"Do you have a big family?" I asked. "Kids and all that?" He had been so gentle, cleaning Fred's face; it was the gesture of a father.

Chandler laughed. "Oh, yes. A lot. They're all grown now, though, spread out, living their lives." I nodded. He was probably a good dad. People who had lots of kids tended to love kids.

"Detective Miller asked if it would be all right for him to come over this evening," he said. "With his partner, Detective French. She's a woman," he added, nodding at me.

"Fancy that," I said. "They actually allow women to be police down here?"

Chandler nodded and smiled a bit. "You got me," he said.

I put my cup down. "I want to know what's going on here. The police thought it was suicide. Even Fred told me it was suicide at first."

Chandler shrugged. "It seemed open-and-shut at first glance. Suicide note. Sloppy, um, job of..."

"Hanging," I finished. I sipped my tea. What a civilized visit. Tea and cookies and suicide. Or murder. But the police were coming over, so I opted to leave the coke balloon firmly where it was for the time being.

"But of course within a few minutes the medical examiner knew..."

"That she was murdered."

"Right." He paused. "Fred called you right away, he told me, before they told him the truth, that she did not take her own life. And soon after he was arrested, so..."

That explained his frantic message on my voicemail. I thought about Lisa, the ticket agent at the airport, telling me that my sister hadn't committed suicide. I shivered.

"Miss Cleary – may I call you Danny?"

"Sure."

"Danny, do you think I could get a real drink?"

I found myself actually smiling at him. He looked tired suddenly, and his suit almost looked rumpled. He and Fred were probably pretty good friends, or close to it. He said he had met him at a benefit, and he knew Ginger. And the way he had cleaned Fred's face at the jail, it was the gesture of a kind and gentle man. "Let me see if I can scare something up."

Five minutes later, we were both drinking Grey Goose over ice.

"And how exactly is it that my brother-in-law was charged so quickly?"

Chandler cleared his throat. "Perhaps we should wait for the detectives…"

"Chandler. May I call you Chandler?"

"I'd prefer it."

"Chandler, why did they arrest Fred?"

He looked down at his glass and drained it. He grabbed the bottle from the ice bucket to his left and topped up my glass, and then filled his nearly to the brim. "His DNA. His was the only DNA recovered from her, uh, the body."

"Oh God," I said. "But how could they possibly have gotten DNA this early? Doesn't it take weeks? Or months?"

Chandler nodded and took a generous swig. "It used to, and in most jurisdictions still does. There's a very new technology – it's called RapidHit, or RapidDNA, I believe, something close to that. Some police forces around the country have bought it and are testing it. It can turn DNA around instantly, apparently. Ninety minutes or something like that. Palm Springs has one, and they aren't very far away. And in a case like this, with Fred and Ginger being so…"

"Rich," I finished for him.

"Yes," he said. He looked like the word was distasteful to him. In my experience, rich people don't like to use the word "rich." Especially in front of the poors. "You'd have to talk to the District Attorney, or maybe the detectives can help you. But all I know is that DNA analysis was done only about forty-eight hours after the… event."

"The event," I said. I got a flash of my sister hanging from a shower rod, and for a moment I thought I would scream and never stop.

"As this is all just now happening, I am going to have my team study the legalities of using this technology in court, its accuracy, possibly a constitutional challenge. We do have our work cut out for us." He took a long swallow of vodka. "But even if we get this technology excluded, they will still be doing old-school DNA testing. And let's face it, it probably is Fred's DNA. They were apparently... intimate before your sister left the house that evening."

Oh God. Oh my God. How do people get through things like this without drugs, I thought. Why don't they all just go mad? I needed to smoke crack. I needed to get him out of here.

"This looks very bad for him," I said. Concentrate on Fred for a minute, the police are coming, then within maybe thirty minutes I'll lock myself in a bathroom, one of the far upstairs ones, and smoke. Hopefully until my heart explodes.

No, not that much. After I kill whoever killed Ginger. Then I would gladly let my heart explode. It was on its way already.

Chandler York looked at me. "Danny. Don't worry. Not to toot my own horn, but I'm the best at what I do. I have a team dedicated exclusively to proving that Fred Lindquist did not murder his wife."

"Then who did, Chandler? Who do you think did?"

Chandler York put his glass down on the coffee table, a low, wide thing made of teak. What was this doing here, I found myself thinking. Ginger had always said she hated mid-century modern. He leaned his elbows on his knee and swivelled his head around to look at me. "Who do you think did it, Danny?"

"I don't have a fucking clue," I said. "How the fuck should I know? Ginger was my twin, but I haven't been here in three years. My life has been sort of, uh, chaotic since I saw her last. I hardly talk to her, really. How should I know?"

"Danny," Chandler said. "You haven't seen the note yet." He drained the rest of his glass of straight vodka in one swallow. "You haven't seen the bloody note."

The doorbell rang, and before I could move, I could hear Rosen talking to some people.

"Detectives Miller and French, Danny," he said. I brightened up a bit at the use of my name. Miss Cleary was getting old, but not as old as ma'am.

I stood and held my hand out in my best lady-of-the-manor fashion. I was faking it of course, taking it all from movies and *Dynasty*. Pop culture to the rescue. Chandler didn't get up from the couch, just leaned forward to grab the Grey Goose and refill his glass. I found it a vaguely endearing gesture, that he felt so at home here, and that he was obviously taking this situation hard. He and Fred could be best buddies, as far as I knew. And as far as I was concerned, that was a good quality in a defence lawyer.

Note to self: become buddies with a good defence lawyer. One never knows when it'll come in handy, apparently.

For my part, the crack craving was beginning to ease a bit, giving way to a slight Grey Goose buzz and a profound desire for oblivion in the form of sleep, not drugs. It was a new feeling. Novel, one might say.

Detective Miller was such a cliché it was like I was shaking hands with Columbo crossed with the actor Gabriel Byrne. Nicotine stains on the index and middle fingers of his right hand, tousled black hair that could really do with a wash. I liked him immediately. Didn't trust him – he was a cop – but I liked him. Detective Amelia French, on the other hand, seemed like a real hot shot. Expensive suit, expensive highlights, expensive rock on her ring finger. She couldn't have been much older than thirty or so – maybe a dozen years younger than Miller – but she wanted to let me know who ran the show. I took an instant dislike to her, and from the slight look of distaste she gave me when I got the old cold fish handshake, the feeling was mutual.

But to be fair to her, I probably wasn't in my best making-friends kind of mood. And I was pretty sure I did still have vomit in my hair.

"Can either of you tell me who the fuck really killed my sister? And why you've got an innocent man in jail? And why Social Services took my nephews, when there were people here to take care of them?"

Miller looked at me and smiled. "Get to the point, why don't you?" he said. He flipped his keys around his index finger. Nervous tic. Definitely a smoker.

"Want an ashtray?" I said to him.

"Do you mind?" he asked, sitting down and making himself comfortable. He looked like he was in for the long haul. I was glad I had taken off my vomit-stained t-shirt. But the jeans were still pretty messy. And why did I care? Jesus. I must really need a hit if I was looking for some kind of distraction in a quick flirt with the homicide detective assigned to my sister's murder.

"This is my brother-in-law's lawyer," I said, motioning to the couch. "Chandler York." Chandler waved half-heartedly with his glass.

"We know," she said, looking around the room as though she was a Secret Service Agent and I was the President. She flipped the drapes to one side.

I looked around and grabbed a green glass *objet d'art* which probably cost more than my rent, put it in front of Miller, sat down next to him and took a cigarette out of his pack. "Sorry," I said. "I just ran out."

"You'll pay me back," he answered. I shrugged. I doubted it. I also doubted that Fred and Ginger would have allowed smoking in the house, but I figured these were exceptional circumstances.

"Who killed Ginger?" I repeated.

Detective French, satisfied that the room was clear of potential perps, flopped herself down on the couch opposite us. "Fred Lindquist killed his wife," she stated flatly. Chandler sighed heavily.

"No," I replied. "He did not." I took a long drag of Miller's Marlboro. "And what about this suicide note someone made her write? It's addressed to me, he said." Chandler nodded. He was looking tired. It occurred to me to wonder if him swilling Fred's Grey Goose constituted billable hours, not that I gave a fuck. "Can I see it?"

Miller shook his head. "Not yet," he said. "You will eventually see it, or a copy of it. Maybe tomorrow," he added.

"Why do you think Fred didn't kill your sister?" French asked. She had gotten up and was pacing, giving off an air of impatience with all of us. But then she smiled, and all of a sudden she was beautiful. Smile more, honey, I thought. Catch more flies with honey, and all that.

"Because I've known him since I was, oh, eight years old. Because my sister was the most trustworthy person on this fucking *planet*" – I slammed my glass down on the coffee table, hard, spilling Grey Goose. Shit. "…and like she did, I would trust this man with my life. With the life of anyone I loved."

I caught the two detectives giving each other the eyeball. I thought maybe they should go now. And Chandler, for that matter. I had the small matter of a balloon of drugs to attend to. Tomorrow I would find out more. Tomorrow I would do some of the coke to perk up and my brain function would improve, and I would start putting the pieces together. But right now, I needed crack.

"Guess we're done here," Miller said, moving as if to go. "We'll leave you to your…" he gestured to the vodka. "You must be very tired. We can do this tomorrow."

Everyone paused for a minute as we heard a car squeal up out front. I hung my head for a couple of seconds, exhaustion overcoming me. It was only what… ten at night? But that's one a.m. Toronto time, and when was the last time I had slept more than three hours at a stretch?

Crack, anyone?

Darren came in, even before Rosen could get to the door. He glanced at the detectives, but spoke to me.

"The boys," he said. "They're missing. Someone took the *boys*."

4

Five years earlier

Jack and Ginger were in the pool, playing with the twins.

"Marco," Jack called out.

"Polo," Matthew yelled. He and Luke were six, and worshipped their uncle Jack. I had married him when they were just babies, and we flew down to California every few months or so to visit.

Fred and I sat on beach chairs next to the pool, watching them. Fred's skin was sunburnt, but I was turning a nice golden brown.

"You guys have all the luck," Fred said, comparing our skin. "Why, pray tell, was I cursed with two red-haired parents?"

I watched Ginger splashing around in the pool. Hyperactive six-year-old twins, and she looked like a slightly more robust Elle MacPherson. If I didn't love her so much, I'd have hated her. Being fraternal and not identical twins meant that while, in our case, we looked very much alike, we had been hatched from two different eggs. And she got the prettier one.

I watched Ginger lifting Luke in and out of the water, her long brown arms glistening in the sun. Unlike his brother, who was four minutes older, Luke wasn't a water baby.

"Hey," Ginger called over to us. "Darren should be arriving soon."

Fred made a noise at the back of his throat, which I chose to ignore. Darren had just become successful, the band that he had formed at nineteen now actually appearing on the Billboard charts. He looked every inch the rock star suddenly, all blond curls and expensive sunglasses.

I closed my eyes against the California sunshine, and debated going inside for sunglasses. I didn't want to look at Fred, who had been acting strange since Jack and I had arrived a couple of days earlier. The gentle, geeky boy who had doted on my sister in high school had become a millionaire many times over, and he had hardened into someone I was no longer quite comfortable with.

When I had said this to Darren on the phone the night before, his explanation was that money is a soul-destroying, corrupting influence. He said that there aren't many laid-back multi-millionaire entrepreneurs floating around. I somehow doubted that Fred was still reading Yeats to Ginger before bed.

Still, Ginger had said nothing by way of complaint against him, and I was sure she would talk to me if there were serious problems. I thought I had caught Fred looking at her with something approaching disdain, once or twice. Before now, the only look I'd ever seen on his face when he gazed at his wife was a kind of wonder that such a beautiful creature existed.

Something started dripping on me, and I yelled.

Jack was standing over me, shaking his wet hair – what was left of it – onto me. He had a big smile on his face. He loved coming down here, loved Ginger and the boys almost as much as I did. He certainly seemed to have more time for playing with them than Fred did. Jack grew up in foster care, and while he didn't like to talk too much about it, I knew that he loved the closeness of my family. Like us, he was from Maine, and had been taken away from his own parents at the age of five. He spent the next twelve years on a working farm with apple orchards, he'd told me, with foster parents who housed six or seven other displaced kids. He left for university at seventeen and never looked back. He rarely talked about his childhood, and I had learned not to push him about it. He just got quiet for a day or two and seemed sad. I felt almost guilty to have had a well-adjusted childhood full of love, and I didn't want to push the issue.

"You shithead," I said to him. I grabbed his hand.

"Ignore her, boys," Jack called over his shoulder. Matthew and Luke were standing behind Jack. They followed him everywhere. "Your aunt Danny has a potty mouth."

"Potty mouth, potty mouth," Matty started yelling. Like Ginger and me, the boys were fraternal twins. They were both tall and hearty like the Clearys, and physically confident. Neither of them seemed to have picked up much from Fred's gene pool, which he always said made him very happy indeed.

"Sorry, boys," I said. "Your uncle Jack makes me say swear words sometimes." Matt plopped himself on the edge of my chair and picked up my book. Unselfconsciously, he leaned against me and started reading. I looked up and gave Jack a look which said, *don't get any ideas, fuckface.* Jack had been making noises about us having kids, but I was in my twenties and I didn't feel quite ready. But the sweetness of having a child's weight leaning trustingly on me caused my eyes to water. Jack noticed, and kissed the top of my head, and then Matty's.

From the front of the house, we could hear the enthusiastic beeping of a car horn, a light, tinny sound. Probably an expensive import. Probably Italian. Probably Darren.

Matthew got up and ran into the house, followed by Luke, who had jumped out of the pool upon hearing the car, like a loyal dog who hears his master coming home from work.

It had to be Darren. If they loved Jack, they worshipped Darren.

Five minutes later, he appeared through the French doors at the back of the house. Matthew was dangling in a fireman's hold over Darren's shoulder. Luke was riding Darren's other side, his little legs trying to wrap around Darren's narrow waist.

"Delivery for the Lindquists," Darren called. "Would somebody please sign for these?" The boys giggled happily, helplessly, as Darren dumped them both gently on the soft grass behind the house, and started tickling them.

Darren was going to be such a great dad someday. Fred got up and shook Darren's hand, and Jack hugged him, that manly, back-slapping kind of hug that always touches me.

"Keeping my sister in line?" Darren asked him, and I got out of my chair.

"Hey," Jack responded, peeling Luke off his leg and picking him up. "She just won her third straight fight. She's keeping me in line, these days."

It was true. Under Jack's tutelage, I had started boxing, then mixed martial arts. I had a knack for it, and against Jack's better judgment, he had started to train me. Over the course of just over a year, I had gone from being a gym bunny to a woman with a bit of a bloodlust for fighting. I wasn't sure that Jack was all that happy about it, either. He had been a bit quiet lately. But down here in California, all that had seemed to wilt in the bright sun. I didn't ever want to leave.

"Don't you believe it," I said, hugging my little brother. "Hey, D."

Darren hugged me extra tight. I missed him. He rented a place in Toronto, where Jack and I lived, but he had been on the road for a long time. "No matter what happens, I'll always be taller than you." It was something he said to me every time we met after a time apart. I always teased him about being younger and less experienced than me, and he came back with the lame height thing.

"Hey, Beanpole," he said. He kissed my forehead. I shot up so quickly as a kid that at nine I was by far the tallest kid in the class, and it stayed that way until seventh grade. Dad had started calling me Beanpole, and it stuck.

Some things never change. It was comforting.

Fred seemed to snap out of his current mood, and within an hour he was happily barbecuing steaks and burgers, and Darren and I played water polo with the boys, while Ginger and Jack played backgammon by the pool.

I started laughing so hard at Darren's attempts at spiking the ball that I swallowed some pool water. I started coughing, laughing at the same time.

"Hey, Danny," Ginger called. "Breathe, why don't you?" The boys thought that was hysterical.

It was a nearly perfect day.

It was the last one I would be able to remember.

Soon after that visit, the demons haunting Jack began to take him over, the paranoia and psychosis became more pronounced, and nothing would ever be the same again.

5

Darren filled us in, while Detective French paced and talked quietly and urgently into her cell phone.

A woman with my I.D. and matching my description had showed up at the facility where the boys were being housed until family could collect them. She had convinced seasoned social workers that she was their aunt, Danielle Cleary, and was taking them home. She had had identification and the correct paperwork. The boys, the social worker said, had seemed to know the woman, and were happy to go with her. She was about my height and weight, and had choppy dark hair like mine. Said social worker had even phoned the number she was given for detectives who were responsible for the case, and was told with all seriousness that she should release the boys to this woman's custody.

Detectives Miller and French, of course, had never heard of any of this. And after thorough checks with the Newport P.D., no one else had either. And according to the social worker, the business card was a standard-issue Newport Beach Police Department card. She knows them, sees them all the time, and didn't see anything amiss.

An Amber Alert was being issued. I could hear sirens in the distance.

Ginger's boys were gone. Somebody had kidnapped the boys.

A part of me broke quietly as I listened to Darren. I stopped being able to take it in. I needed to get high. I needed to fuel my body with a bit of sleep and a bit of food.

And then I would get out of this house, and find whoever did this. Whoever took the boys had to be the person, or people, who had taken my sister from me. Missing children should mean that every law enforcement agency in the state should be looking for them. They would find them, or I would find them.

Either way, I was going to kill them.

Half an hour after Darren told us about the boys being taken, while everyone downstairs went into action, I quietly pleaded headache and emotional fatigue, and excused myself to lie down for a moment. No one particularly seemed to notice. Darren was speaking to Miller, trying to be calm, and Detective French was talking loudly to someone on her phone.

As soon as I got to my room I closed and locked the door and ripped my jeans and underwear off. In seconds I was in an undignified position, retrieving the balloon of drugs from between my legs. Quicker than you could think possible – and with more certainty of movement than I'd had in days – I pulled an old pair of yoga pants from my bag, and rooted around in the various plastic bags I'd thrown in for the seemingly-innocuous, disassembled parts of a homemade crack pipe: a small bottle of Tylenol (with one or two in it, in case my bag got searched) that had a hole gouged in the side, a few Bic pens (to empty the ink cartridge to use as the mouthpiece), and in my travel sewing kit, needles, elastics, a few inches of duct tape and a bit of tinfoil. I threw it all in my toiletries bag, along with the balloon, and before I could go looking for a bathroom, noticed that this bedroom had an en-suite.

Perfect and perfecter.

I rinsed the balloon and emptied it – two grams of coke, and a rock of crack cocaine, not quite an eightball. It was all I could get my hands on before I left, and in truth all I felt comfortable bringing. My general lack of paranoia regarding my drug use meant that I wasn't clear on the laws around what amount constituted intent to distribute, but I was pretty sure that this wouldn't meet it. My fingers nimbly put together my pipe. I realized I didn't have a screen or any cigarette ash to use as a screen but I was too close to relief in the form of crack to go and find the cigarettes I had thrown into my suitcase at the last minute, light one, and generate some ash. This was down and dirty but it would still work.

I broke off a tiny chunk of rock and placed it on the pierced tinfoil and lit it.

Heaven.

My grief faded as the high shot through my synapses and down to my fingertips. I closed my eyes. This is what would help me get through the next days, the next weeks. I could do what I needed to do – see my family, find Ginger's killer, kill Ginger's killer. I couldn't do too much, I couldn't binge on it. I would be sensible and controlled. Just enough to let me do what I had to do. After that, nothing else mattered.

I was probably in the bathroom for half an hour, sitting on

the edge of the tub with the exhaust fan on, taking another hit or two until the bit of crack was reduced to crumbling black ash. I washed my face, brushed my teeth, stuck my head under the tap to wet my hair and get the worst of the vomit out of it. I would have a shower once I had had a quick sleep, and by then Darren and the police might even have the boys back here, and I could do what needed to be done. I hadn't done enough crack to stay awake, not being as tired as I was. I carefully put the pipe and the drugs in the Ziploc baggie I had brought for my shampoo, left my shampoo on the edge of the tub, and went back to my room. I closed the door.

Alone and high.

I slowly lay back on the bed. I closed my eyes and let myself drift.

There were voices in the room, a man's voice, and a woman's. I couldn't quite recognize who they were, or what they were talking about.

I opened my eyes, and I wasn't in my room at Ginger's house. I was somewhere else, somewhere I had never been before. Something was around my right arm, around my bicep. It hurt. I looked down and there was a belt tied around it, a woman's belt, but not one of mine. And in my left arm was a syringe. I looked at my hand, at the strawberry birthmark between my index finger and thumb.

Ginger's hand. Not my hand, but Ginger's.

I was Ginger.

I was crying. Ginger was crying. The woman was slapping the inside of my elbow.

"There," she said. "Right there. I showed you how. It'll be easy. It'll be beautiful."

"No," I said. I looked at Ginger's hand, at the syringe. "My boys." I could feel tears running down my face, and a sadness at a level I had never before experienced.

"You're saving your boys," the woman said. She was gentle, but insistent. She slapped the inside of the elbow again, the long tanned arm I stared down at. "You must do it now."

And I did. I knew I had to, so I let her lead my hand with the syringe to my arm, and her finger pushed my thumb over the plunger.

I felt it immediately, a rush to my brain, something beautiful for a second before the purity would stop my heart and my brain.

I looked at the woman. I saw her face.

"Look at her eyes," someone said. "They're brown." Then I closed them, and it was over.

It was the most comfortable bed I had ever slept in. Scratch that, it was the most comfortable bed ever *made*. Artisans in a hillside village in South America must have spent a year putting this bed together by hand. It had probably cost more than a car. It *should* cost more than a car. It was light out when I woke up. Someone had come in and put a blanket over me. Darren? Rosen? I hoped the fan in the bathroom had taken any crack smell away.

The dream came back to me in patches but I put it out of my head. Here and now. Here and now, my twin sister was dead and I didn't know if her sons had been kidnapped by murderers.

Downstairs, Darren and Miller were sitting in the living

room. It almost looked like they hadn't moved since I went to bed. Two uniformed cops were chatting quietly by the front door, take-out coffees in their hands.

Darren motioned for me to sit down next to him on the couch. He put his arm around me and kissed my head. Between the two of them, they filled me in.

The boys' kidnapping was all over the news. The FBI had been called in and a command post was being set up, along with lots of equipment in the dining room to record all phone calls in case of a ransom demand. Everyone was looking for the twins. Darren and I had been asked to not leave the house. We were to leave the search to the professionals. The police had even contacted our brothers Skipper and Laurence and advised them not to fly down, and to take extra precautions for their own safety.

Without saying so directly, it was obvious that they thought we might be targets as well.

But Fred was still in custody. DNA is DNA, and due to the sensational nature of the crime – beautiful Newport Beach matron murdered in a no-tell motel on the wrong side of the tracks – and Fred's wealth and profile, all testing had been rushed. The police believed that the woman who took the boys could be Fred's accomplice. He was being questioned.

No matter how angry at me Fred had seemed the night before, I simply couldn't believe that he was capable of a crime of passion, especially against Ginger. But the police were right, if the phony suicide note was addressed to me, and somebody had bothered to pose as me – fake I.D. and all, and an elaborate enough network to pull off pretending to be police detectives in one of the wealthiest areas of the world? I was pretty certain that somebody wanted to get my attention. But other than to break the hearts of everyone who loved me, I couldn't figure out why I would be anyone's target. I had nothing anyone could want. I was a divorced crack addict on the verge of bankruptcy who rarely left my crappy apartment. Even I could see that my life was pathetic. I might have had some illegal habits, but I doubted that the bank that had issued my Visa card was going to go to these lengths to fuck with me.

I leaned against Darren. I knew that I needed food, and I needed a shower and probably some caffeine, if my body could handle it. I needed my sister to come into the room and tell me that this was all a bad dream, some kind of drug-induced psychosis. I closed my eyes, willing the cravings to pass. I needed crack. I needed a new life. I needed my sister to be alive. I needed Matty and Luke to be brought back here, safe and sound and without anyone having touched them. Because if anyone hurt those boys, I didn't think I'd be able to manage. I'd lost my parents and my twin sister, and my husband – whom I still loved, and always would – was following the demons living in his brain. If my nephews were lost, my twin sister's twin sons, all I could imagine was losing any humanity I had left in me, and turning into a killing machine. Then I could let myself disintegrate into a million tiny pieces and disappear into the ether.

I needed to talk to Gene. Regardless of how fucked up he was, he was my best friend. Outside the family, he understood me better than anyone in the world. At least these days, since Jack and I were no longer, and I had nose-dived into druggie oblivion.

I excused myself from Darren and Miller, mumbling something about a shower. There was a phone on the bedside table. I hadn't bothered to bring my ancient cell phone with me down here; it was a 90s-style flip phone and I doubted it would even get service here. I was old school, used a landline. I sat up in bed and dialed my own number. He was probably still there. As crummy as my place could be, especially after one of our benders, it was still better than Gene's. He had keys, and usually spent most of his time there.

I let it ring until the voicemail picked up, then hung up when I heard my own voice. I tried again with the same result. Then I called Gene's number and let it ring ten, twelve times before giving up. He didn't have a machine. He never wanted to be found. True addicts, people as far along as Gene was – which was even worse than I had gotten, despite my best efforts – only wanted to be found by their dealers. When, of course, they didn't owe them money.

"Fuck," I said out loud.

I stepped into the shower and the blood seemed to seep back into my veins. Sleep in the best bed ever constructed, hot water, and the prospect of anything that Marta might have to eat in the kitchen brought me around enough to make coherent thinking a little more possible.

I threw on a short black jersey skirt and a sleeveless black silk top. It was the closest I had to anything that fit me. Somewhere in the back of my head, I was thinking that this outfit could take me from whatever dive bars I might have to hit to look for the low-lifes my sister had apparently been associating with, and also not be out of place when – when, not if – we found the boys. I had no intention of staying in the house all day. And I was pretty sure they couldn't prevent me from leaving. If they did, I'd call

Chandler. I was pretty sure he liked me, and might throw me a bit of legal advice at the family rate. I threw on an old pair of sandals – with a pang, I realised that they were probably Ginger's – that I found sticking out under the bed. It made me wonder if Ginger hadn't been sleeping with Fred anymore. I liked wearing them.

Before going downstairs, I went into the bathroom, made sure the sink counter was dry, cut a couple of quick lines of coke and snorted them with my last twenty.

I went down to the kitchen.

"Wow," I heard a voice behind me say. Officer Miller appeared behind me in the kitchen. With a shower under my belt, I noticed that he looked a little less rumpled than he had the night before. He must have gone home and gotten some sleep as well. "You look… different."

"No shit, Sherlock," I said. "I don't have puke in my hair." I wasn't in the mood to get all Flirty McFlirty-Pants with this guy. Last night, maybe for half a second, when my defenses were down and with Grey Goose in my system, I might have looked at him differently. Today, he was another suit. And he had one function: to find my nephews and lead me to my sister's killer, or killers, so I could do what I had to do.

"How did you sleep?" he asked, pulling up a stool at the big island in the centre of the room.

"Let's see, what other meaningless comments can we make," I replied, opening cupboards looking for a mug. Coffee was on. "How about, are you an alcoholic? Did your father spank you? Did you have eggs for breakfast today?" I knew I was being a shit. I couldn't seem to stop myself. "Please tell me there's news of Matthew and Luke," I said. I found a mug and looked down into it. Tears were leaking out of my eyes. Dammit.

"I'm sorry, Miss Cleary," Miller said. "We got a BOLO out on the car that this woman drove away in with the boys, but we only got a partial licence from the video surveillance." I looked at him. He took an apple out of his pocket and took a small bite. "As happens after any Amber Alert, we have had dozens and dozens of calls, and a team of officers sifting through them."

"Most of them crazies, I suppose," I said.

He nodded. "But it only takes one real lead," he said gently. "Everyone in the state is looking for those boys." I nodded. I didn't trust myself to speak.

Marta bustled into the room. "Coffee," she said, pointing at the pot. "*Con leche?*"

"Um. Sí. Thanks. Lots of *leche*," I said, patting her on the shoulder as she very kindly pushed me away from her work area. Detective Miller grinned at her.

"Marta," I said, taking a seat three stools down from Miller. "Can I please get some food? Um? Breakfast?" Even with coke in my system, I wanted to eat. It was either grief, a crack replacement, or a bone-deep knowledge that I would need my strength for whatever lay ahead.

"*Sí! Sí!*" Marta swiped at the back of her face with her hands and wiped them on her apron. Very slowly, she said, "This morning, I make churros." She pointed to a large, fragrant basket sitting right in front of me. My sense of smell wasn't what it used to be, and I wasn't used to food just sitting around, unless it was an open bag of stale popcorn spilling onto my carpet at home. Suddenly, the smell of deep-fried dough with sugar slammed into my brain and I thought I would faint from the sheer joy of it.

On the plane, I'd eaten because it was there, and once it was in front of me it tasted good. But this? This was heaven. A plate appeared as I was shoving my second churro into my face, washed down with coffee. I could hear Darren arguing with someone in the living room, and I was aware of Miller watching me eat, but at that moment, all I could do was consume. Food as crack. Huevos rancheros, fresh pineapple and two more churros filled the gap. In the minutes it took me to eat Marta's breakfast, I thought of nothing else.

"Wow," Miller said again. "Never, and I mean never, have I seen any woman eat that much, that fast." He was looking at me with something approaching awe.

"Whatever," I said, adding to my feminine appeal by belching. Loudly.

Marta smiled and patted me on the back as she refilled my coffee.

"Marta," I said. "Thank you. Thank you so much. That was the best food I have ever had, ever." My eyes filled with tears. My God. What was happening to me?

My tears, of course, set Marta off again, and she hugged me like I was her little girl. Which set me off even more. Still sitting on my stool, I rested my head on her sturdy shoulder and cried.

"Go," Marta said over my shoulder, waving Officer Miller away. "Vamoose." I heard him leave the room, clearing his throat.

I kept crying. For losing my parents three years ago, so suddenly and horribly. For giving up on Jack. For the mess I'd made of my life, from which I wasn't sure I could ever recover. Or ever wanted to. And for Ginger. And Fred and the boys. Do people ever recover from loss like this? At that moment, I was sure the answer was no.

The only answer, then, was revenge. Swift, brutal revenge on whoever had done this to my family. And then, if I got away with it, I could escape, go back to Gene, the rock and the pipe, and live my life my way. Until I died.

And if I didn't get away with it? I was in jail anyway.

But there was no way, I decided, pulling away from Marta gently, that I was going to let Darren help me. He had a good life. He wasn't like me, and there was no way I was going to let him spend the rest of his life in jail. And even if that didn't happen, I knew it would change him so profoundly that he would never be himself again. No way.

"Beanpole," Darren said, coming into the kitchen and taking in the scene of me cleaning up my swollen red face at the sink, with Marta patting my back and cooing in Spanish. "You okay?"

"Never better," I answered drily.

"Good point," he answered. He sat down on one of the stools and grabbed one of the last churros from the basket. "Can you fucking believe how good these are? I'm going to get fat if we stay here." His voice was too loud, distracted. He was trying to put a brave face on this nightmare, and I loved him for it. I turned and leaned against the sink, looking at him. Marta patted me one last time, smiled brightly at Darren, and left us alone.

"So what the fuck is going on," I said.

Darren took a deep breath. "Okay. The good news is, there's a security tape of Fake Danny getting the boys into a minivan outside the home," he said. "They have her license plate, or some of it, and they're running down leads."

"Running down leads," I repeated. "Yes, Miller told me."

Darren looked tired. "I heard Miller say something about Fred maybe having an affair. Maybe he wanted to take the boys and start a new life, and this Fake Danny is his girlfriend. I don't know," he finished. It all seemed so implausible. Fred?

"Why? Why would they kill Ginger? Why not just get a fucking divorce if that was the case?"

"Money. Fred's rich. It's California. Ginger gets half of everything. Would have gotten." Darren wiped his hands clean of sugar, over and over, obsessively. He shrugged. "I don't believe it either, in case you're wondering. But I don't know."

"Oh," I said. "Oh." We were quiet for a minute. I felt a wave of nausea, and waited for it to pass before I spoke.

"But, Danny," Darren said. "They have Fred's DNA. In her," he finished.

"I know." I felt sick. "But he was her husband. They must have had sex before she went off to meet her killers. They must have."

"Yeah," he said. "Right, and in the absence of any other suspects…"

"The police really had no choice but to arrest Fred," I said. "I think somebody must be framing him. And they kidnapped the kids to get more money or something."

"And taking the boys from the house would have been a lot harder than taking them from a setting where they're all together, and no one knows them," Darren continued. "This place is always crawling with people."

"I noticed," I said. Other than Rosen and Marta, there was Driver Derek, and a gardener was buzzing around out back.

Something else was bothering me. Too many pieces didn't

make sense yet, but there was something bigger that was just out of my reach. Crack brain. Too many integral synapses which no longer fired.

"And the fake suicide note to you, they figure—"

"Yeah," I interrupted. "I already thought of that. Anyone knowing them would know that Ginger loved her family. And if anybody did research on us, I would be the easiest target to be involved in something messy. Maybe they'd think I had something to do with it, put them off the scene for a bit. Or something," I finished.

Darren stood and stretched. He really did look done in. "Probably, Beanpole. Likely. But still, it doesn't make total sense."

"No," I agreed. "I mean, not to be too, you know… self-aggrandizing…"

"Self-aggrandizing," Darren said. "Good one."

"Thank you." Thank God for cocaine and food. I marvelled that I could sound almost normal. Inside, I was howling in pain. "Anyway, really, aside from being a fuck-up and all, why me? I mean, you're a musician. You're – I mean, you were – close to Ginger. Musicians get up to all sorts of shit."

Darren shrugged. "Have you fucked anybody over recently?"

"Other than myself?"

"Obviously." Darren did a couple of jumping jacks, one of his staying awake tactics.

I thought. "No. Not other than a couple of pissant drug dealers to whom I owe pocket change."

"Pocket change?" Detective Miller was standing in the doorway, probably having stood outside listening to our whole conversation.

"Arrest me," I said, pouring myself more coffee. "You must have known I was an addict."

"How much money do you owe?" Miller wanted to know. He grabbed the last churro. Bastard.

"Couple grand?" I said. I wasn't sure. "About fifteen hundred to one guy, a few hundred to another. Nothing major."

"That's relative," Miller said.

"It would cost more than that to plan this sort of shit, let alone carry it out," I said. "Jesus. My guys are scumbag drug dealers, not evil criminal masterminds. This isn't Pablo Escobar we're talking about here."

Miller grabbed a little notebook out of his inside suit pocket and slid it, along with a pen, across the counter to me. "Their names, numbers, and anything else you can tell me about them."

"No," I said.

"Excuse me?" Darren said. "Why not, Danny?"

Good question. "Because," I said. "Because I know they didn't have anything to do with this; it's absolutely ludicrous. And I won't rat these guys out."

"Honor amongst thieves?" Miller said, eating his churro calmly.

"Fuck you, Detective," I answered. "I'm a lot of things, but a thief isn't one of them." Inappropriate emotion, perhaps, but nothing made me more crazy than the world's assumption that all addicts are depraved and degenerate.

He shrugged. "You know what they say? About how you can tell an addict is lying?" He swallowed the last bite. He looked at Darren and me, who were staring at him. "His lips are moving. Or in this case, hers."

"Go fuck yourself, Detective. Or better yet, stop hanging around here and do your job. Find our nephews."

He stood up and grabbed his notebook, shoved it back into his pocket. "Are you telling me that you are not cooperating with this investigation?"

"No," I answered honestly. "I just don't want to rat out my only sources. Toronto will be pretty dry when I get back there, if I do."

Miller started out of the room. "Wouldn't that be a shame," he said over his shoulder. Darren got up from his stool and gave me a sad, disappointed look, then followed Miller out of the room.

Whereupon I took my coffee mug, poured the dregs into the sink, and smashed it as hard as I could onto the tile floor. Marta came running.

"Sorry, Marta," I said to her. "Sorry." She looked at me, then down at the floor.

"You sad?" she asked me, getting the broom. I hadn't moved.

"Yes, Marta, I am sad," I answered. "But now I'm something else. I'm mad."

I hugged her one more time, whispered another apology into her ear, and left the room.

6

I snuck back up to my room to grab my purse. Detectives Miller and French, along with two other men in plain clothes who I could only assume were also law enforcement of some variety, were talking very seriously with Darren. They didn't seem to notice me pass the doorway on my way to the stairway. Upstairs, I grabbed my purse and checked my wallet. Great. Nothing but two credit cards that I just hadn't gotten around to cutting up. When collection agencies are after you for non-payment, credit card companies tend not to let you use their cards much anymore. And my debit card. It was possible that my monthly support money from Jack had gone into the bank. I couldn't remember the date. I could never remember the date.

I definitely needed some cash. A girl needs her walking-around money, my mother used to say. Pin money, she called it. Except in this case, it was my money I was going to need to get around and start doing what I had to do. I couldn't sit around here any longer, waiting for something to happen. Ginger had died at a motel called the Sunny Jim in Santa Ana. As far as I was concerned, this was the place to start. I knew there would be cops swarming the place. But if the woman who had kidnapped the boys was impersonating me, then I was going to jump in. Bad enough that Ginger had been killed. Bad enough? The worst thing I could imagine happening had happened, and in some moments I felt as though I was sleepwalking through a nightmare.

But now Ginger's boys had been taken, and my name had been used to do it. It had to be up to me. I owed it to Ginger. On a million different levels, I owed it to her. She loved me so much she had, if Fred was telling the truth, travelled some distance down the path I was on, to know what I was going through. To feel my pain better, to help me? I would never really know. Maybe when this was all over and if I didn't make it through whatever happened, I would see Ginger again, and I would know everything. I hoped so. I hoped that would be the outcome, at that moment – find the boys, kill the people who were doing this, and whether in that act or from continuing on the trajectory I was on, I could die too. And just maybe Ginger would be there, waiting for me.

Either way, my troubles would be over.

I didn't know where Darren was supposed to be sleeping, and besides, he undoubtedly had his wallet safely tucked into the back pocket of his jeans where it always was. But he might have extra cash in his suitcase. Or a credit card – I could always forge his signature, and he always just used D.A. Cleary on his cards, instead of Darren Andrew. (He liked the connotation, he said.) I had just been accused of being a thief, which I truly had never been. But I was resourceful, and I figured I might as well be hung for a sheep as a lamb.

My room was directly at the top of the wide staircase. Purse in hand, I kicked off Ginger's sandals and carried them, hoping nobody would hear and remember I was up here. I crept down the hallway, glancing into open doorways. This was only the second floor, and I remembered Ginger saying that the boys' room was on the third. But was that the old house, the one in Huntington Beach? Fuck.

The first room I tried was definitely just a spare room. Not a personal touch anywhere.

Next to this was a bathroom. I heard Darren at the foot of the stairs calling my name, so I called out I'd be down in a minute. I ducked into the bathroom and locked the door. I wasn't ready to go back down there and try to talk to strange police people.

It smelled like Ginger. I opened the medicine cabinet, and there was a half-empty bottle of her old standby perfume, Chanel No. 5. A hairbrush with a few of her hairs still caught in the bristles. Nivea, of course. I touched everything, softly, not moving anything. Breathing deeply, I closed my eyes.

Idly, I opened the cabinet under the sink.

A large box of Tampax at the front made me smile. Made me a teenager again, back in the bathroom at home in Maine with Ginger. I squatted down and removed it. There was a travel case with a few small bottles of shampoo and an old dried-up bar of Pears soap. Ginger was very brand-oriented; fickle she was not, even with her soap. The basic detritus of a woman's life. A messy woman's life. I smiled and settled more comfortably on the floor, rifling through my sister's things.

At the back was a plastic grocery bag. I pulled it out.

Inside was a wig. A short black spiky wig. Good quality too; seemed to me like it was made from human hair.

Funny, I thought. One of the reasons I had wanted to dye my hair black in the first place was so that I wouldn't look so much like Ginger. Even though she lived a couple of thousand miles away from me, I didn't want her in any way associated with me, for her sake. And it seemed like she was trying to look like me.

Makeup. Loads and loads of it. Bright red lipsticks, kohl eyeliners, fake lashes, some still in containers, some pulled off and just thrown in loose, like dead spiders. A pair of torn stockings. A cheap, trashy bra. Very unlike my sporty sister.

But which smelled, even a foot away and with my limited olfactory sense, like Chanel No. 5.

At the bottom of the bag was a cheap plastic wallet.

I realized I was sweating as I pulled it out, and I pushed my bangs off my face.

Inside the wallet, there were twenties. And fifties, and tens. A few dozen bills at least, thrown in haphazardly, crumpled. I held my breath. There was more. Two credit cards, an American Express Platinum card and a MasterCard. They both looked new. Both bore the name Danielle Cleary.

I turned them over. Both with a close approximation of my signature.

I realized I was barely breathing, and I also realized that I was about to pass out. Since I was a kid, this has happened to me at moments of great stress – I will stop breathing without realizing it, until I actually faint. It's embarrassing to admit, but there you are. My name is Danny Cleary, and I am a swooner.

I threw everything on the floor and fished around in the wallet. There was one more piece of identification.

A California driver's license, bearing the name Danielle Cleary. With a picture of Ginger, wearing the black wig that was sitting on the floor in front of me, skin paler than I can ever remember her having, and red lipstick. And gaunt. Like me.

Like I had become.

For a few seconds, I started to hope. Ginger could be alive. She went and got her sons yesterday. Something had gone seriously wrong, gotten very seriously fubar, but she was out there somewhere. She was not lying on a cold slab in the morgue.

She was out there, alive, and in trouble. She needed me, was calling out to me.

It was the last thought I had, before something cracked behind me, and the whole world went black.

"Danny. Danny."

I thought it was Gene for a second. I thought D-Man was outside and I had passed out on the couch waiting for him. D-Man was outside, and I was having a cat nap before our next delivery. Gene needed twenty bucks for Bruno.

"It's in my wallet," I said, clearly enough. Or so I thought.

"What, Beanpole, what?" Darren was shaking me. "I'm calling 911."

He started to move away from me, and things were clear again. I was on the bathroom floor. At Ginger's house. All around me were the things I'd found in her vanity. Except the plastic wallet, which I could feel under my butt.

I tried to sit up. "Someone must have hit me."

"No, Bean," Darren said. I was starting to be able to focus on his face. "You had one of your fits."

That's what my family had called my fainting attacks: fits. Like I was an eighteenth-century epileptic. It was a family joke. Ha freaking ha.

"No," I said. "I didn't." I always knew when I was about to faint. I had a few seconds of a weird sort of carbonation feeling in my brain, like club soda had been funnelled into my head. I tried to sit up. "Ow." The back of my head throbbed. In one particular spot. This was not how I woke up from my, um, fits.

"I was looking for you. I checked your room, then I saw this light was on with the door closed, and the door was locked… Danny, you know you're not supposed to lock bathroom doors. I had to break it down." He sounded very, very tired. And scared. "We need to talk about next steps. We need to talk about the boys. You need to be part of this. You can't wander around locking doors."

"A girl needs her privacy," I answered. This time I was able to sit up, with Darren pulling my arms. I adjusted my weight a bit so that my butt was still covering the wallet. I didn't think about why, but I didn't want him to know about it yet.

"What is all this crap?" Darren asked, looking at the stuff on the floor.

"I don't know," I said, chucking stuff back inside the sink as though none of it had any more import than the Pears soap. "I came in to pee and I thought I smelled her in here. Some of her stuff is here. I wanted to look at it."

Darren sighed and sat back against the closed door. "Oh, Beanpole," he said. After a pause, he said, "This is kinda weird, when you think about it."

"Yeah, well, so color me weird," I answered, moving my butt a little more.

"No. Ginger and Fred have a huge bathroom off their bedroom. It's, like, palatial. Why would she have her stuff in here?"

Why indeed.

I felt the back of my head. "Another one for you, then," I said. "Go," he said.

"Why, if I just had one of my fits, do I have a huge goose egg on the back of my skull?" I poked it again. "Jesus."

Darren reached over and touched it. I flinched. "Yes," he said slowly. "You do. Are you sure you didn't have it already?"

I looked at him. "No, doofus, I did not have it before. Ow." I prodded it a bit with my fingers. "The door was locked, Darren. The door was definitely locked. You know that yourself. And I think I'd remember if somebody had broken the door down and conked me over the head." I was feeling giddy. Ginger might be alive.

Darren looked sadly at me. "Bean. Did you score?"

"When, exactly, would I have gotten crack and smoked it, fuckbrain?" I said. There's nothing more frustrating for an addict than to be actually telling the truth for a change, and not to be believed. "Darren."

He looked at me for a minute. "Okay."

I looked around the room. There was a window, but there was no way I wouldn't have noticed someone come in that way. And short of crawling out of the toilet...

"Oh fuck," I said. "The shower."

The large Jacuzzi tub/shower combo had a dark maroon shower curtain pulled back. I thought maybe I had registered the curtain being closed when I walked in, but who could remember? I had a lump the size of Delaware on my head.

"I don't feel so good," I said.

"Me either," Darren said. "What is going on here, Danny?"

"No," I said. "I mean, I really don't feel so good. I'm going to heave." I had my hand on my stomach.

"I'm not leaving you alone again," he said.

"There's no one here now, unless they're in a drainpipe. They must have gone out the window. Now stand outside the door and plug your ears." Darren had a sensitive gag reflex. If he heard or saw puking, it would start him off. He had to be very careful going to movies.

One look at me obviously told him that I meant business, and he did what I said.

As soon as he was out of the room, I climbed to my feet slowly. My purse was on the floor behind the door, half spilled onto the ground. More evidence, as far as I was concerned, that someone had conked me on the head and taken a flyer out the window – it was on the second floor, but even I could manage a jump from this height. I made sure the window was locked, and as quickly as I could with a pain in my head that was starting to gain momentum by the minute, I chucked the plastic Ginger/ Danielle wallet into my bag.

Then I proceeded to throw up for real. I didn't have to fake it for Darren's benefit. I thought I was losing the lining of my stomach. I rinsed out my mouth and splashed water on my face. Darren was knocking on the door.

"Danny? You okay?"

When I opened the door, Detectives Miller and French were standing next to Darren.

"EMTs are on their way, Miss Cleary," Detective Miller said, all business now. "Tell us what happened." Detective French motioned for me to come out of the bathroom. As soon as I did, another cop, or investigator or whatever, appeared from behind her, a tall Asian guy, and as I looked behind me, I saw that he was photographing the room. Just like on CSI.

"I don't need an EMT, and I don't have health insurance down here," I said. For some reason, I was too embarrassed to tell him about my financial status. Not that he didn't probably already know. Tell him I'm a crack addict? No problem. About to go bankrupt? Shameful.

"I'll pay for it," Darren said, at the same time as Miller was telling me that arrangements would be made.

"Like a funeral," I said. "Arrangements." I felt sick again. There was going to be a funeral, at some point. We were going to have to bury Ginger. What did she want done? Cremation? I couldn't remember if we had ever talked about it.

Then everything became even more chaotic, as two EMTs arrived on the scene. They sat me on a chair in the hallway and forced me to do a few follow-the-finger kind of tests – preliminary neurological tests, they said – and poked at my head. It hurt.

"That hurts," I said. We were in my bedroom now, and second techie was in the bathroom now, dusting for fingerprints or something.

"This is definitely a recent trauma," the female paramedic told Miller. "The skin is newly broken back there. Not much, she's not bleeding much, and head injuries bleed like a mother— I mean, head injuries tend to bleed profusely. But it's definitely new, and we're going to have to take her in and check for concussion or other injuries. But I think she's fine." The male EMT was bustling around, taking my blood pressure and in general getting in the way. "Ha," I said. "Told you somebody hit me."

"How did this happen," Darren said to Miller. All of a sudden he looked threatening again. I was seeing a whole new side to my brother in the last twenty-four hours. "With a house full of cops."

Miller sighed. "I honestly don't know. Officers are securing the perimeter." He looked down at me. "How do you feel?"

"Other than a headache, fine," I answered truthfully. I did. It surprised me. I wanted crack. Later I would smoke some crack. If I could get away from everyone, I would go to the Sunny Jim, where Ginger died, and I would smoke. The thought made me stronger.

Miller was leaning over pretty close. I could smell Old Spice and cigarettes. I liked it.

"There are too many people in this house," Darren said. "Who all was here? And I haven't walked through this whole place yet. Is there another way out, other than the front stairs? I haven't seen anything."

Miller shook his head. "There's a third floor, which of course is being checked now, but unless we hear something from one of my men in the next five seconds, I think we can assume that it's empty."

At that moment, a cop from far, far down the hallway, around the corner and out of sight, yelled, "Third floor, clear!" It was kind of exciting. Anything to take me out of my head. My head was not a good place to be.

Miller smiled. "See?" He leaned against the wall. "Within a couple of minutes the house and property will have been checked. It is possible that the man who did this to you—"

"Or woman," I interrupted.

"Do you think it was a woman?" Miller asked quickly.

"No. I mean, I have no idea. But I wanted to be politically correct."

He nodded. "The perpetrator could have come in a second-floor window from a ladder and left the same way. This house," he said, looking around, "has a lot of rooms. But there are more than a dozen officers on the property at the moment, apart from myself and Detective French. We'll find something." He patted my knee gently, as the EMTs insisted on loading me onto a stretcher. I had my purse clutched tightly onto my lap. I made sure it was zipped up.

Darren was pacing. He followed my stretcher down the stairs, telling the EMTs to take it easy. Under the circumstances, it was comforting. It had been a long time since someone had looked out for me like that.

Outside, Darren tried to climb into the ambulance with me. "No," I said. "Darren. Go to the morgue."

"Hey, drama queen," Darren said. "You're not that bad. I think you'll make it."

"F-U-C-K-U," I said. I closed my eyes. The headache seemed to be getting worse. "Go and see Ginger. Okay? And find the boys. Please. And take one of the detectives."

"Why?"

"I have a bad feeling about this, Darren. Please. Just take Miller. Or French. She's kinda hot, if she smiles at you," I added, just before the EMTs closed the doors.

"I noticed," Darren yelled. I laughed and closed my eyes.

I could feel Ginger with me. She wanted me to laugh. She had the most generous soul of anyone I had ever encountered.

And I would find whoever took her life, and took the boys. I promised Ginger that, as we rode to the hospital.

7

Obviously a slow day in the E.R. I was seen right away, and it was determined that I did not, in fact, have a concussion or any other brain damage.

"Can I get that in writing," I said to the doctor. "About the brain damage, I mean. I might need to prove that some day." The Cleary sense of humor: my nephews have been kidnapped and my twin sister murdered, but I will still crack wise. Inappropriate coping mechanisms? Me?

The doc looked at me. Apparently, he wasn't used to our brand of humor.

"I will of course forward copies of our reports to your family doctor," he began, and I stopped him.

"Not necessary. Let's get this whole payment thing out of the way so I can get out of here, sweetie. Okay?"

Darren had said that he would pay, but I wanted to try something. At the front desk, I pulled the plastic wallet I'd found at Ginger's out of my purse. I handed the billing secretary "my" American Express card. She swiped it through a scanner next to her computer. There was a short pause, during which I realized that I hadn't put on deodorant after my shower that morning.

"Thank you, Ms. Cleary," the woman said, glancing at me politely as she handed me back my card. "You have a nice day now."

"I surely will," I answered in my best California accent. Being in Orange County always did that to me. "Thank you so much." And with that I walked out the emergency room door and into a cab someone was just getting out of. Good luck for me – taxis in Orange County are a rare occurrence. As I opened the back door of the car, I saw two cops enter the emergency room. I figured they might be looking for me.

I settled in, and sighed. A taxi. My home away from home.

"Can you take me to a bar, please?" I said to the driver. "Something within a couple of blocks of the Sunny Jim Motor Inn." The driver looked at me in the rear view. So did I. I didn't look all that bad, considering. Sleep and food on one side, getting conked on the head and throwing up on the other. It might have been a draw, but I think the sleep and food had won out.

We drove for about ten minutes, out of the stretch of office buildings where the hospital was located. I had no idea where we were. I had been down here more than a dozen times in the years Fred and Ginger had lived down here, but we didn't tend to do the hospital tour.

Soon we were out of Newport, somewhere in Santa Ana, maybe. Definitely not as pricey as the palatial digs I had just left. More my territory, really. Small strip malls, all with adobe roofs. Lots of fast-food joints and Korean nail places. Target. K-Mart. 99 cent stores.

The sun was bright but not directly overhead. It was mid-afternoon by now, I guessed, but I didn't wear a watch, and the taxi didn't have a clock.

"How much further?" I asked the driver, just as he made a sharp right turn. We passed a bail bonds place, and for one of the first times in Orange County outside of a parking lot, I saw people on the street. Mexicans, mostly. A couple of girls who might have been hookers, fanning themselves, laughing, and pointing at something I couldn't see down an alley.

"Here we are," the driver said. He pulled up in front of the Sunny Jim without pulling in. "Lots of places to go around here." He pointed up the street. "There is a nice place," he said. "Have a sandwich and a *cerveza*, and nobody bother you there. You are a girl," he said, looking worriedly in the rear view. I like people who state the obvious. Bless.

The fare was twenty-five bucks, and I gave him two of the twenties from the plastic wallet. Share the wealth and all that. *Noblesse oblige.*

"*Gracias*," the driver said, when I indicated that I didn't need change. "But, lady," he said. "You sure you want me to leave you here? You meeting somebody? Your man?"

"Don't you worry, Jorge," I said, reading his name off his cabbie license. "I'm meeting my sister."

I stood in front of the motel where my sister had died. Other than police tape over the door to one room, the Sunny Jim looked to be business as usual. I stopped at the office entrance for a second, considering taking a room, but I wasn't ready for that. Not yet. First, I wanted to take in some of the local color.

If Ginger had died here, maybe she had hung out around here. I had drugs in my purse, and money to rent a room. I badly wanted to be high, to erase everything and watch sitcom reruns and drift away.

But here I was, and this was more important.

I walked in the direction Jorge had indicated. An old Mexican man stood on the street, cowboy hat shading his eyes as he gazed into the distance at something I couldn't see. My head was pounding again now. The doctor at the E.R. had given me nothing stronger than two Tylenol, which hadn't even dulled the pain. I was used to stronger painkillers. I passed another bail bondsman. A pawn shop. Then, Lucky's Bar and Grill. I was glad it wasn't a Grille. I didn't like Grilles, but I was quite fond of Grills. I was pretty sure that this wasn't the place that Jorge had been pointing to, but either way, somebody in this place was getting my business. Closest bar to Sunny Jim's, as far as I could tell, and I looked enough like Ginger – particularly the Ginger who had apparently been trying to look like me, according to the fake driver's licence – that my presence might provoke some reaction. Either way, I could use a drink.

I wished I had thought to stick my sunglasses in my purse. I'd grown unaccustomed to daylight. I like my face covered. Note to self: buy shades.

Lucky's was the kind of place that didn't have windows. I understood places like this. A lot of women would be nervous, walking into a strange dive bar, in a strange, down-and-out neighborhood. But this? This is what I was made for.

It took me a few seconds to adjust to the dark interior after the harsh sunlight outside. I paused in the entrance, for effect. I knew I looked okay, and patted myself on the back, metaphorically, for wearing what I had. Any worse, and I could have been mistaken for a whore. Any classier, and I would have been a target, a rich *gringa* who'd gotten lost on her way to Laguna Beach. As it was, in my little black sleeveless top and skirt, I could be anything. It was all up to me.

I was on. Showtime.

Once my eyes adjusted, I saw that there were half a dozen people at the bar, one woman among them. The bartender was Caucasian, and big. Mean-looking biker-type. Two of the guys at the bar were white, two, from what I could see, were Mexican, one black, and the woman? I couldn't see her well enough yet.

But well enough to know it wasn't Ginger.

I made my way to the bar, confidently but not like I owned the place. The bartender looked at me.

"Jack and seven, please," I said, pulling a twenty out of my purse. I put it on the bar and lit up a cigarette. Nobody else seemed to be paying much attention to the smoking bylaws here, so who was I to argue? I wasn't a full-time smoker despite the crack addiction, but put me on a barstool and I'm Joe Camel.

The bartender slid an ashtray my way. Good start. If he'd pegged me as a cop, he would've told me that there was no smoking in his establishment.

My drink was weak, but it would do. I stirred it with the straw once or twice, then chugged it back in one. Let it sit for a minute.

"Let's do that again," I said, pushing the twenty a little further across the bar. He hadn't taken it yet. He made me another. I rested my forehead on my fingers like I had had a long day, or a headache, which I did. This, I had to approach with caution.

The two white guys were stealing glances at me, then talking quietly to each other. Nobody else had spoken a word since I came in, but I didn't have the feeling that it was because of me. There probably wasn't an overabundance of witty banter flying back and forth here. Maybe the happy hour crowd provided more amusement, but somehow I doubted it.

"Miss," one of the white guys said after about ten minutes of all of us staring at the same football game. "Miss?"

"Sorry?" I said, as though he was disturbing me from a deep reverie. In fact, this was what I had been waiting for.

"Can my friend and I buy you a drink?"

I looked at them. Both about my age, early thirties-ish. Blue-collar, if they had any collar at all, which I doubted. They seemed respectful. They weren't assuming I was a pro, just maybe hoping one of them would get laid.

"That's nice of you guys," I said, smiling earnestly. "But I'm not sure I'm the company you're looking for." This way, I thought, I could weed out the potential johns. "You know how it is."

"Troubles," the other guy said, nodding into his beer.

"Troubles," I agreed. You don't know the half of it, brother. We all sat silently for a couple of minutes. Good. Nobody was going to hassle me here. Within fifteen minutes, I was part of the woodwork. If I stayed on this stool long enough, I'd be a regular.

I sighed heavily, as if regretting my anti-social behavior, and ordered another drink. "And a round for those guys," I said to the bartender. "Thanks, guys. Thanks for not pushing me." I let a tear roll down my cheek. I was officially an expert at the crying thing now. I rooted around in my bag for a tissue, and one of them lit my cigarette for me, as though I was his sister.

That was it. We were friends now. Ten minutes later, I was shooting pool with Dom and Dave. I figured I'd give it a bit. If

Ginger had been in here, I thought these guys would maybe have mentioned something to me about our similar appearance, if the photo on the fake driver's licence was anything to go by. And even if they didn't know her, they must know the 'hood.

But as a stranger in a dive bar – which are almost always populated by regulars, no matter where in the world you go – you don't start getting nosy right away. Not good for one's health.

For someone who has spent as much time in bars as I have, it's amazing that I don't have better pool skills. I was a pretty good baseball pitcher in high school, and more than a good volleyball player. I had fantasies about being a female MMA fighter, if I could ever get past the crack thing and rebuild some muscle.

But pool? Forget it. For whatever reason, I could barely break the balls. As it were.

Dom and Dave forgave me, though. They were old school. Women were mothers, sisters, girlfriends, or whores. I was none of those, but once I was out of the whore category, as far as they were concerned, I could have been any of the other three. The others at the bar barely glanced over at us. Good.

The boys each beat me handily, of course. "I know when I'm outclassed," I said, pulling up a chair and putting my feet on another, watching them play. Dom went into the bathroom every ten minutes or so, returning a bit more animated each time. Ah. A kindred spirit.

Cocaine. Where there was coke, crack couldn't be far behind. And maybe, just maybe, Ginger had scored in here, in her – what? Quest to become more like her twin? Ease her own pain, despite anything Fred had said to me in jail? Suddenly, watching Dom bouncing back from the men's room in his Vans, doing some kind of pseudo-thug walk, I felt as though I needed to know that nearly as much as I needed to find who killed her. Why had Ginger come to places like this? Why was she wearing fake eyelashes, for God's sake? I had never once even seen her in mascara.

Dave, however, didn't seem to be on the same wavelength. He wasn't going to the bathroom with his buddy, and he wasn't talking a mile a minute either. I wondered if he knew about his friend's habit. Far be it from me to break it to him. I bided my time. At one point I excused myself and went to the ladies', which surprised me by being much cleaner than I had anticipated, and did a couple of quick bumps of coke off the back of my hand.

I had to stay sharp, after all.

Then on impulse, I locked myself back in the stall, took all the money out of the plastic wallet, quickly separated it into denominations, and put it into my own wallet.

Finally, they finished a game when Dave sunk the eight ball and went to the bar to order another round for us, then waved that he was going to the can.

"Dom," I said. "Cut a girl a break?"

"Sure," he said. "Can I do for you, Big D?" They had taken to calling me this, because even at 5'10", I was taller than both of them.

"Got a little bump for me?" I didn't need it, of course, but Dom didn't need to know that. And there's nothing like sharing narcotics to bond people. I figured if I could get Dom away from Dave, smoked or snorted a bit with him, he might know something about Ginger. Anything. At least he would have heard gossip, right? A woman being killed days ago in the motel practically next door? And if she was into any kind of drug scene around here, he could be useful.

Dom sat up straighter and looked at me. "I don't know what you're talking about," he said. He glanced around the bar nervously.

"I'm not a cop," I whispered, smiling into his eyes. "I'm just a girl with some troubles, and you know I'm not from around here." I stopped smiling. "Look. For all I know, *you* could be a cop. But I'm telling you straight here, Dom – I prefer the rock, it's been a few days, my sister is dead and I need it." My nails were making crescent moon shapes in my palms. Dom wiped his palm across his mouth.

"Dead?" He patted my knee and shook his head. It's hard to look sad, though, on cocaine. "Okay," he said slowly. "I'll see what I can do to hook you up. But not around Dave. He's pretty straight, and I just got out of a program," he explained. He looked closer at me. "You got cash?"

"Some," I said. I was wary. He seemed like a good enough guy, but the cash in the plastic wallet might just disappear if I advertised it. And I hadn't even had a chance to count it yet.

"Where you staying?"

"The Sunny Jim," I replied, without hesitating. "I mean, I will be."

He looked more closely at me. "You don't seem like a Sunny Jim kinda girl," he said.

I shrugged. "The Four Seasons is full," I said. He laughed.

"Here comes Dave," he said. "Be cool."

"Cool is my middle name," I said, grinning, happy happy happy. Oh, happy day. Dom giggled and all of a sudden I trusted him again.

Let Darren and the millions of police look for Matty and

Luke their way. I was going to find them my way. Even if it was at the end of a crack pipe. This is where it started for Ginger, and the Sunny Jim was where it ended.

And once I settled into the motel room, with or without Dom, I would call Darren. I knew it was cruel to make him worry any more than he was already. But he could focus on the boys, and I could focus on Ginger. Besides, it was all the same. Whoever killed Ginger either took the boys or had something to do with it. The law of averages didn't allow for that kind of coincidence.

Dave came back with our drinks, and the three of us sat shooting the shit for about ten minutes. I was sitting on pins and needles, willing Dom to get up and go to the payphone to call his guy.

"What time is it?" I asked Dave. I still didn't know, and bars like this tended not to put clocks behind the bars. Too much of a reminder to the clientele that they were getting loaded when they were supposed to be eating dinner with the ball and chain. Dave looked at his watch.

"Almost five. Shit. Shit. I've gotta bust a move, guys," he said. "I'm late for work."

Work? He was more than half in the bag. I hoped he wasn't a bus driver.

"Where at?" I said, adopting their grammar. That's me, a barstool chameleon.

"Pawn shop, two doors down," he said. "Hey. Come see me later."

"Cool. I will," I said. I got up and gave him a sisterly hug. "Thanks for distracting me from myself, Dave. You're good people." People who hang around in bars like this make friends easily. Sometimes it's actually real. This is how I met Gene, and he was about as close as it got.

Gene. Where the fuck was he? As soon as I got a room, I would try calling him again.

"How much you want," Dom asked as soon as Dave had walked out. Good. No messing around.

"A ball?" I said. An eightball. Three and a half grams. In Toronto, it went for anywhere from two hundred to two hundred and fifty bucks. But I knew it varied wildly, depending on supply and demand and where you were. "How much?"

"Two hundred," he answered decisively. "But, Big D. You gonna share with a brutha?" I laughed. I was happy. I was going to smoke crack. And I was going to find something out about my sister, and where the boys were. A package deal. The only way to fly.

"You betcha," I answered. Even if I didn't want to try to milk Dom for info, I wasn't a huge fan of smoking alone. "How long's it gonna take? For your guy to get here?"

"She's already here," Dom said. "You got the two hundred? All I got left is about half a gram of powder, but I'll throw that into the mix. Got no cash left, only ten for gas."

"I feel you, my brother," I said. I did, too. If it wasn't for the windfall courtesy of my sister, I'd be in the same boat. Thank you, Ginger, I thought. You always did come through for me. I had my purse on my lap under the table. I counted out ten twenties by feel under the table, folded them up in my fist and pretended to hold Dom's hand so I could pass the money to him. Dom nodded, got up and sauntered into the men's room. He would have to count the cash before he talked to the dealer.

Who was obviously the only woman at the bar, if she was already here. She was so good, she hadn't so much as glanced our way the whole time, as far as I could tell. From what I could see, it looked like she was nursing a cola, or maybe it had booze in it. She was a Latina of some variety. From the glimpses of her profile, she wasn't young, and wasn't old either. Dressed respectably enough, in decent jeans, new-looking sandals, and a modest white shirt.

Dom came out of the bathroom and slid onto the stool next to her, leaned over as though to kiss her cheek, and then I could see him whisper to her as he dropped what was obviously the money into her purse, which was sitting on her lap. Dom nodded in my direction, which pissed me off. What if she was an undercover cop after all? I had to trust him, though.

I'd done these deals in public before when D-Man was out of stock, but this was new territory, and I liked being the observer. Without turning around, the woman fished around in her purse as though looking for a tissue. It was fascinating to watch. She was undoubtedly counting the twenties, and at the same time grabbing the eightball. Dealers who work out of bars tend to do that – they only carry certain pre-packaged amounts, so if you want half a ball, for example, you're out of luck. She pretended to blow her nose delicately on a tissue, then placed the tissue on the bar and asked the bartender for another drink. While his back was turned to reach into the fridge behind him, Dom grabbed the Kleenex and put it in his pocket.

Done. Simple.

I was finishing my drink when Dom came back to the table. "We're on?" I said.

"We are right the fuck on," Dom answered. "Let's go and have us a party, Big D."

"I like how you think, Dom," I replied as we walked out of the bar. I turned and waved goodbye to the bartender as I left, and he waved back knowingly. He either knew about the deal and kept his eyes shut to it – and got a cut, which was most likely – or he was innocent of the whole thing and thought Dom was going to get lucky.

The woman was looking at the TV behind the bar, and didn't glance in my direction once. That I could see. But I had no doubt that she had me memorized, sized up and classified. If she was worried about me, she would have been out of there by now.

Or I would have been on the bathroom floor with a knife in me.

Dom wanted to drive to the Sunny Jim, but I told him no.

"You're a bit drunk there, sweetie-pie," I said. "I don't ride with no drunks. You feel me?"

"That's cool," he said, putting his keys back into his pocket. "Everybody's got their quirks. It's only a couple of blocks down," he said.

"You have a pipe?" I asked, stopping. Shit. Making one would require a visit to a convenience store and ten or fifteen extra minutes, and in the excitement back at the house I didn't think to grab my own.

"Do I have a pipe, she wants to know," Dom said to the sky. "Girl. What kind of man do you think I am? Of course I've got a motherfucking pipe."

I laughed. Oh joy. And I found it amusing that the closer he got to smoking crack, the blacker this white boy was sounding.

114

Ah. America.

I had a flash of Ginger, and Darren, and even Detective Miller as we approached the motel office. Ginger was dead. I had a weird burst of pre-crack elation – Darren couldn't reach me, I didn't have a cell phone. For all I knew, the police had found the boys by now. I had met a new friend, and he had an eightball and a pipe in his pocket. I would get high, and I would get information. At some point I would call Darren because I knew he'd be worrying, but I wasn't going to tell him where I was. Even if I found what I was looking for. Especially if I found what I was looking for. It was possible Dom had some kind of idea of who had killed Ginger. It was possible I would find out who killed my sister, who took my nephews. But first I would get high.

And in eight or ten hours I would be crashing like a derailed freight train. But who cared, because right now was all that mattered.

This was the hotel where my sister had been murdered. There were two or three other motels within walking distance, but this was where I had to be.

"I would like your finest room, please, sir," I said to the man behind the counter. He was obese in a way that you usually only saw on American reality television. Like soon he wouldn't be able to move and he would become fused to his couch.

"Wow," he said. He grabbed a key from behind him, not taking his eyes off me. Or standing up either. That would have been a lot to expect. "You look like somebody."

My heart beat faster. "How much? Somebody who?" My hands were sweating as I rifled through my purse.

"Seventy a night, laundry facilities on the second floor, two dollars a wash, two dollars a dry," he replied. "Somebody dead."

"What?" I was counting out the cash, hands shaking. I shoved eighty at him. I wanted to get out of there, but fast.

"You look like somebody who's dead," he repeated.

"Thanks," I said, snatching the key from the counter. "You know how to flatter a girl." I knew what he meant – I looked like Ginger, especially if she was trying to look like me. But had he seen her body? Did he know her?

Dom and I walked quickly to Room Four, and it was only my need for the pipe that stopped me from going back to talk to the desk clerk again.

Later, I told myself. When I wasn't feeling any pain.

Once inside the room, Dom and I didn't waste any time lighting up. All conversation was gone now. It was all about getting high as quickly as possible.

I took the first hit and held it in, closing my eyes. Thank you, thank you. The smoke filled my head, my limbs, and my heart, making everything easier to bear. Dom turned the TV on. I let myself be high. I sat and looked at *SpongeBob SquarePants* and thought about what I would say to Dom, how I would ask what I wanted to know. I had to be careful, doubly so because of being high. Even I knew that.

About an hour later we'd gone through half the eightball. I didn't feel quite as chatty as I usually did on crack. Either we were smoking a huge amount, or Dom was pocketing some. I found I didn't really care. I lit another hit and closed my eyes again, savoring the rush, thinking about sending Dom out for more. It was only, what? Six-thirty or so? Maybe seven? Surely that dealer chick would still be at the bar.

When I opened my eyes, Dom was standing over me, his fists clenched.

"Who the fuck are you," he said. He didn't look so friendly anymore. I coughed. Crack lung. "Your name isn't Danny."

"Yes, it is," I said. "I swear." I really hoped he wasn't going to hit me. I tensed my thighs, ready to tackle him and avoid a punch. I didn't know if my body would work or not, but I had already been hit once in the head today.

He threw the plastic wallet into my lap. When had he gone into my purse?

"That," he said, pointing to it, "is not a picture of you on there. That's a picture of Danielle." He cocked his arm back as though to land a good blow at the middle of my face.

"Wait, wait," I said, as calmly as I could. The crack had slowed down time. I was sweating, and my heart seemed to be going too slowly. Way too slowly for being high. "That's my sister." Dom didn't put his arm down, but he looked unsure.

"What do you mean," he said. "She's dead."

I started to cry for real. "Did you kill her?" So much for staying cool and collecting information.

"What?" Dom was yelling now, but he'd put his arm down. "Fuck are you talking about? Danny was my *friend*."

"Your friend," I repeated. I wasn't crying anymore. Crack brain. I couldn't process what was going on. Sometimes I felt more coherent on crack, able to make great mental leaps. This was not one of those times. My brain felt slow and foggy. Too slow and foggy, in fact. Something was wrong.

"Wait a minute," Dom said. He moved away and sat on the other bed looking at me. "When you first come into the bar,

117

Dave and I, for a minute we both thought that you was Danielle. That you *were* Danielle," he corrected himself. Was it just me, or was he speaking in slow motion? "But then we saw that you weren't as pretty. No offense," he added.

"None taken," I said. None was. I wasn't as pretty as Ginger. "Her name is really Ginger."

Dom shook his head. "Nope. Her name was Danielle." I didn't wonder why Ginger had used my name. It made sense. I was her twin, and I was an addict. For whatever reason, Ginger was becoming me.

"My name is Danielle. Well, Danny. Remember?"

We continued with this Who's-On-First routine for a bit. I knew Ginger. She didn't do anything by half measures. If she was going to live like me, she was going to become me, ID and all. And as much as she loved me, I thought that loving her boys as much as she did meant that she wouldn't, couldn't, do the things she had done as Ginger Lindquist. She had had to leave Ginger altogether to be in a place like Lucky's, or the Sunny Jim. If, indeed, she had even gone there under her own steam.

"Did my sister used to go into that bar?" I asked Dom. "Is that how you know her?"

"Lucky's? Yeah. She come in about six or eight months or so, I guess. Maybe more. She took a shine to us. She was like one of us."

I was lying down on one bed by now, and Dom on the other. We were both on our sides facing each other, trying to talk. I couldn't figure out what was wrong. My tongue was getting thicker.

"Dom," I said carefully. "Did that dealer know Ginger? I mean, Danielle?"

"Yeah," he said. His eyes were closed now. "They were sorta friendly, I guess you could say. Not a lot of women come in, you know?"

"Dom. Dom," I repeated, as loudly as I could. He seemed to be sleeping. "That taste like crack to you?" Crack has a particular taste when you inhale the smoke. Sometimes it has a faint baking soda taste to it, if it has been cooked with too much. But usually not. And this tasted like something else, but I couldn't remember my words. And the effect had been the same.

Dom didn't answer. "Dom," I repeated. I closed my eyes, too. "I think we might be in trouble."

8

I woke up and it was pitch black outside, but a lamp was on in the room. I started violently throwing up on the spot, my head turned to the side. All over the polyester bedspread, the floor, myself. I was a puker from way back, long before drugs. A puker, as well as a fainter. Anything could set it off. First day of my period, certain smells and tastes. Cilantro, for example.

I kept my eyes shut as my body emptied itself.

When I opened them, I started shaking.

Dom was on the other bed, soaked in blood. It seemed to have come from his mouth, but there was so much of it, I couldn't be sure. His eyes were bulging open. He was so white he looked blue.

There was no doubt he was dead. I didn't have to check.

He was the first dead body I would ever see.

Something caught my eye in the mirror. "Hi, Danny!" was written there, in large friendly script. With blood, or red lipstick.

I didn't own a red lipstick.

I looked down at myself. I was covered in vomit, and there was a hypodermic needle in my arm, taped there to keep it in place. The plunger was down. I ripped off the tape and took the needle out and applied pressure to my arm in case it bled. Throwing the needle across the room, I moved quickly to the phone. I was wide awake and more alert than I'd ever felt in my life. I stepped on Dom's blood on the carpet, and it squished under my bare feet. I retched again as I picked up the phone. No dial tone. Nothing.

"No!" I was shouting. I slammed the receiver into the phone over and over. "No, no, no." I ran past Dom and crossed myself. Jack had been Catholic, and I had picked some of it up by osmosis.

Wrenching open the door, I ran outside, barefoot, covered in puke and some of Dom's blood, I could see now, splashed onto my bare legs and feet. Had I killed him? No, no, no.

"Help," I was yelling, running toward the office. I cut my foot on something in the parking lot and kept running. "Someone call the fucking cops!"

A couple of girls on the street moved forward to get a look at what was going on, and a man who looked like he could be dealing walked quickly in the other direction. Toward Lucky's.

Before I reached the office, a police car and ambulance careened into the parking lot, sirens blazing. Fuck, I thought. That was fast.

Detective Miller got out of the car, Detective French right behind him. I pointed at the room. "He's dead! He's dead in there!" They rushed past me and into the room, guns drawn. A paramedic approached me with a silver foil blanket.

"Ma'am?" he said cautiously. "Where are you hurt?" He looked like he was scared I was going to spray HIV-tainted bodily fluids all over him. I didn't blame him.

"I'm fine, I'm fine, go get him, get him!" I yelled, pointing at the room. A crowd was starting to form. The paramedic wrapped the blanket over me. It seemed important that someone went in to take care of Dom. I knew he was dead, but I didn't want him in there alone. Someone in a uniform should be in there. All the uniforms in the world should be in there.

Poor Dom. Oh, God.

"We have to wait until the officers indicate it's okay to enter," he said calmly. "Please come and sit down so I can check you out." He led me over to the back of the ambulance. I sat there as he flashed a light into my eyes and asked me a few questions to determine if I was of sound mind. What was my name? What year was it? Who was the president? Another EMT was taking my blood pressure. Second time in one day. He frowned at the reading, got me to lie back, and did it again.

"Do you suffer from hypertension?" the second EMT said.

"High blood pressure? No. I mean, I don't think so."

Where were Miller and French? They hadn't come out of the room yet. I started shaking again. Then my body seemed to take over, and the shaking turned into convulsions. I was aware of everything, but I just couldn't stop my body from moving. The paramedics snapped into action, strapped me onto the gurney, and one of them slipped something into my arm.

"Stay with us, Danny," one of them was yelling into my face. He was too close, and it made me panic more. My body wrenched back and forth, up and down. The paramedic was talking on a walkie-talkie or something as he ran around to the front of the vehicle and started it up, sirens on again. I closed my eyes and gave in to my body. "Danny! Danny! What did you take?"

I could hear him, but I couldn't talk. But the shaking was slowing down.

"She's responding to the drip," the EMT yelled to the one in the front. "Danny. You're an IV drug user. Is that right?"

I shook my head. I'd never put anything into my arm. Just up my nose and into my lungs.

"Danny, there's a bruise and a track mark on your arm," the paramedic said, more gently. "We're here to help. You don't have to lie. We've seen worse."

"Somebody drugged me," I managed to say. "I woke up with a needle taped to my arm." EMT guy relayed this info to the front, and I could hear that guy radioing ahead for the hospital to inform the police. "It was just supposed to be crack, and it was crack, but I think there was something else in it."

"Don't worry, Danny," the paramedic said to me. He was cleaning the vomit off my face. "We'll be at the hospital soon. You're going to be just fine."

"I don't think so," I said. "But thanks for saying so."

I was admitted to the hospital, poked for blood, given an EKG, six stitches on the bottom of my foot, cleaned up, fed some clear broth and given something to relax me.

"Ativan?" I said, swallowing the pills the nurse handed me.

"You know your pharmaceuticals," the nurse said, no expression on her pretty face.

"Everybody has to have a hobby." I was just closing my eyes when Miller and French walked in.

"I'm in a private room. I can never afford this," I said. I was pleasantly sleepy.

"You're under police protection here, Danny," Miller said.

"There's an officer outside this room." He indicated the bed. "Mind if I sit?"

"What about Dom," I said, nodding for Miller to sit. "I don't suppose…"

"He's dead," Detective French said. She was standing at the foot of my bed with her arms crossed. Miller shot her a look.

"That note on the mirror," I began, but French cut me off.

"Written in your friend's blood," she finished crisply.

"The twins?" Oh God. Please tell me they're safe. Please, God, let them be safe. I was out getting high. No matter what I had told myself, I was doing drugs while the boys were still missing. What would Ginger say?

"You tell us," French said. "You sure you have no idea, Ms. Cleary?"

I sat up straighter. "Lady, what is your fucking problem," I said slowly. "I didn't kill him, you know. You might want to brush up on your people skills. In the space of the last several days, my twin sister has been murdered, my nephews have been kidnapped, I was attacked in a bathroom, and then drugged, while someone two feet away from me died from whatever knocked me out. It's a good thing I didn't choke on my own vomit."

French looked out the window. Miller spoke up.

"Danny," he said gently. "That man did not die from an overdose, or a tainted dose. Someone held him down, while someone else cut off his tongue."

"And left him there, unable to move, while he bled to death," French finished quietly. "They gave him a blood thinner, first, to speed up the process." She was still looking out the window.

"Oh my God, oh my God." I grabbed Miller's hand and held

it tight. "Why didn't they kill me too?" I wished they had. But maybe not like they'd killed Dom. "Oh God, poor Dom, poor Dom; he was a nice guy, too. He knew my sister."

Miller looked over at French, who took a notebook out of her back pocket and started writing. "How do you know that, Danny?"

The drug was working its magic, and there was nothing in the world, nothing I wanted more than sleep. "Please," I said. "Can we do this tomorrow?"

Miller started to say no, but I was already drifting out. Just before I went under, I heard Detective French's voice. "She's two steps ahead of us," she said, and then I slid into oblivion. Finally.

9

*G*inger was patting at the back of my head with something, gently.

"You did a real number on yourself this time," she said. She very softly punched me in the shoulder. "Good thing you can handle it."

"I didn't do it to myself," I was trying to protest. But she was busy writing something down in a notebook. There was a tube down my throat. Why was there a tube down my throat?

Ginger was singing something as she wrote in her notebook. I was listening to it as hard as I could. It was "King of the Road." We'd always sung this when I was growing up. The whole family.

Ginger looked at me as I tried to sing along. "Don't you remember the lyrics?"

I was trying to nod, but she cut me off. "Get some rest, ma cherie amour," she said. I tried to laugh. We used to sing the Stevie Wonder song together.

I couldn't do anything through the tube in my mouth. It was so frustrating, and I tried to pull it out and I kept pulling and pulling, but more and more tube kept coming up, until I realized that I was pulling out my own intestines. It vaguely bothered me.

"Danny," Ginger was saying, gurgling through the blood that was seeping down her face. *"Find it."*

"Hey, fuckface. Beanpole," Darren was saying. My eyes were open. My head hurt as though I'd been hit on the head by a two-by-four swung by David Ortiz, aka Big Papi.

Hey. I'm a baseball fan. So sue me.

"Hi," I whispered, looking around.

"It was horse tranquilizer," Darren said. "Cooked into the crack."

Ketamine. Nearly anything could be mixed together to get the effect addicts wanted. So many addicts, so many amateur chemists. "Get right to the point, why don't you," I replied. My voice cracked a bit. I was very thirsty. I looked around, and Darren grabbed a glass of water sitting next to my bed and put it up to my lips. I drank, and it tasted like springtime in the Alps.

"Thank you," I said, leaning my head back and wincing. Oh yeah. The knock on the back of my head.

"The doctor who let you walk out of here yesterday is going to be in big trouble," Darren said conversationally. "You were supposed to be held here."

"They ain't built a jail that can hold me, homes," I said. Darren laughed. He got up and kissed my forehead.

"Do you have any fucking idea how worried I was yesterday? How worried everybody was?"

Everybody. Oh Christ. This meant he had told Skipper and Laurence.

"The twins?" I said. Darren shook his head. He didn't look

like he'd slept. I closed my eyes.

"Did you see Ginger?" I asked. My voice was hoarse. Darren passed me more water.

"I did," he said. When I was finished with the straw, Darren filled the glass again with the pitcher on my bedside table and took a big swig. "I saw her."

"It wasn't Ginger," I stated. "Somebody who looked like her?"

"Danny," Darren said gently. "It was definitely Ginger. Okay? It was Ginger."

Then he sat down on the edge of my bed and cried. Hard. Not like, I didn't get the promotion and my wife is leaving me kind of crying, but it's the end of the world as I know it kind of crying.

"Oh, Darren," I said. I sat up, with difficulty, the pain in my head stabbing in different directions. "Darren. I'm so sorry. I'm sorry."

"Danny," he said. "Don't ever do this to me again."

"Get hit on the head?" I said, fingering the bump back there. Ouch.

"Take off and not tell me where you're going. Disappear, Danny." He was crying full out now, like he was eight years old. "I can't do this by myself. Don't leave me by myself."

We sat like that for a while. I patted Darren's back like Mom used to do, and promised him that I would never, ever leave him again. That even if I was going to do something stupid, I would tell him, or bring him. For the rest of my life, amen.

I knew even as I said it that it was a promise I might not keep.

"She didn't look like her, Beanpole," Darren said, trying to clean his face up. I was so proud of him for not apologizing for crying, or trying to hide it. My heart was swelling so much with loving him that I thought I would burst. "I mean, it was Ginger. Don't get any wrong ideas. But… it wasn't our Ginger."

"What do you mean?" I asked quietly, still stroking his back. I was frozen inside, but I didn't want to interrupt his flow.

Darren shrugged. "She looked… homeless. Not cared for."

"But she was in a morgue. They must have cleaned her up."

"I don't know," Darren said. He got up and walked to the end of the bed. "Danny. Don't take this the wrong way, okay? I love you more than any other living person."

"I know," I said. I did, all of a sudden. And it made me want to live.

"She looked like you, Danny," he said. "She looked like you do, right now."

I looked at my hands. "Darren. I still haven't seen the note." He wandered to the window and looked out, not saying anything. He glanced outside the room.

"Detective Miller is here. I think he wants to be the one to show it to you."

Danielle, my sister, the note started, and I laughed and cried. Ginger had always loved Elton John's song "Daniel."

I'm sorry that it had to end this way. I know it's going to hit you hard, and I wish I could change what's happening.

You have chosen a way of life. I wanted to see what you saw. I wanted to change my life. I wanted to take it all back. Except the boys. Okay, Danny? Not the twins.

I'm in so much pain, Danny. I've tried so hard to be strong like you.

Take care of the boys. Please. I don't know if Fred can.

You are the wind beneath my wings. Ha, ha. Except that I mean it. You are.

> *Love and Kisses,*
> *Ginger*

P.S. Find Jack.

Ginger had written it. It was weird, and I would have to process it later, alone, but it was most definitely her handwriting, and the in-jokes were Ginger. The music stuff, the "Danielle, my sister" and "wind beneath my wings" stuff. The syntax was hers, though it rang a little strange. But she was being made to write it, sometime before that needle went into her arm. It didn't make much sense to me, not really. But she was still writing to me, even if they were telling her most of what to say. She was talking to me.

I had to find her boys.

"Detective Miller," I said, looking up at him after reading the note a few times. "I want to tell you something, and I want to know if I can trust you." Darren had gone to call our brothers and tell them I was all right. Or alive, at any rate. Detective French wasn't around, for which I was grateful.

Miller rubbed his palm across his forehead a few times quickly. "Danny. I don't know if you can trust me."

"What a shitty answer," I said.

"If you're about to confess that you know something about your sister's homicide and want me to keep it in strictest confidence between the two of us…"

"Get over yourself," I said. "If I did – which, of course, I do not, idiot – I wouldn't tell the likes of you." My head was pounding worse than ever. Didn't they dispense pain medication here? In this establishment?

"Okay, then," Miller said, crossing his legs. He looked like he wanted a cigarette. Join the club, my friend.

"What have you figured out about Ginger's life? I mean, in the six months or year or whatever?"

Miller sighed and uncrossed his legs, leaning his elbows on his knees. "Danny. I don't believe you had any part in your sister's murder," he said.

"Why, thank you," I said.

"But I do believe that you were involved in her death," he continued.

"Oh," I said, after a pause.

"For some reason, Ginger became Danielle," he said. "She managed to get I.D. in your name. We're still working on that, but it's not that hard if you have money and connections. She lost a lot of weight, changed her appearance."

"She was still prettier," I said.

Miller shrugged. "Personal taste," he replied.

"Bless," I said, smiling. It hurt my face to smile. I stopped.

"What?"

"Nothing. Bless your heart. We used to say it back home."

"Danny," Miller began slowly. He took my hand. Oh dear. "In light of your nephews' abduction, Fred's lawyer was able to get him another bail hearing, and he's been released. He had to surrender his passport and he'll be wearing an ankle monitor. But other than you and his lawyer, no one visited him in jail. At the moment we can't prove he had anything to do with whoever snatched his sons."

I nodded. I couldn't think straight. No surprise there.

"But the DNA," I started, and Miller nodded.

"Yes," he said. "And without giving everything away, that's obviously a big part of the prosecution's case. But he *was* her husband," he added. "It'll be easy enough for him to explain that away, I would think."

"But you still think he did it," I said.

Miller squeezed my hand. "Danny, I'm really sorry, but I'd bet my life – and more importantly, my pension," he smiled, "that Fred Lindquist killed your sister, and that he's the mastermind behind his sons' disappearance."

"One way or another, we have to get them back," I said. I would think about the rest of it later. Ginger was gone. Right now, we had to make sure her boys were safe. Somehow, in my addiction and my grief for Ginger, I thought that they would be fine, that this was all some very bad practical joke, or a misunderstanding. The boys knew who took them. The police had said that. So if the boys knew the woman, she would take care of them.

It wasn't until now, until Dom's death, that I realized that this might be different than that. Bigger.

"We will," Miller said. "I have a feeling that this is going to get a lot harder for you, before it becomes easier. Do you know what I mean?"

"Not really." I tried to shift, make myself more comfortable. It wasn't working.

"Danny," Miller said again. "We think whoever kidnapped the boys was also involved in Dominic's death."

"And they drugged me," I said.

"You took tainted drugs," Miller corrected. "You chose to buy and consume drugs, and they were mixed with animal tranquilizers. We haven't proven that it was meant for you." He squeezed my hand. I hadn't realized that he was still holding it. "The drugs could have been meant for Dominic Pastore alone," he continued. "After all, he's the one who was murdered. But whoever killed him, saved you."

My head was coming off my body. "What?"

"Danny. Didn't anyone talk to you about this yet?" I shook my head. "That needle in your arm was basically an amphetamine cocktail, with adrenaline. You were meant to come to. In fact, I'm not sure why you didn't wake up when they were killing Dominic," he said. "But whoever did this didn't want you to die."

"Not yet," I said.

"Not yet," he agreed.

I thought for a second. "Was it the same person who hit me in the head at Fred and Ginger's place? In the bathroom?"

Miller shrugged. "We found nothing, other than a ladder and a few footprints under the nanny's window. But the nanny's been gone for a month now."

"Why?" I asked. "Why has the nanny gone? They have twin boys. They have a butler, for Christ's sake. And a driver, and a maid, and a gardener. Where's the fucking nanny?"

Miller looked at me. "We're checking into it," he said.

"Did the coroner finish a toxicology screen on Ginger?" I asked.

"Yes," he answered slowly.

"And?"

"Heroin. But much too pure. It probably would have killed a seasoned junkie, let alone a first-time user like your sister."

I breathed. "Could you ask the nurse to get me something

for my head, Detective?" I said.

"Call me Harry," Miller said. He looked like Columbo again today. I almost liked him again today. He got up and went to the door, out to talk to the nurse. "Hey, Danny?"

"Yo," I said, my eyes closed.

"You up for this?" I opened my eyes, and he looked at me. He reminded me of Darren, for a minute. "You're at the centre of a very big shitstorm."

"Harry," I said. "I was born for this. Couldn't you tell?" I shut my eyes again.

"Yes, Danny, I could tell," he said. He started to open the door.

"Hey. Harry," I called out. He turned around. "Watch out for my brother. He's not as…" I waved my hand.

"Tough as you are?" Miller said. He was smiling but serious.

"Something like that," I answered. Miller paused in the doorway.

"I have a lot more questions for you," he said.

"I know," I said. "And I have a lot more for you, too."

"But right now?"

"Yeah. Sleep."

I closed my eyes and sighed deeply. I could feel Miller watching me for a minute before he slipped away.

I woke up hours later. It was dark, but I wasn't alone. Miller was sitting in the corner of my room on a chair. He smiled at me.

"You seem pretty accident-prone," he said. "I thought I'd better keep an eye on you. Besides," he added, "I'm not much of a sleeper." Join the club.

I held my hand out and he took it. I pulled him closer, so he was sitting on the bed. "I don't know what I'm doing," I said.

"I know," he said. He pushed some hair off my forehead.

"I like you," I said. "I don't know why."

"Thanks. I like you, too."

He kissed me, and it was nice. More than nice. And under the circumstances, very, very weird. I liked the faint taste of nicotine in his mouth. There was something strangely familiar about it. About him.

But there was nothing about him that reminded me of Jack. That was a good thing. And a bad thing.

"Lock the door," I said.

And he did.

Sex in a hospital bed is about as comfortable as it sounds. Even while it was happening, I felt like it was more about forgetting than any real feelings of desire. I was half aware that I was using Miller as a crack substitute and he was a nice guy. He didn't deserve that. In the real world, when my twin sister hadn't just been murdered and my nephews hadn't been abducted by someone posing as me, I might have even fallen for the guy.

If, you know, he wasn't a drug-hating cop and I wasn't a cop-hating junkie.

I pretended to sleep afterwards. When Miller left the room, I tried to clear my mind. The last two days had taken their toll on me – aside from the hit on the head, I had consumed my fair share of crack mixed with a substance that could have killed me, and then a nice injection of an amphetamine cocktail. My new friend had had his tongue torn out of his living body, two feet from me, while I was unconscious a few feet away. I had six stitches in my foot from broken glass I had run through in the motel parking lot. My sister was dead – really dead, apparently, though I had hoped otherwise.

And it seemed that I had just had a quickie in my hospital bed with the detective in charge of the investigation. In the grand scheme of things, it was nothing, and I knew enough about my own addict psychology to know that he was a drug substitute. But I still felt disgusted with myself.

I knew that eventually, despite the police telling them to stay away, it would only be a matter of days before my other brothers would arrive at my bedside. Between all three of them and the power of their collective charm and influence, they would find out everything they could from the police about the investigation – both Ginger's murder and the boys' disappearance – and they would probably find me a nice rehab facility down here. Drug rehabs were a grown industry in Southern California, and having me stuck in a hospital bed after my little adventure at the Sunny Jim would give them the perfect opportunity for me to detox and get talked into some facility in Malibu that catered to entitled drunks, trust fund coke fiends, and oxyheads.

I could be protected, guarded, cleaned and polished. And returned to what? My apartment in Toronto with my cigarette-burned old couch and walls that reeked of smoke. No job and no real friends left who weren't addicts.

No Jack. No Ginger.

I remembered the pledge I had made with Darren on the plane. I was going to kill whoever was responsible for this. There was even less hesitation in my heart now than there had been then. Not only had this happened to Ginger, but it had happened because of me, and whoever did it was watching me. Closely. I had no idea why, but whatever it was about, Ginger had known. She knew, long before she was killed, that something was going on that involved me. She hadn't just been involved to try and save me from a future full of crack. She was my twin sister, three and a half minutes older. She had died, in part, so that I wouldn't have to.

I was sure of it. My heart started to pound.

I ripped the sheet and blanket off myself and tried to stand. My foot was bandaged – the stitches. Where were the painkillers? I sat back down and pushed the button to ring for the nurse.

"What's the problem?" a stout, middle-aged woman said, approaching me a minute or two later. Her skin was the color of mahogany, and had the same sheen. She was beautiful. If a little cranky.

"Can I get anything to help with the pain?" I asked. "My sister was murdered and my nephews have been kidnapped and I have to help." I was babbling. I was sincere and yet somewhere in the back of my brain I knew I was playing her, and felt ashamed. But I knew that if she knew the whole story, she would forgive me. "What's your name?" I asked her.

"Wanda," the woman answered, pointing at her name tag. She motioned, slightly impatiently, for me to lean back on the bed. I did, and she gently took the dressing off my foot and looked at it. I said nothing. She then checked the chart hanging at the end of my bed, and moved closer to check the dressing on my head. She snapped her pen decisively.

"Well," she said. "I'll get Dr. Ortiz to pop in and check you out. See if we can do something for you."

"Wanda," I said. "How long will that take?"

She looked at her watch. "This hour? Forty, forty-five minutes. You're not critical, you know," she said, looking at me. There was a lot behind that look. Nurses know drug-seeking behaviour when they see it.

"Yes," I said. "I do know. But," and here, I'm ashamed to say that I cried a little, and I didn't have to try. It was a new, but honest, skill. "Wanda. I'm scared. My sister's dead. I've been through a lot. I need some help," I said. "You have family?" I asked her, reaching for the tissues on my bedside table.

"Do I have family," she asked the ceiling. "Honey, you don't even know," she answered. I nodded, encouraging. "Four kids, four sisters, a mama, and a daddy in a wheelchair," she said.

I stopped crying and smiled. "Shit," I said. Wanda laughed.

"Shit," she agreed. We looked at each other.

"You love your family?" I asked her.

"What do you think," Wanda said. She played with her I.D. badge, which was pinned to the pocket of her scrubs.

"I don't know. But I do," I said. "My sister Ginger was murdered, and whoever did it is either trying to kill me, or pin it on me, or send me a message," I said. "I'm not from around here, you know."

"No kidding," she said dryly. "I could tell by your tan."

"Ha," I said, smiling at her and looking at my deathly pale limbs. "I've made some mistakes, these last couple of years. I need to make things right. For my sister."

Wanda was still as a statue. She looked at me. "What do you want," she said.

"I just need some painkillers," I answered. "Nothing too strong, but not by IV. Just a couple of Percocet before rounds."

"Just Percocet?" She looked at me. "Do you know how regulated narcotics are in hospitals these days? I do know that you have a protective detail at the door, so I guess I believe your story. At least some of it," she said. "But I am not putting my job on the line for you."

"Fine," I answered, throwing the bedclothes back. "Tylenol then. Lots and lots of it."

10

I wasn't sure Wanda would come back, or if she did, if she would have Miller or the cop at the door with her. I gave it 50-50 odds whether she would rat on me so I couldn't leave.

In twelve minutes – but who's counting – she returned with a heated blanket, inside of which she pulled a set of Hello Kitty scrubs. And two Tylenol.

And gave me a look that said I had better not complain. So I smiled, popped the Tylenol and pulled on the scrubs.

"He's gone to the washroom," she said. She wasn't looking at me. "If you're going, go."

"Will you get in trouble?" I didn't know why I was asking, as it wasn't going to make a difference to whether I left or not.

She shook her head. "I'm the mean-ass bitch around here," she said. "They would never believe I helped you. Besides, not my job to be anybody's warden."

I moved differently in a nurse's uniform. Thank God it wasn't Wanda's – hers would have been approximately four inches too short in the legs.

"Wanda. Did I ever tell you that I love you?" She hadn't brought underwear or a bra, and I didn't know where my clothes were. She looked at me, wearing sandals and Hello Kitty scrubs, my hair sticking straight up.

"Beggars can't be choosers," she said, and smiled at the sight of me. Her smile made my heart lighten. Out in the world, people were kind. People wanted to help you. There were people like Wanda. I had renewed hope. It was a nice feeling. I hoped it would last.

"If my brother Darren somehow talks to you privately," I reminded her, "you can tell him what happened here. And tell him I'll get in touch. But nobody else. Okay?" My foot hurt. I was wondering how I was going to pull this off.

I walked straight out the door, into fluorescent lights.

Nobody stopped me. Trying my hardest not to limp, I walked in the opposite direction of the nurse's desk at my left. I had my purse swung over my left shoulder, but I doubted that my – or Ginger's – wallet was in it anymore. That would have been too much to hope for.

I found my way to the lobby, saw a bank of payphones, and paused. I didn't really have a plan, as such. Find Ginger's killer? Check. Find my nephews? Yes, and quickly. How? Fucked if I knew. And in the meantime, I had to evade both the police – difficult, and my brother – next to impossible.

Nobody was looking at me, that I could tell, so I picked up a phone and rooted around in my bag for change. I dialed Fred and Ginger's number. At the same time, I cursed Darren for not having a cell phone. What kind of self-respecting musician wanders the globe without a cell? My ancient one was one thing – I never went anywhere, and I had a landline, and at least I did own one. But in this day and age, for someone like Darren to not have one was more annoying than charmingly quirky.

Rosen answered. "Lindquist residence," he intoned.

Take a break, Jeeves. "James," I said. "It's Danny." I had no idea why I had decided to trust him. Lack of choice, I supposed.

I could hear a sharp intake of breath. "Are you all right?" he whispered into the phone.

"Peachy," I answered. "Hospitalized. Being tended to." I thought the FBI would be listening to every word. I had to be careful now. "Is my brother there?"

"Yes," he answered. "Mr. Lindquist has been released from jail. Bail, they said," Rosen continued. "And the detectives are in an uproar."

"Why?"

"Because he never arrived here from prison. He's gone. Missing."

"Oh, Christ," I said.

"I'll tell Darren that you telephoned. Perhaps you could try again in a little while." And he put down the phone.

What the hell was that all about?

I went into the public washroom near the entrance of the hospital and locked myself into a cubicle to regroup. I pulled the Hello Kitty scrub pants down and peed while I thought. Multi-tasking. Grabbing my purse, I rooted through loose Kleenex and change, an eyeliner and a tube of lipstick, until I hit pay dirt.

The plastic wallet was gone. The police must have taken it as evidence, at some point. I was beyond relieved that I had transferred the cash to my own wallet, and it seemed to be all there. I counted. Five hundred and forty dollars left. After spending two hundred on the faux-crack yesterday, a bunch of rounds of drinks and seventy for motel hell.

I opened the Altoids tin where I carried my stash, and held my breath. I always kept a bunch of real Altoids in it, on top, in case anyone checked it. And because I like to have fresh breath. I should have just over a gram of coke, and most of an eightball of good old ketamine-free Toronto crack tucked away underneath.

It was there. And without further ado, I used a useless Visa card to quickly and quietly scoop out some of the coke from the wrap of paper and snort it. Better than Tylenol any day of the week, and it would help me get clear.

I would have to be careful with the rest of the money. Five hundred and forty dollars doesn't go all that far for an addict on a mission. Though I was pretty sure I wouldn't be risking any street-bought crack anytime soon. Being drugged with horse tranquilizer and then adrenaline and amphetamines will sometimes do that to a girl, I guess. Take away that old adventurous spirit with regard to buying street drugs from strangers. I knew I would start craving it again by tomorrow, though, but tomorrow was a whole day away. I had enough of my own crack to get me through the next couple of days, if I didn't binge.

Besides, the way things had unfolded so far, I was far from sure I would still be alive then.

Exiting the stall, I went to the mirror and assessed the appearance. Could I be taken for a nurse finishing her shift? I was pretty pale, but what else was new. My hair, however, was in dire need of a wash – I had shampooed it the morning before, but a lot had happened between then and now, including throwing up twice and of course, being knocked on the head. They had cleaned me up at the hospital, but had neglected the hair. I wet it down as much as I could, sticking my head under the tap for a few seconds. I hoped nobody would come in. I slicked it back and noticed that the blonde roots were starting to show through.

That's when Detective French walked into the bathroom.

She looked as surprised to see me as I was her. Before she could react further, and without thinking, I crossed the three or four steps between us and punched her in the chin. As hard as I could. Which had the desired effect of her slumping straight to the ground. She hit her head pretty hard against the bathroom wall before she did.

Despite what you see on TV, most people will go down with one punch, especially if they're not expecting it. It was something I'd learned from Jack, who had been a bare-knuckle boxer in his youth, before becoming respectable and getting his Ph.D. I checked to make sure French was breathing, and then decided it would be a good idea to amscray, and quick.

Assaulting a police officer. Good one. I was pretty sure I might be in a bit of trouble before this was all over. With French's temperament, she'd probably try to pin attempted murder on me. I could just hear Darren's eyes roll. But it didn't matter. None of that mattered. What happened to me after I found the boys and killed whoever had them, whoever killed Ginger? I couldn't care less.

I opened the door and sauntered out. Be cool, I told myself. I didn't look around for Miller. He might not notice me in this uniform, if he was milling around out here somewhere. An old lady in a wheelchair sat near the entrance.

"Let me help you, dear," I said, and wheeled her through the doors. A nurse escorting a patient outside. What could look more natural?

Luckily, the woman didn't protest. I realized that she must have had senile dementia or something. She just turned around and smiled at me, and her smile broke my heart.

"Hi," I said, when we were outside. "My name is Wanda." I looked down and noticed Wanda had actually pinned her nametag to the Hello Kitty scrubs. I looked for a cab stand. It was a different entrance than I had come out of yesterday.

"Hello," she said. She stuck out her hand. "I'm Doris."

"Nice to meet you, Doris," I said, shaking her hand. "Are you on your way home?" Now that I had her out here, I didn't know what to do with her. I glanced back inside to see if any irate relatives were rushing after her, but all I could see was my own reflection in the glass.

"I don't know," she said simply.

I had to get out of here. I saw a cab. Again, with the taxi luck.

"Doris," I said, rooting around in my purse. "I'm sorry I brought you outside. I thought your ride was here. This is for your trouble." I shoved a twenty into the old woman's hand and turned to go.

"Bye, Wanda!" Doris called after me. "Don't take any wooden nickels!" I turned around and waved back at her. She was waving her twenty in the air. Dear God, I found myself praying, take care of this lady.

As I was climbing into the back of the cab, a police car approached the hospital entrance, sirens blazing.

"Hi," I said to the driver. "Fashion Island, please. Macy's

entrance." I had been to Fashion Island with Ginger every time I'd come down here. I knew it couldn't be too far from here – I was pretty sure it was somewhere in Newport. It was a huge, fancy-schmancy shopping centre, if you like that sort of thing. Which Ginger had at least tried to, that kind of thing being expected of her down here. Very expensive, very Orange County. I would have been just as happy for a K-Mart, but if I was a nurse living here, I couldn't exactly ask a cab driver to take me to the nearest K-Mart, without knowing where one was. It might stick in his head. So, Fashion Island it would have to be. And I could be lost in there for a while, and get myself some real clothes. I have never been known for my shopping prowess, so I was pretty sure it was the last place anyone would think to look for me.

"Thanking you," the Sikh driver said, and pulled away. And I was thanking God that English wasn't his first language. He wasn't going to try with the small talk.

Twenty-five dollars later, we were there. It could have been worse. This time, I handed the driver forty and asked for ten back. I couldn't afford to keep handing out twenties like they were candy on Halloween.

In Macy's, I wandered around, feeling safe for the first time in a couple of days. I looked at clothes, trying to decide what look I wanted to present today. Slutty? Or like a buttoned-down business chick? I settled on casual. Big surprise. I bought a pair of skinny jeans and a nice black t-shirt. Ginger's sandals were going to stay. I took some time trying on bras, because despite all the weight loss, I still had breasts, and I didn't like them moving around so freely. Sends the wrong message to the male of the species. I didn't want any undue attention.

I took the clothes to a cashier, and fished money out of my wallet.

"Your poor hand," the woman said. I looked at it. My right hand was swollen, the knuckles looking like raw meat. As soon as I looked at it, it started to hurt. Of course.

"Long day in the E.R.," I said, smiling at her.

"Must've been a very long day," the cashier said, handing me my change.

"You don't know the half of it," I replied, ruefully, as though I had been treating gunshot gangbangers all night and had had to subdue them by force.

"Have a good day, Wanda," she said as I walked away. My heart stopped for a second, until I remembered the nametag.

"I'll try," I said.

I changed clothes in yet another public restroom, hoping I wouldn't have to punch anyone else out today. Though I didn't like her, I hoped Detective French was okay. She was probably only out for a few minutes, unless hitting the wall had done some damage. Highly unlikely. Her head seemed way too hard for that.

With new clothes, a touch of makeup and my hair still slicked back, I didn't look half bad. But then again, my standards aren't tremendously high. I did a quick, energizing bump of coke in a stall when the ladies' room cleared out, and walked back into the mall.

Wealthy young matrons in expensive yoga gear and six-carat diamond rings walked around with shopping bags, looking as serious as though this was a board meeting at Exxon. For them, shopping wasn't just a pastime, it was a serious necessity, up there with two or three hours of exercise a day and a good plastic surgeon. Another world. I might as well have been in Bali, or Greenland, so far was this from my existence. But this was Ginger's world.

Or it had been. Until she had turned into me.

I saw a clock near a huge fountain. It was almost noon. I looked for payphones, but in this land of five-year-olds with iPhones, it took a long time to find one. I went into an upscale chain restaurant and ordered a Caesar salad and a glass of white wine. The phone was just outside, but I needed a little something to fortify myself before I made the necessary phone calls. And I needed change.

Two glasses of wine later, I called the house again. Darren answered.

"Thank God," he said, whispering. "I was just about to call the hospital to fill you in. Have you heard what's going on here?"

"Frankly, no," I answered. I didn't bring him up to date on my daring hospital escape yet, and I didn't bother mentioning talking to Rosen.

"Fred's gone," Darren continued. He sighed into the phone. I could hear Marta crying in the background. I wondered what she was cleaning. "He was being driven back here by Chandler York, you know, his lawyer?"

I knew.

"The police were here waiting for them, you know, to put on the monitoring bracelet around his ankle. But apparently they pulled into a gas station on the way back from the jail, and somehow Fred got Chandler's gun and forced Chandler to get out of the car when they stopped for gas."

"Fred?" I said. "Lindquist?" I could hear my voice raise an octave. Fred was about a foot shorter than Chandler York, and in no kind of physical shape. But then again, a gun changes the playing field pretty dramatically.

"Fucking place," Darren was saying. "Everybody carries guns around."

"He's a criminal defence attorney," I said. I felt sorry for Chandler; I had kind of liked him. "Can you blame him?"

"Anyway, he took off in Chandler's car," Darren continued, ignoring me. "They already found it a couple of miles away in a Target parking lot."

"Fuck off, Darren," I said. "No way."

"Way," Darren said. "And they shut the shopping plaza down, the whole nine. They think Fred was picked up there by somebody. I hate to say it, but it looks like Fred was behind all this after all."

"He was in jail when I got hit on the head."

"Well they know somebody else is in on all this. I mean, the woman who took the boys, right? And you know. The drug thing yesterday. That guy…"

"Dom," I said. "His name was Dominic." A tear leaked onto my face, and I brushed it away. "What about the boys?"

"Nothing. There's nothing on that yet. They don't know who the woman is," he said. "The license plate from the car that she took the boys away in was a dead end."

"Maybe Fred has them," I said. "Maybe he ran away to be safe, and took the boys with him somehow. Maybe there's a big—"

"Danny. Fred killed Ginger."

I was silent, thinking hard. It was too much. Not Fred. "Who's there at the house?"

"Just James and Marta," Darren answered. "Along with about ten cops."

"Miller and French?" I ventured.

"Nope," Darren answered. "No sign of them yet." Thank God. So far Darren, at least, didn't know that I'd slugged a cop. Or, for that matter, had sex with one in my hospital bed. "Listen. Are they letting you out now?"

I took a deep breath. "They already did. In a manner of speaking," I said slowly.

"Danny. Where are you calling from?"

I trusted Darren with every fiber of my heart and soul. True, I didn't want him to get in trouble like I was in, but that was out of love.

But I did not trust whoever else might be listening in on the phone. Someone in that house had bonked me on the head twenty-four hours ago.

"I can't tell you, Darren," I said. "Trust me, I would if I could."

"Don't even think about doing this, Danny. There's nothing to prove here. We know Fred killed Ginger. You can't find the boys by yourself. It's up to the authorities now." He sighed. He sounded exhausted. "There's a lot of people here. It's good. They seem really on it."

"What about what we talked about on the plane?" I said. I realized I was speaking too loudly. Cocaine. A couple of women pushing strollers glanced at me, and I rolled my eyes, as if I was talking to my wayward boyfriend.

"That still holds," Darren said quickly. "Danny, that holds more than ever. But for now, as our brother-in-law is in the wind, I want you back here at the house." I hesitated. Maybe I should just go back to the house, hang out with Darren for a couple of days, recuperate. Physically and psychologically. I had an en-suite, and Darren didn't know I had drugs with me. I could escape and get a bit high here and there, tell him I was sleeping. It would make sense; my twin sister had been killed and my nephews were missing. Not to mention I had had a physical ordeal. Sleeping a lot would be what a real person might do. And maybe it would help to be around Darren. There wasn't anyone who loved me more than he did.

No one alive, that is.

But in reality if I went back to the house, there would be no quality time, or chance to get high. In very short order I would be arrested, charged with assault and battery on a police officer. I sort of hoped that I would be given a pass, and wondered if there was a legal loophole that involved temporary insanity due to bereavement and drug withdrawal.

Besides. I realized that I felt safer hiding in plain sight than I would at Fred and Ginger's house. And I wanted to finish what I started. Let my instinct guide me.

"Danny?" It was Darren's voice again.

"Darren, I love you. When you talk to Skip and Laurence, you tell them I love them too. Okay?"

"What are you going to do," he said, sounding resigned. "You remember your promise."

I thought for a minute. "Darren, I don't trust this phone, where I am right now," I said carefully. I hoped he understood that I didn't trust who might be listening at his end. "It doesn't feel lucky. Do you know what I mean?" Silence on the other end for a few seconds. "No," he said, slowly. "I don't."

"I might be feeling lucky again in a couple of hours," I continued. Jesus. Was it me on coke, or was he being slow? Probably me on coke. "Before I come back, I need to feel lucky."

"Okay," he said. "Okay. Hey, Danny?"

"That's me," I said.

"Don't take any wooden nickels," he said.

That's what the old lady at the hospital had said to me an hour and a half ago. All the hairs on my body stood up. Creepy.

"Why did you say that?"

"I don't know. It's an expression, you know. A figure of speech? Meaning, be careful? Stuff like that?"

"You've never said it before," I said.

"Whatever, freak," Darren said. "Hey, Danny – I hope you're feeling lucky in a couple of hours. Like you said."

Don't blow it, Darren. "Yup. Talk to you later," I said. I hung up.

And unless my brother was on a totally different planet than I was, he would be meeting me at Lucky's Bar and Grill in two hours.

11

I went back into the restaurant to have another glass of wine and kill an hour. My foot was also hurting – the Tylenol Wanda had slipped me was wearing off, or wasn't that strong to begin with. My salad was long finished, but I asked for another menu, along with another glass of wine. I figured I should have some protein, if I was going to go around beating people up. Or worse. I ordered a medium-rare cheeseburger and fries. The appetite was coming back, despite the couple of bumps of coke. I changed the chardonnay to a Shiraz and settled in. I debated becoming an alcoholic instead of a crack addict: it would be cheaper, and more socially acceptable. I was quite enjoying my little wine buzz.

And it helped me put pain and fear and worry off to the side, and concentrate on what I had to do. Once my nephews were safely back with us, and Ginger's killer or killers were dead, I could break down and mourn. Preferably with Gene, and a room full of crack. And not until then.

I had been idly glancing through a copy of the *Los Angeles Times* that someone had left behind, but I put it down and looked at the women lunching around me. One of them caught my eye – she looked like I did, a few years ago. When I was fit and strong, and teaching a women's self-defence class at my local Y, in addition to having six or seven clients that I trained every week. When I ran three or four miles every other day.

Before my split from Jack, and the orgy of low living that had followed.

I tried not to think about Jack, and I was pretty sure that he was doing his level best to not think about me, either. After I had left him, he stayed in Toronto for about a year before packing up and taking a job in Bermuda, then Grand Cayman, then back to Bermuda. He was a risk analyst for a very high-end hedge fund, the kind that you needed four or five million to get into. I had loved the contradiction of him: the street fighter with a Ph.D. in mathematics. He wasn't pretty to look at, but that's always been my thing. I'd take the late great James Gandolfini over the Brad Pitts of the world, any day of the week. Show me a barrel-chested guy with size-seventeen neck who reads good books in his spare time, and I'm on my back like a bug. Or I was, until my sex drive went the way of my bank account.

Thinking about men made me think about Miller. Harry. What was happening there? The last days had been chaos and hell, but somehow my mind kept going back to Miller, the unexpected interlude in the hospital, the rumpled, vaguely sexy mess of him. And him a cop, no less. I knew it was a coping mechanism. I'd always been like that – even before drugs, I got through trauma by thinking about, and doing, totally random and inappropriate things.

Then I remembered Gene. I motioned to the waitress that I'd be right back, and limped back to the payphone to try him. Note to self: buy a phone card.

Again, I tried my place first, and Gene answered on the first ring. He sounded anxious. He must be waiting for D-Man, I thought.

"It's me," I said. "Sorry. Nothing outside for you yet."

"Thank God," Gene said. I heard the pop of his Zippo. He inhaled deeply on the other end of the line. "What the fuck is going on down there?"

"Nothing much," I said. "And by that I mean, someone I was partying with was murdered last night, while I was three feet away. Plus, someone drugged me, and not in a good way, if you know what I mean. Oh, and someone came out of my sister's shower and knocked me unconscious. And today? I punched out a detective and left her in a ladies' room." I put my forehead against the cool phone. "It's good to hear your voice."

"Oh, wow, you too," Gene said. "I can't really take in what you just said yet, but are you at this moment okay?"

"I am, at this moment, okay. I am having a few glasses of wine and a cheeseburger, then I'm meeting Darren for drinks." I neglected to mention that I was going back to the bar where some sinister female drug dealer had sold me poisoned crack.

I filled him in, briefly, about Fred and the boys. I sounded remarkably calm.

"Oh." I could hear him smoking furiously. His manner of smoking always reflected his state of mind. Which, by the sound of it, was agitated. No wonder. "Danny. Something weird is going on here too. I don't want to trouble you, but…"

Oh fuck. "Gene. Tell me right now. Wait. Are you high?"

"I was," he said. "Our friend gave me credit. But I am very much not, right now."

"You okay?"

"Danny, someone called here. A woman," he said. "For a second I thought it was you." I stopped breathing and waited for him to continue. "I was asleep. You know?"

I knew. His sleeping was legendary. After a bender, he could sleep for thirty hours.

"Anyway. She asked for Danielle. Not Danny. I said you weren't home. Then she said she knew that, but she wanted to try anyway. She asked me to pass along a message to you. She made me write it down." I could hear him leafing through what I was sure would be a holy mess on my coffee table. "She said, 'Tell her I'm taking the twins on a trip.' Then she said to tell you, 'You're it.'"

"I'm it?"

"You're it," he said. "Danny. I gotta go. D-Man is on the other line. Call me back, okay? Please. I'm not going anywhere." And he hung up.

The twins. Ginger's boys. This was the woman who had kidnapped the boys.

My mouth went dry and I kept my hand on the phone, trying to think past the pounding of blood in my ears. I fished around in my own wallet for Miller's card. He had written his personal cell number on it. Surely he wouldn't be able to trace where it was coming from, but even if he could, this was more important. I squinted at my own writing, but when I got through, it went straight to voicemail. Maybe he was catching up on sleep himself.

"Miller," I said. "Danny Cleary here. Tell Detective French I'm sorry. Really sorry. I just had to get out of there and take care of some things alone." I told him exactly what Gene had said. "Tell the RCMP or the Toronto police or whoever that they have my permission to put a tap on my phone. Not that my permission is probably needed. But if you hear hints of any illegal activity not pertaining to this case, can you give it a pass? Or do whatever you have to do.

"But please. Find that woman. Find the boys. I'll be in touch." I paused a minute. "And by the way, that was fun." I'm such a romantic. I hung up. I quickly called my own number back to warn Gene, tell him to maybe go back to his own place for a bit until this all blew over. I got my own voice on voicemail. Gene must have run downstairs to pick up from Bruno. He couldn't check my messages, he didn't have my password. I would call him back.

I went back inside, where the waitress was putting my food on the table. I wolfed it down as though it would be my last meal. I was kind of hoping that it wouldn't be. I found myself wanting, more than anything else, to call Jack. I needed Jack. I missed Jack, especially after the thing with Miller the night before. I felt like I had betrayed Jack, despite separating so long ago. But when his head was on straight, when he wasn't fighting his own demons, he was the best person in the world to help others fight theirs. But time wasn't on my side; I had to keep calm, keep my wits about me and think.

I kept my food down. This was a good thing, after all the shit that had been in and out of my system recently. The red wine and red meat seemed to perk me up, too. I could never understand how vegetarians had any energy whatsoever. Of course, not eating for days at a time while smoking crack had had the same effect.

I limped through the mall and found a funky store which had relatively cheap, costume-y clothes in the window. Inside,

I picked up a blonde wig and tried it on. It was the color of my natural hair, but it was long. I tried it on.

"Wow," the teenaged salesgirl said, smiling at me. "You rock that wig." She played with her nose ring, which looked new. And sore.

"Do I? Do I rock this wig?" I laughed. It was cheap, so I bought it. When the salesgirl put it in a bag, I stopped her. "Wait," I said. "I'm going to wear it out of here. Freak out my girlfriends."

"Well, you look like a different person, that's for sure," she said, handing me my change.

"That's the idea," I answered.

I slowly made my way around the huge shopping centre, trying to figure out where there might be a cab stand. It was Southern California, though, so they were few and far between, when they did exist. I finally asked at a mall information booth, and they pointed me in the direction of the valet stand outside the restaurant where I'd just eaten. Figured.

On my way there, I passed a kitchenware store. On an impulse, I entered and bought a knife. A small one, but sharp. It wasn't meant for the purpose for which I might need it, but I figured it would do the trick. Having it in my purse made me feel a few degrees better. I knew I had to stop spending money, but a little peace of mind seemed like a good investment at the moment.

"Do you know where the Sunny Jim motel is?" I asked the cab driver. He was a skinny white guy in a torn death metal t-shirt. I was pretty sure he'd know the general area.

"Uh. Yeah," he said. He turned right around and looked at me. "You sure you want to go there?"

"Actually, I'm going up the street from there, but I lost the address," I said. "I'm directing a photo shoot over there. I don't know that neighborhood."

"I didn't think so," he said, clicking on the meter. We listened to Skid Row most of the way there, with one Metallica tune thrown in. I always did like James Hetfield's voice. The driver was surprised when I sang along.

"Women," he said, smiling at me in the rear view. "They can always surprise you."

"Don't you forget it, buddy," I said, tough-girl friendly. I realized that I'd missed interacting with people, after all this time holed up with Gene doing crack. And another out-of-body moment: was I really conversing with a person, and smiling, and not screaming?

The driver dropped me in front of Lucky's. "You know this place?" I asked him.

"Nah," he said, making change for me. "The chick and I, we stay in and play video games mostly. I'm a recovering alcoholic," he said.

"Really? Well. Good luck with that. Working the Twelve Steps?"

He nodded. "I'm on step eight. Making amends," he said.

"That would be a hard one."

"It is," he said. "You have yourself a good day, miss." Miss. Put on a blonde wig, and the ma'am was out the window.

Lucky's was the same as it was the day before, but missing at the bar was one female drug dealer. And Dave wasn't here, either. I was hoping he would be. I wondered if he knew about Dom yet.

I wondered if anybody here knew about Dom.

The bartender was the same, though. He was watching football, again, and barely glanced in my direction when I entered. Huh. And as far as I remembered, blondes had more fun.

I scanned the room, my eyes adjusting to the dark after the bright sunshine outside. Still hadn't bought shades, and I'd just spent a few hours at a mall. A guy in a baseball cap at the bar turned around. It was Darren.

"Since when do you wear hats?" I said, sitting on a stool next to him.

"Since when do you wear wigs?" he retorted. I ordered a cranberry and soda. Darren was drinking beer. He raised an eyebrow at my order, but looked pleased enough. I was a bit tired after my three glasses with lunch, and figured it was best to take it slow.

"I'm practicing moderation," I explained to him.

The bartender showed no sign of recognizing me from the day before. He brought me my drink without a word and went back to the game. Chatty guy. I looked at the game for a minute. Pats and Jets. I hate football.

"Is this where you got it?" Darren asked me quietly. I shook my head at him, and headed for a table at the back, near the pool tables. Where I'd hung out with Dom and Dave yesterday. It seemed like weeks ago.

"Yes, this is where Dom got it. There was a chick here yesterday. Looked Latina. Mexican maybe, or Puerto Rican. I don't know." I took a long swallow of my drink. Cranberry juice without vodka. Who knew.

Darren leaned over and gave me a hug. I was worried about

my wig slipping, so I just patted him on the back and pushed him away.

"Where did you tell the cops you were going?" I asked him.

"For a drive," he answered. "I'm not a prisoner. They couldn't force me to stay in the house." He looked at me more carefully. "How are you feeling, anyway?"

"My foot hurts like a sonofabitch," I said, holding out my bandaged right foot. "And look at my hand." Darren admired the swelling and bruising, while I told him about punching Detective French.

In my family, minor injuries were things to be admired in others. Nothing like wiping out while crossing the street and almost being hit by a car so that you could have a funny story to tell. When Darren leaned down to examine my foot closely, I saw something sticking out of the waistband of his jeans. He was wearing a leather jacket. It wasn't the hottest day in Southern California, but for those of us from northern climes, it was positively balmy.

Darren was wearing the jacket to hide a gun.

"Where did you get that?" I said calmly and quietly.

"Rosen," he answered.

"Ginger's butler gave you a gun?" It wouldn't be the oddest thing that had happened in the last days, I supposed.

"Loaned," he answered. "Yes. Actually, it turns out he's more of a bodyguard. Former Israeli army. It's a Desert Eagle," he said. I looked at him. "The gun," he whispered. "Israeli-designed, manufactured in the good old U.S. of A." Whatever. He looked at my foot again. "You could use a pedicure."

"When was the last time you handled a gun?" I asked. Dad

had taught us all to shoot when we were kids. Well, adolescents. Some families go to the movies together; the Clearys shot at cans in the gravel pit. I hadn't touched one since, though I knew the boys had gone deer hunting with Dad sometimes.

"Went to a range in South Carolina last month, on tour," he said. "I go once every few months."

"Why do I not know this?" I said.

Darren shrugged. "You telling me there aren't things I don't know about you?"

Touché. "You're not licensed to carry that thing," I said. "You could get in big trouble."

"Uh. Danny? You punched a cop today and left her unconscious in a hospital bathroom. Who, exactly, do you think is in more trouble?"

I told Darren about my phone call with Gene, and the woman who'd called with the messages for me. I told him about leaving a message for Miller.

"I haven't seen him," Darren said, once he digested everything.

"I still don't believe it." I took a sip of my drink. I felt tired, dehydrated and my buzz was slipping away. "Or maybe I do. Darren, I don't know what to believe. But we just have to concentrate on getting the boys back for now."

I was about to excuse myself to the ladies' room to feed myself another bump of coke when the bar door opened.

It was the woman. The drug dealer. Chatting and laughing with Dave. Dave, who yesterday hadn't even glanced in her direction. Who Dominic had wanted to hide his drug use from. I whipped my head back in Darren's direction. I hoped they wouldn't recognize me from body language in the dim light, but long blonde hair does tend to catch people's eye. It's one of the reasons I changed mine. I got tired of never being invisible.

"That's her, isn't it," Darren said.

"Yup."

I thought fast, trying to come up with a clever plan. I couldn't think of one, so I got up and march-limped over to the bar.

"Dave!" I said, kissing him on his cheek. "Nice to see you again." Dave looked confused for half a second – why was this tall blonde chick kissing him? – but then he recognized me.

"Hi," he said. He glanced at the bartender. I turned to the woman.

"We haven't been formally introduced," I said, sticking out my hand. "Danny Cleary. And you are…?"

"Lola," she said. She looked sort of bemused. Like she was enjoying the fool I was going to make of myself.

"Lola," I said. "Right." She ignored my hand. Her voice surprised me – younger than I thought, and with precise, unaccented English. "I like the blonde. It suits you."

"Thank you," I said. "It's my natural color."

Off to my left, I noticed the bartender giving the nod to the other two guys at the bar, who got up and left without a word. The bartender slowly came from around the bar and locked the door behind them, then walked back and looked at the TV again. I willed Darren to stay where he was. If he started flashing his gun around, Mr. Football Fan behind the bar would probably pull out a sawed-off shotgun and blast us all to pieces.

Dave was looking nervously at the woman. "Lola," he started to say, but she shut him up. I stared at them for a minute, then turned to the bartender.

"I don't know if you remember me from last night," I said. "Danny Cleary."

"Lowell," he responded. He didn't offer me a handshake either. How rude. These people needed to be taught some manners.

"Where are my nephews?" I asked, looking Lola in the eyes.

"I have no idea," she answered, eyebrows raised, as though talking to a slightly annoying, slow child.

She couldn't be the woman who had taken them. That woman was apparently my height and weight, and this one was about five feet tall.

"Why did you dose us? Why did you kill Dom?" I said. I could hear Darren slowly getting out of his chair. "Did you kill Ginger too? Do you know where my nephews are?" Lowell put his hands up suddenly. Without looking back, I knew Darren had drawn down on him. Lowell looked pissed off, but not like he was going to do anything stupid just yet. He didn't want a nervous-looking pretty boy getting all trigger-happy.

"Dom's dead?" Dave said. He looked at the woman. "Lola. What the fuck?"

"Shut up, idiot," she hissed at him.

Then quickly and suddenly, Lola reached across the bar, obviously to grab a gun or weapon behind it. Before she could finish her reach, I grabbed the back of her head and slammed her face into the bar. Hard. As hard as I could, which was pretty hard. Three times. Blood poured out of her face. Her nose was broken. I hoped it hurt. A lot. I held onto her head. My blood was pounding.

"Dave," I said, not taking my eyes off Lola, "do not move. Do you hear me? You stay right the fuck where you are, or my brother will shoot you in your stupid head." I glanced at the bartender, whose mouth hung open as he looked at Lola. "That goes double for you, meathead," I said to him. "Sorry. I mean, Lowell." I got the impression Lola was the alpha dog around here. He was used to taking orders from women.

I twisted Lola's arm behind her back, almost at breaking point. She grunted.

"Are you behind all of this?" I asked her. I pushed her arm a little bit further. There was a rush of blood to my head, a pounding of rage and adrenaline.

I had never felt better in my life.

"Bitch, you'd better say something," I said, "or I am going to break your arm, and then my brother is going to shoot off your kneecap. Then how will you blow the big bad dealers in the alley for your crack supply?"

Lola spat blood into my face. I jerked her arm up further, and the sound of it breaking was like a branch snapping off a tree in a dry forest. She screamed. We were all silent for a minute. It wildly occurred to me that there might be someone in the kitchen, but I saw the sign on the bar that said "No Food To-Day."

"Danny?" Dave was speaking off to my left, very quietly. I glanced at him quickly. Both of his hands were gripping the bar, and his eyes were wet.

"Yes, Dave," I said calmly.

"Is Dom really dead?"

In a couple of sentences, I told Dave what had happened the night before. I believed that he didn't know anything. He wasn't smart enough to be that good an actor. And being in grief myself, I recognized the real thing in him.

He nodded, crying. "You bitch. You bitch," he was screaming at Lola, who I was still holding by her hair. She was moaning and trying to rock back and forth, but I held her head tight. I wanted to rip her hair out of her head.

"Danny," Darren said behind me. "I'm going to ask Lowell here a question."

"Shoot," I said. I smiled at the bartender. "Whoops. Sorry, meathead. Didn't mean that literally."

"You know why we're here, don't you," Darren said. "Did you know my sister?"

"Tall bitch? Looked a bit like that one?"

I could hear Darren breathing. Even Lola was silent.

"Yeah, I knew her," he said slowly. "How could I forget her? That bitch gave me the best head I've ever had." Before the last word was out of his mouth his hand had moved below the bar.

"Darren, gun," I yelled. In the same moment that Lowell managed to get the sawed-off shotgun from under the bar and point it, Darren fired.

Lowell slammed back into the bottles behind him, the top of his head spraying onto the mirror.

I looked at Darren. He was still holding the gun as though he expected more bartenders to pop up behind the bar like ducks at a fair.

The big man disappeared behind the bar, which was now red and slick with his blood. I threw Lola to the ground, where she screamed as her broken arm made contact with the floor.

"Darren. The back door. Quickly. You too, Dave," I said, pulling Dave up by the back of his shirt. Darren grabbed him and handed me his gun.

"I don't need it," I said, waving him off. I picked up my purse and pulled the knife from it. Lola tried to kick at me from the floor. I kicked her kneecap as hard as I could, and leaned down, the tip of the blade at her throat.

She looked at me, knowing it was her last moment to live.

"You'll regret this," she said. "They will get you."

I couldn't be sure. I couldn't be sure how involved she was. I wanted to kill her, I wanted to slice her throat, I wanted to punch her until every bone in her face was broken. But she could be a pawn. She could be just a low-life pawn. I couldn't be sure.

"They've already gotten me," I said. "They killed my sister."

Instead of cutting her, I kicked her in the stomach. With my bad foot. Then I threw the knife back into my purse and hobbled after the boys.

12

I hopped, skipped and ran to the car. Darren had thoughtfully parked in the alley behind the bar. He was driving a vintage red Fiat Spider convertible. He'd shoved Dave into the miniscule backseat.

"Get in!" Darren yelled.

"Shut up," I said. I hopped over the passenger door and slid into my seat as Darren pulled away.

"Observe every fucking road rule, Darren," I said.

"No shit," he said. He was shaking. "Light me a cigarette."

He didn't smoke, but I didn't comment. I lit two, difficult in a convertible, handing one to Darren and one to Dave, who was cowering in the backseat. If you can't start smoking after killing somebody, when can you?

"Unobtrusive car," I commented. My ears were ringing, but my hands were surprisingly steady. Everything seemed too bright.

"It's Southern California," he said. I could tell by his voice that Darren was feeling the exact same way. Shock.

"Rental?" My voice sounded high and unnatural.

"Nope."

"You bought it?"

"Yup."

"With cash?"

"Of course," Darren said.

"Wish I was a rock star," I said. Everything seemed too vivid. I hoped I wouldn't pass out. The wind would help. Darren laughed, too loudly.

Dave, emboldened by the cigarette gesture, piped up from the back. "Where are we going?"

We all pondered this. "Do we have a plan?" I asked Darren.

"I was hoping you would," he said. "I plan on getting drunk, myself."

I nodded. It was as good a plan as any, and I said so. We needed to regroup.

"But we need to find somewhere to stay," I said. "Probably not wise to go back to the house."

"No," Darren said. He looked in the rear view. "Dave? You there?"

Dave looked petrified of Darren. "Yes," he said.

"Feel like going to Palm Springs?"

"Never been," Dave said. "I'm supposed to be back to work."

"Sorry, pal," Darren said. He threw his cigarette overboard. "I think you might be taking a sick day."

I pulled off my wig and stuffed it into my purse. And we cruised down to Palm Springs.

The scenery on the way from Orange County to the desert is breathtaking. Red rocks, mountains, acres of windmills. And traffic.

"Rush hour," Dave called from the backseat. He was probably getting bugs in his mouth. Convertibles are overrated, if you ask me. I kept turning around to see if anybody was following us, but with the amount of traffic, it was an impossible task. I'd never tried to see if anyone was tailing me before. Except maybe keeping an eye out for police when I was scoring, and even then, I was pretty foolhardy.

Darren had been silent for most of the trip. He had his sunglasses on, so I couldn't see his eyes. I wondered how he was feeling. It was his first time killing someone. At least, as far as I knew. He handled it well enough that I was starting to have my doubts. But me? I was feeling just fine, other than the obvious injuries, and for the fact that Ginger was really dead. But as for regret about what had happened at Lucky's?

None. Zero. Nada. And if that makes me a bad person, so the fuck be it.

There was no doubt in my mind that Lowell the bartender had had some knowledge of, if not hand in, what had happened to Ginger or Dominic or the boys, or all of it. At the very least, by locking us in with him and his piece behind the bar, he was making a choice. And Lola? Whatever her role, she was in deep, and my only regret was that I didn't have more time to get information from her. I was glad I hadn't dragged her along with us, though. Would have been hard to conceal an unwilling passenger in a tiny convertible. Criminal mastermind, my brother was not.

We got into Palm Springs proper and cruised the ten or twelve blocks of the strip. It was beautiful weather in the desert, and tourists were everywhere. I had been here before, with Ginger. It was one of her favorite places.

We didn't discuss where to stay. Darren pulled onto a street parallel with the strip, where some of the lesser-priced hotels were located. We pulled into a mid-price motel with lots of palm trees and a pool.

"Ginger and I stayed here one time," Darren said. "With Fred and the boys. We swam in that pool. Few years ago. Before chauffeurs and butlers. Or bodyguards," he corrected himself.

It was my second time staying in a motel formerly frequented by my sister. I hoped it would be more successful than the last time.

Darren and I discussed room arrangements. "One room," he said. "You, me and Dave here. Two beds, and then Dave and I can get cozy. Right, Dave?" He grinned over the backseat at our passenger-slash-hostage.

"Really? I have to stay with the boys?"

Darren took his sunglasses off. "Danny. You think I'm going to let you stay in a motel room by yourself right now? Uh. No."

"How 'bout you, Dave? Ready for a slumber party?"

Dave smiled. "This is a nice place," he said. "Do you think they'd mind if I swam in that pool in my boxers?"

Darren and I looked at each other and laughed. It felt good. "Dave. My man," Darren said. He was laughing a little too long, a little too loud. "You and I are going to need to do some shopping."

"Me, too," I said. "I bought this outfit at Macy's today," I said to them. "What do you guys think?"

Darren stopped laughing. "You've got blood on you," he said. "Good thing that shirt's black." I looked down at myself. I did have blood on me. On the way up, I had tried to clean the blood off my face in the car, with a little spit and a tissue. I hadn't checked my shirt.

Dave suddenly leaned out the side of the Fiat with his head down, looking like a puppy. "You guys crazy or something?" He seemed weirdly resigned. I figured he was probably in shock. He just found out his buddy had been killed, but at least he knew we didn't do it.

Darren and I looked at each other. "Maybe," I said.

Dave nodded, as if he understood.

"Well," Darren said, getting out of the car. "You kids stay in the car. I'm going to get us a room!" He tossed me the keys. "Danny. Move the car, maybe?" He indicated spaces further from the road.

"Copy that," I said. I slid behind the wheel of the Fiat. I hadn't driven in a while, and forgot how much I loved it. Even just across a Days Inn parking lot.

Twenty minutes later, all three of us were ensconced in a twin double room. It was decent if bare bones, but the pool, which we could still see out our window into the twilight, looked inviting. Darren ordered a pizza and wings, and two four-packs of soda.

"I want a swim," I said. I had an urge to scour myself with chlorine.

"Not yet," Darren said. "First, we need to talk to Dave here. How you doin', Dave?"

Dave was lying on one of the beds, a wet washcloth over his eyes. "I'm getting a migraine," he said. His knock-off Nikes were hanging off his toes. He didn't even have the energy to kick them off. He looked twelve years old, all of a sudden, and I felt a motherly pull towards him.

"We'll get you some pills later," Darren said. He rooted around in the desk drawer and pulled out some Days Inn stationery and a pen.

"Danny. We need to think now. Okay? You okay?" It was serious Darren again. I was starting to wonder about these mood swings I'd seen in him. That, or it could have been seeing him shoot someone's head off today.

Not that I'd behaved like a Girl Scout myself. I could still feel Lola's hair in my hands. I was glad I had broken her nose. And her arm. But still, I was glad I hadn't killed her when I had the chance. That was something I was pretty sure you couldn't come back from. It was what I had wanted to shield Darren from. Obviously that plan hadn't worked out very well.

"Okay. I'm ready," I said. I looked at Dave, who looked fast asleep now. Darren made a move as though to wake him, but I stopped him.

"Let him sleep for now," I said. "He just found out his best friend was killed last night." Not to mention being kidnapped by the killer and his sister, who were, for all he knew, on some kind of *Natural Born Killers* spree. If he could sleep, good. Better than hysterical screaming and running for the door.

"Since we were five," Dave said from under the washcloth. So much for my powers of observation. "We grew up together. We were foster kids together." He rolled over with his back to us. I looked at Darren and he looked back at me, and nodded. We left him alone.

On a sheet of paper, Darren and I wrote:

Dead People
Ginger
Dominic Pastore
Lowell the Bartender

Injured People
Danny
Detective French
Lola aka Drug Dealer

Persons of Unknown Whereabouts
Matthew and Luke
Fred
Fake Danny

People Who Might Know Something
Detective Miller
Detective French
Dave
Lola
Fat desk clerk at Sunny Jim Motel
All of the Persons of Unknown Whereabouts

"Huh," I said, after we finished the list. "We've made progress."

"Who should we talk to first?" Darren said, leaning back on his elbows. He rubbed his eyes. His jacket was hanging over a chair, and he was wearing his jeans and a Nirvana t-shirt.

"Darren. Where the fuck is the gun," I said. Darren looked at himself, then at me, then grabbed the keys where I'd thrown them on the desk, and ran out to the car. Three minutes later he was back, holding his gun in his hand.

"Are you insane?" I said. "Didn't think to hide that maybe?"

Darren shrugged. "Off season. No one around." He put the

gun carefully on the desk. I looked at him.

"Darren. We might end up having to go to jail."

"We might, at that," he said. "How you feel about that?"

"That I would rather not," I responded. "But I need to see this thing through." I examined the bottom of my foot. I wished we had Advil for pain. Or something stronger. I sighed, suddenly feeling the crack urges come back to hit me again square in the chest.

Funny thing, that. A little uber-violence had erased the urges for a while, more than anything else ever had. Now that I was calmer, I wanted my real drug.

"I didn't see anything," Dave piped up from the other bed. Darren and I looked at him. He removed the washcloth from his face. "You guys don't have to worry about me. That Lola…"

"What about Lola, Dave? You two seemed pretty cozy when you walked into Lucky's."

Dave sat up. "I've known Lola a while," he said. "She's been coming into the bar maybe a year? Maybe less. Everybody knows she runs a few things through there. But I didn't think she was bad people." Two fat tears appeared and ran down his cheeks.

"Did she know my sister?" I still wasn't sure how much Dave knew.

"Your sister is Danielle, right?" This again.

"Was. Ginger, actually. Danielle is my name."

"Danny is your name," Dave corrected me. He wasn't going to be on *Jeopardy* any time soon. It took a while, but between us, Darren and I managed to make Dave understand that I was not my sister, and she was not me.

"Did Lola know Ginger?" Darren asked him.

"Ginger. Weird," Dave said slowly.

"Dave," I said, flopping myself down on the bed. "Please."

"Yeah, yeah, they knew each other. Ginger started coming into the bar. We don't get a lot of girls at the bar," he said. "Ginger started coming in, and around that time I think is when Lola started hanging out there. They were pretty tight. At least I think they were. Ginger gave Lola's sister a job, even," Dave said. Darren and I looked at each other. "Taking care of her kids," he continued. "Lola's sister, she's different than Lola, that's what Ginger said. She wasn't in the life. She didn't do drugs or anything. She was going back to school or something or other. Literature?" He then went bright red, as though he had insulted me, or insulted my sister, by talking about our drug use. "Jeanette. That's her name. I remember 'cause it was my first girlfriend's name."

There was silence for a minute. The mystery nanny. The mystery nanny who took the kids. Jeanette.

All of a sudden I remembered my dream. When I had turned into Ginger. Or she had turned into me. I remembered the voices in the room. I closed my eyes, and tried to remember if I had seen faces. Figures. Anything. But dreams fade.

"What does Jeanette look like?" I said quietly.

"I dunno. Not like Lola," Dave said. "I think they weren't really sisters. Maybe they were adopted? Or in a group home or something when they were kids, like Dom and me? Her sister is more white. Looks a bit like you," he said, gesturing at me. "Tall like that. Not as pretty, though," he said, smiling a winning smile. "I only ever saw her one time. She didn't hang out at Lucky's."

Someone knocked at the door. Darren checked through the peephole and I hoped there wasn't a gun on the other side. Luckily, it was the pizza guy, and if he was packing heat, he didn't let on.

"Hey, Dave," Darren said, once we were all tucked in to a couple of slices. "Tell us everything you know about Lola and her sister."

"And our sister," I added.

"After that, can I have a swim?" Dave said. He bit the point of his second slice. "You guys are pretty cool."

"After that, you can swim all night if you want," I said.

"In your underwear," Darren added.

That night, I slept like the dead. No dreams, either. And when I woke up, I didn't want crack. Immediately. I wanted coffee, Advil and Marta's churros, but crack didn't occur to me for, oh, about twenty minutes.

Progress.

I lay in the semi-darkness, squinting at bright sunlight breaking through a gap in the heavy drapes. I wondered where the twins were, if they had slept last night, how scared they were. I closed my eyes and tried to pray, but my soul didn't feel clean enough. I could hear Lola's arm breaking.

Darren and Dave were both still sound asleep in the next bed, Darren's arms and legs hanging off the bed, with Dave sprawled across most of it. I wished I had a camera, and a reason to blackmail my brother.

The night before, Darren and I agreed that one of us would have to call the house in the morning. There might be news about the boys. Besides, no doubt half the police in Southern California would be looking for us, and Darren hadn't checked in with Skipper and Laurence since yesterday morning. We didn't know what story Lola would tell the police, the truth or not. Or whether she would have even gone to the police. She might have gotten out of Dodge and gone to some underground crackhead doctor and had her arm and nose set. Her type tends not to like the authorities. In my experience.

I hoped Lucky's didn't have security cameras somewhere. It seemed highly unlikely, given the shady nature of some of the goings on there, so I decided not to dwell. But ballistics would show what kind of gun had killed the bartender, and I didn't know how long it might take Rosen to crack and tell Miller that he had loaned Darren his trusty sidearm.

"Shit, shit, shit," I said quietly as I got into the shower. Everything had happened so fast in the last couple of days, and I, at least, had acted on nothing but pure gut instinct. Which was about to get both Darren and me thrown into jail for the rest of our natural lives.

But we did have more information, courtesy of our new best friend Dave, than we had the day before.

The motel might not have been much, but the shower was killer. I forgot about everything for a few minutes and let hot water run over my head. There was even shampoo and conditioner. I was almost content, for five full minutes.

Which lasted until I came out of the bathroom with a towel wrapped around myself and one in a turban on my head, and saw Darren standing at the desk, looking down at it in horror.

"The gun," he said. "The fucking gun. It's gone."

13

Darren shook Dave awake. "Hey, fuckhead! Wake the fuck up! Where is it?"

Poor Dave took a second to wake up, even with a crazed former gunman yelling in his face. I couldn't imagine him getting to work on time with a normal alarm clock.

"Where is it?" he said, sitting up. "Where's what, dude?"

"The gun, Dave, the fucking gun!" Darren was shouting. The clock said it was eight a.m.

"Darren. Be quiet," I hissed. Someone in the next room yelling about a gun at eight in the morning tends to alarm the tourists.

"Where did you put it last," Dave said. "Look there."

I laughed. I couldn't help it. I may have had a touch of the old hysteria.

Darren, however, didn't see the humor in the situation. He was rummaging around on the floor, amongst the empty pizza boxes and soda cans that the boys had thoughtlessly left strewn everywhere. Having a sore foot, I had declared myself exempt from clean-up duty. It was there, I was sure. Dave wouldn't have taken it – if he had, why hadn't he shot us in our sleep and made off in the Fiat? Or brandished it threateningly if he was a bad guy?

I helped Darren search, and after a toddle to the bathroom in his boxers – which had seen better days, I could not help noticing – so did Dave. We looked under both beds, even using a helpful little penlight Darren had on his keychain. We looked in the two wastebaskets, and in the pizza boxes, and Dave even shook the soda cans, as if David Blaine had come in during the night and hidden the gun there. We stripped both beds and piled the bedding up in a corner. Darren even looked in the toilet tank.

"What is this," I said. "*The Godfather*?"

"Danny," he said. "You are not appreciating the seriousness of this situation." He was sitting on the bed I had just slept in. Dave's boxers weren't the only thing in the room that had seen better days. The mattress, without its cover, looked like the Black Dahlia might have been cut in half there.

"No, I am. I'm just hysterical," I said calmly. "This is one of the ways in which it manifests itself."

"So what happened to the gun?" Dave said. "Someone must have come in while we were sleeping and took it." He was pulling on his clothes.

Darren and I exchanged a look. It seemed like a simple impossibility, but there was no other way around it. We had all seen the gun on the desk when we went to sleep, sometime around midnight, and eight hours later it was no longer in the room, or on any of our persons.

"At least we all have our tongues," I said brightly, and wished I hadn't. Dave looked like he had been punched in the gut.

"Oh God, I'm sorry, Dave. I'm so sorry," I said. I sat down on the other bed where he'd sat down abruptly. "I'm just scared. Okay? I'm just scared."

"'S'okay," Dave said. "Hey, Danny. Did you and Dom have a good time? You know… before it happened?" His eyes were bright and wet.

"I gotta say, Dave, it was one of those great nights," I said. "We laughed like fucking idiots. We had a ball." Dave nodded.

"That's good," he said. "I didn't think he was doing shit again, but I'm glad at least he was having fun." I nodded and rubbed Dave's back.

"We need to get out of here," Darren said after a minute. "Somebody's following us. Somebody is fucking with us."

"It's possible that someone saw you running around the parking lot with a gun, and decided to break in here and steal it during the night." I said. "There are lots of shady characters out there who would love to have a gun that wasn't registered to them."

"That's true," Dave said helpfully.

"Let's get breakfast," I said. "I think they have an omelette bar here. What could happen to us at an omelette bar?" The boys nodded. It was irrefutable logic.

We walked quietly through the motel to the dining room, and I thought about the twins. I knew they were still alive – there was no way they weren't; I couldn't think of a single endgame that would involve anyone wanting to kill Ginger's kids. And I just felt that they were alive. I knew it. But they would be a handful, two pre-teen boys, especially two pre-teen boys who were being taken from their home by someone other than family, immediately after the brutal death of their mother.

More and more, I thought that Fred and Lola's sister, this Jeanette woman, had done it all. There was something that didn't feel right about it, but the pieces fell into place. But the idea of sweet, gentle Fred having anything to do with killing my sister sent a wave of bleak sadness over me. It felt like I wouldn't be able to breathe much longer.

Just get the boys away from him, I kept thinking. Get those boys away from Fred and Jeanette, if they have them, and after that, you can smoke crack until your heart explodes.

The thought was comforting.

The only other people in the breakfast room were two overweight couples with fanny packs, and an elderly lady, who held onto her table as though there was about to be a 7.6 earthquake any second. Dave opted for only cheese in his omelette, while Darren and I had the works: broccoli, onions, jalapenos, whatever mystery meat was going, plus three different kinds of cheese. The appetite, she was back. If I didn't get back to my old workout/fighting schedule, I was going to start looking like one of those tourists from Kansas. In a blonde wig.

"Why are you bothering with that thing," Darren said. "Nobody here knows you."

"Obviously someone does," I said, draining my second cup of coffee. "Unless we weren't the only people who had guns stolen last night. Maybe we should file a report!"

Darren ignored me, and declared that he was going to the lobby to call Fred and Ginger's place. He wanted to get a word in with Rosen. He pulled out his wallet and passed a handful of twenties to me.

"Go shopping," he said. "Get yourself a change of clothes. And for Dave too," he added.

"Sweet," Dave said. "Thanks, man." Darren paused a second, and threw another few twenties down. "Look nice, okay?" We agreed to meet at the pool in an hour, hour and a half tops, and ascertain our next move. Darren even used the word "ascertain." Which concerned me.

Dave and I took our time over coffee, not saying much. He was quite restful company. Not overburdened with the need for witty repartee. Trusting. Docile. Willing to go with the flow.

He made me want to get a dog.

We wandered into the bright desert sunshine, and walked the short block to the strip. There was a plethora of tacky tourist crap side by side with pricey, funky boutiques. Darren and I spent fifteen minutes or so window shopping, before he lingered for long minutes in front of a shop that sold novelty t-shirts.

"He, uh, said I could get a new shirt, right?" Dave said, carefully not looking at me.

"Sure, buddy," I said. "Take your pick. Beavis and Butthead? Lynyrd Skynyrd?"

"That one," Dave said. It was plain white. Nothing on it.

"Oh," I said. "Okie dokie." We went in, and Dave rifled through the rack until he found a medium. It swam on him, but he asked the cashier to put his old one in a bag. He wore the new t-shirt proudly out of the store.

"You're a man of contradictions, Dave," I said.

"Trying to blend," he said. I stopped in another store a block away and quickly outfitted myself with some new underwear, a white sleeveless sundress and a pair of white Keds. Comfort was the order of the day, and I was so over the flip-flops I'd stolen from Ginger's place.

"We better get back for the meeting," Dave said, looking at the ratty Timex he wore.

The meeting. I smiled. "Right you are." On the way back to the motel, I bought a blue bathing suit, just a basic one-piece. I wanted to swim, and I had a smidge more modesty than Dave about jumping into a public pool in my underwear. Walking back, I thought I understood the phrase "retail therapy" for the first time. I felt close to Ginger, walking these streets. She was watching over me. I could feel it. She would help us find the boys.

That, or it was just wishful thinking, helped along by drug withdrawal and grief.

Darren was by the pool, chatting up a female bartender who had set up outside for the afternoon.

"My compatriots," he said, in greeting. "Melissa, I would like to introduce my sister, Gretchen, and her husband, Doug." He stared Dave down, daring him not to get it.

"Hi!" Dave said, sticking out his hand and speaking loudly. "Doug. Doug... Douglas."

"My husband just had a couple of mimosas," I said to Melissa, shaking her hand. "It's part of his charm. The Doug Douglas thing, for example." Melissa laughed uproariously. She didn't get out much, I was pretty certain. That, or Darren had charmed her halfway out of her panties already. Come to think of it, I was sure it was the latter. "Hey. Bro," I said to Darren, poking him hard in the back with my fingernail. "I talked to Mom this morning, and I have to fill you in." I looked at Dave and Melissa, who didn't look like they had a clue between them. "Will you guys excuse us for two secs?"

Melissa and Dave were cool, and Darren walked twenty feet away. I didn't have to say anything.

"What," he said. "I was bored." He was chewing a toothpick.

He looked anything but bored. He looked like I'm sure I looked when I was about to do crack, or some other behaviour to distract myself from what was really happening.

"What's happening at the house?" I said.

"I told Rosen that we'd headed up to Oakland following a couple of leads," Darren said. He waved at Melissa. He even winked. I rolled my eyes so hard my head hurt.

"Oakland?" I said. "Leads?" I said.

"Keep the police off our trail for now," he said. "If they're looking."

"Anybody find Fred? The boys?"

"Nobody is telling Rosen anything," he said. "The cops are there, but Miller is conspicuously absent. And French of course is in the hospital."

"What? I only hit her once," I said. Darren looked at me.

"Didn't I tell you last night?" he said. "Somebody broke into her house later in the evening and shot her. She's in intensive care." I went dizzy for a second. I wanted badly to call Miller. He was probably busy trying to find whoever shot his partner, but as far as I was concerned, the likelihood that it wasn't related to Ginger and the boys was slim to none.

"Any messages on the mirror?" I asked.

"Not that I know of," Darren answered.

"We need to head back up there," I said. "I need to talk to Miller and tell him about Lola and her sister, or whoever she is."

"And how are you going to say that you came by that information?" Darren said, looking intently at me. "By breaking her arm and her nose while I shot someone?"

Good point. "No!" I said. "Dave! We can tell him that Dave

185

told me everything! I went looking for Dave after Dom was killed."

"Could work," Darren said. "But Dave… he needs to be coached." We looked over at him, both of us wondering what stories he was telling the lovely Melissa about his life as Doug Douglas. I sighed.

"Got anything better to do on the drive back?" I asked.

We decided to give ourselves twenty minutes for a quick dip. As we were about to have Dave lie for us, we agreed to spend a little time keeping him on side, and a swim was all he'd asked for after we effectively kidnapped him the day before. We'd checked out of the hotel, but I changed into my new bathing suit in the bar restroom, and tried to ignore my pale legs. And the fact that I kind of definitely needed to shave. Whatever. I did laps, Dave did cannonballs into the deep end, and Darren continued to flirt with Melissa.

I watched how much he was drinking, and realized I would be the one driving back up to Orange County. Me, the sober one. Who knew.

Dave and I rousted Darren from his barstool perch, bade our farewells to Melissa, and headed for the car. We were all quiet – Darren was recovering from murdering someone yesterday, I assumed, as well as worrying about the twins and having enjoyed a nice spell of daytime drinking. I just wanted crack. I had pushed myself in the pool, trying to forget everything. Dave looked around the parking lot warily as we approached the Fiat.

There was a vanload of tourists unloading luggage twenty

feet away. Four or five little kids were throwing a Frisbee at a scrawny hound who was barking furiously, ecstatic. It was a beautiful, perfect day.

"You okay there, Dave?" He was even walking differently, as though he thought he was being filmed and wanted to make a good impression.

He nodded. "Think we can put the top up though?" he asked. "I think I got too much sun." He did look a bit red, and we had a drive ahead of us.

"Probably not a bad idea anyway," Darren said. "Less visible." He and Dave wrestled with the Fiat's canvas roof, which turned out to have a large tear along the top.

"I see you performed a full inspection before purchasing, Darren," I said.

"I was in a bit of a rush," he said. "I've never bought a car while illegally carrying a firearm before. I might have neglected some of the due diligence on this one."

Dave settled himself into the miniscule backseat and we buckled in.

"So we go back to the house and call Miller?" I said.

Darren nodded. "I really don't think Lola would have told anyone," he started to say, when I heard a noise from the backseat that was unsettlingly familiar. I had heard it the day before just before Lowell the bartender's head exploded. I turned my head with my eyes half closed, expecting not to still be alive by the time I could look.

A gun. Sticking through the back of the headrest into Darren's neck. The sound was the safety being released.

"Drive, Danny," Dave said. His voice, the cadence, it was

all different. Simple-minded Dave was long gone. "We have somewhere we need to be."

And without another word from anyone, I pulled us out of the Days Inn parking lot, and we headed north.

14

We cruised out of Palm Springs, all of us silent for a bit. I was glad to be sober, because I knew I needed my faculties about me. Darren was sitting with his shades on, his face absolutely still. He was slouched down, his legs spread, every inch the rock star.

You'd never know he had a gun held to the back of his neck.

I looked at Dave in the rear view, trying to meet his eyes. He looked out the front windshield and ignored me. The hand holding the gun was steady. Gone was the simple-minded slacker who hung out at a sleazy tavern and supposedly, at least, worked at a pawn shop. The way he held his body was different, more self-assured and strong. In the space of a few minutes, he no longer looked like you could push him over with your pinky finger. Everything about him was different. I kept thinking of the movie *Primal Fear*, with Richard Gere and Edward Norton, where you think Norton is a hillbilly simpleton, until he morphs into his real self. A ruthless killer. Dave even looked a bit like Edward Norton.

I wished I had called Miller last night after all, and told him where we were. I didn't have to tell him about the bartender. Miller was a straight arrow and he would probably have had to turn us in for any crimes, but dying in the desert before finding the twins and avenging Ginger's murder didn't sound like my cup of tea either.

"So what did you do with the gun last night?" I said. "We tore that room apart."

"Put it in the safe in the lobby."

The sun was even brighter this afternoon. Waves of heat shimmered across the highway. Darren cleared his throat, but didn't say anything.

We passed out of Palm Springs, into the desert. "Hey, there's a sign for Cabazon," I said. "Anyone up for some outlet shopping?" Ginger had dragged me down here before. A couple of acres of upscale outlets in the middle of the desert, with a casino nearby, Cabazon is heaven for tourists with holes burning in their pockets.

No one responded. "Look!" I continued. "McDonald's!"

Dave sighed heavily. "I am sorry about this," he said.

"Who are you?" Darren said. He didn't move anything but his face when he spoke, which is when I realized that he was more afraid than I had thought. Sunglasses hide a lot.

I was able to keep my mouth shut. I tried to think. Was Dave a Fed? Or a cop? But if so, why would he go through last night's charade? Even if he was somehow undercover trying to solve the kidnapping – and I was almost hoping that was the case, that he was FBI and just taking us to a field office or something – why wouldn't he have identified himself by now? Did he get caught out without a weapon, and after the horror show at Lucky's yesterday, didn't feel safe taking Darren's gun until we were out cold?

Soon enough we saw a sign for an exit that would take us over to Joshua Tree National Park.

"U2's greatest album," Dave said. "Also, our destination. Take this exit, Danny."

I looked in the rear view but Dave's eyes were hidden by his sunglasses.

"I really didn't want to be in this position," Dave was saying. He was still looking straight ahead, his gun at the back of Darren's neck. "You two surprised me yesterday. I didn't think…" he trailed off. I saw his point. He hadn't really thought either Darren or I had it in us to kill. And as far as he knew, I had killed Lola after he went out the back door.

"Live and learn," I said lightly. "Ginger was our sister. My twin. They have our nephews. If you fuck with us, you will regret it." I felt strong as I said it, and I meant every word. But with a gun pointed twelve inches away, it came out sounding hollow.

"Are you law enforcement?" Darren asked. "Is Dave your real name?"

Dave didn't answer.

We drove for a bit, through scrub and weird moon-like trees that, it turned out, were actual Joshua trees. Who knew.

"We're going to pass a ranger booth," Dave said. "You could try and give a signal to the attendant that something is going on here, but I wouldn't. I think you're going to want to, uh, take this meeting." I glanced at him and he seemed to be actually blushing under his sunburn.

"Take this meeting?" I said. "You must be FBI."

"Take a meeting. In the desert," Darren said, finally. "At gunpoint."

We approached a park entrance booth. The gun had moved, presumably under Dave's thigh. I rolled down the window. "Hi there," a friendly young woman inside the booth said. "Will you folks be camping tonight?"

I wondered how often campers turned up in two-seat Fiats. But this was Southern California. Go with the flow.

"Nope, just catching the sights," I said. I smiled. Darren leaned across me and took his sunglasses off.

"Hi," he said. He beamed his million-dollar smile at her. "My sister isn't a fan of the outdoors, miss," he said. "For her, sleeping under the stars means picking up actors at bars in L.A." I punched his arm, and the girl laughed.

"Right," the young woman said. She leaned through her little window and peered more closely at Darren. "I recognize you, don't I?"

One of his band's videos had been in rotation six months or so ago on the music channels. I didn't know whether Darren had made himself so visible by habit or design, but in either case, Dave cleared his throat.

Darren nodded quickly at him and looked back at the pretty young woman at the gate, who was running her hands through her hair. I tried very hard not to roll my eyes. "I hear it all the time, but unless you've sat in on one of my sociology lectures at Berkeley, probably not."

"You're a prof?" the girl said. She looked skeptical.

"No tenure yet, though," he said. He leaned back in his seat and waved as she passed me my change and a map of the park.

"Well good luck with that." I could tell she was thinking of changing her major, if this was what the sociology profs looked like. She continued with some kind of welcome to the park but I was already pulling away. I could hear Dave readjust in the miniscule backseat. Sure enough, the gun came out again.

"Really?" I said. "Do you really think that's necessary?"

"I've seen your fighting record," he said. "And I saw you both yesterday."

If Dave had seen my fighting record, it meant he had obviously done a fair amount of research on me. It's not like I went pro or was even a real contender in the ring; I doubted Google would have much to say about me. How in the hell would he know that?

We all kept quiet for a bit. The car glided through a part of the desert that looked like it was the moon. Huge, smooth rocks, and bizarre, leafless, misshapen trees dotted the landscape. It was past midday, and the sun was unrelenting, even at this time of year. Everything seemed yellow. I wished the roof was down, or the Fiat was air-conditioned.

We drove for longer than I thought possible. How big could this park be? I looked around for other vehicles, and so far hadn't seen any. Had someone rented out the whole place to murder us? At this point, it seemed as likely as anything did. I just drove and tried to stay calm and centered.

But another part of me was tensing my muscles. Girding my loins for battle. Ginger always liked to say "girding my lions for battle." I glanced at my feet to see if my new sneakers were tied tightly.

Ginger. I wondered if maybe Dave had been the man in the room with her, in my dream of the moments before Ginger's death. Or was it Fred? Lowell was the only one of them who had seemed like he had it in him; he had just looked bad. Dave certainly wasn't who I thought he was a few hours ago, but at the moment everyone I knew was surprising me. I glanced at

Darren. He looked back at me and smiled. It was the kind of smile that made me feel part of something. Not alone in the world. I needed that smile, at that moment.

"Here," Dave said. He was checking an iPhone. "Pull over here." We all sat in silence for a minute. I tapped my fingers on the steering wheel.

"Can we get out, at least?" I was antsy and the car was too small. I hadn't adjusted the seat properly for my height. And if I was going to be shot, I'd rather be standing up outside when it happened.

And then of course it occurred to me that if Darren and I got out and shut the doors quickly Dave would be locked in the car. The top was up and it would be too difficult and awkward to climb out of that non-existent backseat easily or gracefully, even for someone of Dave's size. But then I looked around at the landscape. We could run, but there was nowhere to hide closer than a hundred yards away, and with a gun and the Fiat's canvas roof, Dave could be out of the car in a few seconds.

I knew Darren was thinking the same thing. I could practically smell his wheels turning. But he'd also had more than his fair share of drinks by the pool, and although he was athletic enough, he wasn't the fastest runner in the world, a fact which Ginger and I had teased him about mercilessly when we were kids.

Ginger. A wave of pain took me then, and for a minute I thought I would pass out from it. The sheer misery of missing her, of being clean and sober and not feeling Ginger out there felt like a kick in the solar plexus.

I must have made a noise because Darren grabbed my hand.

"No touching," Dave said.

Something clicked in my brain at that second. Someone getting between me and a member of my family. Almost before Dave got the words out of his mouth, without thought or hesitation I reached around, knocked the gun out of his hand and elbowed him sharply and efficiently in the face.

While he was knocked back holding his nose, I picked up the gun.

I looked at Dave, who had blood spurting from his nose. His head was slightly lowered, one hand trying to catch the blood, but his eyes never left me. I raised the gun and pointed it at him.

The whole thing had probably taken three seconds.

"No, Danny," Darren said. I got the feeling he didn't want to touch me while I was like this, in case the lightest touch on my arm could jolt me into squeezing the trigger.

"How does it feel, motherfucker," I said. I released the safety. My voice was calm, and I don't think my heart was even racing. "Surprise," I said softly.

Darren opened the passenger door and stepped outside. I held the gun steady on Dave while Darren shot his seat forward and grabbed Dave's arm.

"Get out," he said. "I don't have to tell you not to do anything stupid, or my sister will shoot you. And in the mood she's in, I think she'd probably start at your ankles and work her way up." Once Dave was out of the car, I leaned back and grabbed his phone. He'd dropped it when I grabbed the gun from him.

Oh God, for some crack. My kingdom for some crack.

The sun was merciless and the air was far drier than anything I was used to. An east coast girl, I much prefer humidity with my heat. And we had no water with us. In the desert.

"What do you think, leave him here and go?" I looked at Dave. Darren had made him sit on the ground cross-legged with his hands on his head. He looked like a fourth grader who'd been hit in the face by a baseball. Without the gun, he looked weak and harmless. But I certainly wouldn't be making that assumption about him again anytime soon.

"It is hot," Darren said. "I could use a cold one."

"Afternoon hangover?" I asked sympathetically. "They're the worst."

"My own fault," Darren said. "Hair of the dog would be nice though." I turned right around. There wasn't another vehicle or person in sight.

"Shoot him first, do you think?"

"Hard to say," Darren replied. He leaned against the car and pulled a pack of cigarettes out of his back pocket. He lit us each one. I thought of Gene.

"Since when are you buying cigarettes?" I wanted to know.

"Since Dickhead Dave over there and his buddies murdered our sister and kidnapped our nephews."

"Fair enough," I said. "Fair enough." Dave took his hands off his head and looked about to say something. I walked forward a couple of paces and put the gun to his head. "Dave, I think my brother told you to keep your hands on your fucking head."

My voice cracked. My hand was shaking. I realized that my face was wet. I was crying.

I wanted to kill him. I wanted to put a bullet in his head and leave him for the carrion. I wanted it so badly I could taste iron in my mouth, I could taste the smell of his blood and the metal of the gun in my hand. It was a part of my body at that moment, an extension of my arm, as though by just thinking about how badly I wanted revenge, I could end this man who sat in the dirt in front of me.

But he had brought us here for a reason. It could have been to kill us – this place was pretty deserted, after all – or maybe there was someone else coming. He had checked the time a lot.

Besides, if I killed him now, we couldn't get any information from him. And he obviously had some to give. I took a step back, the gun still on him.

"Where does Fred have the boys," I started, and then I heard an engine.

"Ask him yourself," Dave said. He looked up at me, his nose a pulpy mess. His voice was nasal, and he sounded very, very tired. "Just ask him yourself."

I backed away from Dave and towards Darren and the car, as a dark sedan slowly approached us. I put the gun slightly behind me on the off-chance it was a lost tourist, but my thumb was resting on the safety. I had had enough surprises for one day.

There was a long moment of quiet. The engine of the sedan turned off, but the glare of the sun made it impossible to see who was behind the wheel.

Fred Lindquist, my brother-in-law, possibly the murderer of my sister, got out from the driver's side and stuck his arms in the air nervously. I moved my gun hand out from behind my back but kept it at my side. Darren put his hand on my arm.

Then Detective Miller got out of the passenger side holding a weapon and trained it on Fred.

"Well, boys," I said, "it looks like we've got ourselves a party."

15

"Now this," I observed, inhaling deeply on my cigarette, "would be a good time to smoke some crack."

All four of the men looked at me.

"Danny, you have to keep it together," Fred said. He turned to Miller. "Can I put my arms down now? You've already frisked me. I'm not going anywhere." He gestured around him.

As I walked toward Fred, I could see Miller nodding, in my peripheral vision. Before anyone could say anything, I slapped Fred, as hard as I could.

Silence. To his credit, Fred barely flinched, and I watched as a red mark formed on his pale, freckled skin. I didn't know if I had ever slapped anyone before. Punching or kicking was more my style, but my knuckles were still swollen from Detective French the day before. I walked over to Miller, who reached out one arm as if to embrace me, but it didn't seem like the moment for intimacy. "How did you find him? And why is he here and not in jail?"

"He will be," Miller said. He looked worn out, done in, the dark circles under his eyes even darker than usual, and I had a sudden desire to step into his arms after all. I wanted to rest my face against his neck and smell the rumpled, nicotine scent of his skin. Crack replacement, obviously. "In fact, I shouldn't be here. I don't have much time, I have to take him in. But," and he looked at Fred, who was standing feet shoulder-width apart, hands clasped behind his back and staring straight ahead, as if he was in the military, "he said he had arranged to meet you here. So I was a little, shall we say, concerned." He looked at Dave. "Who is that?"

"Fucked if we know," Darren said.

We quickly told Miller about how I had met Dave as Dom's buddy, and about Darren and I being taken at gunpoint to the desert. We neglected to mention the carnage at Lucky's. If Miller didn't know already, it didn't seem like the moment to bring it up. My head felt ready to explode.

Dave's real identity could wait. I wanted to hear what Fred had to say.

Darren and I approached him, and I grabbed my brother's hand. I knew how he felt, but touching him made me feel it even more strongly. This man had helped Darren with his math homework when Darren couldn't pass tenth grade calculus to save his life. He ate most of his meals with us from the time he was sixteen because his depressed, widowed mother didn't cook.

I thought Darren was going to hit Fred, and obviously Fred did too. He stood his ground and looked straight ahead. But Darren sighed.

"Well, you're caught," he said. "You are hopefully going to spend the rest of your life in jail. What was so important that you had this dickwad" – he gestured back at Dave, who was still sitting cross-legged in the dirt – "pull a gun on us and bring us here?"

"I hired him," Fred said. "I hired him to follow Ginger. When she started disappearing."

I looked at Dave. "So you're some kind of private investigator?"

Dave shrugged. He looked like he was going to say something, but he stopped and gingerly touched his nose.

"Hands on your head," Darren said, glancing at him only briefly.

"We don't have much time," Miller said. "I have to get him back or there will be another manhunt, and I would prefer not to lose my badge. Or go to jail with scum like him," he added, nodding at Fred.

"You need to get the boys back," Fred said. He was looking at me, then at Darren. "Please."

I looked at Fred. He was a ruined man. He did not look like a man who had carried out the murder of his wife and kidnapping of his sons.

"Gladly," I said. "Where are they?" Darren looked at me. I shrugged. "Benefit of the doubt," I said.

"Toronto," he answered quickly. "At least, I think they are." He leaned against the car, and Miller took a step nearer him. Fred waved his hand as if to say don't worry. "And so is Jack."

"Jack?" Darren and I said, at exactly the same moment. In a less disturbing moment, it might have been funny.

Fred nodded, and glanced at Miller. "I need to make this quick, and you need to hear it. I know you hate me. I don't blame you. I did something horrible to Ginger. But I didn't kill her."

I breathed deeply, trying to slow the racing of my heart so that I could hear him above the blood pounding in my ears.

"You know we had a nanny," Fred was saying. "Jeanette."

I looked at Dave. "Lola's sister," I said. He nodded.

"I was the one who wanted Ginger to get a nanny. She didn't want to. She didn't care if the house was chaos or if the boys ran around like savages. She said it made a house a home." Fred sounded odd, not like himself. Since when did he care about a messy house? But there was a catch in his throat. "I was rich and getting richer, even in this economy. Did Ginger tell you about my business?"

"We don't care about that," Darren said. "Just tell us where the boys are." He nearly yelled the last few words and it seemed to shock all of us.

"Yes. Well I wanted us to have a nanny so Ginger could spend more time on herself. There was no reason she should have to work as hard as she did, running after the boys, you see?"

"Ginger loved running after the boys," I said. "What did you want her to do, spend more time shopping and getting her nails done?" How did Jack have anything to do with this?

Fred ignored me. "Anyway, I asked around for recommendations and Jeanette came really highly recommended by my lawyer, and she had great references. She was a hit with the boys from the get-go. And with Ginger, too. They were more like friends than anything." He cleared his throat. "She kind of made herself indispensable around the house. To all of us," he said. He cleared his throat.

"You had an affair with her," Darren said. I stopped breathing and looked at Fred. He opened his mouth to say something, then looked down at the ground.

"Ginger had gotten so distant. She was so worried about you, Danny. And she told Jeanette about you. All about you, and Jack. And then when we were, um, alone," Fred said, face red, "Jeanette would want to know all about you and drugs and Jack and where he lived and money and… I just thought she was fascinated by our… colorful family."

"Ginger and Jeanette started leaving the boys with Marta and going off, sometimes overnight," he said. "Ginger started losing weight, and she was distracted all the time. She wasn't Ginger."

"Jeanette got her into drugs?" I said. "Is that what you're saying?"

"You and Jeanette got her into drugs, Danny," Fred said. "If you weren't her twin and she hadn't had this need to feel everything you were feeling, none of this would have happened. None of it."

Darren walked over to Fred and looked like he was going to hit him. Miller stopped him, said something about it being a bad thing if he brought the prisoner back beaten up.

"The boys," Darren said. "Hurry up, Fred. I can't stand to look at you much longer. Even if you didn't kill Ginger, you're the one who got her killed."

"I hired Dave to find out what Ginger and Jeanette were up to," Fred said. "Turns out they were going to some dive bar and buying drugs and going to the Sunny Jim motel to get high. And who knows what else," he added.

"They weren't up to anything else," Dave said. He was still sitting cross-legged on the ground, but he'd removed his hands from on top of his head. He looked as comfortable as a person could be under the circumstances. "At least, Ginger wasn't."

We all looked at him.

"As far as I could tell, Jeanette was taking over Ginger's life.

The weaker Ginger got, the stronger Jeanette got."

"Like a vampire," Darren said.

Dave nodded. "Kind of, yes. She made sure the boys loved her. She seduced Fred. And then, of course, she went for the money."

Money. Of course. It's always about money. Sometimes I wish we could burn it all and run the world on the barter system. But we'd still have the haves and have-nots, I suppose. Still have women bartering their bodies for whatever they needed.

"How?" I croaked.

"Blackmail," Fred answered simply. "Turns out she had filmed our, uh, time together."

Darren spit on the ground. Fred ignored him.

"And when I wanted to end it, and tried to fire her, she demanded money. A lot of it."

"A million," Dave said.

The rage started in my brain like buzzing bees.

"And did you pay her?" I didn't recognize my own voice.

Fred nodded. "Yes," he said. A million dollars. I shook my head.

"But it didn't stop," Darren said.

"She still wouldn't leave. She still had the tapes of us together. And I couldn't tell Ginger. I just couldn't. I hired him," he nodded at Dave. "And I just waited. I couldn't stand the stress, and what having Jeanette in our house was doing to Ginger. I was going to tell her," he said. "I was. But then… she just didn't come home one night."

I didn't want to think about that. I would think about that later. I would smoke crack and think about that later. My heart felt sore. It actually felt broken, like a sharp cracked rib in the middle of my chest.

"So what does this all have to do with the boys being in Toronto?"

Fred nodded at Dave, who said, "Can I stand up now?" He was looking at Darren. "I'm unarmed and outnumbered. All I was supposed to do was get you here." Darren and I looked at each other, and I shrugged. Darren nodded at Dave, who climbed to his feet slowly. Not a bad idea, faced with the guns Miller and Darren had. "Jeanette boarded an Air Canada flight from LAX the same day she took the boys. I don't know what she told them to get them to cooperate, but I do know that they got on that plane. Before the Amber Alert had gone out," he added. He looked at me. "And Jack MacRae is in Toronto right now, staying at the Four Seasons."

"Oh," I said. Jack in Toronto. I wondered how long he'd been there, but wouldn't ask.

Dave nodded at Fred. "According to my client, Jeanette asked a lot about Jack. There are several possible scenarios we're looking at. She knows Mr. MacRae has significant capital, so she could be using the boys as some kind of leverage to get money from him. Fred tells me that he told Jeanette a lot about Jack."

I couldn't look at Fred. I imagined him engaging in pillow talk with a woman who wasn't my sister, talking to her about my husband. I clenched my fists, took a deep breath. I could hear Ginger telling me to breathe. So I did.

"There is another possibility, of course," Dave was saying. He kicked at the ground, and for a second he looked like the slacker I'd met at Lucky's. "Jack could be involved in this. You left him, and he took it badly? And he's got mental health issues?"

"You are joking." I turned and looked at Fred. "You really think Jack would hurt those boys? In a million years? No matter what, Fred, no matter how far off the reservation he might have gotten, he loves those boys as much as any of us do."

"Danny," Fred said, almost gently, "people change."

"Fred would like us to go to Toronto, Danny," Dave said. I looked at him. "Jack will at least see you, and if he doesn't know anything about the boys or Jeanette, it wouldn't hurt to put him in the picture."

"I know Jeanette will get to him," Fred said. "She was… very curious about him."

I looked at Darren, who nodded at me.

"I'll go," I said.

I looked at Miller, who had been unusually quiet during this. He called me over with his eyes, and I went. Darren was standing six feet from Fred now, talking quietly, and I knew he didn't trust himself to get any closer to him.

"Are you sure you want to do this?" Miller was asking me. His eyes were soft. "If this Jeanette is there and she did kill Ginger – and I'm starting to think she might have at least had something to do with it – then you're walking into a lion's den." I could tell he wanted to touch me, but this still could not be a worse time for a gesture of affection.

I nodded. "Yes," I said. "If he's right," I said, nodding in Fred's direction, unable to even say his name, "then I've got to go up there and get the boys. When they're safe, I'll deal with Jeanette."

"Deal with?" he said.

"Give her a stern talking-to." Miller nodded. No point

in putting him in a position where he had any moral qualms about letting me go into what could, by my own hand, turn into a war zone.

"Keep in very close touch," he said. He tried to smile. "I'll worry."

I nodded. "I'm still not sure how much of this is true," I said. "This isn't the Fred I know. He's changed."

Miller shrugged. "I didn't know him before, of course, but it seems like this Jeanette character has a pretty bad influence on people." He looked at Fred and Darren talking, and lowered his gun. With one hand he fished a cigarette out of his shirt pocket and managed to light it. "Lindquist is going to trial. If I get found out for this little expedition, I could lose my job."

"So why did you?"

He inhaled deeply and grinned at me. "I want to get the girl in the end," he said. "Seems worth the risk. Besides, it's not like Lindquist will tell anyone. He's the one who wanted to come here."

I smiled, or something like it. Too many conflicting emotions. Right now, I just wanted the boys back, and safe. And now Jack was in the mix. And this was complicated.

But then again, I seemed to run towards complications.

I patted his arm and turned to Dave, who was watching us closely. "So you're coming with me?" I said.

"No," he said. "You're coming with me."

"You can trust him, Danny," Fred said to me. Darren came over and ruffled my hair. I felt so tired suddenly. I felt like I could lie down and sleep for a year. "Really."

"High praise coming from you," I said. "You fucking prick," I said. "You goddamn cheating, lying, fucking prick." But I was weary, and so were my words. And if Dave worked for Fred, at least he was trying to get the boys back, which made him an ally in that, at least.

I looked at the men around me. Darren, Fred, Miller and Dave. Of all of them, Dave was the one whose well-being I cared the least about. A perfect companion, then, for the task ahead.

"Okay," I said. "Let's go find the boys."

16

We drove in the two cars to a private airfield in the desert. I rode with Dave and Darren, while Miller escorted his prisoner.

In our car, at least, we were silent. I closed my eyes, found myself breathing deeply and holding it, then exhaling slowly. It might have looked like a relaxation exercise, but I was pretending I was inhaling crack. If you hold your breath for a really long time and then exhale very slowly from deep in your lungs, you get a teeny, tiny rush. For now, I would take it.

Dave said that Fred had a private plane on stand-by. A rental, he said. Fred didn't own it.

"Pfft. I thought you said he was rich," I said. "Where's the Gulfstream?" Dave laughed.

We all got out of the cars. My skin felt burnt and raw and dry, a nice match for my insides.

"Time for you to go," Fred said. Back to Toronto. Back home to my apartment, and Gene, if he was there. And D-Man.

And maybe Jack. And please God, Matthew and Luke.

And Jeanette. I was going to put a stop to this. To her.

I stood still for a minute, letting myself bake. I felt like this dry sun could erase me, shrivel me up and take away my rage.

For a few moments I welcomed it. I felt nothing, and it was like a blessing.

Darren and Dave seemed to have come to a sort of truce. Darren pulled a bag out of the Fiat's backseat, with the few bits of clothes and toiletries I had picked up in Palm Springs. Darren was civil enough to Dave, considering an hour ago Dave had a gun pressing into the back of his neck.

"Take care of everything here," I said, hugging my little brother. He held onto me tightly.

"It should be me," he said into my hair. "I should be going."

I shook my head. "Don't be stupid. I'm the one Jeanette was impersonating. Jack is my husband. It has to be me, Darren. Jeanette called my apartment for a reason. To let me know the game is on back there. Whatever her plan is, it's got to do with me somehow."

Darren nodded.

"And it's you Jeanette seems to want to play with," Fred said. "Maybe because of Jack. If he's her next target, you're the one standing in her way. Like Ginger was," he said. He looked down and wiped one hand over his face, a weary gesture. Whatever happened to him now, he would never fully recover from this.

And he needed to use me as bait to get the boys back.

I nodded. I understood. In his shoes, I don't know that I would have done any differently.

"But promise me one thing," I said. "Somebody has to trust me with a gun up there."

Dave looked at Miller. "We'll talk about that on the plane," he said.

"I didn't hear that," Miller said. "Really."

I decided I didn't care what anybody thought. I went to Miller and hugged him, briefly. "I might need it," I said.

"I hope not," he whispered.

"Me, too," I said. "Make sure everybody keeps looking for the boys up here," I said to him. "We don't know for sure they're still in Canada."

"Of course," he said. "The Feebs are all over this like white on rice." I didn't want to think too much about that, about what they might have heard over the phone at the Lindquist house in the last thirty-six hours. He must know I was in some kind of trouble here – not least of which for punching Detective French – and if I could leave, then leaving I should do.

"Thanks for everything," I whispered.

"Hey, this isn't goodbye. It's see you later," he said. I nodded and stepped back. Fred and Darren were staring at us. Dave was looking politely in the other direction.

Darren was rubbing his face. "Okay," he said slowly. "Okay."

"We have to go," Dave said. "The plane is waiting." He handed me something. My passport. I looked at Dave, and he shrugged and looked almost embarrassed.

Darren hugged me. "I'll take care of things here. Stay in contact. Promise."

"I promise to get the boys back."

"And stay out of trouble," he whispered back.

"Ha," I said, wiping a couple of stray tears from my face. "You know better."

Darren grinned. "That I do." We licked our right thumbs and touched them, like we used to do when we were kids.

"Hey, Danny," Darren called out as Dave and I walked

towards the plane. He made a sideways "V" with his fingers and tapped his chest twice, gang-style. "Peace out."

I did the same, laughing. "Right back at you, idiot," I called, and walked with Dave towards the plane.

17

The best thing about flying on a private plane is that you don't have to wrestle with taking off your shoes before boarding, or get patted down by a female security officer who looks like a prison guard. The pilot introduced himself to us, shook our hands, introduced us to the rest of the flight crew – a ridiculously handsome co-pilot and an extremely cheerful young steward – who were laid-back and funny and seemed genuinely pleased to see us.

We settled into our seats, and despite everything, I was impressed. Not bad, I thought. If this was going to be my last time flying, might as well go out in class.

I looked across at Dave. He glanced up at me, smiled the polite smile you might give someone sitting across from you on a train, and went back to a studious perusal of the laminated menu card we'd been handed by the steward.

"So," I said. "Was the gun really necessary? Do you suppose? You couldn't maybe have let us in on the fact that you're, whatever you are – a private investigator, a Navy SEAL, a soldier of fortune, whatever – while we were at the hotel last night? While I comforted you because Dom died?" I took a sip of water from the bottle the steward had placed in front of me. "You really chose the wrong profession, by the way. You're Oscar-calibre."

"Look, Dom really was my friend from way back," he said. "I've known him for years. I got him in rehab last time. When I found out he was killed…" Dave slapped the menu down. "I'm sorry. I have a client. I had to wait for instructions from my client. You and your brother didn't give me a second alone last night. And the timing was important. I had to get you to that airfield. The fact that Detective Miller caught up with Fred slowed things down a bit, but I think the fact that Miller, uh," Dave cleared his throat, "obviously admires you greatly was lucky."

I blushed. I couldn't help it. I've never been one for the PDA, but I'd needed to say goodbye to Miller. I'd given myself even odds at getting out of this in one piece. Getting the twins to safety might mean I'd be sacrificing my own, and I was fine with that. I owed it to Ginger to keep her boys alive.

"Do you believe Fred?" I asked him. The steward brought us champagne and I took mine gratefully. "Or do you think he's in on this with Jeanette?"

Dave looked at me steadily. "At this point, it doesn't really matter what I believe," he said. "Mr. Lindquist has paid me very well. I don't do this kind of work very often. Involving children, I mean." He drained his champagne in one draft, and raised his eyebrows at the steward for more. "I don't care if he's involved. I do care about getting the children to a safe place."

I sat for a moment and looked out the window as we took off smoothly. I looked back at Dave.

"I believe you," I said. "I'm not sure why, since you've done nothing but lie to me since I met you, but I do."

Dave nodded. "Good," he said.

"Tell me what you need me to do," I said.

"Eat," he said. "And tell me everything about Jack."

"Everything?"

"Everything. We're not going anywhere," Dave said.

I met Jack MacRae at the gym. I'd been drifting through my early twenties after college in Toronto, doing a little office temp work here and there and dating smart, if boring, banker types.

Hey. I was blonde, fit, and had that cheerleader exterior. Those were the guys who asked me out. The kinds of guys I liked – smart, geeky guys, not unlike Fred – normally didn't look twice at me, figuring me either for an airhead, or that I would never go out with them. Or both. I didn't care that much. I was having enough fun. I had my certification to train, and I took on a few clients from my gym – usually skinny but under-fit female executives who wanted to "tone" their sagging butts. Before I got hold of them, they would spend an hour and a half a day on the StairMaster or treadmill, burning calories, and losing even more weight. Emaciated and flabby. No muscle. I would explain that strength training was the only way to buff up. Serious weight training, not flinging around those pink three-pound dumbbells most women then seemed to think was enough. If you under-eat and over-exercise and don't work on building muscle, your body consumes it. Then you become a brittle little thing who can't pick up an umbrella.

But I digress.

I had been lifting in the men's part of the gym for a year or so, but I never talked to anybody there. My social life was full enough, and I took working out pretty seriously.

But I noticed Jack. Everybody noticed Jack. He had a giant aura about him, if that doesn't sound too spacey. He wasn't that tall, maybe a touch under six feet. And he was big – very big. Could bench-press more than any other guy in the gym, but didn't brag about it. Did pull-ups without seeming to get fatigued, and handstand push-ups. Which, for a man of his size, was pretty impressive. He wasn't one of those bodybuilder types, trying to get all their muscles cut so you could slice a tomato with them, and dropping body fat down to three percent to compete in tournaments. Jack was all about power.

He approached me first, but it wasn't a pickup. He'd noticed that I was lifting heavy for a woman with my build. I'm an ectomorph, naturally lean, with more of a runner's body. And I didn't use a spotter, because I felt like I wanted to be macho. Stupid, and Jack told me so. He showed me some new routines, split-sets that I hadn't done yet, or periodization. Boring if you're not a lifter.

We hung out at the same times, and just naturally worked out together. Jack didn't talk much, but when he did, I liked what he had to say. Dry, understated humor. I found myself thinking that he would fit right in with the quirky Clearys, except for the fact that he was fit, when people my sibs and I brought home tended more to the nice-and-nerdy.

I was the one to ask him out. It took all my nerve to do it, but at the end of one sweaty set, I said, "Let's go out for dinner." Just like that. Having been, I am ashamed to admit, one of those women who are used to being pursued, it took a lot of chutzpah to say those words.

"I can't, Danny," was all he said. After I finished blushing, we continued working out, and it was another month before I said anything personal. I asked him if he had a woman.

"No," he said, and told me to put another ten pounds on my bar, to not be such a sissy. Strike two. Hey, I was just asking. Exchanging human interaction with a friendly acquaintance.

That winter, there were a series of muggings in the area of our gym, young gangs of teenagers swarming people coming out of bars or out of the subway, robbing, and often beating them. It was heavily publicized, but I didn't feel touched by it. Besides, I felt like Superwoman, with all the working out. But Jack took to walking me home, because I lived about four dark blocks from the gym, and we almost always worked out at night. One night I said something cocky about almost wishing some snot-nose kids would try to steal my bag. Blah, blah. Big talk.

"Shut up, Danny," Jack said quietly. "Don't wish that. You're one woman, and there are whole groups of those kids. And you might be strong, but you don't know how to fight worth a damn, I bet."

"So teach me," I said. Those were the words that sealed the deal with Jack and me. And really, changed my life forever.

The first time Jack took me to a boxing gym, I loved it. He showed me how to throw a punch, hit a heavy bag, how to move. I felt like a moron, of course, because I was used to being good at things physically, and this was a whole new skill set. But punching something full force, once I knew how to do it without getting hurt? Pure adrenaline. He helped me get my wrists and forearms stronger, so that I could hit harder. Soon, I was skipping some of my weight training sessions so I could go and train at the boxing gym with Jack. And even though Jack and I were still only buddies – and buddies who didn't talk about our personal lives – I stopped dating and concentrated on this and only this. Plus the clients and two-day temp jobs I would do to make money. I didn't live high off the hog. My apartment was rent-controlled, I read my books from the library, and I never ate out.

Without telling me, Jack entered me into a small match with one of the few other women who worked out there. Layla, her name was, and I remember joking with her that she'd better not be as good as Laila Ali. Layla just smiled and told me that she was going to "clean my clock." I laughed, because I had never heard anyone actually use that expression, and I've always been overjoyed when I hear something like that used in a serious context. Blame the Cleary sense of humor.

But Layla, not being a Cleary, didn't think my laughter was so funny, and what was supposed to have been a little training match with the newbie, for her, became a real fight. Within seconds, I took a right hook across the side of my face. Despite the face guards we wore, it made me go down and see stars.

And got my blood pumping. Rage slammed through my brain. Even though I knew that hitting me was her objective, and that we were in a ring and therefore it wasn't a sucker punch, I saw red. I was back up. And I went at her. And at her. I got her against the ropes and kept hitting until Jack pulled me off her. He was trying not to smile, I could tell.

"You need to work on your jabs," was all he said for a while.

I was euphoric. It was the proudest moment of my life. Jack fed me half a roast beef sandwich and some water in the change room, which we had to ourselves. I was literally jumping up and down with excitement. I wanted to do it again tomorrow. Or maybe the next day. Even though my jaw was pretty sore from that first punch.

Jack sat quietly listening to my elation. "Looks like you're a fighter," he said. "I think we should go further, and I don't mean with boxing. I mean, we should teach you some other martial arts. Like Krav Maga would be good for you, that's Israeli, or ju-jitsu…" I had stopped listening. Jack said I was a fighter.

And with adrenaline still pumping through my system, I kissed him. "I do want to go further," I said, when I let him up for air. I think he understood what I meant. And after holding my shoulders and looking at me for a minute, he decided to come around.

So we went further. In every way there is to go further. He taught me everything to know about fighting, which was a lot. And I taught him how to have fun with life. Not to take things so seriously.

Our wedding, four months later, was City Hall all the way. Two strangers as witnesses, and I didn't even tell the family until it was all over. Jack became my life, and while I was dying for everybody to meet him, I wanted him to myself.

It wasn't until after we got married that I really learned about him. How he was raised in foster care, but he didn't like to talk about that. At twenty he'd gone looking for his real family, and found them; he could see from one look into the squalid living room how things were. The people who had made him were still together.

He saw a man who was his double, but twenty years older, sitting in a living room that stank of cigarette smoke and sweat. A huge paunch hung over his belt, and he hadn't shaved in a while. Jack's birth mother, on the other hand, was obviously soused, and just as obviously being beaten around on a regular basis. She had bruises yellowing around one eye, and the remains of a fat lip. And when she brought Jack in a beer, she was holding her arm at an odd angle. Jack knew it was broken. Recently. And hadn't been set.

Jack got up off the couch, politely took the beer from the woman called Doreen who wanted him to call her Mom, and escorted her back to the kitchen. He picked up the phone and called 911. Doreen was apparently too far gone down the rye bottle to realize that he'd done it, but Mitchell, his birth father, was not. He came charging into the kitchen, yelling at Jack to mind his own goddamned business, how he should have drowned the baby at birth. He took a swing at Jack, but Jack ducked. And belted his father a good one in his gut.

Jack wasn't really a fighter yet, but somebody who plays hockey and wrestles tends to know how to handle themselves.

Jack stood over his father, who was lying on the floor, in the throes of a heart attack. The minute and a half of excitement and exertion, plus the punch, had finished what a lifetime of bad living had led to.

When the cops and ambulance came, it was obvious what was up. Doreen was sitting on a plastic lawn chair in the kitchen, rocking back and forth and trying to hold her rye bottle with her broken arm. Jack told them the truth, and they believed him. One look at Doreen told them all they needed to know. He walked out of that house, he said, knowing that if he had any of that man's genes, which he obviously had, then he shouldn't be allowed to be near women. Jack had already figured out, in sports, that he had strength, but he also knew that he had a tendency to violence when provoked. He didn't want to lose control of himself. Ever.

Which is why it took me so long to get him to see me. But once he saw me fight, he said he knew that we were actually soul mates. He recognized things in me that he saw in himself. It was rare, he said, to find these qualities in women. He wanted to teach me to take care of myself, so that I would never, ever wind up anybody's victim.

We were happy, for a long time. We married when I was twenty-five, and my late twenties were for the most part, the happiest time of my life.

Jack started boxing and wrestling more seriously, and he took to it like, well, like I did to crack later. He was a few years older than me, and was finishing his Ph.D. in mathematics and his thesis involved the Computer Science department and had something to do with Artificial Intelligence. He won some big award in the department. I met a couple of his colleagues at school; happy, nerdy types. I liked them, but Jack and I were happy alone together. But they all told me that Jack was in for something big one day. "Very big," one guy said to me, one of Jack's mentors. "He has the capability to develop systems that change the world." Yeah, yeah, I thought. Those nerds with Asperger's – gotta love them, but they were always so hyped on their own intelligence.

But then Jack slowly started to change, in alarming ways. He started whispering to me in bed at night about a shadowy cult-like group who tracked his movements. At first, I was terrified, alarmed. He had worked on some super-secret stuff when he was doing his Ph.D., and up until now I had no reason to disbelieve anything Jack had to say, about anything. I became a little frightened, for both of us. I shredded everything that might have any of our details, and became much more aware of my surroundings when we were out. I even went online looking at spyware, trying to see what equipment was out there for people who might want to do Jack harm.

But then things changed.

If we were in a restaurant, he started to believe that people at the next table were taping our conversation, even when they had been seated having dinner before we arrived, and we hadn't planned on going to that restaurant. I began to see that his fears were delusional, that he was paranoid in a very frightening way. He would come home and tell me that somebody was following him. He developed extreme road rage when he was driving. It scared me. He scared me. Sometimes, if I tried to reason him out of his delusions, he would put his face nose-to-nose with mine and yell at the top of his voice, enumerating the details of his conspiracy theory. It was so frustrating for him if I didn't believe him that I tried to. I tried to see logic in his assertions. After all, he was so much smarter than I was, right? He was Jack. He was all-powerful.

Eventually, I took him to the hospital, when he agreed that something was wrong. He thought he was clinically depressed because he had taken to spending days in bed, unable to get up. The doctors diagnosed him with schizophrenia.

That's when our world collapsed. They put him on Haldol, an antipsychotic, plus Zoloft and Ativan. A dangerous mixture for him, as it turned out, and he became much worse. Bad enough that I was seriously concerned for my own safety, should he decide that I was the enemy. Then, through a year of trial and error, he was on lithium and Ativan, for when he got anxious.

Through all of this, we were both still fighting. For both of us, it released a lot of aggression. On other people. I wouldn't let him do any real fights, worried about the effects of his drugs and what he could do, or have done to him, but he sparred all the time and worked hours every day on developing his body. And so did I, but I found myself leaning toward defensive fighting. I didn't want to tap into my own rage; I had seen his. And I figured that if he kept going the way he was, I might need to defend myself against him one day.

Eventually, it all became too much. Some of the family came to visit, and Jack decided that Skipper's wife Marie – an elementary school teacher – worked for the CIA, and he banned her from the house. He wouldn't let me use the phone for days at a time. He would cry and beg me to help him, but he had stopped taking the lithium, and refused to go back on it. He had to be sharp, he said, when They came calling for him. He became obsessed with the cult or group that he believed were following him, some organization that bled people of their money and then bled them of their lives. Jack thought he was on their hit-list. He was sure of it. He changed our phone number to an unlisted one and insisted we move.

After one long, harrowing night, during which I saw that Jack was even starting to think that my calm attempts at reasoning with him made me the enemy, I packed up some things and moved in with a friend. He left me alone for a while, then called twenty, thirty times in a row, crying, begging me to come back. I did.

It took six months of this, before I was worn down enough to actually leave for good. Jack was in the process of getting rich quick in the meantime. Despite, or perhaps because of, what was going on in his head, he could sit at his computer and work for twenty hours writing code. Odd behaviour in geniuses has long been accepted, I learned. And the rate of this kind of mental illness is much higher in the higher-I.Q. brackets.

"At least I don't have to worry about getting it," I joked to Darren on the phone.

I didn't take much money from Jack in the separation, other than monthly support for a few years. His own lawyer thought that was crazy, with what Jack was worth by then. But taking away the only person in the world Jack trusted – myself – I couldn't take away his money too.

I spent the first six months crying. Then I dusted myself off and began my new life as a barfly, then addict. My new lifestyle consisted of doing vast quantities of drugs and watching movies for thirty-six hours at a stretch. I liked it. Nobody bothered me. And on crack, the only problem you have is finding more crack, and the money to buy it with. Makes life very, very simple. And after my years with Jack, simple was what I needed. Wanted.

Until now.

"And that, Dave – if that's even your real name – is what I know about Jack MacRae," I said. "I could tell you more personal things, but I don't think that would help."

"So he doesn't trust easily, or fall in love easily," Dave said, looking at me. He touched his nose gingerly. I could tell it wasn't broken, but it probably wasn't feeling so hot, either.

I shrugged. How could I answer that? How easily does anyone fall in love?

"Do you think he could be with Jeanette?" Dave asked. He looked distinctly uncomfortable, as though he hated asking personal questions. Odd, for a guy who did this for a living, and only hours ago had had a gun on me.

"I don't know," I said slowly. "I didn't even know about his foster family; he barely mentioned them. But if he's harming those boys in any way…" I looked out the window, looked at the clouds. "No. Jack loves those boys."

I was trying to make my voice normal. Thinking about Jack was one of the reasons I had started doing drugs in the first place. This wasn't helping.

"Do you think he could be a danger to others? I mean, outside a staged fight?" Dave asked.

I took a deep breath. "Yes," I said. "If confronted, he could be a wild animal."

"In my experience," I continued carefully, "Jack wanted people to be able to protect themselves. He was a huge righter of wrongs, in his book." I paused for a second, then looked at Dave. "But I haven't seen him in nearly three years. I don't know what's happened to his brain. I don't know what kind of drug cocktails they've got him on now, or if he's running around without any meds."

"What about the boys, Danny? If he has the boys?"

"Children fall under Jack's wing of protection. If he has them, which I doubt, but if he does, then they are absolutely safe."

"But if he believes that we are the enemy coming to get the kids?"

"Then watch out us," I answered. We sat in silence for a minute, thinking about this.

"Is he proficient with firearms?" Dave asked.

"He wasn't when I knew him," I answered. "But again…"

"Yeah. Three years."

"Well," Dave said, "I know you can still fight."

"That was one thing. Lola was a sitting duck," I said.

"A sitting duck who was very quickly reaching for a gun," Dave said. "And what about me? I had a gun on you one minute, and the next?" He pointed at his face.

"I can probably still handle myself okay," I said slowly. "But I haven't trained in years now. I don't have muscle left, or speed, not really. And against Jack?" I waved my hand.

"Unless he trusts you again," Dave said.

"And if he doesn't, you had better give me that gun and some refresher lessons. Or you are going to have another dead Cleary on your hands."

I got up to go to the washroom and do a couple of lines of coke, which was now nearly gone. When I got back to my seat I looked out the windows, and watched the lights of Toronto as we approached landing.

18

The plane landed at the small airport on Toronto Island. A quick ferry ride to downtown Toronto, where another car would be waiting to take us to my apartment. No waiting for luggage, no lineups for customs. It was clearly the only way to fly.

Note to self: buy a private plane.

Neither Dave nor I had any bags. Or any jackets, for that matter. I was still in the sleeveless sundress I had bought in Palm Springs early in the day, what seemed like weeks ago, and Dave in his thin white t-shirt and jeans. I wanted to brush my teeth so badly it was nearly crowding out grief and crack cravings, and I knew I needed a bit of sleep before hunting for Jack and Jeanette. I only had my purse, and I only noticed Dave had a wallet when he checked it on the ferry back to the terminal at the foot of Bathurst Street.

"You're going to need clothes," I said. Gene had a few things at my place, and he and Dave were of a similar size, but I wasn't sure I was quite forgiving enough to be offering him clothes. And it was cold in Toronto, but not bitter cold. Just regular, brisk autumn cold, the kind that makes you want to hug your jacket around yourself as you rush down the street. The kind of evening where you break out the gloves. Dave and I stood in line for a taxi, shivering, but it wasn't long until we were sailing up Avenue Road towards my apartment. As we cruised through the quiet neighborhoods on the way to mine, there were leaves that had blown into the street, all set now and turning into mulch.

I loved it. I was not cut out for unrelenting sunshine. In this weather, I thought, I could make my brain work better. I could find the boys. I would find the boys.

And I would stay away from D-Man and Gene until they were safe. After that, all bets were off.

Dave and I had agreed that he would come to my apartment with me and check if it was safe. If it was bugged. If there were sufficient deadbolts. That Jeanette wasn't hiding in a closet with a Glock. Then he would repair back down the road to Yorkville and check into one of the pricey hotels on Fred's dime, give the concierge a credit card and his sizes to get him some clothes, and we'd start fresh in the morning.

All the way up Avenue Road I was thinking about Gene. I hadn't had a chance to warn him we were coming. I didn't know if he was at my place, but I kind of doubted it. He usually didn't stay there more than a day or two, so he'd probably gone back to his place by now to sleep it off. I hoped. I hoped he wasn't still sitting on my couch watching the game show channel, taking hits from the pipe. For one thing, I didn't want him to be surprised in the middle of a perfectly good high by me walking in with a stranger in summer clothes.

I was feeling strong and the goal of getting my nephews back was keeping me that way. But the fact of a rock of crack sitting directly in front of me with a pipe and lighter at the ready would be a test I knew I would fail.

I had the cab drop us off at the side door, jabbering away about how my place might be a mess, that's the way I'd left it, and warning him that my friend might be there. I didn't give a shit if Dave was appalled by my living conditions or not, but apologizing for a messy place is hardwired in.

We exited the elevator at the fifth floor, and Dave walked ahead of me. His hand was behind him, resting lightly on the grip of the gun in the back of his jeans. Somehow I hadn't noticed it. A t-shirt and jeans, and I hadn't noticed a gun, and obviously no one else had either, or there would have been cops everywhere in the cab line-up at the ferry terminal. Either way, I was glad to see it. The hallway was hushed and empty, and I fumbled with my keys and opened the door.

The living room was neat, tidy, and empty. I exhaled. Gene had cleaned up, a rare feat for him. Bathroom, the same. The bedroom door was closed. Dave opened it with one motion, his gun drawn.

Gene was tied to the bed. Something was stuffed into his mouth, and his face didn't look much like a face anymore.

I pushed past Dave, who tried to restrain me. He settled for checking the closet and under the bed.

Gene had been beaten past all recognition. I took the gag out of his mouth, and his mouth just stayed open, limply. His eyes were closed, and I checked for a pulse. I was pretty sure I could feel one.

"He's alive," I said. "Call an ambulance." Dave grabbed the phone beside the bed and dialed 911, while I held Gene's hand. Dave pushed me away and took over, clearing Gene's airway and talking loudly to him. He pulled his shirt up and examined him for other injuries. His chest was dark red and purple, and his skinny torso looked slightly misshapen on one side.

"Broken ribs," Dave said. "I don't know what kind of internal injuries he might have." He felt again for Gene's pulse. Then felt again, more intently.

"It's gone," he said. He leaned over Gene, tilted his head back, and gave him CPR. I could hear the ambulances speeding up Avenue, their sirens wailing. I counted every time Dave pushed with his interlaced palms over Gene's sternum, then breathed into his mouth. I prayed he knew what he was doing.

I buzzed the paramedics in and ran down the hall to the elevator to wait for them. Within minutes, they had Gene on a stretcher. He was breathing on his own, but wasn't conscious.

Dave flashed some kind of badge at one of the EMTs as we were rushing back towards the elevators, and I heard them say that they were taking him to Toronto General. Dave said he'd meet me there, and I just nodded.

My brain registered the badge and filed it away for use later.

The paramedics hooked Gene up to an IV drip in the ambulance, and I held his hand as we sped back down Avenue Road to one of the hospitals on University. We pulled into Toronto General. One of the paramedics gently turned Gene and found his wallet in his jeans pocket and tossed it to me. "Hang on to that for him," he said. "We'll need his information." I ran behind the stretcher as they took him down the hall for examination and testing, but they wouldn't let me go into the room. Dave found me, and led me to chairs in the hallway outside where they were working on Gene.

"Jack?" he said to me.

I shook my head. "He could do the beating. But he wouldn't tie anybody up first."

Dave actually took my hand, gently. "Danny. If Jack is as sick as we think he is, we don't know what he would do anymore." I nodded. Dave went and got me a coffee. I was so, so tired all of a sudden.

"Thanks for helping Gene," I said, staring into my paper cup. Dave shrugged. I waited for someone to come and tell me something.

Gene was the most gentle person I had ever met. Kind, funny, and fucked-up, he had never intentionally hurt a soul in his life. But he didn't really have the skills to live in a harsh world.

"I don't trust you," I said. I thought about the badge, and for some reason kept it to myself for now.

"I know."

"But you saved his life, maybe."

"You're welcome," Dave said. We sat in silence. Finally, a doctor came out of the room.

"You here for this man?" he said, indicating behind him.

"Eugene Gold," I said. "Yes."

"Your husband?"

"No," I answered. "My friend."

"He's lucky to be alive," the doctor said, sitting me down on the bench and ignoring Dave. "He has three broken ribs, and most of the bones in his face are broken."

Oh God. I wanted to be sick.

"But the most dangerous thing is the damage to his liver and spleen. He is having a hard time breathing on his own, so we had to put him on a respirator. We're taking him for x-rays now, and CT scans," the doc continued.

The doctor patted my hand. "We have a plastic surgeon on staff. If there are no internal injuries that we have to see to first, he'll take a look at your friend and see what we can do about putting him back together." He paused. "Do you know who did this?"

"No," I said. "I just found him like this. I just got back from California tonight." The doc shook his head and started moving away from us.

"Oh! Doctor," I said, rushing towards him. "You should know. He's an addict. Crack cocaine. In case you need to know."

He nodded. "Stick around. The police will want to talk to you."

Dave and I took turns sleeping on uncomfortable banks of chairs in a patients' lounge. I paced and searched through Gene's wallet, trying to find his mother's phone number. I had never met her, but I knew she lived in the wilds of Northern Ontario someplace. His father was dead, and he had no brothers and sisters.

"I can't find anything," I said to Dave. "Other than me, his mother is all he has. And I don't know how to find her. I don't know her last name; she's remarried." I put my head in my hands. I felt the bump on the back of my skull. It was still tender. I winced.

"Sorry about that," Dave said. I looked at him.

"You did this?"

"Yes," he admitted. "I came in through a window. We needed to find out more about Ginger, about where she'd been, and with whom."

"And I walked into the bathroom, and you had to jump into the shower," I said.

"I heard you coming down the hall, but it was my only choice. Actually," he said, "I thought you might be Jeanette Vasquez for a minute. That's her last name, by the way. Jeanette Vasquez. From the back, you look remarkably alike." Great, I thought. I look like a sociopath. "But either way, I had to get out of there without anyone seeing me. I didn't do too much damage, did I?"

"No," I said. "You're a wily little fucker, you know that?"

"Yeah," he answered. "I know."

When the police found us in the waiting room, I told them that I was being escorted home from my sister's funeral, and came home to find Gene on the bed. No, he didn't have any enemies that I knew of. No, I didn't either.

I crossed my fingers for that one.

Knowing they would hear it from the medical team, I told them that Gene was an addict, and that I had been one too. I said I was clean, but that Gene probably wasn't. I intimated that it might have had something to do with a drug deal gone wrong.

"I don't know who he buys from," I said. I crossed my toes this time. "He doesn't sell it, it's just for his own use. If somebody beat him up over it, it's because he owed them money or something. But I don't know who." I still felt like I should protect D-Man, because I knew he was in no way capable of this.

Dave was silent during all of this. One of the cops asked him who he was.

"Can I talk to you over here?" he said to the older cop. They moved across the room, and I saw Dave flash his badge at the guy. I heard him say something about being a friend of the family, and that I'd been cleaning up my act. I didn't deal with the dealers anymore. He gave his word that we would cooperate with any investigation, and assured the cop that I had been in his presence for the last three days. No phone calls had been made to Toronto, to any dealers or otherwise, he said.

The older cop nodded. They probably didn't care much anyway. Another junkie beaten up over drugs. A day in the life.

The police left, and Dave returned and sat back down.

"Thanks," I said.

"Don't worry, Danny," Dave said, looking straight ahead. "We'll find them."

"I might have to kill her," I said. "Jeanette. You going to give me a problem with that?"

"I'm not so quick sometimes," Dave said. "I miss a lot." Not so quick, my ass. I hoped that if push came to shove, Dave would be in my corner.

I nodded and closed my eyes again. "You going to show me your badge?" I said.

"Which one would you like to see?" Dave said. "I've got about eight I think. No, nine." He sounded sort of amused. I snorted. It really didn't matter who he was, as long as he was going to help me get the boys back. If he was, in fact, law enforcement of some kind – which I thought unlikely; he was way too good – and he wanted to arrest me when this was all over, he could give it his best shot.

I think I slept for a while. I had a hospital blanket over me when somebody shook my knee. Dave nodded at the door.

The same doctor we'd talked to earlier came into the lounge. He sat down as though his knees were bothering him. There was blood on his scrubs that hadn't been there before.

"We have to remove his spleen," the doctor said. "It's ruptured. There's a great deal of internal bleeding. Your friend is in surgery now. Dealing with his face will have to wait, I'm afraid."

"Is he going to live?" I asked.

"We hope so," the doctor said. "He's got good people in there. But you should go home and rest. Come back tomorrow. He'll be out for a long while." And with that he patted my hand again, and left the room.

I put my head between my knees. I was pretty sure I was going to have one of my fits. I could feel Dave's presence beside me, and I was glad he was there. But I wanted Darren. Or Ginger. I gulped in air, and tried not to cry, because breathing unsteadily like that would surely make me faint.

"Danny. Breathe." I could hear Dave's voice like it was a long way away. I breathed.

When my head cleared, I sat up slowly. "I need sleep," I said.

"Yes," Dave agreed.

"Then tomorrow morning we're coming back here."

"Okay," Dave said.

"After that, you're going to give me a refresher lesson in shooting."

"Yes."

"We're going to get the boys back. And then I'm going to kill her."

"And if Jack is somehow involved?" Dave said quietly.

"He's not," I said, but my heart skipped a beat.

19

When we got back to my apartment, I didn't want to look in the bedroom again. I knew my sheets had blood on them. Gene's blood.

"I'm sorry," I said to Dave. "I'm taking the couch. I need sleep. I can't..." I waved my hand at the bedroom. "Clean sheets are in that closet," I said, pointing at the hallway. "There's a spare toothbrush in the medicine cabinet, and..."

"Danny. Go to sleep," Dave said. "I'll stay awake for a while and make sure you're okay, then I'll catch a few hours." He double-checked the door and locked the windows, even though I was on the fifth floor. He closed the blinds, and put my desk chair up against the door, in case anyone managed to break in while we were sleeping.

"At least we'll wake up," he said. He smiled.

"Isn't it preferable to die in your sleep?" I said, making myself comfortable on the couch. I didn't even remove my clothes.

"It's preferable not to die," Dave corrected me.

"Good point," I said. I spent half a minute thinking about Miller. I wished he was here with us. And that's the last I knew until morning.

* * *

I woke to the smell of coffee brewing. And eggs frying, with onions. I sat up.

"Hi," I said. Dave was wearing one of my aprons. Well, my only apron. Jack had bought it for me during our first year of marriage, when I decided to teach myself how to cook. It didn't go quite as well as the fighting had, but I could put together a mean protein shake.

I sat on the couch, waking up. Dave brought me coffee and eggs, all of which I consumed without a word.

"Gene made it through surgery," Dave said, shovelling eggs into his face. For such a skinny little guy, he sure enjoyed his food.

"Really? You called?"

He nodded. "An hour ago. He's in recovery. We can see him later today."

"Oh thank God," I said. "Thank you," I said to Dave. He nodded and returned to his eggs. I finished eating, and put my feet on the coffee table and lit a cigarette. Dave looked disapproving.

"Hey, it's my apartment," I said.

"I know. But you're supposed to be in training," he said.

"I've always smoked," I said. "Even when I was fighting." I took a defiant drag, which of course had to be one that made me cough. Dave grinned.

"Fuck off," I said. But in a friendly way.

Dave looked at his watch. "I'm going to have a shower," he said.

"Clean towels in the cupboard in the bathroom," I said, not moving. I was glad to be home. Dave nodded, and a minute later,

I heard the shower. I luxuriated on my couch for a minute. My books were here. My clothes. My things. And Gene was going to be all right. Well, maybe not all right, but he would live. I felt it. And the twins were in Toronto, and I would find them.

But Ginger was still dead.

I got up and went to my computer to see if Darren had sent an update. I clicked my mouse to remove my screensaver, and what was waiting for me on the screen made me stop breathing.

A photo of Matty and Luke sitting on a gray cement floor. No restraints that I could see. A large window in the background, but I couldn't see anything behind it, no buildings. The boys looked like they were trying to smile. Luke looked like he'd been crying. There was no message, no words. I didn't want to click on the image anywhere, in case it disappeared.

I stared at the picture, touching the screen. Ginger's boys.

When I heard the shower stop, I yelled for Dave. He came out with a towel around his waist, his gun in his hand.

We looked at the screen. The boys looked so grown up now. The last time I'd seen them was three years ago.

I tried to focus, take my eyes off the boys and look for anything around them that might hint at where they might be. I was pretty sure the photo had been taken in Toronto – the phone call hinted that the boys were here, and the sky outside the window was gray. Southern California hadn't seen a sky like that since they went missing. The window behind them was large, square at the bottom and oval at the top. It looked like it reached from almost the floor, to well above where the picture ended. It must be a warehouse, or a loft. Some kind of downtown studio space, maybe?

"Danny," Dave said slowly. "It's time to call Jack."

I nodded. It was.

I made Dave stay in the living room while I made the call from my bedroom. I told him not to bother picking up the phone to listen in – Jack's instincts were infallible, and he would know if someone was listening. Besides, Fred trusted that I wanted the kids to be safe, almost as much as he did.

Dave said Jack was staying at the Four Seasons, but I decided to try his house in Bermuda first. I didn't need to look at my address book. Somehow, even though I never called Jack, I had his numbers firmly lodged in my brain. I called his home first, hoping against hope that he was there and not mixed up in any of this. A woman answered on the first ring. By the sound of her accent, a Bermudian woman.

"Can I speak to Jack, please," I said.

"Not here," she said, as though she had better things to do.

"Can you tell me if he is at his office?" I asked politely.

There was a pause. "Who is this, please," the woman said.

"It's his ex-wife," I answered. No point in beating around the bush.

"He is not with you?" the woman answered. My heart skipped a beat.

"No," I answered. "I'm in Toronto. I need to speak with him."

"He flew to Toronto, missus," she said. "If you talking to him, you tell him Irene's mother is sick? I need to be going home."

"I'll tell him, Irene," I said. "But I haven't heard from him. Do you know where he's staying?" I held my breath.

"Hotel," Irene answered. "Sometimes at the Four Seasons Hotel up there." She sounded distracted.

"Thanks, Irene. I hope your mother is okay," I said.

"You and me and God," she said. "Bye, missus." And she hung up.

The second I disconnected, Dave was back in the living room. He handed me a gun.

"Here," he said. "You have ten minutes. I'm going to teach you how to use this thing."

Dave gave me the idiot's guide to the Sig P220 38. Obviously I didn't get to actually shoot it in my tiny apartment but Dave made sure I knew how to use it. Hopefully I wouldn't have to.

"It's big," I said. I tried to make it feel comfortable in my hand, make it feel like an extension of my arm.

"It's not the smallest," Dave agreed. "But it'll fit in a purse easily."

I changed clothes to go find Jack. I rifled through my closet and found a pair of indigo denim jeans that he loved. I hadn't worn them in a long time, and while they were big on me now, I had put on a couple of pounds in the last days. I pulled on a pair of black leather motorcycle boots and a black turtleneck. And a black leather jacket, to complete the look. I even put on makeup, some eyeliner and mascara, and pale lip gloss. Very early sixties, Emma Peel-*Avengers*. I fluffed up my hair, and wondered whether to stick the blonde wig on. My hands were shaking, but I wasn't scared. I was just nervous to see Jack.

I would always love him. I knew that the day I left him, and I knew it would never go away. I also knew that love didn't solve everything.

And if Jack had anything at all to do with Jeanette kidnapping the boys – or God forbid, what had happened to Ginger – I knew that I wouldn't hesitate. I would do what I had to do.

"Wow," Dave said. "You look great." Somehow, the way he said it, I knew he was gay. Which was perhaps why I felt so comfortable with him.

"Thanks," I said quietly. Dave went back to staring at the computer screen, at the boys.

He gave me a cell phone. "I'm going to stay here," he said. "Call me as soon as you can. No matter what." He looked me in the eye. "Danny. Keep the objective in mind."

"Get the boys back," I said.

"Get the boys back," Dave repeated. "And don't get killed in the process." Impulsively, I kissed Dave's cheek.

"Thanks again for Gene," I whispered into his ear.

Dave hugged me, and I let him. "Call me," he said, and I left.

20

I love hotels. I always have. Long before I had any money, I chose to drink in hotel bars. There's always something about them, some impermanence that has always appealed to me. Jack felt the same way, and sometimes we'd just walk down to the Park Plaza, before it morphed into a Hyatt, or here, to the Four Seasons. Sometimes we'd get drunk enough to get a room.

And sometimes we'd go to a hotel because Jack thought our apartment was being bugged.

I managed to hail a cab on Avenue Road and went to the Four Seasons. Standing in the lobby and failing any other brilliant idea, I went to the front desk, and asked for Jack MacRae's room. The chipper young blonde behind the desk was ecstatic when she found him in her computer. "Shall I ring up to the room for you?" she said. She conveyed the impression that nothing else would give her greater pleasure.

"That's okay," I said. "I'll just run up to the room and surprise him."

Cindy behind the desk looked sad. "I'm so sorry," she said. "We can't give out room numbers without our guests' permission." I nodded. Of course.

"Then please ring him for me," I said. I patted my bag, making sure the gun was in there. And the knife. I was petrified, and excited. I hadn't seen Jack in nearly three years. "Tell him it's Danny."

"Thank you!" Cindy said, as though I'd done her a great favor. I wondered what drugs she was on, and whether I could get some. She hit a few buttons and was obviously listening to ringing on the other end, through her headset. "I'm sorry," she said. "Mr. MacRae seems to be unavailable. Would you like to leave a message?"

"No," I said quickly. "I'll just… wait." I wandered away from the desk, after Cindy implored me to have a great day, and to let her know if I wanted her to try again for me. I decided that a cocktail was in order. Jack might be all day, doing business or doing Jeanette Vasquez. One drink would loosen me up.

That, and a quick bump of cocaine in the ladies' room.

I went into one of the Four Seasons' lounges, which, despite being the more casual, less expensive dining option, was more expensive than anywhere I'd frequented in a couple of years. I sat at a table for four, and watched the power brokers do their power brokering over low-fat bison burgers. I ordered a glass of Sauvignon Blanc and perused the menu. I was surprised that I had an appetite, after the eggs earlier. I was considering the bison burger myself when I realised someone was standing over me.

"Danny," Jack said.

He looked like a million bucks. He wore a black suit with an open-collared white shirt. He always did have trouble with ties. He looked like he had just shaved.

I stood up and hugged him tight. "Hi," I whispered. That's

242

me, always knowing what to say in difficult situations.

Jack hugged me back. We stood there long enough to block the waitress's path, and to make a few people around us turn to look. This Jack didn't look like he belonged with a chick in jeans and motorcycle boots. We broke apart, finally, and I indicated that he should sit down. The waitress appeared with my wine, and Jack ordered club soda.

"On the wagon," he said. "Figured out booze and meds didn't go so well together."

"Oh," I said. He seemed fine. Coherent, affable, calm. Nary a twitch nor a darting of the eyes to be seen. He wasn't drumming the table with his fingers or shifting around in his seat. "You look good, Jack."

"Thanks," he said easily. He looked at me. "Wish I could say the same, Danny."

"Ouch," I said.

"You'll always be the most beautiful woman in any room," he said gently. He shut his mouth and shook his head, looking at the table. He was always emotional. I loved that in a tough guy. We sat in silence for a few minutes, during which time I stared out the window onto Yorkdale Avenue, trying not to cry. The waitress brought Jack's club soda, and was about to ask us if we wanted to order food, until she saw the look of us. She skedaddled.

"Where are the boys, Jack?" I said, after downing nearly half my glass of wine in one gulp.

Jack shook his head.

"So you do know," I said. I had an urge to slap his face, as hard as I could. But I knew better.

"I might," Jack said. He rubbed his head, which he still kept shaved. "That's why I'm here. In Toronto." He looked at me, tearing again. "I'm so sorry about Ginger."

I looked at him. I couldn't speak.

"You don't…" he began. He stared at me. "You think I had something to do with killing her."

I started with the tears again. I was embarrassed, and waited to get myself together to speak.

He plopped the menu back on the table in an impatient gesture I knew well. My tears seemed to make him angry. "I could never have hurt Ginger," he said. "You know that."

And I did. For a minute I felt such shame at thinking that Jack could ever hurt my family.

"But, Danny, this is all my fault. All of it. If it weren't for me, none of you would be on their radar. They're after me, now. I need to make them think I'm with them, if we want to get Matt and Luke back."

I took a deep breath and held it for a minute. The waitress hurried over, ready to take our order. We were more interesting than the business people around us, I could tell. She probably had a bet with the bartender about what was going on here. I shook my head at her and gestured to the menu, indicating that we weren't ready to order.

If Jack didn't seem so otherwise calm, and if the world of the Clearys hadn't been brutally turned upside down in the last week, I would have thought this was just more of his disease-fuelled paranoia. Even as it was, I couldn't be sure it wasn't.

"Who is?" I said. "Jeanette? Who else?"

Jack took a fast gulp of water. "Not sure. Probably Lola – she grew up in the house with us. Little woman, Ecuadorian…"

"Yeah," I said. "Met her." And broke a couple of her bones. But we'd get to that.

And then I realized what he'd said. "Grew up in the house with her?" I had to remind myself to breathe. In and out, and repeat.

"Yes," he said.

"Wait… what? What the fuck is going on?"

"Danny," he said. "I told you I grew up in foster care."

"With Lola?" What? I put my hand on my chest to try to calm my heartbeat. Breathe.

"Why haven't you told me this before? I always wanted to know about your childhood." I wondered briefly, panicked, if this was Jack's madness again. He seemed so sane, but I hadn't seen him in so long.

Jack looked at me. "Danny, this is… evil, I'm about to tell you about. I wasn't going to bring that to you. To have you thinking about this, worrying about this. And some of it… is going to make you sick. You would have left me," he said simply.

I took a deep breath. "I'm all ears," I said. I motioned for the waitress, and ordered a bottle of wine for myself. "Start."

He was five, Jack explained, when the state had removed him from Mitchell and Doreen Harper's house. Jack had started school that year, and while Doreen made an effort in September to keep her son clean and fed and to school on time, by the beginning of October this had all but vanished. Jack would walk the two miles to school because at even that early age he had learned to be embarrassed about where he lived, by the rusty cars out front and the broken windows covered with boards and plastic sheeting. Jack's new school clothes never got washed more than a couple of times, and it didn't take long for the school principal to notice how the child never brought a lunch to school, and instead sat outside alone while the other kids traded sandwiches. It didn't take long for Jack to be removed from his parents; while the wheels of bureaucracy can move slowly, the fact that neither of Jack's parents seemed able to meet the most basic requirements imposed by the state of Maine meant that within a matter of weeks, Jack was living at The Orchard.

Jack thought he had died and gone to heaven, he said. He shared a large bedroom with three other boys, sleeping on a comfortable top bunk where he could look out the window at the stars every night. One of the older boys helped Jack with reading, and his foster mother sat at the head of the table every night while everyone held hands before their meal, saying grace. If one of the kids couldn't help giggling or scuffling, they weren't punished with anything more than a kindly frown. There were chickens to feed and a couple of friendly mutts, and even three horses. Jack thrived on the healthy food and open air, and company of other children who had also come from difficult beginnings.

"I didn't have to be ashamed," he said. I was drinking wine and we hadn't ordered food yet. I couldn't take my eyes off Jack while he was speaking. I was trying to take it all in so intensely it almost felt like I was hearing with my eyes as well as my ears. "I went to school in clean clothes. I got plenty of food. And Corinne, my foster mother? She was – well she was great. She wasn't overly effusive or huggy or anything, but there was never a moment with her when I didn't know she cared about me. A lot. About all of us." Jack grabbed a piece of focaccia from the bread basket and tore it into little pieces. "You know what, Danny? You know what we did together, as a family?" He laughed. "We played board games. Every Friday night we played Monopoly or Clue or Operation. We always had two or three different games set up and Corinne popped popcorn, and all you could hear was kids laughing."

Tears welled up in his eyes, and in mine. The things I had taken for granted in the Cleary household. I cleared my throat.

"What about Corinne's husband?" I asked. "Did she have one?"

"Michael," Jack said. "He was great, too, back then. He travelled a lot for work though. At least in the first few years I was there, he was only home for one week a month. But when he was there, it was different. Still good, but different." I grabbed a piece of bread and looked for the waitress. I wanted so badly to hear all this, but I could feel my stomach starting to make noise.

And I knew that something very bad was coming. Not only because Jack was somehow mixed up with Jeanette and Lola, but because he had never told me this before. Something very, very bad must have happened to him.

"He was a giant figure, you know? I mean, he was a fairly big man, tall and strong, but it was more his – I don't know, his aura, I guess. At dinner, he would just talk about what he'd seen on the road, and the people he'd met, and he'd talk about his theories of... well everything, I guess."

"He had a captive audience, huh," I said.

Jack smiled, and it seemed the waitress was at our side in a second. Jack ordered us each a rare steak, which both pissed me off and pleased me. I had actually decided on the rare steak, but I hated the presumption. But I didn't want to interrupt his flow, so for once I kept my mouth shut.

"Danny," Jack said, when the waitress fluttered away, "that's pretty much it. He had something that people wanted to listen to. He would sit in the evening and rail against the government, and taxes, and how we all had to stand up for ourselves, to own our voice.

"Corinne was a tough nut, but when Michael was around, she was pretty much obedient. He wasn't violent, but there was just something about him. He didn't much like Corinne's religious leanings, for example. When he was around, there was no grace at the table. That kind of thing.

"A lot of kids in foster care, they eventually get returned to their families, for whatever reason. That happened in our house sometimes. Sometimes, if one of the kids was especially mouthy or, I don't know, didn't fall under Michael's spell? He would return them to the system. It's easy to do. He and Corinne seemed to have a great relationship with the caseworkers who came to visit, and why not. I mean, those of us who were there were obviously going great. Academic achievement was important to them, but it wasn't the only thing. Michael always stressed finding what we were good at, no matter what it was, and being the absolute best at that one thing."

I listened, paying as much attention as I could, while a dominant part of my brain was occupied solely on how much I missed Jack. Wanted to touch him. Was relieved that he wasn't a bad guy.

"Then Corinne got sick. I was twelve. She died."

"Oh God," I said. "Baby, I'm so sorry."

He shook his head and looked around for the waitress, and

when she scuttled over Jack, after a pause, ordered a Diet Coke.

"Cancer. Anyway. After that, everything changed. Everything. Michael stayed home with us and barricaded himself in his room for days at a time, getting one of the girls to bring him in food. And…" He shook his head.

"And…?" I asked. I dreaded hearing what he might say.

"Jeanette was his favorite. She was just turning twelve when Corinne died. I remember that, 'cause we didn't wind up celebrating her birthday. I think – well I know, Danny, I mean I know – that he was messing with her."

"Oh shit." Fuck. Why did stories always end like that? What was wrong with people?

"I mean, when Corinne was around, everything was so – I don't know, innocent I guess. But it's like Michael lost it. He started talking about The Family like we were something really, really special. And he was the head of it, you know? We all owed him our lives, as far as he was concerned. And I mean, for most of us, we really kind of did."

"No, you didn't," I said. "You could have wound up somewhere else, somewhere better."

Jack shook his head. "No. I had a lot of amazing years there. The best years of my life. Until I met you," he added, seeing the look on my face. "But then he started treating us like acolytes, and the girls were like his own little harem. Corinne would have just – well she would have died before anything like that would have happened. And Lola, Jeanette's best friend in the house, her little puppy dog – well Michael didn't really like Lola, but he was so into Jeanette that he *allowed* Lola to do things for him." Jack shook his head at the memory.

"Oh my God," I said.

"Yeah." He folded his hands on the table. I could tell he was trying hard not to fidget. "Danny, I was turning thirteen when Corinne died and all this started to happen. I was a runt. I just kept my head down, listened, and didn't make waves. But, Danny – Jeanette was my sister. Sort of."

"Oh God," I said again.

"Jeanette thought Michael was God. I think that whatever he was doing to her, had been done much worse when she was very little. She really thought she was just his favorite – which she was – and it was like she was flattered by the attention. I didn't know what to think. I hadn't exactly come from the best role models myself. And Michael seemed to love us."

"Was he – did he stop working? What did he want? How did he support all of you?"

Jack shook his head. "At the beginning, I'm not really sure. I mean, I was a kid. I remember there was some life insurance or something, from Corinne. And then – well, it didn't take long before Michael started lecturing us about The Family, and everything we did had to be for the good of The Family, and if we worked together we could have anything and everything we ever dreamed of, and show the people who had abandoned us that we were a force to be reckoned with. Those of us over twelve had to start bringing money into the house. That was fine with me – I was always a little capitalist. I got a paper route."

I smiled. This, I remember him telling me.

"But the money had to go into the family pot. We were allowed to keep ten percent, like a reverse tithe. Danny, the thing is, while it sounds crazy, other than the Jeanette thing – which

I, for one, just tried to ignore – a lot of it worked. He gave self-esteem to a bunch of kids who had none. We cooked and cleaned together and we still played games on Friday nights."

"Sounds nice," I said. "That part, anyway." I couldn't get the image of a man who would have had to have been in his thirties at the time, taking a twelve-year-old girl into his bed.

"Eventually things got weirder, though. Michael set up a quota – any kid over twelve had to bring in a certain amount of money each week, and he didn't care how we got it. Stealing, whatever. Then he started a chocolate-bar scam – you know, kids wandering around shopping malls selling chocolate for a youth group or whatever? Well, every Saturday a few of us got dropped off at a different part of town and we had to pretend we were selling chocolate in support of our local 4-H club, or whatever he thought up that week."

Our steaks came, but I barely noticed.

"It was still fun. I mean Michael had a whole elaborate system of rewards for kids who brought the most money into The Family. He had a great sense of humor, though not about himself – he couldn't take a joke on himself, that's for sure."

"It sounds like he was building his own army of misfits," I said. I cut into my steak. Beautiful.

Jack talked about starting to realize, when he was fourteen and thick in the grip of adolescent hormones, that Michael was encouraging Jack to have sex with one of his "sisters." They weren't related by blood, Michael told them, so there wasn't anything wrong with it. Michael told Jack that it was a reward because Jack was bringing a significant amount of money into the house – he was tutoring students in math after school and on weekends, and of course he only kept his ten percent.

"One early evening I was in the stable, mucking out the stalls. Jeanette came in – I guess I would have been turning fifteen by this time, so Jeanette was fourteen – and without a word she pulled me away from what I was doing and…"

I put my fork down.

Jack didn't look at me. "Danny, I was a kid, a horny kid who had been told that this was normal. It was my first time, but of course Jeanette knew what she was doing." I thought I was going to be sick. I closed my eyes and counted to ten. I couldn't blame Jack, I couldn't. He was a kid, he didn't know any better.

"I'm sorry, Danny, I'm sorry, but you have to know this. This is key to what's going on right now."

"Yup," I said. "Keep going." I sipped my water. I needed my head to clear up a bit, or I was scared I would do or say something I would regret, and all I should be doing was focusing on getting the twins back.

Jack and Jeanette became obsessed with each other, like any other young couple in love. Jeanette would sneak out of Michael's room in the middle of the night and climb up to Jack's top bunk. There were fewer boys now, Jack told me, and the bottom bunk was empty. After six months or so, Michael took Jack aside and told him that this was okay – as long as Jack kept being a "strong member of The Family," things like ready access to whatever girl he wanted could be his. So Jack and Jeanette kept up their nighttime assignations, and things continued, as happily as they could.

"You've got to understand, Danny," Jack said. He finally took a bite of his steak. Blood was congealing on his plate, and I lost my appetite. "This was my normal. I didn't know any different, really. I mean, I went to school and everything, played baseball, all the normal things guys do. But we had no TV in our house, no visitors, no other family. Our moral code was Michael's."

I nodded. I tried to understand.

One day, however, Jeanette didn't crawl into Jack's bed, and not the next night either. When Jack saw Jeanette over breakfast the second morning, he saw that she had bruises on her throat, and she was quiet. When he tried to touch her, she jerked away and continued cooking bacon.

"I went to Michael right away. Michael said that physical violence was only called for against our enemies, never The Family. But Michael explained that Jeanette wasn't bringing in her fair share, that at her age – fifteen, at this point – she had to earn her tithe." Jack stopped, and laughed. I didn't like the sound of it. "Her tithe, can you imagine?

"Michael had set up dates, as he called them, for Jeanette. Pay dates. He was selling her. I guess on the second night, the man got too rough with her. Tried to choke her."

Jack's voice was low, and I had to lean in to hear.

"I skipped school that day, and Michael and I talked for hours. He told me that he had a dream of creating a sort of empire, a business model of multiple income streams. That's what he called us, by the way – income streams. He said he saw something in me, knew I was smart, a leader, and as he had raised me, he knew he could trust me. He said that for those of us who stayed loyal to The Family, you know – untold riches and success could be ours."

"Sounds more like the mafia than a cult," I said.

Jack smiled. "Sure. An even more twisted one, where you

bring in broken kids and train them up to follow." He pushed his plate away. I had never seen Jack leave a steak on his plate. "Anyway. That was the day that I knew that I would leave Michael, leave this place, and never look back. I would take Jeanette with me. I didn't tell Michael that, of course. After our talk, Michael decided that we had a piece of business to conduct."

I stayed still. I didn't know if I wanted to hear what this piece of business could be.

"Michael drove me out to the farm where Jeanette had been hurt the night before. Some rich rancher had died and left everything to his shit-bag son, and Michael said the son was blowing through his father's money so fast there would be nothing left in a year. Michael said the guy was actually doing drugs. Michael thought people who did drugs were the lowest strata of society. Bottom-feeders, he called them."

"And him a pedophile," I said. "Nice."

Jack continued. "I was full of rage. You know?"

I nodded. I knew.

"Michael pulled up this long, winding driveway. On the mailbox it said 'Heart's Content.' He named his fucking house Heart's Content. This almost made me want to kill him more than anything else. " I laughed. I couldn't help it. I knew the feeling – when you have hatred in your heart, anything can feed it.

"This skinny fucking idiot opened the door in his bathrobe, with a cocktail in his hand. It was early afternoon, just after lunch, and this guy didn't look like he'd been to bed yet."

I fiddled with my wine glass. Been there, done that.

"I didn't know how to control my temper yet. I just looked at this guy, just stared at him for a minute. I know he said something to me, but I have no idea what. Then before I knew what I was doing, I was pounding him down. Punching. Kicking. I remember the glass in his hand sort of smashed against the wall and I caught a piece of it on my forehead." Jack showed me the tiny scar that I'd noticed hundreds of times before and never bothered to ask about. He'd been a hockey player, after all.

"Then Michael was behind me. He stood there watching me, with his arms crossed, this – look on his face. Approval, I think. I'm still not sure."

Someone cleared our plates, but I barely noticed.

"When I was done, the guy was pulp. I mean, he was still breathing, but his face was nearly unrecognizable. My hands weren't much better." I looked at Jack's hands, which had touched me so gently. But I had also seen what else they could do.

"Then Michael kind of moved me aside and crouched down, whispered something in the guy's ear. I couldn't hear him. Besides, my blood was still up. I couldn't hear anything. Michael went into the kitchen, cool as anything, and came back with a bag of ice for my hands. Then he disappeared down the hallway. He was gone for minutes – I don't know, maybe five, ten minutes? When he came back, he was carrying a gym bag, swinging it from his hand like he was on his way to a racquetball game, not a care in the world." Jack stopped for a minute and shook his head. It was all I could do not to reach over and stroke it.

"Michael just stepped over the guy on his way out like the guy was a piece of dog shit on the ground, and he led me back out to the truck. He sort of threw the gym bag on my lap and when we were on the road he told me to open it." Jack ran his hand over his mouth, which seemed dry. "It was money, Danny.

Bundles of twenties and fifties. There was about a hundred and fifty grand in that bag. Sitting in that truck, it just hit me: Michael knew. Somehow, he knew what this guy would do to Jeanette, and he knew what I would have to do to the guy. He knew.

"Michael just laughed and laughed, driving home, like it was the best day of his life. Which it probably was. I remember saying something about the police – I mean, wouldn't the police be after me? Wouldn't the guy call the cops? And Michael assured me that it wasn't possible. It was all taken care of."

I drank my water and looked down. It was all becoming too, too clear.

"That was it, for me. That was the moment that I knew I was out. But I also knew that I couldn't let Michael know that. If I let him know that – well, I had a feeling I would end up worse off than that fucking miserable prick in his dead daddy's mansion ."

"How much longer were you there?" I asked quietly.

"Two more years," Jack answered. "I graduated early, got the scholarship, but didn't wind up going to that school. I had been planning for a while, you understand." He ordered a coffee. I shook my head. "I knew I was going to disappear. If Michael thought I was at Berkeley, I would always be there for him. I had my papers ready. I had saved up for nearly two years, for good fake papers."

"Oh." Somehow, I hadn't thought of that. Jack MacRae was not, of course, his real name.

"Scott," Jack said, half smiling at me. "Harper."

"Scott, huh," I said softly. "Nice to meet you."

"Scott is dead. He died twenty years ago. But – well, they found me. And you. And Ginger and Fred." Jack looked squarely at me.

"Right," I said. "Right."

21

Jack and I sat and talked for another hour or so. How he had gone to school in the Midwest under the name Jack MacRae.

"How did you pick it?" I asked. I smiled at him, trying to see a Scott Harper in there.

"When I was very little, I remember Doreen saying her mother was Scottish," Jack said. He smiled. "And I just always liked the name Jack."

"Me too," I said, and realized I was whispering. Jack grabbed my hand.

"Danny, you have to hear the rest of this," he said. "All of it." I nodded.

Jack had gone through his young adulthood as happily as he could. He worked hard. He had girlfriends here and there, but the messed-up nature of his earliest relationship haunted him. He left the States and took a job in Toronto. He had what he called "flashbacks," periods of paranoia that Michael and the others had found him. He didn't trust anyone – until me. And Ginger, eventually, and Fred. But no matter how happy he was with me and my family, fear and paranoia were his constant companions. He told me he didn't remember things about some of our marriage, at least towards the end when he unplugged our phone unless it was absolutely necessary, and insisted that we keep the drapes closed, twenty-four hours a day.

Then after we'd split, Jack had really gone off the rails. Six months of calling me, thinking he was being followed daily, then in a moment of clarity, he said, he checked himself into a hospital.

"In the States," he said. "Good private hospital." I nodded. He could afford it.

He stayed there for three months, he said, during which time the psychiatrists had him on a pharmacological regimen that seemed to suit him. They said he wasn't schizophrenic, just severely bipolar, with paranoid delusions.

"Oh, is that all," I said.

When he got out, he continued working. Took the gig in Bermuda, then on Grand Cayman, then back to Bermuda. He didn't socialize, he said. Other than a few "paid companions" here and there, he kept to himself. Information I didn't need to know. It got lonely in Bermuda, he said. An island of 65,000 people, and the ex-pats and locals had a very strict divisive line. Ideal, in a way, for a loner like Jack, but at the same time, not anonymous enough. He said he didn't really talk to anyone during that time. Once or twice a year he'd phone a couple of his buddies from hockey back in Canada, but that was about it. "Fighting?" I asked. He nodded slightly.

"Just enough to keep my hand in," he said. "Getting old."

"Working out, though."

Jack smiled. "Of course." He took a swig from his glass. "Then," he said, "Ginger called."

He said she was lonely, that Fred was away all the time. She was concerned for him, she said. And wanted to talk about me.

"She knew, Danny," Jack said. "About the crack."

"I know," I said. "Jack. I'll never be able to shake this guilt."
He looked at me for a minute, and put his hand over mine.

"Danny," he said. "You're going to have to. You have responsibilities." I nodded. I wasn't sure what they were, but he was probably right.

"Continue," I said. I let his hand stay on mine, until he decided to move it.

Jack and Ginger talked on the phone once a week or so, for a few months. He was getting worried about her, sensing there was a lot she wasn't telling him about what was going on in California. She would never talk about Fred, but she talked about the boys a lot.

"Did you know Matty came first in his class last year?" Jack said. "He's a smart kid."

"No," I said. "I didn't know." There was so much I didn't know. A fresh wave of guilt washed over me, and made me nauseous.

"Don't throw up, Danny," Jack said. He knew me well enough. "Stay calm."

"I'm fine," I said. I took a sip of his soda, and nodded for him to go ahead.

Jack decided to go to California and see Ginger and Fred and the boys. Take a holiday from the islands and see what life was like in the real world. When he got there, he said, he knew something was wrong. This was not the Fred he knew when we were married. He was paranoid, angry, never home.

And Jeanette was living there. As the nanny.

Jack shook his head. "The second I saw her, Danny..."

Jack stopped. "It was as though the world had ended, for the second time."

I didn't know whether the first was when he left The Family, or when I had left him. I didn't think I wanted to know.

"At first, I didn't know how to play it," Jack said. "When I was finally able to get Jeanette alone – and she did a lot to prevent that – she pretended she didn't know who I was, that she had never seen me before. She pretended so well, and it had been so many years…"

"You almost believed her," I said.

Jack nodded. "Well, not really, of course. But my head…"

"Yeah," I said. "I know."

"Ginger and Jeanette were thick as thieves," Jack said. "Did everything together. Ginger told me she never wanted to hire a nanny, wanted to take care of her own kids, but Fred insisted."

"So I gather," I said. A fresh wave of anger at Fred made me close my eyes.

"But once Jeanette was there? Ginger loved her. They had fun. And I couldn't figure out what the game was. I mean, Jeanette seemed to really love the boys, and I knew Ginger loved having her there. And… well, I liked seeing her too," Jack said. He looked at me. "You left me."

"Oh my God, Jack," I started to say, but he stopped me.

"Danny, I'm sorry. I understand. I shouldn't have said that. It was just – I was vulnerable."

I didn't want to hear this. I had to hear this.

"She told me that she'd stayed with Michael for five years after I left, but things were never the same. And she knew Michael wouldn't let her leave of her own accord, so she started saving her bits of money until she could get far away."

Despite my hatred for the woman, I shivered. I could imagine what she had had to do to earn that money.

"We had a little thing again," Jack was saying. "I was lonely. It was nothing." Jack looked at his hands and squeezed them together until the knuckles went white. It had been a long time since I had seen that gesture. "Ginger never knew. Or – oh God, I think she didn't. I hope Jeanette never told her. It was just brief. But, Danny, Ginger told me that Jeanette had been recommended by a friend of theirs, of hers and Fred's. It was a fluke, as far as I knew. I mean, how could it not be? Jeanette never saw a picture of me around the house either, and said she had no idea of my connection to the family."

"And you believed her?" I put my glass down. I needed crack. I couldn't deal with this. "The one time you choose to put your paranoia aside."

"Ginger's not much for pictures," Jack continued. "I mean, you and I had been split for a while. How could she know about your sister? I thought that was too paranoid, even for me." He rubbed his hand over his face. "Obviously I was wrong," he said.

Pure bloodlust. That's what I realized I was feeling. I wanted so badly to hurt this woman, to give her a small taste of what she had done to the people I loved. And I wasn't feeling quite as warm towards Jack – or Scott – now either. How could he believe that woman?

"What about the drugs," I wanted to know.

"I don't think they were doing drugs yet," Jack said. "I mean, Ginger knew you were. She talked to me about how worried she was, how you wouldn't let her fly out and visit you. But Ginger still looked like Ginger. Maybe a tiny bit thinner, but really, she was doing the whole Orange County thing, and I could see how Fred was pressuring her to be a different person. I tried to talk to him, you know, man to man and all that crap Fred likes," Jack said. "But he wasn't listening. Seemed paranoid."

"She was blackmailing him," I said.

Jack nodded. "I know that now," he said. "It was all just starting. It was after I left that the drugs happened, and… all the rest of it." Jack looked around for the waitress.

"And now they're after you," I said. "Michael's after you."

"Ten thousand a day, Danny," Jack said. "That's what I'm paying to keep the boys alive." He gazed at me. "I left. I left and didn't look back, and I know that man wants me dead. But he hasn't finished milking me yet."

For one wild and shameful moment, I thought about how much crack ten thousand dollars would buy. Enough for oblivion.

"Why did they keep me alive?" I wanted to know. "Why didn't they kill me when they killed Dominic?" I had filled Jack in on my adventure at the Sunny Jim.

"For me, I think," he said. "If you died, I'd just go after them. As much as I love the boys, I wouldn't have been able to…" He stopped and shook his head.

"Jack," I said, and stopped. He was my husband. He was paying to keep the twins alive. I had a flashback to having sex with Miller in the hospital, and felt something like shame.

"Where are the boys," I said gently. "You said you knew."

He shook his head. "No, I didn't. I know that Jeanette has them, and I know that they're in Toronto, and I think I know where. But I'm not sure." We were silent for a minute. "They want me back. Jeanette wants me back. Michael wants to take what I have, and come back into the fold, according to Jeanette. One big happy family again. When I saw Jeanette at Ginger's she told me she had no idea where Michael was, hoped he was dead. I actually believed her."

I felt sick.

"I broke Lola's arm and nose yesterday," I said conversationally.

"Oh, Danny. This is not good for us," he said. "Lola was like Jeanette's little sister, the whole time we were with Michael. They had a special bond. This isn't good," he repeated. But at the same time, I could see that he was a little proud of me. I told him about the events of the last days. It felt so good to talk to him, to tell him everything. Almost everything.

Jack motioned for the waitress. He ordered me another glass of wine, a Shiraz this time.

"Sexist pig," I said. "You didn't even ask me."

"I always did know what you need, baby," Jack said, in his Barry White voice. I laughed out loud.

I looked at Jack, the man I had never stopped loving. I watched his face, the crinkles around his eyes, the funny dent in his head above his left ear. His big strong neck and shoulders. He wanted to know about how I got into crack. It wasn't much of a story, and I told him.

"Oh, the old story," I said. "Girl leaves marriage, very sad, starts drinking too much at neighborhood watering hole, meets fun new friends who do cocaine. Then fun new friends start doing crack, and girl doesn't see how she can hurt herself any further, so she jumps down the rabbit hole. She thinks she can climb back out anytime she wants. She can't."

Jack grunted. He wanted to know if I was seeing anybody.

Miller? Gene? I didn't know what to say to Jack about either of them.

"By your pause, I am guessing yes," Jack said. "Who's the lucky guy?" He looked out the window casually, as though we were discussing the weather. I could see a muscle in his temple twitch.

I decided to leave Miller out of the equation. "I have a friend," I said. "Not what you think, but not exactly not either," I said. I looked at Jack. I believed him, of course I did. I wanted to. But what would Jeanette have to gain by beating Gene to a bloody pulp? "He's in the hospital," I ventured.

"Overdose?" Jack asked, not without a bit of bitterness.

"No," I said. I told him about Gene being tied to my bed, about his face, and having to have his spleen removed. Jack listened, as only Jack could do.

"I'm sorry, Danny," Jack said. "I'm sorry for you, but not for him. Is he the one who got you started?" Into the life, he meant.

"What does it matter?" I said. I wished someone would clear the table. I'd only had a few bites, despite my appetite, and now the meat looked extra bloody, whilst we were talking about Gene in the hospital. "Did you have something to do with this?"

"No," he said. "Why would I bother beating some crackhead?"

Some crackhead. "Good point," I said. "Low-life, right? He got what was coming to him."

"That's not for me to judge," he said. "But if it was this guy who got you hooked on crack, I'm not sorry he's in the hospital."

"You got me hooked on crack, Jack," I said. The waitress was at the table to take the plates away. She picked them up and moved quickly. She couldn't wait to get to the bar and fill the staff in on the new development. "Dealing with you. I needed to escape."

Jack stayed still for a second, then grinned. "Ever hear of Florida?" he said. "Or Hawaii?" I laughed.

"What do we do now?" I said. Somehow, I had come here ready to kill Jack to get information on the boys, and now he was my ally. I didn't second guess myself about it, either. It felt right.

"Let's go up to my room and discuss it," Jack said. He didn't look to me like he wanted to do any more discussing.

"Okay," I said, grabbing my purse and standing up. "But don't use too many big words. I haven't had many discussions in a while."

"It'll come back to you," Jack said, and motioned for the check.

And it did.

22

Jack and I fell asleep, after. The heavy drapes kept out the daylight. The bed was glorious. I was feeling a twinge of something like happiness. I was feeling like I was back where I belonged. Next to Jack.

But Ginger was gone, and we had to get the boys.

When I woke up, the clock said it was nearly six p.m. I hadn't called Darren today, or Dave, who was probably still waiting anxiously in my apartment. Jack was still sleeping, snoring his profound rattling snore. It was like white noise to me. I curled up around him and closed my eyes, wishing that I could erase the last couple of years. I started crying then, for all the mistakes I'd made. For Jack, who had endured unimaginable pain due to the demons in his brain and the devils in his past. But especially for Ginger, who had jumped down into the abyss after me. Whether she was being led there by Jeanette Vasquez or pushed by Fred, or maybe just to get away from her own pain, I might never know.

Jack woke up and pulled me tight into him. I cried myself out while he stroked my hair.

"I kind of like this dark mop," he said. "Suits you."

We lay in silence for a while. "I'm paying money into a

Toronto bank account," he said. "That's one of the reasons I know she's here."

She. Jeanette. My evil twin. She had found her way into our bed.

"I hired some people to find out where she is," he continued.

"People?" I echoed.

"People," he said firmly. Case closed on that one. "But I don't want them going in, guns blazing."

"The boys might get hurt," I said. I sat up. "Jack."

Jack pulled me back down and curled himself around me again. I let my mind wander, allowing myself to enjoy where I was, trying to forget the sound of Lola's arm breaking, or the feeling of Dom's blood squishing under my feet.

And Miller. I would think about Miller later.

We talked a little, small talk. We both knew we had to get up and go. We just drew it out a few minutes longer. I told him about Irene's mother being sick. Then I told him I had to call Darren, and Jack got up and went into the shower, telling me to give his best to my brother. They'd always gotten along, until Darren got a little overprotective of me when Jack went nuts.

I sat up in bed and phoned Fred and Ginger's number. Rosen answered on the first ring.

"Lindquist residence," he said, in his neutral accent.

"It's Danny," I said.

"People are worried about you," Rosen said quietly. "You left your apartment six hours ago."

"But who's counting. I'm fine," I said. I wasn't sure what to tell him. "Can I speak to my brother, please?" Rosen didn't argue. Darren was obviously close by.

I told Darren everything. Well, not everything, but he got the gist.

"So right now, it's all about finding Jeanette Vasquez," he said slowly.

"Yes," I said. "She's got the boys. I'm sure of it."

I heard the shower shutting off, and Jack singing "My Way."

We were silent for a second. "How's Gene?" Darren asked.

"I have to call and check," I said. "I'm going to do that right now."

"With Jack there?"

"Not much choice," I said.

"You sure he's okay? Jack, I mean?" Darren said.

"Pretty sure. Pretty very sure," I said, smiling as Jack came out in a Four Seasons white dressing gown, looking very pleased with himself.

Darren told me that Detective French was conscious, and remembered me belting her, but nothing else. There was a warrant for my arrest.

But nothing, he said, about the incident at Lucky's.

"I don't know who to trust," I said.

"Whom," Darren said, and I cursed at him. It was like nothing had changed. It made me feel good. I told him I'd call him right after finding the boys. I told him that would be tonight. I knew it. I felt it.

I put the phone down and took a drink from Jack. He was having a Coke.

"What now?" he said.

"I have to call the hospital," I said. "Sorry."

"S'okay," Jack said. "I just had my way with you. I guess I can be generous to the poor sap in the hospital."

He kissed me, and it was like the last few years hadn't happened. But they had, and I had to deal with it. We both did.

I got through to the front desk at Toronto General, and asked for the status of a patient named Eugene Gold. The operator put me on hold, and I listened to a public service announcement about hand washing. It said you were supposed to wash your hands for the amount of time it would take to sing "Happy Birthday." Useful. A couple of minutes later, a woman came on the line and identified herself as Mona. Said she was a nurse in Intensive Care.

"Intensive Care?" I said.

"What is your relation to Mr. Gold?" she asked.

"I'm his, you know. Friend," I said. Jack got up and washed his hands. I didn't hear him singing "Happy Birthday."

Mona sighed. "Mr. Gold has contracted an infection," she said. "Doctors are keeping him unconscious until it can be cleared."

"Is he going to be all right?"

"We certainly hope so," she said. She told me that I could call back in the morning and check on his condition, then she hung up. When Jack emerged from the bathroom, I told him what Mona had said.

"Couldn't have happened to a nicer guy," he said.

"Come on," I said. "Gene is good people. He's just damaged. You can afford to be emotionally generous. All I've ever wanted is you." Then hot tears started down my face. It was all too much. I wanted to get back into bed with Jack and forget it all. Ginger had said in her note, "find Jack." I knew now that she meant because Jack was the key to all this. But I also knew that she loved him, and when he got so sick she was one of the only people in his life to stick by him. She wanted me to be with Jack, as long as he was well. And he *was* well. Other than the horror we were dealing with, he seemed healthy and composed.

Jack and I would do this. We would get the boys. I would kill Jeanette. Or maybe I wouldn't have to now. Maybe it would be enough that she goes to jail. Would Ginger really want me to have all this violence on my soul? Then Jack and I could be together again. He was medicated and fine. And as it turned out, a lot of his paranoia back in the day was actually real. What was the old line? Is it paranoid if they really are out to get you? And if I had Jack, I wouldn't need crack. I actually laughed out loud.

Jack was coming over to me, a smile on his face, when his phone rang. We looked at each other, and Jack snatched my hand away before I picked it up.

"Yes," he said. I watched his face. He was listening.

"Thanks. I'll take care of it," he said, and hung up.

"We're on," he said. "Jeanette is in position, alone with the twins."

"We're going to get them?"

"Yes, Danny. We're going to get them."

Jack pulled out some clothes from his suitcase, and motioned for me to get dressed.

"Do you know how to shoot that gun in your purse?"

"How did you know?" I said. Jack smiled at me.

"Danny," he said. "You kept it in your lap when we were in the bar. And look at it." I did. It was thrown on a chair in the room, and through the fabric of the too-small purse, the outline of something hard and gun-sized was apparent.

"Oh," I said. "I was good at target shooting when I was a kid."

"That was long ago and far away," he said. "You have a lot to learn, babycakes. And I have approximately half an hour to teach you."

My second gun lesson of the day. A record.

Jack picked up where Dave had left off in the morning. But I still didn't get to shoot the thing. The Four Seasons tends to frown on guests shooting firearms in the hotel. An archaic rule.

"Shouldn't we call somebody?" I said. "You know. The police?"

Jack shook his head. "I don't know. I don't know who Jeanette has in her pocket. Or who's in on this with her." He pulled on some black pants and a black t-shirt. Commando gear. He looked like a bulked-up version of Rosen, actually.

"This whole thing is a viper's nest," he said. "I want to make sure we get the boys out of there safely. After that, we can have every law enforcement agency in the western hemisphere on these people. And we will. But Jeanette is unstable. She has been manipulated and been manipulating, her entire life." He was pacing a bit, which made me nervous. "That's why I am going in. Just me. She wants me back. I'm going to get in, disable her, get the boys, get out."

Disable her. I'd love to disable her. I thought about Dave, back at my apartment. I told Jack about him. Despite Dave having saved Gene's life, and my instinct that he was on side, Jack wasn't convinced.

"He had a gun on you, on Darren," he said. "He sounds like he's part of this, Danny. I really don't know how deep this goes. Until all this started happening, I had made it my business to stay out of the way of Michael and any of these people. I could have had them investigated long ago, but I wanted it all out of my life, out of our lives. And look how that turned out." He checked his ammo.

"Look," Jack continued. "I'm going to leave calling the police up to you. I guess it is unlikely Jeanette has many contacts here, but we can't be sure. And I don't know about this Dave. I don't know who to trust."

"Whom," I corrected.

"Fuck you, babycakes," Jack said, and I hugged him. "I need her to think that I'm coming after her because I'm in love with her, despite everything."

"Despite the fact that she's charging you ten grand a day to keep your nephews alive."

"Yeah," he said. "Despite that. She's playing that as though it's all on Michael and she's still his pawn. Listen. I might have to act the part."

"She's going to be kissing you and shit, I suppose," I said.

"If I play my cards right," he said. "Do you want the boys back or don't you? You need to carry your gun and stay hidden. We'll scout out the location, then you can wait outside and I'll signal from the window if you should come in for the boys. Or call the cops." So many variables. I suppose that's what happens, when you're dealing with highly damaged psychopaths.

Jack gave me his cell phone, and instructed me not to answer any incoming calls. He set the phone to vibrate before he gave it to me.

"Goody," I said. "I have this, while you're in there fucking Jeanette."

"I'm not going to fuck her," he said. "I don't think I could, anyway."

"Stud," I said.

We left the room half an hour before Jack was supposed to be at Jeanette's hiding place, an old loft somewhere between Sheppard and Finch, off Yonge Street. Jack got his rental car, a black Escalade, out of the public parking lot next to the hotel. He was worth more than God these days, but he still wouldn't let a valet park one of his cars.

Traffic was ferocious, but Jack was one of those effortless drivers; smooth, calm, and with an unerring instinct for the best route. We drove up the Don Valley Parkway to Lawrence, then got off onto Avenue Road. On the way, Jack explained that he had learned to shoot in Bermuda, out of boredom, and because it was a skill he didn't have yet. I knew there was more to it than that, that there was probably still an element of paranoia. I let it pass. But he didn't have a gun with him in Toronto. It's difficult to get a firearms licence in Canada, which is one of the reasons it's named one of the best places in the world to live. It's a peaceful society. I did not, however, feel that way now.

We drove from Avenue Road to Yonge Street. We weren't far from where D-Man lived, but I opted not to inform Jack of this. He might want to make a pit stop to give someone a beating to get his blood going.

At Yonge and Sheppard, I looked out the window at the new movie theatres and trendy restaurants that had opened up in the neighborhood. When I first came to Toronto, the area was considered to be a no man's land, strictly for new Asian immigrants and lower-income families. Now, trendsetters from downtown would occasionally make the twenty-minute subway ride from downtown to try one of the newly reviewed restaurants in the area. 1960s- and 70s-era apartment buildings were making way for overpriced condos and lofts. I was expecting Jeanette to have one of these places, but instead Jack kept driving a couple of blocks north, past the well-lit developments, and turned left onto a dark side street. There was a dingy bar on the corner, and a homeless shelter two doors down. A 24-hour convenience store was across the street. Other than that, there was no one on the street on a chilly November evening, and we were out of the trendy loop.

Jack pulled over to consult the address he'd written down at the Four Seasons.

"Get down," he said, firmly. "We're here." This screwed up our plan a bit. We were going to circle whatever block the place was on, suss out which window I could see. But without meaning to, Jack had pulled into a parking spot right by the entrance.

I slumped into the space in front of my seat gracelessly, thankful that he had rented an Escalade. I couldn't imagine myself doing this in Darren's Fiat. Jack took off his leather jacket as he opened the car door, and threw it over me casually. If someone was looking out the window, they wouldn't have thought a thing. I hoped.

"Window on this side of the street," Jack mumbled, pretending to lean in and grab his keys. "If I put my hand flat on the window, come in. Stay down," he said. "I may go up the fire escape and see if I can see what's going on in there, before I go knocking on the door. See if anyone else is there."

I didn't have to say anything. Jack knew I heard him.

Jack walked away, and I stayed down. I put my hand into my purse and pulled out the .38, and stuck the knife into the back pocket of my jeans.

After ten minutes, I felt safe enough to stick my head up. We were parked thirty feet or so off Yonge Street, equidistant, I judged, between Sheppard and Finch. Jack had gone left, which meant that Jeanette was above the crappy-looking bar on the corner. The boys were probably up there too. I tried to see if the window looked like the windows in the picture, but I could only see the side of the building. The back and front windows were out of my sightlines.

Crouching in the footwell of a pricey SUV isn't as glamorous as it sounds. I'm not short, but nobody would find a comfortable position here. And I knew that we were parked in such a way to make any movement on my part dangerous. We had stumbled onto this place by a bit of fluke, without any prior knowledge. If Jeanette Vasquez decided that she didn't trust Jack and wanted to check out his vehicle, I was in perfect view for her.

To occupy myself, I sang old standards in my head. My parents had reared us on Cole Porter and the Gershwins and Irving Berlin. I sang every Frank Sinatra song I could remember, especially the 60s swinging ones. I sang old Dinah Washington tunes, and Billie Holiday. I sang every song I could remember from Porgy and Bess. Crouched in the footwell of a Cadillac Escalade on a side street off Yonge Street in North York, I covered as much of the American Standards Songbook as I could remember.

Jack, as far as I knew, was fifty feet away, with the woman who murdered my sister.

I kept glancing up at the windows. I couldn't see anyone in the window, and certainly not Jack giving his signal. But this was taking too long. Far too long.

I held the gun in my hands. I warmed it up, until it felt

like part of me. I put it to my cheek and let my tears wet the barrel. I prayed. I hadn't prayed in such a long time, and it wasn't something I let anybody know about. Not Jack. Not Darren. Not Ginger. But I talked to God about Matthew and Luke, and I prayed for forgiveness for what I was about to do.

I hoped Ginger would forgive me. I hoped Jack could. I wished I could be a different person. But I wasn't.

I was going to kill Jeanette Vasquez.

I got out of the car.

23

The back door to the building was unlocked. I heard Dire Straits playing, but it was from the bar downstairs. "Sultans of Swing." Good song. Mary J. Blige's "Family Affair" started next. I debated just going into the bar, 'cause those guys had their groove on. And it would be safer. But instead, I went up the back stairs.

I walked on the outside treads of the stairs. They tend to squeak less; any rebellious teenager will tell you that. I held the .38 in my right hand, against the stairwell. I had Jack's cell in my jacket pocket, still, I hoped, set on vibrate.

There were three doors at the top of the stairs. I paused for a second, knowing that I might only have that long before somebody came looking for me. Outside, I had done the math. Jack said it was the middle apartment. I crept along the hallway, as quietly as my motorcycle boots would allow. The first apartment I passed was totally silent. I kept going, trying to keep my breath shallow.

I paused before the second door. I could hear Elton John singing "Tiny Dancer." I have nothing against Elton John, but it wasn't my favorite. Hold me closer, Tony Danza. I looked at the door. It looked flimsy, but then again so did I.

I listened at the door, and got nothing other than Elton. Leaning back, I leaned on my left leg, and shot my right leg out, hard, into the door. To my surprise, the door popped open. No one had locked the deadbolt.

There was no reaction inside. I leaned against the outside doorjamb, the Colt held against my chest like both Dave and Jack had told me. I was trying to control my breath. It seemed, at the moment, like my most important priority. Good not to have one of my fits just now, if I could help it.

Elton John morphed into Lynyrd Skynyrd. "Free Bird." I hoped Jeanette wasn't trying to send me a message.

I stuck my head into the doorway for a minute. I registered a regular living space: neutral-colored carpet and furniture. Kitchen to the right. And a long hallway. The music was coming from there. No one, no matter how far down that hallway, could have missed the door busting in. But there was no sign of life.

"Jeanette Vasquez," I yelled. "Show yourself." I hoped my voice sounded stronger than I felt. I threw my purse into the hallway and talked to it as though it were a cop. I was hoping to fool Jeanette into thinking there were a few of me.

Down the hallway, I heard a crash, like breaking glass. I released the safety on the gun. My heart was pounding so hard that I thought it would come through my chest.

"Jeanette," I yelled. "This is Danny Cleary."

I held the gun ahead of me. I was trying not to shake. For a long minute, there was no sound.

"Well, as I live and breathe," a woman's voice said. "Danielle Cleary."

A woman started down the hallway. She was holding a small

body in front of her, a gun to his head. It was Luke.

"Hi, kiddo," I said to him. "You might not remember me. I'm your Aunt Danny." I looked at the woman. "Hi, Jeanette." Luke was looking at me with wide eyes. He'd been eight when I'd seen him last, but shock and fear can do a lot to a person. Especially a little person. I tried to smile at him reassuringly, but tears were streaming down his face. He looked so much like Ginger.

I felt my heart break, right there and then in my chest.

"Fred was right," Jeanette said. She paused and looked at me. "You do look like shit. You're much better looking in your pictures."

"How's Lola?" I said. "Maybe the broken nose will help her looks a bit. Anyway, tell her hi for me, will you?" My mind was spinning. Where in the hell was Jack?

I had no idea what Jeanette looked like before, but she had obviously gone to some effort to look like me. Like I did now. Short, choppy dark hair, roughly the same size. Pale skin. And I wasn't sure from this distance, but her eyes looked blue. Like Ginger's.

"Tell her yourself, doll," Jeanette said. I heard a shuffling in the hallway, and I adjusted my stance. I tried to smile at Luke. I probably didn't do a very good job, because he looked like he was going to start to cry all over again.

Eleven years old. His mother dead, his nanny holding him hostage, and his aunt waving a gun around. I don't know much about child psychology, but once I got these kids away safely, I was pretty sure we were in for some heavy-duty family counselling.

But first I had to save their lives. We could worry about their psyches later. And where in God's name was Jack?

Lola appeared in the doorway, holding Matthew in front of her as Jeanette had done with Luke. He looked lethargic and dopey. Maybe he had just woken up, or maybe he'd been drugged. I could feel my respiration increase and I tried to slow it down. Lola's arm was in a cast and a sling. Good.

But no. If Jack hadn't known Lola was here, and had come in here not expecting her... something bad had happened. Too much time had passed.

"Hi, boys," I said. I tried to listen for Jack down the hall. "Wow, we've been looking all over for you! I've come to take you home." Well, close enough. Back to family, anyway. Where their home would be now wasn't my immediate concern.

Luke started towards me and Jeanette hauled him back by his shoulder. Not gently.

Lola was looking daggers at me with the black eyes she must have gotten from the head-butt I'd given her on the bar. But she wasn't armed, that I could see. Matthew was her shield. I made eye contact with him, tried to make sure he knew I was there to help him, and to stay calm. There's only so much non-verbal communication you can engage in with a frightened eleven-year-old who may or may not remember you very well.

"Danny, it's a hoot to meet you in person. It really is. But we were kind of hoping that you'd be sitting by the bedside of your crack buddy. Eugene, is it?" She smiled, and if I didn't know she was a psychopath, I would have thought she was a perfectly friendly-looking person. Someone to have a latte with after spin class. If I had ever done such a thing.

"Was that really necessary?" I said.

"No," Jeanette said. "But you hurt Lola, so we had to hurt someone of yours. Haven't you ever played a game before?" She squeezed Luke's shoulders. "Boys, your Aunt Danny is silly. She doesn't understand the rules." They did it together, then, Jeanette and Lola. Beat and tortured Gene, in my bed, in my apartment.

Matty reached over and tried to grab Luke's hand. It was something Ginger and I would have done at their age, to comfort each other. But Lola jerked Matt away, and he looked like he wanted to punch her. His little fists clenched by his sides.

I could see which twin took more after his auntie. I hoped it wouldn't get him in trouble.

"Rules," I said. I was listening for any more movement in the apartment, but there was none. Had Jack gone into the wrong apartment? "I must have missed the memo."

"Well we don't have time tonight for all that, Danny, but let's just say that your part is at an end. The fact that you were such a loser druggie made Ginger so much easier to control," she said. "I got a friend to recommend me to Ginger and Fred as the absolute ideal nanny. But there was poor Ginger. She wasn't just any old Newport matron, going to Pilates and lunches. She really did want to know, to really *know*, what you were doing to yourself. She said it was a twin thing." She smiled at Lola. "Lola and I were close growing up and we're close now, but we're not even related, and this twin shit is strong. Right, boys?"

"Yes," Matthew said, with venom. "And you had better not hurt my brother."

At this, Lola slapped the back of Matthew's head.

The blood was there again, pounding in my ears.

"Keep your filthy hands off my nephew," I said to Lola. My voice sounded calm, almost pleasant. "Or do you want me to break your other arm?"

Lola raised her arm as though she were about to hit Matty

harder this time, and I pointed the .38 in her direction. "I'm an excellent shot, bitch," I said. "Try me."

"Lola, chill," Jeanette said. "Let me finish here." Lola stuck her arm back down abruptly. If I had had any doubt who the alpha was here, it was clear now. She sighed, as though this were as frustrating as getting stuck in traffic on your way to a pedicure appointment. "You were a means to an end, okay? It was never really about you. We got Fred. It didn't work out quite like we had planned, but the payday was decent enough. But finally, there he was, the golden goose, my first love, and so rich now! So we have much bigger fish to fry now."

"Stay away from Jack," I said, but it was hollow. They had the boys. They were holding the cards.

"You mean Scott? Yeah, I don't think so. But look, it's been great meeting you. But we have your nephews, and he loves these boys. I don't really need you anymore, Danny. Scott is here, and we're going to be one big happy family. Aren't we, kids?" Luke was trying desperately not to cry, and Matty looked like he was figuring out what to do.

"It ends here for you," Jeanette said. She almost sounded apologetic. She looked me in the eye as she released the safety on the gun she had at Luke's head. "Put your gun on the ground." I was trying to think quickly. If I put the gun down, Jeanette would shoot me dead on the spot, of that I had no doubt. But the boys would be safe for now, at least. Whatever happened after this, Jack would protect them, probably better than I ever could. But where was he?

I kept my eyes on Jeanette as I slowly leaned over to place my gun on the floor. I thought it would be the last thing I ever did. I was expecting the shot at any moment, and hoped the boys would close their eyes. I wouldn't see Darren again. Or Laurence, or Skipper, or Jack, or Gene, or Miller. I looked at Matty and tried to smile. *Close your eyes*, I mouthed. Luke's eyes were already closed.

I heard something in the hallway. Jack, oh God, please be Jack. They had probably tied him up.

A shot. A shot from somewhere behind them, and I dove for the floor and grabbed my gun.

Lola went down screaming.

Then, pandemonium.

"Matty, behind me, now!" I yelled, and he obeyed without hesitating. Good kid. Jeanette was still holding the gun carefully to Luke's head. But she wasn't smiling anymore.

Jack.

Jack stumbled into the room from the dark recesses of the hallway that he had shot from. He had his weapon in one hand, trained on Jeanette. There was something in his mouth, something wound around his face, something to keep him from yelling out and warning me. It looked like black stockings. He wasn't trying to remove it.

One hand was holding the gun.

The other hand was covering the blood that was escaping from his chest.

It was silent for a moment. I could hear Jack trying to breathe through the fabric on his face. He was covered in blood. He was barely standing.

"Scott," Jeanette said. "I'm sorry," she said. "What did she do?" She actually sounded sad, surprised. In the midst of my shock and terror, I clearly realized that she must not have known that Lola had stabbed him. She had really thought he was hers. For half a second, I nearly felt sorry for her. "Lola. She just... she's got such a temper. So jealous of you." She actually sounded scared, as she looked at him. "Let's just get rid of Danny, I'll get you to the hospital."

I tried to think. Maybe I should just grab Matty and run. Get one boy out, and get the cops here immediately. Ambulances, police, fire, God himself. Save Jack. Save Luke.

Then I saw Lola, lying on her back on the floor, reaching for her gun. Jack was now bent over at the waist, trying to hold his gun arm in the air. He was shaking. He didn't seem to see Lola.

With a swift movement, I turned and shoved Matty back through the door, which was still partially open behind me. I could hear his feet pounding down the stairs, hesitating, then continuing to go. I could hear sirens. The neighbors had called the police. Good.

Lola managed to grab the gun. In my peripheral vision I saw that Jeanette still had the gun to Luke's head, but she was actually looking a little alarmed at how bad Jack looked, and at Lola with the gun. Without hesitation, I pointed and fired at Lola's head before she could get a shot off at Jack, and then before checking to make sure I hit her, I turned the gun on Jeanette.

Jeanette screamed. There was more rage and anger in that scream than I believe I had ever heard before. Other than what I heard in my own head.

Jack was now slumped over onto the floor, and I had caught Lola right above one eye. She stopped twitching the second I noticed where I hit her.

Jack was on the floor. Jack was bleeding. There was way too much blood. It was mixing with Lola's on the floor. It enraged me, his blood mixing with hers.

The sirens didn't seem to be getting any closer, or time had stood still.

Jeanette grabbed Luke and walked backwards down the hallway Jack had just emerged from, still holding the gun at Luke. I didn't trust myself to shoot while she had him. She was crying. I started to shake.

She could hide back there. She wouldn't hurt Luke. She knew Jack would never forgive her. The police would be here in a second. The ambulance would be here.

"Jeanette," I yelled. "I'm taking care of him for you. I'm going to keep him alive, and you can have him. He's all yours. You had him first. We're divorced. Just don't hurt Luke." I couldn't hear anything from the rest of the apartment, above the pounding of blood in my ears.

I ran to Jack.

He was conscious. He was breathing. Barely. I ripped the fabric from his face, his mouth. There was too much blood, there was blood in his mouth. His eyes were panicked as he tried to breathe. Someone had stabbed him in the heart. I placed both hands over the wound, which was sucking. Behind me I heard tentative footsteps and I didn't turn around. I was not going to take my eyes away from Jack's.

Jack wasn't going to die.

Jack was going to die.

Matty was behind me. He sat down on the floor with me. He put his arm around my neck, as I held my hand over Jack's heart, as his lifeblood spilled. I couldn't stop it. I couldn't stop it. I didn't want Matty to see this but I couldn't say anything. I just looked into Jack's eyes, and he was looking into mine with more love than I had ever felt in my life. More, I knew, than I would ever feel again.

"Baby," I said. He was shaking. He was dying. "Baby." I tried to keep his blood in his heart where it belonged. I leaned over and kissed his mouth gently. His blood was on my face.

When his heart stopped beating, I felt it. Mine stopped too. I hoped it would never start again.

When he stopped shaking, when his body was still and I heard the sounds of sirens right outside, I got up and walked down the hallway. I was holding my gun again in one hand. I didn't remember picking it up. In the other I was holding Matty's hand.

"Luke," I called. "Luke." But he didn't respond, because he wasn't there.

All that was at the end of the hall was a bedroom with an open window onto a fire escape.

Slowly I walked back down the hall, putting my gun on the floor carefully. I sat on the floor beside Jack and held his hand, and Matty's, and waited for all the people to come.

24

Matthew and I were sent to Sunnybrook Hospital to be checked out. They wanted to take us in separate ambulances, but Matt wouldn't leave my side, and I certainly wasn't leaving his. We held hands tightly in the ambulance but didn't say anything. I could feel his leg pressed up against mine. He was shaking. So was I.

Jack and Lola, they took to the morgue.

There was nothing wrong with me. Physically, at least. Once they cleaned Jack's blood off me, they saw that I had no injuries. I tried to fight them when they wanted to clean his blood off. I kicked someone, when they tried to clean his blood off me. They gave me a shot of something to calm me down and make me docile. They tested my hands for gunshot residue, even though I told them I shot Lola. They tested me for hepatitis and HIV, due to all the blood – Jack's blood – I'd gotten into my eyes and mouth. I told them they didn't have to test me. It was only Jack's blood.

It was my blood.

Matty was in the same room, on another bed, being checked out. I had threatened the medical staff with a painful death if they thought they were going to take him out of my sight for even a second. I don't know whether they believed me, or if it was Matty's shrill screams when they tried to take him away from me, but they kept us together. Those screams were the only sound Matty had made since I'd seen him when Lola brought him out of the room in the apartment. No words, not even to me, but he kept his eyes on me.

I looked at my hands, sitting on that hospital bed. They were clean now. My right hand was still bruised and swollen from punching Detective French, but otherwise you would never have been able to tell that these hands had tried and failed to staunch the blood of the only man I would ever love. These hands had killed a woman in cold blood. Two days before that, I had beaten her badly, badly enough to break bones. And yet I had no remorse, and I couldn't figure out why. My parents didn't raise me to be this way. A psychiatrist might disagree, might say that my father rewarding me for punching out Darren's high school sweetheart was encouraging later homicidal tendencies. But if I did have those tendencies, they were focused. I enjoyed people. Despite the horror and chaos of the last week, I had made small connections with strangers. Marta, for example. The cab driver who was doing the twelve steps. Wanda the nurse.

Jack was dead. My husband was dead. The last couple of years of our separation didn't seem to matter. My husband was gone. And Ginger was dead. My sister, whom I had loved fiercely, who deserved a happy, gentle, chaotic life with her wonderful sons. Lola and the bartender were meaningless bad guys, and I didn't spend a second worrying about their wasted lives. Dominic Pastore was an innocent bystander. I didn't love him, but he didn't deserve to die. Darren had killed a man, too. I was pretty sure that he was going through something like what I was.

But Darren didn't have the love of his life bleeding to death in his arms.

Jack died trying to save my family. And if I died doing the same? Well, it didn't seem to matter much.

I was glad they had given me the shot of whatever it had been, to calm me down. For once I didn't even ask anyone what it was. Thorazine maybe? I was actually glad it wasn't crack, for once. It kept me calm but not euphoric. I believe I would have lost my mind, perhaps irrevocably, in those couple of hours, if I had been allowed to fully process everything. And seeing that would have damaged Matty even further. Medicated, I could even try to smile at him, as the nurses took his vital signs and took his blood and the doctors performed basic neurological tests on him. They did sexual assault tests on him, and he allowed them to draw the curtain between us for that. He didn't make a sound.

Police came in and out of my room. My impression was that they didn't know what to charge me with. Weapons offences were being whispered around, but I wasn't paying much attention.

When they finished examining us medically, Matty came and sat on my bed with me. We held hands, but didn't speak. We both listened to people in the hallway talking about us.

A nurse came in, finally, a kind older woman. She said that Matthew was going to have to go to his own room.

"No," I said calmly. "He stays with me."

"I am staying with her," Matthew said clearly, and I smiled at him for real. They were the first words I had heard from him, through the whole ordeal.

The nurse left the room, and we could hear someone in the hallway saying, "For the love of God, do you have any idea of what that boy has been through? What both of them have? They aren't to be separated." Whoever that person was, I loved him. I put my arm around Matty and kissed the top of his head.

A minute later, the owner of the voice came in.

"Knock, knock," he said. I thought I recognized him as one of the cops who had come into the apartment where I was sitting on the floor in a bloody tableau with Jack and Matthew. He was fifty-ish, and looked kindly and smart. His name was Detective Paul Belliveau, and he told me that my brother Darren was on a plane, on his way, and that we were both being kept in the hospital overnight for observation. He seemed to feel very sorry for us, and kept patting my foot gently and awkwardly over the blankets.

He seemed like the nicest person I had ever met. Matty seemed to think so too. Paul, as he told us to call him, pulled up a chair next to the bed where we were half sitting, half lying. He told us he had all night, he had all day tomorrow, and we could tell him our story in our own good time.

Matty talked. They had been taken by their nanny. She had fed them, but at the same time, she gave them drugs to make them sleep a lot. Mary Poppins, she was not. He was feeling particularly guilty that he and Luke hadn't fought back. Before they realized that Jeanette was bad, she had convinced them to tell the authorities she was their aunt, so Social Security would release them to her, she said, and they could go home to see Marta and James. She had taken them to the In & Out Burger and bought them food.

But she didn't take them home.

And on the plane to Toronto and for the rest of the time, they were given shots to keep them dull and unable to move much. They slept a lot. They ate junk food. She didn't talk to them much, but other than drugging them, she didn't hurt them either. Another lady came to stay. She wasn't very nice. Jeanette said she was their aunt, but they knew that wasn't true.

Then earlier tonight, Uncle Jack had come into the apartment where they were being kept. He winked at them, they said, to let them know he was going to help them. That's what they figured, anyway. They trusted their Uncle Jack. Jack had spent time with them in California before their mother was killed, had taken them to a Lakers game, to the movies, to a concert in Anaheim. They had all gone to the beach together.

Matt told me he knew they were going to be all right, that Uncle Jack would take them home.

But then Uncle Jack had left their room and somewhere in the hallway he sort of yelled a bit and Matty thought he could hear him fall, but then he fell asleep again.

He hadn't mentioned his mother yet. There were so many layers of trauma, I didn't want to bring her up either. Matt kept asking when we were going to get Luke back. I told him we would. I promised him that I would get his twin brother back.

I hated myself for the promise. I would die trying, but my trying might not be good enough.

He hadn't mentioned his father yet either. There was going to be a lot of pain for this boy. I wished more than anything that I could take that pain for him so he didn't have it.

Paul listened to Matty and wrote a lot of notes. I didn't say anything. I just asked Paul if he would mind coming back in the morning. I wanted to sleep. I needed to escape. A few minutes later someone brought Matty and me some buttered toast and chocolate milk, and not long after that we turned out the lights. I enveloped Matty up as best I could with my body around him. No one was getting to this boy. I couldn't stay awake, but if anyone tried to touch him, I would wake up. He was safe.

"You're safe, and I love you," I said to him, I don't know how many times. I felt his tears, hot on my arm. Over and over I told him he was safe, and that he was loved, until I felt him fall asleep.

And then I exhaled, and I slept too.

In the morning, I woke up with a craving for crack that made me actually dizzy. My opiate-induced pseudo-serenity of the night before was gone. But I had to maintain an outward calm, for Matty's sake. He was sitting in a chair next to the bed, holding onto my hand, holding a comic book he wasn't reading.

A nurse came in to check me. She looked at my foot with the stitches.

"You're going to have a nice scar there," she said. "Oh well. Better than on your face, eh?"

I smiled at her. "Not really," I said. As far as I was concerned, I could have scars covering every inch of me. It would be appropriate, for how I felt. People should shy away from me. No one experiencing this level of pain should look normal.

The nurse nodded, as though she understood, though she surely couldn't know that part of the story. But she'd seen lots of stories in her days as an E.R. nurse, I was pretty sure. "Someone will be in to talk to you soon," she said, and patted my foot.

"No doubt," I said.

I wondered for the first time where Dave had gone. Had it only been yesterday that he had made me breakfast in my apartment? I just hoped he was out there looking for Jeanette and Luke.

From what I could hear, which wasn't much once the nurse half shut the door behind her, police in the hallway were trying to figure out what to charge me with. Matt had made it clear that Jeanette and Lola were the bad guys.

In the meantime, until Darren could come, we were both being kept in the hospital. It was the safest place, they said. And I had a feeling Darren had informed the hospital staff that I was an addict who shouldn't be discharged.

I would never do drugs while Matty was on my watch. But once Darren got here, Darren could keep him safe. And then I could go back to my apartment, or even to a motel, and do what I do. Just for a day. One day. One day of getting high and letting Jack and Ginger go. And then I could go and find Jeanette and Luke.

I had a shower and in the bathroom, put on the clean sweats a nurse had given me. When I came out, Matthew was asleep again. I wasn't the only one who needed escape.

I watched him sleep for a while. I hoped he wasn't dreaming. And then I kissed his hot forehead and promised him vengeance.

25

For the second time in the space of a week, I woke up in a hospital bed with my brother smiling at me. There are worse ways to wake up. I had those this week, too.

"Well, Bean," Darren said. He looked like he'd been crying. "Well. Fuck me, Danny, I don't know what to say." He shook his head, over and over. "Jack, huh. Jack. Shit, Danny."

"Stop, Darren, please," I said. I couldn't deal with comforting Darren right now. I woke up alert, awake, and ready to kill. I could not, would not, go back into the hell of sadness. "I love you, Darren, but I really can't do this." I could hear the shower. Matty had been encouraged by the nurses to get cleaned up, get some real clothes on.

"Okay," he said. "Give me a minute, Beanpole." Darren got up off the edge of my bed, hitched his jeans back over his hips – he had lost weight – and paced for a minute.

I waited. My heart was cold. I had had enough emotion for one week.

"They're going to release Matt today," Darren said, coming back to the bed. "To me."

"Good," I said.

"I'm going to take him to my place," he continued. Darren had a huge rental in hardcore downtown, off King Street. It was nice, but he wasn't there all that much. It was definitely a bachelor pad. "I don't know what I'm going to do about a bed and stuff."

"You'll figure it out," I said. "He'll be safe with you." And Detective Paul had assured Matty and me many times that he would have people watching us all the time, until we found the bad guys and got Luke back. "What about me?"

"They haven't charged you with anything yet?" he said. "They said they want to keep you in another day." I wanted to roll my eyes, because I knew that was Darren's doing, probably aided by Skip and Laurence. I was detoxing, after all, whether I wanted to or not. I didn't need any medical treatment. What? For the six stitches in my foot? The bump on my head? My poor knuckles? Relatively speaking, I had escaped this week with barely a scratch.

"Not yet," I said.

"Well, I have a lawyer friend who'll look after you."

I looked at him. He looked terrible. "How was your flight? Get any rest?"

"A bit," Darren said. He was used to being on the road. Darren could roll with more punches than I had thought.

"I have to find Luke, Darren. I have to find him. Then this can be over."

"We have to find him," he said. I didn't say anything. He had Matty to take care of now.

"How are you, about what happened at Lucky's?"

"I am fine with what happened at Lucky's," Darren said. He looked me in the eye. "I think you're not. But, Beanpole. I. Am. Fine."

"I want you to forget that ever happened, Darren," I said. "If it gets back to us, I did it."

"Bullshit."

I closed my eyes. All I could see was blood. It wasn't the blood that had already been shed. It was bloodshed to come. "This is my fight, Darren, you know?"

"Ginger was my sister too, Danny."

"I know. I know. But she was my twin. And Jack," I stopped. I bit the inside of my cheek until I could taste blood. "Jack was my husband." I took a breath. "And you have Matt now. He needs you. And Luke will need you, when I bring him back. You're more, I don't know… equipped. Equipped to take care of them right now."

Darren laughed, a ragged sound which seemed to match the flickering fluorescent lights. "Are you high?"

"No."

He looked at me. "What happened in there, Danny?"

I closed my eyes for a minute, saw Lola's face just before I shot her. Jack's blood, gushing through my fingers. The boys' faces.

"I'm not going to stop," I said. I was speaking to him, I supposed, but not looking at him. "I'm not going to stop, until it's over. I'm the only one. I know that now."

I closed my eyes and prayed for crack, my one day of crack before the mayhem that I knew had to follow.

"We promised to do this together," he said.

"We did. You did more than your part. Now, you have to be about Matty, Darren. Please. He needs you. They lost their mother, their father is in the wind, and they saw Jack, and what I did to Lola. Their nanny drugged them. They have so few people to trust. They trust you."

"They trust you, too," he said. "Matty can't bear to be away from you for more than a few minutes."

"He'll get over that, now that you're here. When they see me, all they're going to see is murder, and blood. Maybe that's all they'll ever see."

"No, Bean," Darren said softly. "That's not all."

"For now, Darren," I said, "that has to be all. Because right now, that's all there is." I looked at him, dry-eyed and calm. "It's mine now. Do you get it?"

He shook his head, but he didn't say anything.

"Darren. Get me that lawyer. I need to get out of here. I know what I need to do." Darren nodded. He had more contacts in the real world than I did.

He turned around at the door. "Hey, Danny," he said.

"Yo," I said.

"Bear with me on this," he said.

"Okay."

"If I had been killed, instead of Ginger... would you..."

I stopped him. "Darren," I said. "If it had been you, nobody would be left standing." I motioned him back to me. I licked my right thumb, and he did the same. We pushed them together.

"Don't give up on me," I said. "I'll come back from this."

"Danny," Darren said. "If you don't, I won't be left standing. Think about that, okay?"

"Okay, my brutha," I said. I smiled. "Now, go and take care of our boys. Capiche?"

"Capiche."

* * *

Later, Darren took Matty for ice cream while Detective Paul came in and formally arrested me for possession of an illegal firearm. For the time being, at least, it was the only charge. There was enough evidence to show that I had acted in self-defence in the apartment. I had killed Lola while she was going to try for the second time to kill my husband. Detective French had, surprisingly, refused to press charges against me for punching her in the hospital bathroom. And I hadn't heard a word about what had happened at Lucky's.

The gun that Dave had given me was unregistered. I wasn't surprised, of course, but I told the police honestly that it had been given to me for my own safety by my brother-in-law's private investigator – a person whose identity they hadn't confirmed yet, as I didn't have his last name. They believed me that the man existed – they had him on CCTV in the hospital when we took Gene in, though apparently he was aware of cameras, and always had his face averted.

"I have something to tell you, though, Danny," Belliveau said. "I just found out this morning."

I just looked at him. This wasn't going to be good news, or he would have led with it.

"Detective Miller and Fred Lindquist are both missing," he said. After you say they dropped you and the private eye at the airfield; well as you know, Miller wasn't even supposed to do that. But I don't think anybody's too worried about that." I stared at him. "Miller radioed in an emergency code, officer in jeopardy code, shortly after they would have left you. They found his car. They haven't found either Miller or Lindquist."

Jesus.

"This is in the desert, Danny," he said gently. "There's not much around."

"You don't have to tell me," I said. "I was just there." I remembered the baking, dry heat, the relentless sun.

"Fred must have had someone pick them up, or pick him up. Really, they have nothing to go on. At least, that they're telling me," he added.

"How could this happen?" I said. "Miller had his gun. Fred was unarmed."

Belliveau shrugged. "Could be a number of things, Danny. He did get his own lawyer's gun off him when he was being let out on bail."

"Have they checked with Fred's lawyer, Chandler York? He might know something. Those two used to be friends. Well, until Fred hijacked his car, I suppose," I added.

"Yeah, and I guess the man is a nervous wreck. He seems to think Lindquist is having some sort of psychotic break, on some sort of spree."

I couldn't really imagine Chandler York as a nervous wreck. But then I thought of the time I met him, and how he attacked the Grey Goose. Elegant veneer, but who knew, maybe he had a touch of the nervous Nellie. But then again, who could blame him.

So Dave's identity was now in even more question, as he worked for Fred, and no one knew who he was, or his last name. But I remembered Dave with Gene, and at the hospital, and I trusted that he wouldn't be found unless he wanted to be.

And once every couple of hours, I prayed he was out there looking for Jeanette and Luke.

Darren sent his lawyer friend to see me in the hospital before they released me on a Promise to Appear in court on a date late in January, with conditions not to hang out with criminals, or be around any guns, and to check in regularly with the officer who was doing the undertaking. In this case, Detective Belliveau.

The lawyer said it was perfectly fair, and she was only surprised I didn't have any conditions against travelling. I thought that might be Paul's doing. I had a feeling he knew I was going to have to be allowed to travel, because one way or another I was going to do it anyway.

Later that day, Darren took Matty home, and I made a solemn promise to both of them that I would see them in a couple of days. I was getting released later, my legal paperwork was sorted out, and I had put in a call to D-Man and placed an advance order, making sure he was in stock.

I was going to have my day. My one day, with my drug. For the first time since the horror began – other than a couple of hits in the en-suite at Ginger's and the horrible night with Dom – I would be left alone with my drug, and my grief.

Then, I would spend a few days with Darren and Matty, and firm up my plans. I was pretty sure I knew where I was going to look for Jeanette.

I tried not to think. I was waiting for the doc to come and discharge me – and if I knew my brothers, they were trying to make that process as long as possible. I occupied the next couple of hours in taking as long a shower as I could in my little bathroom, and trying to borrow some makeup from a nurse. I wanted to occupy myself in mindless physical gestures. Washing my hair. Endeavoring to borrow a hairdryer, and makeup. Seeing what I could do about getting clean clothes, since my own blood-covered garments had been taken into evidence, and I was getting pretty tired of the gray sweats I'd been wearing.

In a different pair of sweatpants and a t-shirt from a bin the hospital had on hand for the homeless, I sat on my hospital bed. I was antsy. I was going to start smoking crack in a few hours. I wasn't going to sleep on my bed, I would be throwing the bed away that Gene had been nearly killed on. But I would be in my apartment, smoking crack. I couldn't sit still. Finally, I picked up the phone and called Toronto General.

"Eugene Gold, please," I said. "He was in ICU."

"Hold please," a voice said. There were no public health messages this time. Everybody had gotten the hint about the hand washing.

"Danny?" Gene was saying, and I breathed again.

"Gene," I said. I exhaled. "Oh, God. How are you?"

"In pieces," he said. He grunted a little, like he was looking down at himself. "They took my spleen, did you hear?" His voice sounded wheezy. "Gene's got no spleen."

"Yeah," I said. "I was there that night," I said.

"You were?" he said. I told him about arriving back from California, and finding him in my apartment. For the time being, I left out the rest.

"How did it happen, Gene?" I didn't have to ask him who.

He was opening the door, he said, to go downstairs and meet D-Man's backup driver outside and pick up some supplies. When he opened the apartment door, some girl was standing there. Somebody he didn't know.

"I was about to say something to the girl," Gene said. "You know – like, are you looking for Danny, 'cause she's away... whatever. But before I could speak, she tased me." Gene took a deep, rasping breath. It sounded like it hurt. I winced.

"I don't remember anything for a little while, after hitting my head against that table in your hallway," Gene said. "They knocked the wind out of me."

"Probably knocked you out," I said. Poor Gene. Oh God. Crack. I needed my crack.

"Then, next thing I knew, I was tied to your bed," Gene was saying. "I think... I think my nose was broken," he said. He sounded like he was trying not to cry.

No, I thought. No. I will not feel anything. I can't feel anything, anymore.

"There were two of them," Gene said. "Two women. It's embarrassing. Two girls, right? I mean you know I'm a feminist male and all that, but no guy wants to admit he got nearly killed by a couple of girls. One of them – she looked like you. Sort of."

"So I keep being told," I said.

"And the other one was short, really short."

"She's dead," I said shortly. "Her name was Lola." I paused. "Those two have killed people. Ginger. And Jack."

"Jack?"

"Gene, it's complicated," I said. "I'll fill you in on everything, I promise. But first I have to go find Luke."

"Well I hope you don't run into the guy," Gene said.

"What guy?" My heart started beating faster.

"The one who came in at the very end, when they were leaving," Gene said. "He seemed in a rush, or like he was late or something. I don't know. I was in and out by then." I wasn't breathing. I tried to breathe.

"What did he look like, Gene?" I repeated. I tried to avoid knocking over the chair.

I could hear him try to shrug. "Forties? Blackish hair. Tan coat. Smoker. Weathered-looking." He paused. "Sort of like Gabriel Byrne."

Miller. It had to be.

I shut my eyes. "How do you know he was a smoker?" I asked.

"Uh... because he was smoking?" Gene answered, like I was stupid. He paused. "Oh, and just before he left, he burned me with his cigarette. Seemed to think that was hilarious." Gene was crying now.

Oh my God. Oh my God.

I stifled my gag reflex. "Gene," I said. "I have to get off the phone. I want you to sit tight."

"Um. Danny? I can't move. I'm in here for a coupla weeks, anyway."

"Right. Well. I'll call you as soon as I can."

"Danny," Gene said. He breathed in, and it sounded like it took some effort. "I'm sorry." He was crying. "For everything. You know."

"No, Gene," I said. "I'm sorry."

"I love you," he said. We didn't say that to one another.

"You too, Gene," I said. I did.

As soon as I hung up the phone, I fished Detective Belliveau's card out from my wallet, willing my fingers not to shake. I phoned the home number that he'd written in pen on the back. A woman answered.

"Hello," I said. "May I speak to Detective Belliveau, please."

"He's unavailable," the woman said.

"I'm sorry, Mrs. Belliveau," I said. "It's an emergency."

"Aren't they all," she said, but she put the phone down, and I could hear her yelling "Paul." I could hear movement in the background, and heavy footsteps coming down the stairs.

"Belliveau," he said.

"Detective," I said. "Danny Cleary."

"How are you, Danny?" Belliveau said. He sounded like he was sitting down.

"Paul. You need to get here, now."

"What—" he started to say, but I cut him off.

"Detective Harry Miller killed my sister. Or was in on it. And the attack against my friend Eugene Gold. He's here. I'm sure he's here. If Jack was here, and Jeanette and the boys, he's either here or on his way."

I could hear Belliveau chewing on that one. "Get people over to my brother's place, will you? He's got Matty there."

"There's already a protective detail outside your brother's address," Belliveau said.

"Do they know not to answer to detectives from another jurisdiction?" I asked. Belliveau paused.

"I'll be there in half an hour," he said. "Danny. Go into the bathroom in your hospital room, and lock the door."

"Bring me a weapon?" I asked.

"Danny, go into the bathroom, lock the door, and stay away from the door," he repeated.

"We need someone trustworthy protecting Eugene Gold, as well, at Toronto General," I said.

"Okay, okay," he said. "Who do you think I am?"

"You're Superman," I answered, and hung up.

26

I was dialling Darren's number when Detective Harry Miller sauntered into my hospital room.

"Wow," I said. "Hi." I tried to look normal. I tried to look glad to see him. I thought maybe my voice was too loud. I tried not to glance out the two inches of open door to see if the cop was still standing there.

Miller looked changed from days ago, like something the cat dragged in, to quote a favorite expression of my late mother's. His hair was greasy and yet managed to stand straight on end, and his eyes were dry and red.

Ah, I thought. Drugs. Miller is just another fucking junkie.

Of course. Of fucking course. Like to like, and all that.

Miller crossed the room and kissed me gently on the mouth. I responded briefly, or pretended to. This man had tortured Gene, a person I loved, despite everything. He could have killed him.

The fact that I had had sex with him made me want to retch. More, it made me want to bury my fist in his bleary-eyed face.

"Lovely," Miller said. "You're a sight for sore eyes." He looked around my room, as though it held Da Vinci's Code. He paced. Crystal meth, I guessed. Up for days, red eyes, but not sniffing quite as much as a cokehead. More functional than a crack user. Definitely crystal, I decided. Also prone to the violent outbursts. I smiled.

"Lola," I said. "My husband Jack. I guess you heard."

Miller looked around for a few more seconds, before parking himself comfortably into an uncomfortable chair. "Yes," he said. "I have."

"She was in cahoots with Jeanette," I continued. I was doing my level best not to look anywhere but his eyes, but to catch everything else peripherally. Where he might be carrying his weapons. How many paces to the bathroom door versus how many paces to the door to the room itself. Would the cop in the hallway have talked to Belliveau yet?

"Mm," Miller said, as though bored.

"How's Detective French?" I asked. "Should I send her flowers?" I tried to smile, tried for a little flirting. My face, I knew, probably resembled a death mask.

Miller looked at his fingernails for a long time without answering, during which time I wished I had something I could throw into his forehead to kill him dead on the spot.

Miller looked up at me and smiled. He knew I knew. I took a deep breath.

"So, Harry," I said. "How long have you been a junkie?"

"Longer than you," he said.

"Oh, no doubt," I said brightly. "Takes a while to get to your level of depravity." I looked carefully at his hands, waiting for him to make a move. I took a deep breath. "Please," I said. "Tell me you didn't have anything to do with Ginger. Please." It was a small chuckle that did it. A small laugh that spoke of things that he'd seen, and done, and didn't have enough conscience left to feel sorry for.

For the second time in twelve hours, I was in a room with someone who had helped kill my sister.

Miller saw my eyes change at the same time I saw him move his hands. He had the advantage of crystal methamphetamines jumping up his nervous system. But I had pure bloodlust, and rage.

Before he could get the gun out of his waistband, I was off the bed. I jump-kicked him in the head, just missing his nose, then pivoted and kicked the side of his head, hard, with my left foot. I stumbled, then. I was out of practice, weak. Miller's head jerked hard and he grunted, loudly. For half a second I thought I'd broken his neck, but no such luck. He was up and out of his chair faster than I would have thought possible, but then again, I was out of fighting shape. And I was barefoot. I threw a neat punch, but he deftly ducked, and when he stood, a shiny silver gun was pointed at my head.

"Why us?" I said. I was talking to Miller, but I addressed the gun. I kind of hoped the gun wouldn't answer me, though.

"That Jeanette," he said. "She's a spitfire."

"Did you grow up at The Orchard?" I was trying for conversational, which is extremely difficult to do when you have a gun pointed at your head.

"For a while," he said. "Long enough." He shrugged. "However, Daddy Michael didn't much like my habits." I remembered what Jack had said about Michael's opinion of addicts.

"So why, then?" I was still staring at the gun. "Why us, if you're not in The Family?"

"Don't you get it, Danny?" Miller said, shaking the gun at

me ruefully. "Jeanette and Lola, they're my sisters. Well, my foster sisters. We're just like the Clearys. Family loyalty, and all that." He looked at me. "Oh yeah – and money. That too."

Crazy. He was crazy. Maybe crazier than Jeanette.

"When this is all over," Miller answered, "we will have, through you, Jack MacRae's money. Which is a lot, by the way. Not sure you knew that. Plus the cash from Fred, but that's penny ante stuff comparatively. Besides, those stupid bitches spent a lot of that."

"And now you don't have to share the rest of it with Lola," I said. "Just Jeanette." I wanted to find out how many people were involved.

"Well, Lola's out of the share, at least," he said, grinning. "Thanks for taking care of that for me."

The gun was shiny. I was waiting for it to go off in my face. Time was moving very slowly.

Miller was good at reading people. I closed my eyes so he couldn't see my thoughts. For just a minute, it felt like he was superhuman. That they all were.

But if he needed me to get Jack's money, he couldn't kill me right now. If he did, my siblings would get whatever I had. I knew Jack would have left me everything; he didn't have anyone else, and I just knew. With me dead, though, things would be much more complicated.

"You're going to turn around now, and I'm going to handcuff you," he said. "And then we're going to go and meet up with Jeanette and little Luke. Now that Jack's gone, Luke's kind of unnecessary, wouldn't you say?"

"If you want anything from me, Luke will be safely reunited with his brother. If that happens, I'll do whatever the fuck you want."

"You will anyway, darlin'," he said. He sounded like Gene for half a second and I knew I would kill him. As soon as I could, I would kill him with my bare hands. He wouldn't get the clean death of a gunshot.

"There's a cop out there," I said.

"He's on break," Miller said. His face twitched out a smile. I couldn't believe that I had found him attractive. That I had trusted him. That I had – well, I wouldn't think about that.

"I'm barefoot," I said. When Miller looked down at my feet, I took my chance. Springing forward, I knocked his right arm, the one pointing the gun. It went off, and I felt a searing pain across my bicep, like a lick of intense fire. I dove to the floor, and tackled Miller. He wasn't expecting it, and he went down. But he held onto the gun, and with my good right arm, I tried to keep his on the floor. I was sweating, and I thought I might be sick.

Not now, I thought. Breathe, I thought.

Miller struggled to get to his feet, while I used every ounce of my body weight to keep his right arm down. He landed a good punch on the side of my head with his left. It was just above my right ear.

The door flew open, and the young Toronto police officer who was supposed to have been guarding my room stood there, his weapon in hand. It must have been a pretty scene: me, bleeding all over the place, doing my best to pin down a cop who was trying to beat me off him.

"He's dirty," I yelled at the cop. "Belliveau is on his way. Help me restrain him. I'm shot."

The cop probably wouldn't have believed me, would have

hauled me off Miller, had Miller not chosen that moment to squeeze a round out, which missed the officer's feet by a couple of inches. Cops tend to not like to be shot at. They're funny that way. He pointed his weapon at Miller, and took two quick paces forward, kicking the gun out of Miller's hand.

"Get to your feet," the cop said to me. His gun was pointing at Miller's head. With the help of a jolt of adrenaline, I managed to jump back up onto my feet. I didn't like having the young cop's gun pointed anywhere in my general direction. He might try for Miller, and miss. I didn't imagine they put experienced cops on guard duty in a hospital.

The cop spoke into a radio on his shoulder. I didn't hear what he said, because I was occupied with trying not to faint. Miller lay still on the floor. He probably didn't want to be shot either. He was breathing hard, and staring at the ceiling.

"My name is Detective Harry Miller, of the Newport Beach Police Department, in California," he said to the cop, trying to sound calm and commanding. "I came here to question Danielle Cleary for three unsolved murders in the Orange County area. She went for my weapon."

The cop looked uncertain. I would have, too, were I in his shoes.

"Neither of you move," he said. Two nurses came to the door and stuck their heads in, but the cop waved them away.

"This man may be a cop, but he has killed several people, including my sister, and was involved in kidnapping my nephews," I said. "He's also a junkie. Have him tested."

"My badge is in my pocket," Miller said to the cop. "I'm going to get it."

"Don't move," the cop said, but Miller's hand was creeping inexorably towards his jacket.

"No!" I yelled. But it was too late. Before I could see it happening, Miller had pulled another small gun from his inside jacket pocket. I dove under the bed. Three shots rang out, and it sounded like they came from two different guns. I couldn't tell, however, because I had my arms over my head, under the bed. I got my own blood in my eyes. Something hit the floor.

The young cop was lying on the floor, his head inches from mine. Blood was streaming from a small hole in his forehead. His eyes were open and staring into mine. I watched the light go out of them.

"Shit, shit, shit," Miller was saying. I could hear him scrambling to his feet. "I didn't want to do that. That was your fault, Danny," he said. He stood beside the bed. I could see his lower legs when I turned my head. "Get up, Danny. You're going to help me."

Miller didn't give me a chance to respond. He pulled me out from under the bed by my right leg and arm. He was stronger than he looked. Crystal meth, it's a hell of a drug. And I was losing strength by the minute, with the blood that was seeping down my arm.

"We're going to walk out of here," Miller said. He put me in front of him, and put the gun to my head. He was a few inches taller than I was, just enough for his eyes to clear the top of my head. "You are not going to try anything stupid, like trying to fight me or kick me, because if you do, I will shoot you in the head. And eventually I will get the money from your heirs. You know what that means. Messy, right? And then I will proceed to shoot whomever is in the hallway, who gets in my way."

I moved my head in the direction of a nod. The barrel of his gun was pressing into my temple. I didn't want to move much.

"Okay, then!" Miller said, like we were embarking on a great adventure.

We walked into the hallway, Miller's left arm wrapped very tightly around my body, holding me to him, and the right held the gun to my head. Two cops were running down the hallway towards us. Both had their weapons out of their holsters. A hospital orderly was pressed up against the wall, and a patient on a gurney looked wide-eyed.

"Drop your weapons," Miller yelled at the cops. "I will shoot this woman." The cops looked at each other, and didn't drop their guns. They were both trained on him. I hoped nobody was going to try to be a hero, 'cause I wasn't that keen on being shot again.

We proceeded down the hall fairly quickly, Miller keeping his back against the wall with me pressed tight into him. I couldn't move my head, but my eyes were moving wildly, looking for an exit. As much as I didn't relish leaving the hospital as Miller's hostage, I thought my chances were better if we were outside where he might not be so on edge.

We were on the ground floor. Miller backed against an emergency door and pushed through it, still holding me to him. An alarm wailed.

We were outside, and the ground was cold on my bare feet. The cops were behind us in the doorway, ordering Miller to drop his weapon. Unsurprisingly, he chose to ignore them. He moved quickly backwards, and I stumbled. He pulled me tighter into him again.

"We are going to get into that Lexus there," Miller said to

me. "You are going to drive." He opened the passenger side door and shoved me into the car, pushing me over the console until I was in the driver's seat. Miller stuck the keys in the ignition and crouched down, his gun still pointing at my head.

"Drive," he said. I started the ignition, and automatically looked behind me to back out of the spot. I was operating on some fear-based autopilot. All I knew how to do was what Miller said. The pain from my arm was making my brain scream.

I glanced again in the rear view and slammed on the brakes. Detective Paul Belliveau was standing ten feet behind the car, a gun trained on us. He wasn't in uniform. I had never been so happy to see anyone in my life. Even D-Man. Miller screamed at me to keep going and hit my right knee sharply with the gun to get me to release the brake. Belliveau was sprinting, quickly for such a big man, to get out of the way of the vehicle, which was reversing down an incline and picking up speed. Without thinking, I opened the driver's side door, car still in gear, and fell to the ground.

I heard yelling, and shots, but then there was nothing. I passed out, my bad left arm under my body as everything went black.

27

I woke up back in a hospital room. Again.

"They held my room for me," I said. I felt no pain. I gazed to my right and saw that I was hooked up to IV, so some nice opiates were flowing into my bloodstream.

Detective Belliveau was sitting at the end of the bed, looking ten years older than he had the night before. Darren was there too, with a face like thunder.

"Is Miller dead?" I wanted to know. My throat was scratchy, and my arm was bandaged and in a sling. But I was floating on a wispy morphine cloud.

No one answered for a minute, but their faces told me everything I needed to know.

"Fuck," I said, feeling like I was speaking in a dream. "Fuck." How did he get away?

"Fred?"

Belliveau shook his head. He explained that Miller had shot wildly and jumped from the car at the same time I did, and shooting from both guns like something out of a Tarantino movie, managed to get away. Belliveau had thought helping me, lying unconscious on the ground, was more important. It was his instinct, he said.

"It was a bad one," I said. "I don't matter in this, Paul. Don't you get that?"

Paul never took his eyes from my face, but he patted my foot and shook his head. He reminded me of my dad, in that movement. I closed my eyes. No more. No more loss. Morphine. Concentrate on the morphine.

They had found Miller's blood-stained jacket a quarter of a mile from the hospital, he told me.

"So he's wounded, and we don't know how badly," he said. I nodded. Good.

"Pack my bags, Darren. I'm going to Maine. He's gone to Maine. They're all in Maine. Luke is there," I said a little more loudly. Darren and Belliveau looked at me. "King of the Road," I said. I knew I sounded crazy with the opiates, and it made me more impatient. "Destination: Bangor, Maine. The Orchard, Darren. God, how are you not getting this?"

They were both looking at me strangely, and they both looked exhausted. "We are going to keep a protective detail on your family, and Matthew," Belliveau was saying. He rubbed his hand over his face.

Matthew.

"How is he?" I said to Darren. "You should be with him, not here."

"He's in the cafeteria surrounded by about twenty nurses and cops," he said drily. "His mother is dead, he's been drugged, and he watched his precious Uncle Jack die violently. Oh, and his twin brother is still missing. Other than that? Just peachy."

"The house is fully guarded, 24/7," Belliveau added.

"Skipper and Marie are coming to help us take care of them

316

for now," Darren said. I thought he might be saying something else, but I decided to succumb to the drugs, and enter oblivion.

28

Darren had it all arranged.

While Skipper, Marie and a veritable army of security stayed at his house with Matthew, Darren had talked our other brother, Laurence, into going to stay at Ginger and Fred's house in California. It had been decided that there had to be a Cleary presence at the house there, on the off-chance that Jeanette showed up there with Luke. I pictured Laurence pacing, telling bad jokes and getting in Marta's way, and felt comforted. If Luke wound up there, he would be so safe and loved.

Skip and Marie lived in the old Cleary house in Downs Mills, Maine, which they had nearly gutted and renovated. I hadn't been there in three years, but as Darren said, it would be a good home base for the purpose of our trip: bring home our nephew, and kill Jeanette Vasquez.

"I wonder," I said to Darren on the plane. I stretched my legs, which I could almost do. We were flying first class, which was a nice treat, even if it wasn't a private plane. "I wonder how many of them there are." It was the thought that had been going around and around in my head incessantly.

"We're not even sure she's here, Bean," Darren said. "We're

making this trip on Jack's paranoid delusion about a conspiracy with his foster family." Somehow, Darren refused to believe this was as big as I thought it might be. Yes, Jeanette and Lola and Miller may have been Jack's foster siblings, and they had found out who he was, and that he was rich now. They were bad people. But the rest of it? He had a hard time with it.

"Darren, trust me. I just know this." I'd told him about my dream about Ginger, about "King of the Road," and Bangor, Maine. He had an easier time believing in some telepathic twin bond with Ginger than he did in Jack's stories of his childhood. "Still, she must have somebody else here. Michael, maybe? The father, though I hate to use that word? If he's still alive, that is."

I knew I was flying closer to Jeanette and Luke. I knew that like I knew my own name. I trusted Jack, and I trusted Ginger. I closed my eyes.

I felt like once this was over I could sleep for a year or two. Maybe after calling D-Man and getting a nice big unlimited supply of crack. My trusty Altoids tin with my stash was gone, taken or lost at some point in the last day or two. Physically, I had to admit I did feel stronger without it. Perhaps this was a temporary cure for addiction, I thought: hunt down and kill a few sociopaths who seemed to be intent on murdering all the people I loved. Rage and homicide in place of escape and self-destruction.

Still. I knew that after this was over, I would be reunited with crack, one way or another. It was my reward, and for however long I decided to live, my life partner.

I grabbed Darren's hand.

"If anything happens to you," I started to say, but Darren stopped me.

"Bean. Right back at you." He was staring straight ahead. I knew that this had to be all hitting him at least as hard as it had me, but we hadn't had much time to talk. I wanted to get this over with, so Darren and I could spend some time with the twins. "When this is over, Bean?"

"Yeah," I said.

"You're going to rehab."

"Darren," I started, but he stopped me.

"No, Danny. I don't want to hear it. I know you've been clean for a few days now. And I know that just as soon as we finish this, you're going right back to it. And if you think I'm going to let that happen…" He squeezed my hand. "Danny, I lost Ginger. I am not going to lose you too."

I squeezed his hand back, but I didn't say anything. Darren released my hand and burrowed into himself, and slept.

Bangor International Airport is no LAX, and for that I was grateful. It was just daybreak in Maine, and when we landed the sky looked both gray and clean.

"Home," Darren said. He had slept fitfully throughout the flight, while my eyes were now dry and red from long hours awake.

We made our way to the nearest rental counter to get a car, but the customer service rep said he was sorry but they were all sold out.

His nametag told us that he was called Blake G. I wanted to know what the G stood for, but I held back, for once. "Sorry, Mr. Cleary," he said. He made a sad face. "It's December," he said, "and we don't have a big fleet here, as I'm sure you can imagine.

People like to come east for Christmas month. We don't have the Escalade you requested."

"No worries, Blake," Darren said. "What do you have free for us?"

Blake rented us a chrome-green PT Cruiser.

"Very inconspicuous," I said, once we'd thrown our meagre luggage into the hatch. "Good for staying under the radar."

"Something tells me that whoever wants to know where we are will find us anyway, Beanpole," Darren said. "Damn, this thing is awkward to drive." Darren was a low-slung sports car kind of guy, morally and aesthetically opposed to SUVs and other high-riding vehicles. But it was winter in Maine.

A soft snow had started to fall, and the landscape couldn't have looked more different than Southern California if we had beamed ourselves to Mars. I rolled down the windows manually – Blake hadn't rented us a bells-and-whistles model – and took a deep breath of air.

"Wow," I said. "Smell that?"

"What, Bean," Darren said.

"Smells like childhood," I said.

Darren was silent, trying, I presumed, to get used to the new vehicle.

"What exactly are we doing here?" he said, once we were on the highway, heading north. The sun had come out, hard and clear.

"We're going to find Luke and you're going to take him back to Toronto with you. And then I'm going to end this," I answered lightly. "We're going to Skip and Marie's. Home base."

"We are," Darren corrected. "Going to end this."

"Darren," I said, but he interrupted me.

"Why in the name of fuck do you think I'm here, Danny?" he said, and I watched his knuckles turn white on the steering wheel. "Tell me that."

"To get revenge," I answered.

"Right," he said. "But where would I rather be?"

"With your nephew," I said.

"You are correct, sir," Darren answered. "But we made a pact. Remember? I'm in this as deep as you are," he said. He glanced over at me, and I instinctively watched the road for him.

"Somebody needs to take care of Luke and get him to safety. And," I said, to cut off any further arguments, "we need a gun." I was looking in the passenger side mirror. I kept expecting to see someone following us. I hoped that if someone was, it would be Dave. I had a feeling that we were going to need help.

"Correction," Darren said, smoking furiously. "We need several."

After Mom and Dad were killed and the old house was empty, Skip and Marie had offered to buy out the rest of the sibs, but none of us really wanted the few grand any sale of the old house would have given. We all liked the idea of Skip in the place, and knowing he was there made us all feel, I think, like we still had a home to go back to.

Best of all, for Darren and me just now, we knew where the key was hidden, and better yet, where Skip kept the weapons.

Dad had always had plenty of guns, for hunting and target practice, and Skip had kept up the tradition. He didn't have the heart for hunting, didn't have the taste for it, and even less for cleaning and eating the gamey meat. But he liked tradition, and the contents of Dad's gun locker in the basement would still be cleaned and oiled regularly.

"I feel funny about this," I said, as we turned off the paved secondary road and onto the rutted dirt road that led to the old homestead.

"I know," Darren replied. "This thing has terrible suspension." The car was bouncing a lot, but he exaggerated it, bobbing up and down in his seat and making his voice sound all wobbly.

"No, I mean about going to the old house," I said, and saw that Darren had been kidding. "Sorry. I'm a little tense."

"I know, Bean. Me too." We were a few miles away, and the morning had turned sunny and bright. I rolled my window down and stuck my head out, like a dog being taken for a drive. It helped.

"I keep thinking about Dave," I said, after settling back into the vehicle and rolling up the window. We weren't in Orange County anymore.

"Oh, do you now," Darren said. "Oh, *really*."

"Shut up," I said. "You know what I mean. I haven't seen him since I left him at my apartment that day." The day I had gone to meet Jack for lunch. The day we had been in bed together again and I could almost feel what it would be like to be whole again.

The day Jack died.

We were both silent for a minute. I wouldn't think about Jack yet. I couldn't. When the time came – when I had gotten Luke to safety, when I had killed Jeanette and any other of this twisted "family" who might be involved, I would bury Jack my own way. Jack and Ginger. The two biggest loves of my life.

I didn't know how much Dave knew about where things stood now – that Matt was safe, that Jeanette had Luke – or how he knew anything at all. Though I supposed he could be talking to Chandler York, Fred's lawyer. I sincerely hoped so. I made a mental note to call Chandler's office from Skip and Marie's and find out myself if he knew anything at all about Dave or his whereabouts.

We drove another ten minutes in silence, and then we were turning into the old driveway.

"Wow," Darren said. "Place looks the same, huh."

It did, and it didn't. I climbed out of the car and was hit with the old familiar smell of fresh wood, from the mill two miles away. Something about the quality of the light – so different from anyplace else I had been, and so evocative of childhood – made my eyes water.

But the house had recently been painted a nice deep green, and Marie had done a lot of landscaping. Not to my taste, but if you liked fake wooden wells painted bright red and a walkway lined with big rocks painted white, then it was the place for you.

Darren was yards ahead of me, lifting the third rock on the right from the door, and grabbing the front door key from underneath.

"Everybody in Downs Mills knows where that key is," I said. "I don't know why they bother locking it." I hugged myself. It was cold, and the snow had started again.

"They didn't," Darren said, trying the front door. It was unlocked.

My heart started beating faster. I had been kidding about the key – Skip was, for such a resolutely small-town man, pretty security conscious. Only the day before, he had told me that he was thinking about putting a security system into the old place because he was worried about Marie out there on her own when he was in Bangor at the car lot.

Skipper would never have left the door unlocked.

Darren had his hand up, indicating that I should stay where I was, while he checked it out.

"Fuck that," I said, marching toward him. As I did, I heard something, a high-pitched reverberating noise, and a muffled pop, and Darren stopped ahead of me. In what seemed like slow motion, he fell backwards, and I could see the hunter's arrow stuck in his chest, burrowed past his jacket, into a point almost directly in the middle of his torso.

I think I screamed. I know I looked up.

Detective Harry Miller stood a few feet back from the doorway of Skipper's house, *my* house, and in the time I had run to Darren, he had restrung his bow. He was pointing it at me.

In the surreal way that the brain functions in extreme fear and panic, I noticed that he had shaved and had a haircut.

And then I ran, straight at him.

He fired.

29

Miller wasn't as good as he thought he was.

I threw myself over Darren, bounding over him like I was running hurdles, then broke into a somersault, keeping myself as low to the ground as I could while I ran. I had only about thirty feet to cover, but Miller had a crossbow, and it was already strung.

I felt a burning pain in the side of my head, and then I couldn't hear much of anything at all on my right side, but before he could string another arrow, I jumped up the stairs and dived into his legs. Miller saw it coming, knew that's what I'd planned to do, and I could tell that he had tried to ground his legs firmly to give him purchase, but his balance was compromised by trying to restring his weapon. He went down, but not before he managed to kick the side of my head. The bad side. The side that had blood running from it.

I held onto him with everything I had. I held his legs as closely together as I could, and realized that when he fell, Miller had hit his head on the hall table. He wasn't out, but he was stunned. He was moaning. His shirt had pulled away from his shoulder, and I could see a large bandage there. This is where he had been shot. Good.

Outside, Darren wasn't making a sound, which was a very

bad sign. I had to finish this, and get back to him.

The bow had skittered a few feet away from Miller, and he was lying on a leather quiver of arrows that was strapped to his back. But one solitary arrow, the one that he had planned to kill me with, was on the floor, just beyond his head.

I leapt for it, but it meant letting Miller go for a second. His eyes were open, and I could see a bit of blood on the floor. He had cut his head on the table. Head wounds bleed like crazy, but I knew it probably wasn't serious.

Miller grabbed my legs, but I had the arrow.

In one movement, he surprised me by flipping me over onto my back, from my face plant on the floor.

Blood was trickling down his face and onto mine as he wrapped his hands around my throat and squeezed.

I closed my eyes and found myself praying to God and to Ginger as I grabbed the arrow firmly in my hands and plunged it, as hard as I could with the decreasing oxygen to my brain, into his neck. I might not have been able to, had he been able to squeeze even a fraction harder, but the wound on his shoulder had weakened him.

Miller's hands immediately left my throat, and I turned over and coughed, bringing up some bright red blood. I hoped nothing was too injured there. I had to save Darren, and my adrenaline was too high to feel immediate pain.

But I had aimed well. The arrow had gone straight and deep into Miller's neck, but he remained on his knees, making a gurgling sound. His hands went to the arrow. He was trying to take it out. Quickly I grabbed another arrow from the quiver on the floor, but I watched as he fell over to one side, knocking one of Marie's Royal Doulton figurines from an end table onto the hardwood floor, smashing it.

Is she ever going to be mad, I thought, and almost started laughing.

I watched Miller's face. The blood was coming quickly now. With some difficulty, I pulled the arrow out myself, to hasten the process. Looked like I had hit his carotid artery; it was gushing. He was trying to cover his neck but with every bit of strength I had, I speared one hand down into the floor with the arrow. Then I grabbed another, raised it above my head and with a guttural cry and the last of my strength, I crucified his other hand to the floor. Miller looked at me and with the fear and pain, there was something else on his face. Something like pride, or respect. Or at least that's what I told myself.

For the second time in days, I was covered in the blood of a dying man.

I thought Miller almost tried to grin at me. He was aware enough to hear me. I squatted down and put my face a few inches from his. I heard myself saying, "Rot in hell," almost conversationally. Miller shook for what seemed like five minutes, but couldn't have been. Then he went still.

Done.

"Darren!" I yelled, and managed to get to my feet and run outside.

As I ran toward Darren, something from a poem popped into my head. Something about the woods being lovely and dark? I couldn't tell if it was from the silence of the snow and the dark woods surrounding us, or if the arrow that had cut my head and taken a chunk of my earlobe had done even more damage, but outside the world was a muffled, beautiful wonder. And in the middle of it lay my brother, his eyes open and glassy, his whole body shaking.

First aid courses don't tend to prepare you for hunting arrows, and besides, I hadn't taken a class in eight years. Jack had made sure I knew a lot about first aid, though. He said it was only responsible, the amount of fighting we did.

"Okay, Darren," I said, as calmly as I could, "okay. Hang in there. You're not as bad as that, I promise." His eyes were aware enough to follow me, which was a good sign, but the shaking meant that he was either in shock, or heading there. Or worse. I tried to remember what I knew about shock – whiskey? Warmth? I took off my jacket and did my best to cover his centre. At least, the part that didn't have an arrow sticking out of it.

I couldn't take the arrow out. That could kill him, and I didn't feel confident enough that it was the right thing to do. But I could tell by the position and angle of it that it probably hadn't pierced his heart. I was equally aware that it probably had hit his right lung.

"Take care, the boys," Darren said. His voice was a wheeze.

"Stop it," I said. "Take care of them yourself."

For a couple of long moments, I stayed crouched over my brother, holding his hand. As quickly as I had been able to act before, I was immobilized now. Should I try to drag him to the car? I might be able to do that, and kill him in the process. And if the dragging didn't do it, trying to hoist him into the car might. Getting him into the house posed the same problem, though it seemed like a better solution.

One thing was sure: if I left him to lay in the snow much longer, in shock, he would be dead. And soon.

The thought propelled me up. I was wasting precious seconds.

"Darren," I said. His eyes were closed now, and he wasn't shaking any more. But I could hear his laboured breathing. "D! I'm going to call for help. I'll be right back." Without thinking or pausing any further, I ran back to the house. If I had lost my way in those thirty feet, I could have followed the trail of blood I'd left in the light dusting of snow on my way out.

I didn't want to touch my ear. I didn't want to think about it. Adrenaline was keeping me going, and if I stopped, I might never go again.

Miller's body was where I had left it. I had half expected him not to be there, a figment of my imagination, or carried off by unseen forces. But he was sprawled there, obscenely crucified, pinned to the old oak floors, more blood quickly pooling under him. Skip and Marie would never get that out of the wood, I found myself thinking. And also, *I did that?* I had to run past his body to get to the phone in the kitchen, and it looked so big and cumbersome there. He wasn't too large a man, but he seemed to take up a lot of space, lying there.

I had killed him. Almost with my bare hands. As I had promised myself I would. The thought gave me a small burst of strength.

The phone was on the wall where it had always been, but instead of the old black rotary dial that had been there, there was now hanging a cordless phone. I grabbed it, and looked for the talk button, starting to shake myself. I screamed in frustration as I pushed the end button instead of talk, but then I got it right.

Dial tone was there. Thank God. I dialed 911, and put the phone to my left ear.

Nothing. No signal, no dial tone, no dialing. No efficient emergency operator asking me what I needed. Dead. Dead like Darren was going to be.

Then a feeling started creeping along my neck, and the hairs there stood up.

I felt like someone, or something, was whispering into my bad ear, whispering promises of pain and horror still to come. It felt like an evil breeze had blown past me.

I whipped around, but I was alone.

I tried the phone again, and it was dead. Definitely no dial tone this time.

In the couple of seconds between picking up the phone and dialing 911, it had died. Which meant, probably, that someone – or something? – had cut the line.

I looked at the basement door, six or seven feet from where I was standing. Downstairs was Dad's old gun locker. I took the stairs three at a time, twisting my ankle on the bottom stair and landing on my butt on the cold floor. The pain was unbelievable, making the stinging on the side of my face feel like a paper cut. But I didn't stop. I couldn't.

Someone else was in this house. I could now hear footsteps above me. And I was pretty sure it wasn't Miller, risen from the dead.

I half hopped, half ran to the old office at the back of the basement. Despite all the improvements to the rest of the house, down here it was the same dark, dank place it had always been.

Which was good. I knew what I was looking for.

The gun locker was in the back corner, and I fell to my knees in front of it.

There was a loose section of cement in the floor where Dad had always kept the key. He had always locked the cabinet, and I couldn't imagine that Skipper would do any differently. And if I was lucky – if Darren was lucky – he would keep the key in Dad's old hiding spot.

I could hear the footsteps in the kitchen now. Why were they so slow? Maybe whoever it was didn't realize I was down here. But I doubted it.

I found the key, and stood up with difficulty, nearly knocking the whole locker on top of myself as I grabbed it for balance.

The key still fit. I sobbed in relief, and opened the door, grabbing the first gun I could find, an old pistol Dad had first used with me for target practice when I was thirteen or fourteen. It would be unloaded, and I had to find the ammo.

Luckily, Skipper was as organized as our father had been. The ammunition was right where it was supposed to be, in the drawer at the bottom. I pulled out a box of cartridges, and started loading, my hands steady now.

Then Jeanette Vasquez stepped out of the darkness, an AK-47 pointed at me.

30

"You should really have killed me while you had the chance," she said, and my stomach turned over. "Drop the gun," she said. "Do it now, please, Danny." She looked uncomfortable and awkward in winter clothes. Something about her stance made me feel slightly hopeful.

My hand tightened around my gun, and with fingers that were now sweaty, I released the safety.

Off to my right, I could hear chuckling. It was an odd sound, made odder by the fact that I was hearing it only from my left. I seemed to have lost all hearing in my right ear.

"You are one tough nut," a familiar male voice said, descending the stairs. "Really. I am really impressed, Danny."

My knees nearly gave way.

"Fancy meeting you here," I said. I clutched the gun tighter. What the fuck.

I had thought it was nearly over. Save Darren, find Luke, get them both to safety, and I could go back to my life. Or even to rehab, 'cause I owed Darren at least that much, especially now.

But it wasn't over. It was far from over.

I controlled myself, with a greater force of will than I thought myself capable of.

"Hello, Chandler," I said. "Or should I call you Michael?" Chandler. Fred's friend. His lawyer. I flashed back to Fred, standing in the desert, mentioning that his lawyer had recommended Jeanette to Fred as a nanny. I didn't take my eyes off Jeanette's face, hoping she would take her attention off me for one second so I could shoot her. Then him. But no such luck. She didn't even break eye contact with me.

"I love Maine. It's home, as you may know. This is where I raised my children. California has its charms of course, but you know what they say – home is where the heart is."

"What do you want?" I said. I was in danger of losing it. Darren was outside in the snow. He was going to die, and I had a gun pointed at my head. Again.

"What do I want," Chandler said, pacing a bit. I was never going to be able to think of him as Michael, despite everything I knew. He still looked every inch the prosperous, elegant lawyer I had met in Orange County. "What I want, Danny, is for you to put that ridiculous gun on the floor, and I will save your brother's life." He was wearing a dark-gray wool coat and black driving gloves. His hair was slicked back, and he was wearing a white shirt and a dark tie. He looked wealthy. And dangerous.

"What do you mean," I said, still holding the gun.

"Just this," Chandler said. "If you put that gun on the floor in the next thirty seconds, I will call 911 from my cell phone and say that there was a hunting accident out here. Then all three of us will get out of this house and into my car, and we will head back to a little place I keep in the woods out here. Very cosy.

And we will have a talk. You're a wealthy woman now, you know. Or you will be very soon," he said. "Did you know that your husband – my son – left you everything in his will?" I paused for a couple of seconds of silence, keeping the gun in my hand. "Tick tock, Danny," Chandler said lightly. "Ten seconds."

I put the gun on the floor, and my hands in the air. "Call," I said. "Call now."

Chandler tossed me the phone. "You do it," he said.

I half expected to get no signal, but the four bars were all glowing. I dialed 911.

"Danny," Chandler said softly, coming closer to me, "if you say anything I don't like, Jeanette will shoot you, and then go outside and finish Darren off, and she and I will be pulling out of here in just over a minute. Sound good?"

Calmly, I gave the 911 operator directions to the house, and told her that there was a man in the snow with a hunter's arrow in his chest, and that he would die if they didn't get here in minutes. Then I flipped the phone shut as she asked my name and told me to stay on the line.

"Good girl," Chandler said. He motioned for me to toss the phone back to him, and I did.

He caught the phone deftly and stuck it in his pocket, first checking to make sure it was, in fact, 911 that I had called.

"What did you think," I said, watching him. "I would risk Darren's life?"

"No," he said. "You're remarkably loyal. I wish I had known you as a child. You would have made a great addition to our family. Wouldn't she, Jeanette?"

"Always room for one more," she said.

"Where's Luke?" I said. I swallowed. "Please."

"Safe as houses," Chandler-slash-Michael said. "Back at mine having a nap."

Having a nap. Drugged, probably.

"Anyway," he continued, "we'd better get the lead out. As it were," he laughed. "This weather is going to make driving difficult."

We went back up the basement stairs, Jeanette behind us and Chandler gallantly helping me up the stairs. I knew my ankle might have been broken, and I had definitely torn some ligaments. I wouldn't be able to walk properly for a couple of months.

If I lived that long.

Chandler's car was outside the back kitchen door, and I couldn't believe I hadn't noticed it through the window when I came bounding in to use the phone. Sure enough, it was a dark sedan, a Cadillac, shiny under a thin layer of snow.

"Nice car," I said, as Chandler held the door open for me. He followed.

"Have to buy American if you're going to spend any time around here," he replied. "They're all such *patriots*."

"Bastards," I said. Chandler smiled at me.

"You make me laugh, Danny," he said. The car pulled around the house, and I could see Darren lying in the snow.

"Is that why I'm still alive?" I asked. My eyes were stinging. There was simply no way I was going to let this man see me cry. "But no – it's because you think I have money, right? You're going to bleed me like you did Jack?"

"You're alive because you're more valuable alive." Chandler's voice was jovial, nauseating. I looked out the window. He looked carefully at me. "You must be in pain."

336

I ignored him, and continued looking out the window.

"Don't worry," he continued. "You won't be for much longer. That, I promise you."

Darren was probably dead. Ginger *was* dead. Jack was dead, and Gene was beaten beyond recognition and traumatized for life. The pain in my ankle was intensifying, blood was pouring down the side of my head, and I was starting to hear things from a distance.

Let me get Luke to safety, please. Then I would welcome death.

Then I heard the sound of a siren, and within a minute, an ambulance passed us going at breakneck speed, back towards the house. To Darren.

I took a deep breath.

"What are you going to do to me?" I asked.

"Not *to* you, dear," Chandler answered, patting my knee. "*For* you." We drove in silence for a minute. "We have a long drive ahead of us, Danny," Chandler said. "Why don't you try to sleep? You look like you could use it."

And to my surprise, I did.

I came awake with Ginger's voice whispering in my ear, telling me to breathe. "Breathe," she kept saying, over and over.

The car had stopped, and Chandler was looking at me curiously.

"What did you say?" he asked me. "What did you just say?"

I struggled to sit up and become fully conscious. My right cheek was pressed against the cold glass of the car window, but that side of my head felt like it was on fire.

"Nothing," I said.

"She sounded just like Ginger…" Jeanette started to say from the backseat, but Chandler stopped her.

"Never mind," he said. "We're here." He turned the car smoothly into a long wooded driveway. It was overgrown and beautiful. And remote. I shut my eyes and tried to block out the pain from my head and my ankle, and think. Darren would be okay. Darren would be okay. Darren would be okay because I wouldn't be able to survive if he wasn't. And Luke was inside this building, and he would be fine.

And if Darren wasn't okay, if Luke wasn't okay, and I got out of this place, I would hunt down and kill every last one of these people. The thought made me feel calmer, more centred. It wasn't exactly a concrete plan, but I had learned that anger and revenge are great ways to fight pain.

Chandler came around and opened my door. He held out his hand. "It's time to go in, Danny," he said. Jeanette had come around the side of the car, and between the two of them, they helped me out of the car. I did need the help, but I also wanted them to think I was completely unable to move unassisted.

I hoped I wasn't.

With a strength that disheartened me – there was no way I would be able to overpower this man in any way, even if I was twenty-five years younger than him – Chandler half carried me down the long driveway. The light told me that it was mid-afternoon, which meant that we had probably been driving for at least a couple of hours. My brain wasn't working well enough to figure out where we could be, but all I could see were more dark woods.

I thought we were probably still in Maine. This is where it had begun with Chandler and his twisted idea of family. And this is where it would end. And if I died in Maine, that would be okay too. It was also where I began, after all.

The house surprised me by being a lovely wooden cabin, large and sleekly modern. If you had asked me, I would have expected a castle. With a moat. Something more sinister.

This, the main floor, was probably a thousand square feet or so, all open concept without being out of place in the Maine woods. It was what most people's idea of a New England lodge should look like, a place where parties of rich men could come and hunt, and their wives could collect leaves in the woods and read novels on the porch.

Chandler gently helped me into a comfortable chair around the large wooden table. He said something I couldn't hear to Jeanette, and she put the gun down on the counter and disappeared for a bit, then set a cup of hot coffee down in front of me. I sipped the coffee, not caring if they had drugged it. It was hot, and it was good.

Jeanette was busying herself making a fire, and Chandler was looking in the fridge. He took out a big Tupperware container.

"Early dinner?" Chandler asked. "You really should eat something, Danny."

I shook my head, but a few minutes later he put a bowl of fragrant, steaming stew in front of me anyway. It looked and smelled better than anything I had ever consumed. He helped himself to a bowl. Jeanette picked up her gun again and sat at the end of the table glaring at me. Now that we were on her home turf, her psycho-friendliness had worn off.

Chandler dug into his food without talking, and after a minute, during which I told myself that not eating would be counterproductive, so did I. When I had finished the first bowl, Chandler got up and wordlessly filled it again. He sat back down, smiled at me, and continued eating. So did I. With my good ear, I listened for any signs of Luke.

Ignore the woman holding a Kalashnikov at the end of the table, and it would have made a nice, homey scene.

I finished my meal and looked around. Chandler chatted about the weather and the approaching storm. Jeanette continued to glare at me, but she looked tired. She hadn't had any food, or even coffee. Chandler got up and took a bottle of red wine from a small wine rack on the counter, and opened it. He put glasses in front of us, ignoring Jeanette, and poured. I half expected him to toast something, but he took a long swig, and fiddled with a cigarette before lighting it.

"Smoke, Danny?" Chandler asked me, and I nodded, and took a sip of wine. It seeped into my veins, and reacted nicely with the coffee and stew. I could feel myself relax, just the tiniest bit, and it scared me. Chandler lit two cigarettes, and handed me one. I took it. He smiled at me. I was only an occasional smoker, despite the crack use, but it sure seemed like a good time for one.

"See?" he said, smiling. "Not so bad, eh?" He seemed relaxed here, and less imposing.

"Can I see my nephew please?" I touched my ear and winced.

"Oh dear," Chandler said. "Let's get you fixed up, shall we?"

"Please," I said. "Luke. I'll do whatever you want, give you whatever you want. I just want to make sure he's okay."

"He's sleeping, my dear. You can see him in the morning."
The morning. As if I was going to live that long.

Chandler stood up and went into a room off the kitchen,
coming back with a first aid kit.

"Wow," he said, gently cleaning the blood off my head.
"Harry really did a number on you."

"Not as much as I did on him," I said, and Chandler smiled
at me, then laughed. Jeanette did not. She looked angry again.
"Why was he there, anyway? How did you know we'd go to the
old house?"

"We didn't, for sure," he said. "But Harry had spent a lot of
time with you," and here he winked at me, and I tried not to spit
in his face, "and he guessed you would. We'd just dropped him
off earlier today. He was going to set some sort of elaborate trap
for you if you went there. Some Boy Scout stuff which would
have undoubtedly failed. Plus, he wanted to look around, get
some more info on your family. You know, if you didn't agree
to our plan. Then we'd have to get involved with the rest of the
Clearys – what a palaver that would be!" I looked at him. Batshit
crazy. Utterly batshit. "When we went to pick him up… well,
we saw Darren lying in the snow out front, and found what you
had done." He looked at me. "That was quite artistic, if I may say,
Danny. The arrows? Nice touch." He looked impressed, almost
proud, and not at all upset about losing Miller.

I looked at Jeanette. I was glad I'd killed her foster brother.
Give her a chance to feel what it was to lose the people you loved.

"Jeanette, honey," Chandler was saying, "why don't you go
and have a nap. You must be exhausted." He looked at me. "I
don't think we'll need you for a while."

I expected her to protest, but she stood and laid the gun on her chair, and left the room.

I wondered what he would need her for in a while.

"It was ironic, running into you at the house there," I said. I was surprised by how normal I sounded. "I was just thinking, in the car, of calling your office in Newport and asking if you knew where Dave is. You know, the private detective."

"You would have missed me," he said. "And as for Dave – I have no idea. I'm sure he'll turn up eventually." He sounded distracted. He was carefully cleaning the wound, and I found myself gulping down the rest of my wine. The renewed pain had woken up all my senses, and I didn't want that. I didn't want that at all.

So much for finding out anything about Dave. Or who he belonged to.

"Danny," Chandler said, "the arrow tore your earlobe in half, but it's all here. I'm going to have to stitch it."

I nodded slightly. If they were going to kill me in the next couple of hours, they probably wouldn't bother stitching me up. And I doubted they were trying to kill me with lethal stitches to the earlobe.

He stood up.

"You know what, Danny? Why don't we hang on for a minute or so," he said, and I tensed again. He was going to say that there was no point wasting his time in patching me up. "I think you should have some painkillers. Don't you?"

I said nothing. This was it. He was going to drug me, and tie me up, and I would die like Ginger had. I gingerly leaned forward an inch or two and tested the strength of my ankle on the floor. If I was going to die, I was going to die on my terms. I was not going to let this motherfucker and what was left of his merry tribe do whatever they wanted to me. I glanced around, looking for something I could use as a weapon. Could I make it to Jeanette's chair and get the gun? I thought I could. I started breathing more shallowly, hoping for an adrenaline response. Jack had taught me that. It would help with the pain, make it easier for me to bear it and do what I needed to do.

Chandler grinned at me, shaking his head, and picked up the semi-automatic.

"You won't need this, Danny," he said. "And trust me, in very few minutes, you won't even want it. We're going to be best friends, you know. Like family, even."

"Family. That sounds obscene, coming from you," I said. "You killed my family."

"Oh, Danny, I'm sorry about all that. I didn't think that was necessary, not at all, but Jeanette and Harry? Well they did love to egg each other on. And as for Scott, or Jack as you knew him – well, that was his own fault, wasn't it? I mean, if he had just continued to play his part, everything would have been fine. None of this would have happened. Your sister would still be alive and a mother to her boys." Chandler walked around the table. "Besides, when you think about it, you've killed more of my family than we have yours." He took a swig of wine, and loosened his tie, which seemed so out of place here. "But one thing I always taught my children is that we're much stronger working together than we are on our own. Danny," he said, leaning over and patting my hand, "you can be with us. You have great skills. You have wealth now. Lola is gone, and Miller. Lola had lots of loyalty, it's true. Not terrifically bright, though. But

I'll need someone with your skill set. You aren't part of normal society anyway. You know you'll never fit in again with normal people. And you're smart. You'd be much more valuable working with us than you will simply as an…"

"Income stream," I finished for him. I smiled, though it made me feel sick.

"Exactly!" Chandler said. "Exactly." He rubbed his face. "I really hate being scruffy." I looked at him, trying to think. I touched my ear and winced a little more than was necessary.

"Oh, Danny, I am so sorry. I was going to get you something for the pain." He hopped down lightly from where he had perched on the counter, and went into the living room. I watched him, half expecting to feel the muzzle of the gun against the base of my skull at any minute. I still didn't know how many other people could be in this place. I hadn't heard anything, but then again my hearing was compromised.

He returned carrying a tray, and placed it in front of me. When I saw what was on it, I stopped breathing.

A lighter. A pipe. And a nice big rock of crack.

"For you," Chandler said quietly. "My gift to you. For all we've put you through." I looked at him. "Go on," he continued. "Don't worry. It's good. It's not laced with anything. This time." He winked at me, and poured some more wine.

"Enjoy," he said.

31

I wish I could say I hesitated, but I did not.

I wasn't used to regular pipes, but I managed. With shaking fingers, I broke off a decent-sized piece of the rock, and dropped it in, flicking some of my cigarette ash in first to keep it in place. The pipe was a work of art, looked like titanium, shiny and spotless. I took the lighter and tested it. It was new.

Then I held the pipe in my mouth, and lit it.

I could tell, inhaling the smoke, that it was the best crack I'd ever had. Ever would have, even if I lived to be a hundred, and did this every day for the rest of my life. I held the smoke in my lungs and put the pipe down, then exhaled.

Pain? Gone. Euphoria? Check, and double check.

I closed my eyes. Baby, I thought. I'm back. I am back. It was so exquisite that tears came to my eyes.

"You make that look so good, I'd almost be tempted to try it," Chandler said, and without thinking I held it out for him. He laughed.

"No, no, Danny," he said. "I'll pass for now. That's for you."

Everything was fuzzy and bright at the same time, and I almost forgave Chandler for the lying and deceit. He was working on my ear, and for a moment I felt immense gratitude to him. He had let me call the ambulance for Darren, after all, hadn't he? And I did believe that Luke was tucked into bed sleeping. He knew I'd kill him if that wasn't true. I started to turn my head toward him, but he held onto it.

"Don't move, Danny," he said. "I'm about to start the stitches."

"I never knew you could sew," I said. He laughed. He got up and refilled my wine glass, and I took a ladylike sip. I didn't need it anymore, but I thought it best to be polite.

"Thank you," I said calmly. I was trying not to sound as high as I was. I was trying to sound relaxed, calm, and in control.

I was relaxed. One out of three ain't bad.

Without moving my head – I wasn't so high that I had lost my fine motor control, not yet – I took the pipe and relit it, wanting a little more right away. It had been so long. I closed my eyes.

Danny, Ginger's voice said to me, from somewhere. *Danny, you have to stop. Danny. Stop.*

"Am I hurting you?" Chandler was saying. I exhaled, the rush taking me over. "You told me to stop."

I looked down at him, and for a minute he looked really concerned, like avoiding giving me pain was his top priority. "No," I said. "Sometimes I just say that, when I'm getting high. It's like a mantra, I think." My words were coming out slowly, but I thought they sounded okay.

"Okay," Chandler said. "I'm going to finish with your ear."

"Yup," I said, and closed my eyes. I could feel what he was doing, and was aware that there was pain involved, but it was like being frozen at the dentist. I needed to go to the dentist. The thought made me laugh out loud.

"I guess the stuff is good, huh," Chandler was saying. "You're not even flinching."

"It is," I said, gazing at the rock in front of me. It had to be somewhere between three and four eightballs, probably twelve or thirteen grams. Even I couldn't do all that on my own, in one sitting. Maybe he was trying to kill me by overdose. I didn't care. Somewhere in my brain I remembered Jack telling me how much this man hated addicts. But I believed that this batch wasn't tainted.

Danny, stop.

Chandler was finished patching up my ear, and I touched it. A large gauze pad was covering the right side of my head.

"You have medical training?" I asked. He was squatting at my feet now, removing my socks and Ginger's hiking boots. When had I put those on? Oh yeah. Before going to the airport. Back in California.

Years ago.

"A bit," Chandler said. "Army. Back in my misspent youth."

I nodded at him, encouraging him to go on. I couldn't talk yet. I was trying to think. I fingered the pipe, but didn't pick it up.

"This ankle is a mess," Chandler said. "It's very swollen." As he capably but gently pressed my foot and ankle to determine if anything was broken, I watched curiously. Everything else had receded: Ginger's death – and possibly Darren's – Jack, the rest of the family. Even the twins. Nothing mattered but this, this moment. I had to get my head together. I had the largest amount of the best-quality crack I had ever seen at one time sitting in front of me, and I was pretty sure that someone's life was going to depend on my not smoking it.

If Darren made it, he would have told the police, or someone, about what had happened. They would be looking for me. But how? Looking for me in the thousands and thousands of acres of snow-covered Maine wilderness.

If Darren had made it.

Danny. Stop.

I took my hand away from the pipe. Chandler was wrapping my ankle carefully. The gun was on the floor behind him, out of my reach. I couldn't trust my reflexes right now; that much I knew. But would I get another chance as good as this? I figured I would need at least another half an hour to clear my brain enough to be able to function, for my body to respond to my brain's commands and for my brain to figure out the best course of action.

I would get another chance. I would have to.

Footsteps behind me, two sets.

"I couldn't sleep," Jeanette said from behind me. "I thought we should have a real family reunion." I felt a prickle up the back of my neck and when I turned around I saw that she was leading someone into the kitchen. Someone who was blindfolded, shackled, handcuffed.

And had red hair.

"Fred," I said. I tried to think past the crack. "Fancy seeing you here."

Chandler shook his finger at me. "You are slick, Danny," he said. "Cool as a cucumber." I smiled at him, which at least I could manage, with all the crack. "Jeanette honey, let Fred have a seat at the table. And with all of us here, I really don't think he needs such elaborate restraints."

"Yeah," I said. "Fred should join the party." I found myself nodding my head happily, not sure if I really was that high, or I was playing it up to give myself time to think. "He looks thirsty."

"Oh indeed he does," Chandler said. "Jeanette, would you mind…?"

Jeanette looked as though she minded very much indeed, but in a minute Fred was sitting in a chair down the table with his hands free and the blindfold off. She cuffed him to the chair and in the manner of a teenager being told to clean her room, managed not to spill the glass half full of wine that she plonked on the table in front of Fred. She glanced at Chandler and poured herself a glass.

I had to think, I had to think, but it felt like it was too much. Darren was going to die, and Fred, and maybe Luke, if I didn't do this right.

"Stuff is strong," I said pleasantly to Chandler. "Nice."

I looked at Fred then, looked at his eyes and tried to convey a message of apology, and strength, and to give him a *trust me* vibe. Jeanette was watching me carefully, but Chandler had gotten up and was ladling out a bowl of stew for Fred.

Fred didn't look at me. He looked at the table in front of him. He didn't look like he was there at all. He hadn't touched his wine, or moved his hands from his lap after Jeanette had removed the handcuffs. I thought he was probably drugged. Not crack, there's no way he would smoke it, and he certainly didn't look high. He just looked… gone. Broken.

I looked around me as though studying the architecture and design elements of the room. Weapons. In any room, you can find something to use as a weapon to protect yourself. Five minutes ago, I would just have worried about killing Chandler and probably Jeanette and saving Luke. Now I had a catatonic Fred on my hands.

Miller wasn't taking Fred to prison, he was taking him to Maine. They'd probably gotten on a private plane five minutes after we did. Maybe with Lola in tow. A plane that had dropped Miller off in Toronto to help torture Gene.

Fred was here, sitting feet away from me, and he was completely devoid of any means to protect himself. He had never had any physical ability that I had seen, and whatever drug he had been given – or maybe he had just crawled somewhere deep into his head and decided to stay there – he looked docile and defenceless.

Which meant that I would have to be strong. One last time. Just to get Fred and Luke out of this. I had to do that for Ginger. Then, whatever happened to me, whatever I did, didn't matter.

"How long have you been hiding out in the wilderness, Fred?" I asked, as though we were meeting at a dinner party.

"Oh not long, not long," Chandler said. He gently placed the bowl of stew in front of Fred, and after a minute, grabbed a water glass from the cupboard and filled it from the tap. I watched as Fred reached out and grabbed the glass, took a small sip as though he didn't trust it. Then he poured it down his throat. I stared at his Adam's apple slowly bobbing as he swallowed, and tried to think.

Jeanette was reading a newspaper. I hadn't seen her grab it, and I felt like I had lost minutes somewhere. Chandler was whistling happily and was busying himself at the sink. He seemed to be washing dishes. I reached up and touched the side of my head, the side with the bandage. Of course there was no pain, not filled with drugs, but I felt strangely out of balance. I still couldn't hear from my right ear.

I looked over at Fred. He was staring at me, with no emotion. Did he know Luke was here? *Was* Luke here?

"What happened to you?" he said. It came out with a croak. He cleared his throat.

Jeanette looked over at Chandler, who didn't seem to care that we were talking. She went back to her paper.

"Detective Miller," I said. "Darren and I went to Skip and Marie's and he was there."

"She killed him," Jeanette said, without looking up. "Second of my siblings she's killed." She took a sip of wine.

"Now, now," Chandler said. He wagged a soapy finger at Jeanette. "Be nice to our guests, my dear. Danny has just been looking after her own, just like we do. That's why we have come to value her so much."

"If you can't beat them, have them join you?" I said. And smiled. I busied my hands with the pipe, not intending to smoke anymore but I wanted Chandler and Jeanette to think I was nothing but a slave to the crack, malleable.

That was true. But I had to be stronger right now than I had ever needed to be. Once this was over I could do what I liked, and before I left here I would hopefully be able to grab this nice, big, fantastic rock. But right now, I needed a clear head.

I knew I was going to have to smoke a bit more, though. They would notice if I didn't.

At least, that's what I told myself.

Chandler laughed. "Oh, Danny," he said. He grabbed another

bottle of red from a small wine rack over the fridge. "We've already beaten you. We just think you'd be a great addition to the family."

Jeanette stared daggers at me, but said nothing. She licked a finger and made a show of turning the page of the newspaper. Typical passive-aggressive teenage behaviour. Seemed to me like her development had stopped sometime when she was sixteen. Probably had, growing up in this family. I tried to feel some sympathy for her, remembering what Jack had told me, but I just couldn't.

"I have a family," I said, but friendly. "One of them is sitting right over there." I nodded at Fred's end of the table, and for the first time felt a twinge of pain. Good. It meant the crack was wearing off. Pain meant that my brain was clearing up, and messages were making their way from my body. I tried to twirl my ankle around, testing it. Chandler had wrapped it well.

"I'm sorry, Danny," Fred said. He started to cry then, like I had never seen. His chin was lowered to his chest. He was a picture of utter despair and defeat. "It's all my fault. All of it."

"No it's not, Fred," I said. "It's everyone's. Mine, and Jack's, and even Ginger's. We all had a hand in bringing this into our lives." And as I said it I knew it was true. It's was everybody's fault, and nobody's. Nobody except the evil man feeding us stew. I took a quiet, deep breath. "I'm sure Chandler here had this planned for a long time. Am I right?"

Chandler smiled, shrugged modestly. He was opening another bottle of wine. He pulled out the cork and smelled it. "Sometimes a plan just comes together," he said. "Smell that." He passed me the cork. "You can smell Tuscany on that cork." I took a whiff.

"If Tuscany smells like red wine, well then, I'm with you," I said. Chandler pulled fresh glasses from the cupboard and ceremoniously poured us each a glass. Jeanette pointedly ignored him.

"You have a lot to learn, Danny," Chandler said. "You're a very wealthy woman now. You should cultivate an interest in the finer things in life."

"Well this here crack cocaine is pretty fine," I said.

Chandler nodded. "If that's what you want, well of course that's your choice." He was waving the glass under his nose and I itched to reach out and smack it from his pretentious hand. "I've never approved of drugs. But I've always believed – and taught my children, and anyone else who follows me – that you can get whatever you want, if you want it enough."

"And what do you want from us now?" Fred said. "Jack and Ginger are dead. Danny and I are rich and broken. Is this the plan?" I willed him to pick up his spoon – the only utensil, I noticed, that Chandler had given him – and have some stew. He would need his strength, no matter what was to come. And as soon as I thought it he did, as though he had forgotten it was there. Good.

"Fred, I'm glad you asked. I am really, really glad." Chandler looked at us, beaming. "It's getting late. Do you two want to get some sleep, or should we have a chat first? I have a proposition for you both. But we can talk about it in the morning. I make superb blueberry pancakes. I can't wait for you to try them."

I looked at Fred. I knew morning would be best. A night of rest, if I could get any, would help. A clearer head, and time to think. I hadn't had so much crack that I couldn't get a few hours.

Then again, the level of crack in my system just now meant that I was thinking more clearly and I knew I could feel some pain, but in the morning I didn't know if I could count on the adrenaline I would need. The pain in my ankle would be worse in the morning.

And I needed more crack. A fine balance. Not too much, not too little.

"Oh hell, let's chat now," I said. "I'm sitting here with a nice buzz on, and while I'm sure your pancakes are to die for, I might want a nice lie-in tomorrow. It's been a bit of a day." I smiled at Chandler and fiddled with the rock of crack, breaking some of it into small pieces. My hands were shaking. I wanted this crack more than I had ever wanted anything, ever. More than love, more than anything.

"Sure," Fred said. "But do you think we could sit in the living room? And do you think I could get these off?" He motioned to the chains around his legs and the chair. "I'm not going anywhere. But my legs are cramping."

Jeanette looked at Chandler, who nodded at her. She slid her gun over to Chandler while she squatted on the floor and freed Fred's legs. Chandler picked it up and held it casually, but I noticed that he had his finger ready at the trigger.

We made our way slowly into the living room. My ankle was bad. Very bad. But as Jeanette helped me across the room, I exaggerated quite how much pain I was in. Chandler directed me to sit in an easy chair with my bad ankle up on an ottoman. He carefully placed the small tray with the drug gear on a side table next to me, along with my glass of wine, a few cigarettes and an ashtray.

"Quite the host," I said. Chandler looked sincerely pleased at the compliment.

I am going to kill you slowly, I thought, smiling at him. *And if I enjoy it, and go to hell for it, then so be it.*

Fred was on the couch next to Chandler, and Jeanette sat on the floor near the fire, her weapon and the newspaper in front of her.

"Everybody comfy?" Chandler asked. He looked totally at his ease, his feet in slippers on the coffee table. To the manor born.

"Fire away," I said. I looked at Jeanette. "Figure of speech." I smiled at her.

She didn't smile back.

32

It was simple, he said.

"I feel I've gotten to know you both. Well of course, Fred and I have spent a great deal of time together." He clapped Fred on the shoulder. Fred looked sick.

"You both know about my Family." I could hear the capital F. "You've each lost a great deal recently. And for that I am truly sorry." I fiddled with the crack in my lap. I could feel Jeanette look at me.

"Likewise," I said. "For Lola and Miller."

"I won't deny that finding Jack again – Scott, to us – was a great… boost," Chandler said. "I missed my boy, and I won't deny it."

"And his income," I said. I couldn't help it. I smiled and pretended to pack my glass stem with crack, meanwhile letting some of it fall into my lap to be brushed off into the recesses of the cushy chair.

"Touché," Chandler said. He leaned forward and filled Fred's wine glass, and lifted it, questioning whether I wanted more. I shook my head, waving my crack pipe at him. He nodded. "Danny, I've seen how you operate. I'm impressed. As Jack's widow, you'd be very welcome to become part of the family."

"I'm not much of a joiner," I said. "I'm a bit of a lone wolf, to be honest. Besides, I've got quite a lot of my own birth family to be taking anybody else on board."

Chandler nodded. "The life isn't for everybody. Jeanette isn't nuts about all our company all the time. Are you, dear?"

"No," she answered clearly.

"Of course not." Chandler took a sip of wine. "No one is going to force you to do anything you don't want to do. There's been too much of that, in my opinion. I'm getting old! Look at me!" He laughed. He was the only one. "It's simple: you sign over Jack's estate to a charitable foundation that I control. All but ten percent. You keep ten percent. Lock, stock and barrel. Done. Finis. And we all go on our merry way."

"A reverse tithe," I said.

"Exactly!" Chandler said, pleased.

"And if we don't?" Fred said.

Chandler nodded, taking another sip of his wine, savoring it. "Yes, you have to know every part of the deal I am proposing. Well of course, first of all, if you decline the offer, neither of you will get out of here alive. I know what you're thinking!" he said, putting his hand up as though we were interrupting him. "But, Michael, buddy, sure, we can promise you the world and as soon as you let us go we'll go to the FBI." He leaned back. "But first of all, of course we can do this all here and now. Internet transfers and what have you. I assure you, we're quite set up for this. Oh, but, Danny? The timing isn't fantastic on your end. Scott's – Jack's will has to clear before you have access to anything. This will take a little while. You'll recuperate here with us until that happens. Then when the money is in your name, with a few clicks on a keyboard, you can have all this over with."

"I don't want to speak for Danny," Fred said. He shifted a bit and Jeanette watched him carefully. "But you're talking to a couple of people who have lost the people they love most in the world. What if I don't want to play this game anymore? I don't much care if I don't make it out of here."

It hit me then. Fred didn't know the twins were alive. He hadn't seen Luke. He might have thought the boys were killed when Jack and Lola were.

"And maybe, just maybe, I don't want to reward the people who killed my family."

Chandler looked as though someone had spat in his Tuscan wine. As though it was distasteful, during such a pleasant convivial evening, to mention such things.

"You think I haven't thought of that, Fred?" He looked at me. "Both of you. You're not seeing the big picture. How about the twins? If you decide to refuse my offer, then you have a promise from me. And I don't make promises lightly." He shook his head. "You have my promise that anyone you ever loved will be… affected by the Family. In the same way that the people in Jack's life were – you two, and dear sweet Ginger of course."

"And Gene," I said quietly.

"Who?" Chandler looked genuinely confused.

"Her boyfriend in Toronto," Jeanette said. "We paid him a visit." She grinned at me and shrugged her shoulders as if to say, *whoops! I'm such a bad girl.*

I looked at Fred. He had heard what Chandler said about the twins. He had realized that his sons were alive.

"Ah, then you see," Chandler said. "If you opt out, as it were, then you two will have disappeared into these beautiful Maine woods, and no one will ever know where you went. And then the Lindquists and the Clearys – and most specifically your other son, Fred, because of course we have Luke with us – will get visits from my Family over the next years. In various guises, of course. I mean I haven't worked out all the particulars yet." He laughed. "I've been a bit busy lately."

I looked at Fred. He was looking at Chandler with a face that seemed to be unable to register that yes, there is even greater evil than you thought. It *can* get worse.

But your sons are alive. Fred closed his eyes and I could see him get stronger. It could have just been the crack screwing with my perceptions, but I could swear the knowledge strengthened him.

"And if we agree to pay? Is that the end of this? Will we ever see you again?" I lifted up the pipe, holding the end so Jeanette, who was closest, couldn't see how much or little crack was in it. I would still get a little smoke, and a little buzz, from the remainder that was in there from last time. But I had seen her eyeing the rock next to me. She either wanted some, or she was wondering why I hadn't taken a hit in quite a while.

"I've made my case for you joining us, Danny. But once your part is played, you're free to go," Chandler said. "Good Lord, Danny. I'm a man of my word." He took a sip of his wine. "Of course, you know that if you tell anyone about any of this, what I said earlier applies. About your family getting visits from mine."

I lit the pipe and inhaled. There was more crack in there than I had thought. I had to hold it but I tried not to take it too far into my lungs.

I exhaled and the world was bright again. But I still felt clear.

"Where do I sign," I said. I twirled the pipe in my fingers and tilted my head back.

Chandler clapped his hands together. "Wonderful! Danny, I knew you'd see sense. Fred? You on board? Should I open something really special? This might call for a toast."

Time stood still for a moment while we all looked at Fred expectantly.

He opened his mouth to speak.

Then, faster than I would have ever believed he could move, Fred had grabbed the corkscrew from the coffee table, and plunged the business end of it into Chandler's eye.

Before I could think, I yelled for Fred to hold him, while I threw myself off the chair towards Jeanette, using the armrests to propel me.

She was fumbling to get a grip on the gun. It had taken me a second to register what Fred had done. I could ignore the pain in my ankle. I would have to. Chandler had wrapped it well, and the furniture was grouped tightly around the fire. I didn't have far to go.

I still had the metal crack pipe in my left hand and when I knocked Jeanette over, her head close to the open fire, I saw Ginger's face, and Jack's.

I punched the pipe into her eye. It was strong. Sitting in the chair, I had tested it, trying to see how much pressure it could take while I held it in my hand. Funny that Fred had had the same thought. I heard something breaking, and the two men both yelling, and I felt Jeanette's eye pop like a fat grape under my hand. I pushed the pipe in as far as it would go. Blood and ocular fluid flowed out of her eye and onto my hand. I picked her head up off the floor by her hair, and smashed it as hard as I could into the hardwood floor.

I grabbed the gun. Chandler was gone, and Fred was on his knees trying to breathe. His asthma.

"Where did he go, and where's your inhaler?" I said. I was surprised to hear that I was yelling. My lopsided hearing made sound so imprecise. Fred pointed out the back door. It was open. Chandler would have a gun in his car, but if there were more in easy reach in the house I don't think he would have left. "Inhaler, Fred, point," I said. He was bent over, trying to suck air into his lungs. He pointed under the couch. I was on one foot, trying to hold the gun, listening for Chandler to come behind me and registering that Jeanette was stirring. I hadn't knocked her out fully. She started to scream.

I threw myself down and pushed my arm under the couch. It was a mid-century modern-looking thing, and fairly low to the ground. I couldn't see anything and with the sound of Fred's breathing growing more and more labored and panicked, I shoved the gun under the couch to fish around for anything. Fred was dying. I had to get the inhaler. I had to get a phone. I had to get an ambulance, and the police. I had to get everybody.

I felt the barrel of the gun slide against something and as I used the gun to slide the plastic inhaler in Fred's direction I heard something behind me. At the same second I saw Fred grab the inhaler and suck on it, something sharp and heavy landed on my bad ankle. I screamed, thanked God for the crack – I would have blacked out from the pain without it – and flipped myself over with my good leg.

Jeanette was on her knees behind me, one eye socket a mess of gore, blood down her face. For the first time since this all began, I felt a moment of real pity for her. She hadn't had a chance. She had been raised in that house. Her body had probably been sold to who knows how many men.

But when she raised the fireplace poker to hit me again, I shot her with the AK-47. I was just relieved I had known how to fire it.

The blast sent her across the room, with her head and shoulders in the huge fireplace. I gagged and turned over in case I vomited. Fred pulled the gun from me, gently.

He was still trying to breathe properly, but his color was back.

"Get him, Fred."

I wanted to say, don't kill him. Don't have that to live with for the rest of your life, like I do. Like Darren does. Find a phone, call for help, lock the doors, hold onto the gun. No more killing. But I didn't.

Fred ran outside to find Chandler while I lay on the floor and watched Jeanette burn. I couldn't move. I wanted to pull her out of the fire and ask her for forgiveness. I crawled closer but I knew that if I found the strength to drag her out, there was the danger of sparks or fire catching something, and we could all go up. So I left her where she was, closed my eyes, and said a prayer. I hoped somebody was listening to me.

Someone came in the back door. I grabbed the gun and pulled myself back behind the couch. My jeans had been cut by the fireplace poker and I looked at the wound. If my leg had been able to support some of my weight before, I doubted it would now.

Fred called out before he entered the room. "He's gone," he said. "It's me." He walked in, carrying an axe, covered in melting snow. "The car is gone." He stared at Jeanette. "Jesus Christ," he said.

"I know."

Fred ran up the stairs, I knew to look for Luke. I watched Jeanette burn. I felt nothing.

Minutes later Fred came back down and said something about Luke sleeping. Drugged but sleeping. He didn't want to carry him down and see this, he said. He disappeared into the kitchen and came back with a fire extinguisher. "Under the sink," he said. He sprayed in the direction of the fire, and Jeanette, and kept spraying. He was crying. There was white foam everywhere, and the smell of burnt hair, and worse. Fred sat down on the couch so that I was at his feet, and he patted my head. I put my head on his knee, and we sat like that for a long time.

I heard sirens in the distance and I let myself close my eyes. Finally.

33

I got out of the hospital a couple of weeks later.

I needed surgery to pin my leg back together again. My ankle and tibia were shattered by the fall down the stairs at the old house, and then Jeanette's attack. The doctors said I might always have a degree of hearing loss in my right ear, but in the grand scheme of things I wasn't going to worry about it. However, apparently the stitches Chandler-slash-Michael had given me were of professional quality. He wasn't lying about his time in the Army medical corps.

I was in a wheelchair when Laurence took me from the hospital. I didn't quite have the strength to move well on crutches.

Skipper and Marie had flown back with Matty. They were worried that I wouldn't want to come to their house, but they needn't have bothered. I was happy to be alive, and I felt like something at the house had saved me. I was just relieved that they were in Toronto when hell was unleashed at their house.

It could have been much worse. In my bad moments – which were far more than my good ones – I tried to remember that.

Darren was still in the hospital, and the doctors said he probably would be until at least New Year. But he was up, and every day he was able to walk for a few minutes. The arrow had, as I had suspected, punctured his lung, but the ambulance had reached him in time to save it. His back was wonky – it didn't hurt, he said, but he couldn't feel parts of it. The doctors said that with the injuries he had received, numbness was a blessing.

He was in shock, they said, when the ambulance had reached him, lying on the ground in front of the old house. Had it been twenty years ago, he wouldn't have made it.

"Remind me to donate to medical research," Darren said to me in the hospital the day I was released.

"Donate some cash to medical research, why don't you," I replied, and he tried to laugh.

I hadn't talked to Gene, who was still at his mother's, recuperating. When I got back to Ontario, I would go up and see him. I wasn't ready yet to tell him what I'd been through. Laurence had managed to track down his mother's information from the hospital, and phoned to inform them that I was in hospital in Maine, recovering from some injuries.

I told the Maine State Troopers everything, nearly every detail. I didn't tell them about Lowell, but Darren did. It was decided that there weren't grounds to prosecute; in the extraordinary events that unfolded, our claims of self-defence were widely believed.

In the local Maine news, I was identified as "a private investigator from a prominent local family." The state licensing board wanted to know all about that, but I assured them that I had never represented myself as an investigator, private or public. I was a private citizen, and planned to stay that way. As private as possible.

Amelia French sent me flowers in the hospital, and a nice note. It was Miller, of course, who had shot her. She had finally remembered, though the damage he had done to her meant that she was relearning how to walk. She said she wanted to have lunch if I ever found myself back in Southern California. She felt bad that she hadn't seen Miller for what he was, and blamed herself for what had happened.

She'd have to join the club on that one. And no offense to her, but I planned to never go near Southern California, ever again.

Chandler York, aka Michael Vernon Smith, has not been found. The FBI put him on their Most Wanted list. Thorough searches of his home in Orange County and the cabin in the Maine woods uncovered a quagmire of banking details which were going to take a while to unravel. But in the meantime, the authorities froze all assets they could find.

No one could figure out where Dave had come from. Fred paid his fees in cash and swore he couldn't remember his last name, if he ever knew it. In security footage of everywhere we knew he had been – the motel in Palm Springs, the hospital in Toronto – it was apparent that he had been ever mindful to avoid showing his face to a camera. Like Jeanette, Dave had been recommended to Fred by the man he knew as Chandler York, his trusted friend and lawyer. The very fact of him being recommended by Chandler York – aka Michael Vernon Smith – meant law enforcement officers seemed to be of the consensus that whoever he was, he must have something to do with the Family.

But I didn't believe it, and neither did Fred. I remembered he said he and Dominic had grown up in foster care together. Maybe it had been with Michael Vernon Smith? Maybe he hadn't been in on Dominic's murder and split or changed allegiances after that point. Police said no such person as Dominic Pastore had ever lived at Michael Vernon Smith's home, The Orchard, at least through Social Services. But that didn't prove much to me.

All I knew was he had saved Gene's life. Had waited patiently with me at the hospital. And when he had had a chance to kill me, kill my brother, he hadn't.

Skip and Marie managed to get their floors redone before the whole family descended upon them for Christmas and New Year. Miller's blood had soaked into the wood so deeply, and Marie didn't want to cover blood stains with a rug. Skip got the house alarmed, with motion detectors everywhere. I didn't tell him that I doubted anyone in Maine would try to go near the Cleary house uninvited anytime soon.

With Michael Vernon Smith still at large – and in the police's opinion, Dave as well – Fred and I were subtly advised to hire top-notch security for all of our loved ones. Luckily, we had the money to. But with his assets frozen – at least, the ones we knew about – and no other known Family members that I had heard of, I thought Chandler was probably in a small town somewhere, hanging out a shingle as a country lawyer. Until, perhaps, some wealthy people started disappearing. The Feds would be watching.

And so would I. As long as I lived, so would I.

And the twins? Well, they saw their first white Christmas. Along with their father, they spent a couple of hours every day between Christmas and New Year at the hospital with Darren, and we managed to spring him for New Year's Eve. Fred was considering where to take the boys, and where the healthiest place for them would be, after their ordeal.

Maine was high on the list, but Darren and I were campaigning for Toronto.

At Christmas, Laurence informed me that he had reserved a spot for me at a very posh and remote rehab facility on the east coast of Canada. A university pal of his owned the place. I was supposed to go for ninety days, and I decided to do it. I owed it to the people who loved me.

I would go eventually. I knew I wasn't through with the rock. I had to keep my promise to myself, and say my goodbyes to Ginger and Jack in my own way, and that involved me in my apartment, with a few days' worth of crack. I craved crack every single time I felt sad, which was more often than not.

And yes. At the cabin in Maine, while Fred wasn't looking and before the authorities arrived, I managed to grab the huge amount of crack Chandler had given me.

At Christmas, we decided that we would have Ginger's ashes flown to Maine. We would bury her at home, not in the waters off Orange County. Very little good had happened to her there. Wherever Fred and the twins wound up, he was going to take them back to California to see their friends. And to pack up, sell the house, cut ties. And to convince Marta and Rosen to come with them, wherever they decided to go. I told him that I wanted Marta to live with me, if he couldn't make use of her. I would bring her whole family and pay them whatever they wanted. I had the money now, and you don't get cooking – and love – like that every day.

The boys were safe, and my siblings were alive.

All except Ginger.

She continued to talk to me in my sleep, and I continued to listen.

Jack? Well, it would be a long time before I'd be able to think about Jack without more pain than I could possibly bear. Drug-free, at least.

I had done things that changed me. But because of it, some people were dead who should be dead, and some alive who deserved to be.

And now, I knew what I was capable of.

So did Chandler York. Or Michael Vernon Smith. And one day, I would find him.

POSTSCRIPT

Into the second week of January, and I was still recuperating at Skipper and Marie's. I had underestimated how painful and ungainly my leg was going to be while healing. And while I had been prescribed a few Percocet, Marie doled them out in what I told her, only half-jokingly, was a very stingy manner. I knew it was with love. I knew they were helping me, and they loved me, but they were also my jailers – I hadn't managed more than a couple of very quick hits of crack, and the lengths to which I had gone to do that made it nearly – nearly – not worth it.

I fantasized about the day when I could lock my apartment door behind me again, and have D-Man on speed dial. Just those few days. Then rehab. Even Laurence agreed that I couldn't go to rehab as banged up as I now was.

And we all wanted to be near family still, one way or another.

But Marie's cooking was heaven, the boys were still here. I watched them snowshoeing outside and Marie made snow angels with them. They weren't going back to school right away; it was decided that for the rest of the academic year the boys would be homeschooled, and mostly just given lots of love and outdoor exercise. Luke was taking longer to come around, which wasn't a surprise. He had spent time alone with Jeanette and Chandler, without his twin. The night at the apartment, the night Jack died, would have been even more traumatic for him. He was separated from his Matty, possibly forever, as far as he knew. He wasn't doing much talking to anybody but Matty, but I felt confident that would change.

Darren, Fred and Laurence met up in Toronto to sort out some legal stuff for me around Jack's will, get some clothes from my apartment, and do the paperwork to get a continuance on my court appearance – I was to appear by video monitor and had nice statements from Paul Belliveau and a doctor in Maine about the inadmissibility of me travelling yet. I was campaigning for them to be looking for somewhere for Fred and the boys to live, though Skipper and Marie were still pushing hard for Maine.

I was lying in bed one morning, debating whether I was going to start my day with an awkward, surreptitious hit of crack in my closet – the only place I could go during the day; with so many of us in the house, the bathrooms were occupied a lot. Marie knocked briefly and came in, with coffee and a stack of letters.

"Mail call," she said.

I had been getting the weirdest mail since everything about Michael Vernon Smith had been all over the news for the better part of a week. Most of it was delivered to several different spellings of my name, to General Delivery, Downs Falls, Maine. The postmaster knew where I was – everyone knew where I was; my dreams of privacy for the moment had been thoroughly quashed – and they were forwarded. I had people asking me to find their pet rabbit and people asking me to find someone to kill their husband. Those letters I passed to the police, though sometimes after I read them I didn't really want to.

I sat up in bed and took the coffee Marie passed me. The first letter I opened was in one of those old air mail envelopes you hardly see anymore, and was typed on what looked like an actual typewriter. I looked at the postmark, which was so smudged as to be indiscernible, and American stamps had been stuck on at some points in its journey, over whatever was underneath. I unfolded a thin sheet of onion-skin paper.

```
Danny,

    Unlike you, I'm somewhere warm, finally
swimming in my boxers.

    I want you to know how very sorry I am
about your losses. I was too late, and I'll
always have to live with that. I hope you have
decided not to do anything further about our
common friend. That's my job, and you have
done and seen far more than you should ever
have had to.

    But should you need to reach me in an
emergency - if you need help, if he finds you
before I find him - call me at the number below,
and ask for me by my Palm Springs married name.

    Be happy. And please, be careful.
```

Dave. Swimming in his boxers. And the Palm Springs married name? The bartender at the pool that Darren was flirting with. Doug? Dave introduced himself as Doug Douglas.

And our common friend had to be the man I had known as Chandler York.

I knew it. For half a second I wanted to call Darren, call Detective Paul, call the FBI, and whoever else had doubts about Dave. But this I would keep to myself. Even from Darren.

Especially from Darren. I was going to be doing my best to make sure he never had to go through anything bad, ever again. He had killed a man, and lost his sister. He should play his music, be a fantastic uncle, and have his own family one day soon. This life wasn't for him.

I read the letter again and again, something like hope growing in my chest, and resolve. I memorized the number until I knew it as well as I knew the names of my siblings, or the look on Jack's face when he died. It wrapped itself around the pain and love I would always carry for my sister and lodged itself there.

I watched the boys playing outside and decided I would go out today. I was going to go into town. The roads were fairly clear, and I would phone and see if one of Downs Mills' two taxis could come and get me. Skip had mentioned there's a tattoo shop now. I was going to tattoo the number, maybe high up on my thigh, in some kind of a design so only I could read the numbers. The way my life was turning out, I knew that in future someone could do something to addle my brain, and I wasn't taking any chances with this memory. And if I liked the tattoo artist's work, maybe I would have something designed for Ginger, and for Jack.

Perhaps I would cover my body with them.

I reached into the drawer beside my bed and opened my hollowed-out copy of *Anna Karenina*. It had been my hardback edition when I was in high school, and it was still here. I took out my pipe, and my crack, and my lighter, and put them in my PJ pocket. I hopped into the bathroom in the hallway, not bothering with the crutches, holding Dave's letter, folded back inside the envelope. I stood over the toilet, reading it one last time before I burned it and flushed. I watched the ashes disappear.

Then I allowed myself a tiny bit of crack, right there in the bathroom. Marie would probably smell something, but I would say I had burned a particularly nasty letter from some crazy. If she didn't believe me, so be it.

I'm far from perfect. The people who love me know that.

And for the first time in a while, I felt something like hope.

I was a twin once. I was Ginger Cleary's twin.

Don't miss the second part of Danny Cleary's
thrilling story: *Cracked: Rehab Run.*

ACKNOWLEDGMENTS

Getting *Cracked* from my head to your hands was quite a trip – and I mean that in every sense.

But without ridiculous amounts of help, love and support from the following people it wouldn't be here. In some cases, *I* might not be here:

My agent, friend, and brother from another mother, Sam Hiyate. Don't Stop Believin', baby.

My brilliant, wonderful editor Alice Nightingale, who is probably now riding a camel somewhere. In a bikini. And now, and hopefully forever, the wonderful Cath Trechman at Titan, who puts up with me so cheerfully that I wish I could send her daily boxes of chocolate and shoulder rubs.

The lawyers, judges, law enforcement officers, court staff, and other Ministry of the Attorney General colleagues who continue to make my life a hell of a lot more interesting.

The fantastic women of The Rights Factory, past and present, for reading and notes and encouragement, particularly the talented Alisha Sevigny.

My best friend, Marilyn "The Doll" Cleary. One word for you, honey: Bali.

My little modern family: Christos and Lisa. And all my other old friends, who stuck with me through the years of the Bat Cave. I am so goddamn lucky to have you. Nigel, Craig, Shirley, Lynn, Tim, Linda, Vandana, Jenny, Mary-Anne, Jean-Paul and so many others; particularly the late, great Harry Morriss, who died before the book was in print. He was the best of men, and much missed. And thanks of course to all my new friends, who make my life so rich.

My sister Pamela, who probably has this book memorized, and has never had any compunction about correcting me. (I love you, Pam.) My sisters Judy and Isobel, for rarely correcting me. (And unconditional love and support. More intense love and thanks to my three sisters than can ever be expressed.)

And last but definitely not least, The Leslie Clan (sibs and kids): Frank, Theresa, Pam, Judy, Bill, Grant, Isobel, Mike, Aaron, Amy, Connor, Alexandra, Tim, Janet, Myra, Carter, Rosemary, Donni, Laura, Chase, Abigail, Peter, Andrianne, Alana, Andrew, Stephen, Ian and Madeleine. As Mom used to say, we may be crazy, but we've never been boring.

And for those whose lives, hearts and minds have been taken over by addiction: please, do whatever you need to do to stop. It's much better on the other side.

ONTARIO ARTS COUNCIL
CONSEIL DES ARTS DE L'ONTARIO

an Ontario government agency
un organisme du gouvernement de l'Ontario

The author wishes to thank the Ontario Arts Council
for its support during the writing of this book.

ABOUT THE AUTHOR

Barbra Leslie lives and writes in Toronto. Visit her at www.barbraleslie.com, or follow her on Twitter @barbrajleslie.

CRACKED
REHAB RUN
BARBRA LESLIE

After Danny's twin sister was murdered and her nephews kidnapped, Danny crossed North America with her musician brother Darren pursuing those responsible – and being pursued.

Now Danny fulfills her promise to her siblings, and checks herself into Rose's Place, a posh, remote drug rehabilitation facility on the east coast of Canada. Lulled by the sea air and peace and quiet, Danny starts to come to terms with her losses, and imagine what her future will be.

When Danny finds a human hand on the property however, her rural idyll is shattered. In the ensuing media frenzy, Danny's TV executive brother Laurence flies up from New York to visit his sister and Dickie Doyle, a university friend and the founder of the rehab facility. But when Danny and Laurence go to Dickie's cabin, Dickie is gone. And a strange body is trussed up in his bed – minus a hand and foot.

Danny and Laurence race to find Dickie as the killing spree continues – and before they become the next victims.

Coming November 2016

TITANBOOKS.COM

HACK
AN F.X. SHEPHERD NOVEL
KIERAN CROWLEY

It's a dog-eat-dog world at the infamous tabloid the *New York Mail*, where brand new pet columnist F.X. Shepherd finds himself on the trail of The Hacker, a serial killer who is targeting unpleasant celebrities. Bodies and suspects accumulate as Shepherd runs afoul of cutthroat office politics and Ginny Mac, a sexy reporter for a competing newspaper. But when Shepherd is contacted by the Hacker, he realizes he may be next on the list.

"*Hack* is a witty and incisive mystery set in the raucous world of tabloid journalism. Laugh out loud funny and suspenseful—it's like Jack Reacher meets Jack Black." **Rebecca Cantrell, *New York Times* bestselling author of *The Blood Gospel***

"The man is a legend, a master of his craft, and *Hack* is a seamlessly flowing, imaginative translation of these realms, blended together in exciting, suspenseful and oftentimes hilariously moving prose that reads like a conversation while serving as engrossing fiction, compelling insight and eye-opening commentary. It's a joy to read and captures the imagination from the start." ***Long Island Press***

DUST AND DESIRE
A JOEL SORRELL NOVEL
CONRAD WILLIAMS

Joel Sorrell, a bruised, bad-mouthed PI, is a sucker for missing person cases. And not just because he's searching for his daughter, who vanished five years after his wife was murdered. Joel feels a kinship with the desperate and the damned. He feels, somehow, responsible. So when the mysterious Kara Geenan begs him to find her missing brother, Joel agrees. Then an attempt is made on his life, and Kara vanishes... A vicious serial killer is on the hunt, and as those close to Joel are sucked into his nightmare, he suspects that answers may lie in his own hellish past.

"An exciting new voice in crime fiction"
MARK BILLINGHAM, bestselling author of _Rush of Blood_

"Top quality crime writing from one of the best"
PAUL FINCH, No. 1 bestselling author of _Stalkers_

"Take the walk with PI Joel Sorrell"
JAMES SALLIS, bestselling author of _Drive_

"A beautifully written, pitch-black slice of London noir"
STEVE MOSBY, author of _The Nightmare Place_

For more fantastic fiction, author events, competitions,
limited editions and more

VISIT OUR WEBSITE
titanbooks.com

LIKE US ON FACEBOOK
facebook.com/titanbooks

FOLLOW US ON TWITTER
@TitanBooks

EMAIL US
readerfeedback@titanemail.com